THE WORKS OF
BENJAMIN DISRAELI
EARL OF BEACONSFIELD

VOLUME
2

AMS PRESS
NEW YORK

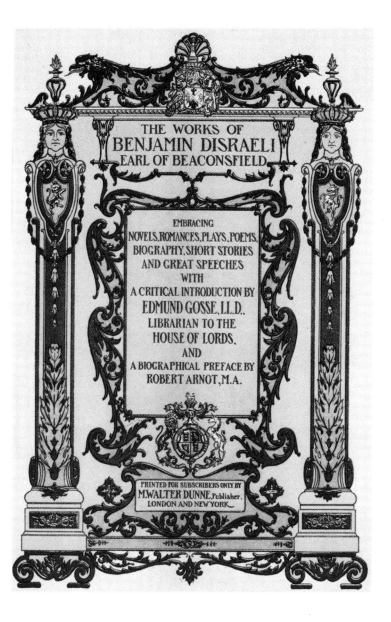

THE WORKS OF
BENJAMIN DISRAELI
EARL OF BEACONSFIELD

EMBRACING
NOVELS, ROMANCES, PLAYS, POEMS,
BIOGRAPHY, SHORT STORIES
AND GREAT SPEECHES
WITH
A CRITICAL INTRODUCTION BY
EDMUND GOSSE, LL.D.,
LIBRARIAN TO THE
HOUSE OF LORDS.
AND
A BIOGRAPHICAL PREFACE BY
ROBERT ARNOT, M.A.

PRINTED FOR SUBSCRIBERS ONLY BY
M. WALTER DUNNE, Publisher,
LONDON AND NEW YORK

AFTER AN ORIGINAL DRAWING BY HERMAN ROUNTREE.

*She blushed deeply, looked down at her horse's neck,
and then turned away her head.*

(See page 305.)

VIVIAN GREY

A ROMANCE OF YOUTH

BY

BENJAMIN DISRAELI

EARL OF BEACONSFIELD

VOLUME II.

M. WALTER DUNNE
NEW YORK AND LONDON

Library of Congress Cataloging in Publication Data

Beaconsfield, Benjamin Disraeli, 1st Earl of, 1804-1881.
    Vivian Grey: a romance of youth.

    (The Works of Benjamin Disraeli, Earl of
Beaconsfield; v. 1-2)
    Reprint of the 1904 ed. published by M. W. Dunne,
New York.
    I. Title.
PR4080.F76   Vol. 1-2   [PR4084]   828'.8'09s   76-12451
ISBN 0-404-08800-7 (set)   [823'.8]

Reprinted from the edition of 1904, New York and London
First AMS edition published in 1976
Manufactured in the United States of America

International Standard Book Number:
Complete Set: 0-404-08800-7
Volume 2: 0-404-08802-3

AMS PRESS INC.
NEW YORK, N.Y.

CONTENTS

BOOK V.
(*Continued*.)

BOOK VI.

CONTENTS

BOOK VII.

CONTENTS

ILLUSTRATIONS

———

BOOK V.

CHAPTER XII.

The Fête du Village.

THE company at the Grand Duke's fête was most select; that is to say, it consisted of everybody who was then at the Baths: those who had been presented to his Highness having the privilege of introducing any number of their friends; and those who had no friend to introduce them purchasing tickets at an enormous price from Cracowsky, the wily Polish Intendant. The entertainment was imperial; no expense and no exertion were spared to make the hired lodging-house look like an hereditary palace; and for a week previous to the great evening the whole of the neighbouring town of Wiesbaden, the little capital of the duchy, had been put under contribution. What a harvest for Cracowsky! What a commission from the restaurateur for supplying the refreshments! What a percentage on hired mirrors and dingy hangings!

The Grand Duke, covered with orders, received every one with the greatest condescension, and made to each of his guests a most flattering speech. His suite, in new uniforms, simultaneously bowed directly the flattering speech was finished.

'Madame von Furstenburg, I feel the greatest pleasure in seeing you. My greatest pleasure is to be surrounded by my friends. Madame von Furstenburg, I trust that your amiable and delightful family are quite well. [The party passed on.] Cravatischeff!' continued his Highness, inclining his head round to one of his aides-de-camp, 'Cravatischeff! a very fine woman is Madame von Furstenburg. There are few women whom I more admire than Madame von Furstenburg.

'Prince Salvinski, I feel the greatest pleasure in seeing you. My greatest pleasure is to be surrounded by my friends. Poland honours no one more than Prince Salvinski. Cravatischeff! a remarkable bore is Prince Salvinski. There are few men of whom I have a greater terror than Prince Salvinski.

'Baron von Konigstein, I feel the greatest pleasure in seeing you. My greatest pleasure is to be surrounded by my friends. Baron von Konigstein, I have not yet forgotten the story of the fair Venetian. Cravatischeff! an uncommonly pleasant fellow is Baron von Konigstein. There are few men whose company I more enjoy than Baron von Konigstein's.

'Count von Altenburgh, I feel the greatest pleasure in seeing you. My greatest pleasure is to be surrounded by my friends. You will not forget to give me your opinion of my Austrian troop. Cravatischeff! a very good billiard player is Count von Altenburgh. There are few men whose play I would sooner bet upon than Count von Altenburgh's.

'Lady Madeleine Trevor, I feel the greatest pleasure in seeing you. My greatest pleasure is to be surrounded by my friends. Miss Fane, your servant; Mr. St. George, Mr. Grey. Cravatischeff! a most splendid woman is Lady Madeleine Trevor. There is no woman whom I more admire than Lady Madeleine Trevor! and Cravatischeff! Miss Fane, too! a remarkably fine girl is Miss Fane.'

The great saloon of the New House afforded excellent accommodation for the dancers. It opened on the gardens, which, though not very large, were tastefully laid out, and were this evening brilliantly illuminated. In the smaller saloon the Austrian troop amused those who were not fascinated by waltz or quadrille with acting proverbs: the regular dramatic performance was thought too heavy a business for the evening. There was sufficient amusement for all; and those who did not dance, and to whom proverbs were no novelty, walked and talked, stared at others, and were themselves stared at; and this, perhaps, was the greatest amusement of all. Baron von Konigstein did certainly to-night look neither like an unsuccessful gamester nor a designing villain. Among many who were really amusing he was the most so, and, apparently without the least consciousness of it, attracted the admiration of all. To the Trevor party he had attached himself immediately, and was constantly at Lady Madeleine's side, introducing to her, in the course of the evening, his own and Mr. St. George's particular friends, Mr. and Mrs. Fitzloom. Among many smiling faces Vivian Grey's was clouded; the presence of the Baron annoyed him. When they first met he was conscious that he was stiff and cool. One moment's reflection convinced him of the folly of his conduct, and he made a struggle to be very civil. In five minutes' time he had involuntarily insulted the Baron, who stared at his friend, and evidently did not comprehend him.

'Grey,' said his Excellency, very quietly, 'you are not in a good humour to-night. What is the matter? This is not at all a temper to come to a fête in. What! won't Miss Fane dance with you?' asked the Baron, with an arch smile.

'I wonder what can induce your Excellency to talk such nonsense!'

'Your Excellency! by Jove, that's good! What the deuce is the matter with the man? It is Miss Fane, then, eh?'

'Baron von Konigstein, I wish you to understand——'

'My dear fellow, I never could understand anything. I think you have insulted me in a most disgraceful manner, and I positively must call you out, unless you promise to dine at my rooms with me to-morrow, to meet De Bœffleurs.'

'I cannot.'

'Why not? You have no engagement with Lady Madeleine I know, for St. George has agreed to come.'

'Yes?'

'De Bœffleurs leaves Ems next week. It is sooner than he expected, and I wish to have a quiet evening together before he goes. I should be very vexed if you were not there. We have scarcely been enough together lately. What with the New House in the evening, and riding parties in the morning, and those Fitzloom girls, with whom St. George is playing a most foolish game—he will be taken in now, if he is not on his guard—we really never meet, at least not in a quiet friendly way; and so now, will you come?'

'St. George is positively coming?'

'Oh yes! positively; do not be afraid of his gaining ground on the little Violet in your absence.'

'Well, then, my dear Von Konigstein, I will come.'

'Well, that is yourself again. It made me quite unhappy to see you look so sour and melancholy; one would have thought that I was some bore, Salvinski at least, by the way you spoke to me. Well, mind you come; it is a promise, good. I must go and say just one word to the lovely little Saxon girl; by-the-bye, Grey, one word before I am off. List to a friend; you are on the wrong scent about Miss Fane; St. George, I think, has no chance there, and now no wish to succeed. The game is your own, if you like; trust my word, she is an angel. The good powers prosper you!' So saying, the Baron glided off.

Mr. St. George had danced with Miss Fane the only quadrille in which Lady Madeleine allowed her to join. He was now waltzing with Aurelia Fitzloom, and was at the head of a band of adventurous votaries of Terpsichore; who, wearied with the commonplace convenience of a saloon, had ventured to invoke the Muse on the lawn.

'A most interesting sight, Lady Madeleine!' said Mr. Fitzloom, as he offered her his arm, and advised their instant presence as patrons of the 'Fête du Village,' for such Baron von Konigstein had most happily termed it. 'A delightful man, that Baron von Konigstein, and says such delightful things! Fête du Village! how very good!'

'That is Miss Fitzloom, then, whom my brother is waltzing with?' asked Lady Madeleine.

'Not exactly, my Lady,' said Mr. Fitzloom, 'not exactly *Miss* Fitzloom, rather Miss Aurelia Fitzloom, my third daughter; our third eldest, as Mrs. Fitzloom sometimes says; for really it is necessary to distinguish, with such a family as ours, you know.'

'Let us walk,' said Miss Fane to Vivian, for she was now leaning upon his arm; 'the evening is deliciously soft, but even with the protection of a cashmere I scarcely dare venture to stand still. Lady Madeleine seems very much engaged at present. What amusing people these Fitzlooms are!'

'Mrs. Fitzloom; I have not heard her voice yet.'

'No; Mrs. Fitzloom does not talk. Albert says she makes it a rule never to speak in the presence of a stranger. She deals plenteously, however, at home in domestic apophthegms. If you could but hear him imitating them all! Whenever she does speak, she finishes all her sentences by confessing that she is conscious of her own deficiencies, but that she has taken care to give her daughters the very best education. They are what Albert calls fine girls, and I am glad he has made friends with them; for, after all, he must find it rather dull here. By-the-bye, Mr. Grey, I am afraid that you cannot find this evening very amusing, the absence of a favourite pursuit always makes a sensible void, and these walls must remind you of more piquant pleasures than waltzing with fine London ladies, or promenading up a dull terrace with an invalid.'

'I assure you that you are quite misinformed as to the mode in which I generally pass my evenings.'

'I hope I am!' said Miss Fane, in rather a serious tone. 'I wish I could also be mistaken in my suspicions of the mode in which Albert spends his time. He is sadly changed. For the first month that we were here he seemed to prefer nothing in the world to our society, and now —— I was nearly saying that we had not seen him for one single evening these three weeks. I cannot understand what you find at this house of such absorbing interest. Although I know you think I am much mistaken in my suspicions, still I feel very anxious. I spoke to Albert to-day, but he scarcely answered me; or said that which it was a pleasure for me to forget.'

' Mr. St. George should feel highly gratified in having excited such an interest in the mind of Miss Fane.'

'He should not feel more gratified than all who are my friends; for all who are such I must ever experience the liveliest interest.'

'How happy must those be who feel that they have a right to count Miss Fane among their friends!'

'I have the pleasure then, I assure you, of making many happy, and among them Mr. Grey.'

Vivian was surprised that he did not utter some complimentary answer; but he knew not why, the words would not come; and instead of speaking, he was thinking of what had been spoken.

'How brilliant are these gardens!' said Vivian, looking at the sky.

'Very brilliant!' said Miss Fane, looking on the ground. Conversation seemed nearly extinct, and yet neither offered to turn back.

'Good heavens! you are ill,' exclaimed Vivian, when, on accidentally turning to his companion, he found she was in tears. 'Shall we go back, or will you wait here? Can I fetch anything? I fear you are very ill!'

'No, not very ill, but very foolish; let us walk on,' and, sighing, she seemed suddenly to recover.

'I am ashamed of this foolishness; what can you think? But I am so agitated, so nervous. I hope you will forget —— I hope ——'

'Perhaps the air has suddenly affected you, shall we go in? Nothing has been said, nothing happened; no one has dared to say or do anything to annoy you? Speak, dear Miss Fane, the — the —— ' the words died on Vivian's lips, yet a power he could not withstand urged him to speak, 'the — the — the Baron?'

'Ah!' almost shrieked Miss Fane. 'Stop one second; an effort, and I must be well; nothing has happened, and no one has done or said anything; but it is of something that should be said, of something that should be done, that I was thinking, and it overcame me.'

'Miss Fane,' said Vivian, 'if there be anything which I can do or devise, any possible way that I can exert myself in your service, speak with the most perfect confidence; do not fear that your motives will be misconceived, that your purpose will be misinterpreted, that your confidence will be misunderstood. You are addressing one who would lay down his life for you, who is willing to perform all your commands, and forget them when performed. I beseech you to trust me; believe me, that you shall not repent.'

She answered not, but holding down her head, covered her face with her small white hand; her lovely face which was crimsoned with her flashing blood. They were now at the end of the terrace; to return was impossible. If they remained stationary, they must be perceived and joined. What was to be done? He led her down a retired walk still farther from the house. As they proceeded in silence, the bursts of the music and the loud laughter of the joyous guests became fainter and fainter, till at last the sounds died away into echo, and echo into silence.

A thousand thoughts dashed through Vivian's mind in rapid succession; but a painful one, a most painful one to him, to any man, always remained the last. His companion would not speak; yet to allow her to return home without freeing her mind of the fearful burden which evidently overwhelmed it, was impossible. At length he broke a silence which seemed to have lasted an age.

'Do not believe that I am taking advantage of an agitating moment to extract from you a confidence which you may repent. I feel assured that I am right in supposing that you have contemplated in a calmer moment the possibility of my being of service to you; that, in short, there is something in which you require my assistance, my co-operation; an assistance, a co-operation, which, if it produce any benefit to you, will make me at length feel that I have not lived in vain. No feeling of false delicacy shall prevent me from assisting you in giving utterance to thoughts which you have owned it is absolutely necessary should be expressed. Remember that you have allowed me to believe that we are friends; do not prove by your silence that we are friends only in name.'

'I am overwhelmed; I cannot speak. My face burns with shame; I have miscalculated my strength of mind, perhaps my physical strength; what, what must you think of me?' She spoke in a low and smothered voice.

'Think of you! everything which the most devoted respect dare think of an object which it reverences. Do not believe that I am one who would presume an instant on my position, because I have accidentally witnessed a young and lovely woman betrayed into a display of feeling which the artificial forms of cold society cannot contemplate, and dare to ridicule. You are speaking to one who also has felt; who, though a man, has wept; who can comprehend sorrow; who can understand the most secret sensations of an agitated spirit. Dare to trust me. Be convinced that hereafter, neither by word nor look, hint nor sign, on my part, shall you feel, save by your own wish, that you have appeared to Vivian Grey in any other light than in the saloons we have just quitted.'

'Generous man, I dare trust anything to you that I dare trust to human being; but ——' here her voice died away.

'It is a painful thing for me to attempt to guess your thoughts; but if it be of Mr. St. George that you are thinking, have no fear respecting him; have no fear about his present situation. Trust to me that there shall be no anxiety for his future one. I will be his unknown guardian, his unseen friend; the promoter of your wishes, the protector of your ——'

'No, no,' said Miss Fane, with firmness, and looking quickly up, as if her mind were relieved by discovering that all this time Vivian had never imagined she was thinking of him. 'No, no, you are mistaken; it is not of Mr. St. George, of Mr. St. George only, that I am thinking. I am much better now; I shall be able in an instant to speak; be able, I trust, to forget how foolish, how very foolish I have been.'

'Let us walk on,' continued Miss Fane, 'let us walk on; we can easily account for our absence if it be remarked; and it is better that it should be all over. I feel quite well, and shall be able to speak quite firmly now.'

'Do not hurry; there is no fear of our absence being remarked, Lady Madeleine is so surrounded.'

'After what has passed it seems ridiculous in me to apologise, as I had intended, for speaking to you on a graver subject than what has generally formed the point of conversation between us. I feared that you might misunderstand the motives which have dictated my conduct. I have attempted not to appear agitated, and I have been overcome. I trust that you will not be offended if I recur to the subject of the New House. Do not believe that I ever would have allowed my fears, my girlish fears, so to have overcome my discretion; so to have overcome, indeed, all propriety of conduct on my part, as to have induced me to have sought an interview with you, to moralise to you about your mode of life. No, no; it is not of this that I wish to speak, or rather that I will speak. I will hope, I will pray, that Albert and yourself have never found in that which you have followed as an amusement, the source, the origin, the cause of a single unhappy, or even anxious moment; Mr. Grey, I will believe all this.'

'Dearest Miss Fane, believe it with confidence. Of St. George, I can with sincerity aver, that it is my firm opinion, that, far from being involved, his fortune is not in the slightest degree injured. Believe me, I will not attempt to quiet you now, as I would have done at any other time, by telling you that you magnify your fears, and allow your feelings to exaggerate the danger which exists. There has been danger. There is danger; play, high play, has been and is pursued at this New House, but Mr. St. George has never been a loser; and if the exertions of man can

avail, never shall, at least unfairly. As to the other
individual, whom you have honoured by the interest
which you have professed in his welfare, no one can
more thoroughly detest any practice which exists in
this world than he does the gaming-table.'

'Oh! you have made me so happy! I feel so persuaded that you have not deceived me! the tones of
your voice, your manner, your expression, convince
me that you have been sincere, and that I am happy,
at least for the present.'

'For ever, I trust, Miss Fane.'

'Let me now prevent future misery. Let me
speak about that which has long dwelt on my mind
like a nightmare, about that which I did fear it was
almost too late to speak. Not of your pursuit, not
even of that fatal pursuit, do I now think, but of
your companion in this amusement, in all amusements! it is he, he whom I dread, whom I look upon
with horror, even to him, I cannot say, with hatred!'

'The Baron?' said Vivian, calmly.

'I cannot name him. Dread him, fear him, avoid
him! it is he that I mean, he of whom I thought
that you were the victim. You must have been surprised, you must have wondered at our conduct
towards him. Oh! when Lady Madeleine turned
from him with coolness, when she answered him in
tones which to you might have appeared harsh, she
behaved to him, in comparison to what is his due,
and what we sometimes feel to be our duty, with
affection, actually with affection and regard. No human being can know what horror is, until he looks
upon a fellow-creature with the eyes that I look
upon that man.' She leant upon Vivian's arm with
her whole weight, and even then he thought she

must have sunk; neither spoke. How solemn is the silence of sorrow!

'I am overcome,' continued Miss Fane; 'the remembrance of what he has done overwhelms me. I cannot speak it; the recollection is death; yet you must know it. That you might know it, I have before attempted. I wished to have spared myself the torture which I now endure. You must know it. I will write; ay! that will do. I will write; I cannot speak now; it is impossible; but beware of him; you are so young!'

'I have no words now to thank you, dear Miss Fane, for this. Had I been the victim of Von Konigstein, I should have been repaid for all my misery by feeling that you regretted its infliction; but I trust that I am in no danger: though young, I fear that I am, one who must not count his time by calendars. "An aged interpreter, though young in days." Would that I could be deceived! Fear not for your cousin. Trust to one whom you have made think better of this world, and of his fellow-creatures.'

The sound of approaching footsteps, and the light laugh of pleasure, told of some who were wandering like themselves.

'We had better return,' said Miss Fane; 'I fear that Lady Madeleine will observe that I look unwell. Some one approaches! No, they pass only the top of the walk.' It was Mr. St. George and Aurelia Fitzloom.

Quick flew the brilliant hours; and soon the dance was over, and the music mute.

It was late when Vivian retired. As he opened his door he was surprised to find lights in his chamber. The figure of a man appeared seated at the table. It moved; it was Essper George.

CHAPTER XIII.

THE reader will remember that Vivian had agreed to dine, on the day after the fête, with the Baron, in his private apartments. This was an arrangement which, in fact, the custom of the house did not permit; but the irregularities of great men who are attended by chasseurs are occasionally winked at by a supple maître d'hotel. Vivian had reasons for not regretting his acceptance of the invitation; and he never shook hands with the Chevalier de Bœffleurs, apparently, with greater cordiality, than on the day on which he met him at dinner at the Baron von Konigstein's. Mr. St. George had not arrived.

'Past five!' said the Baron; 'riding out, I suppose, with the Fitzlooms. Aurelia is certainly a fine girl; but I should think that Lady Madeleine would hardly approve the connection. The St. Georges have blood in their veins; and would, I suppose, as soon think of marrying a Fitzloom as we Germans should of marrying a woman without a *von* before her name. We are quite alone, Grey, only the Chevalier and St. George. I had an idea of asking Salvinski, but he is

(14)

such a regular steam-engine, and began such a long
story last night about his interview with the King of
Ashantee, that the bare possibility of his taking it
into his head to finish it to-day frightened me. You
were away early from the Grand Duke's last night.
The business went off well.'

'Very well, indeed!' said the Chevalier de Bœffleurs; completing by this speech the first dozen of
words which he had uttered since his stay at Ems.

'I think that last night Lady Madeleine Trevor
looked perfectly magnificent; and a certain lady, too,
Grey, eh? Here is St. George. My dear fellow, how
are you? Has the fair Aurelia recovered from the
last night's fatigues? Now, Ernstorff, dinner as soon
as possible.'

The Baron made up to-day certainly, for the silence of his friend the Chevalier. He outdid himself.
Story after story, adventure after adventure, followed
each other with exciting haste. In fact, the Baron
never ceased talking the whole dinner, except when
he refreshed himself with wine, which he drank co-
piously. A nice observer would, perhaps, have considered the Baron's high spirits artificial, and his
conversation an effort. Yet his temper, though lively,
was generally equable; and his ideas, which always
appeared to occur easily, were usually thrown out in
fluent phraseology. The dinner was long, and a
great deal of wine was drunk; more than most of the
parties present for a long time had been accustomed
to. About eight o'clock the Chevalier proposed going to the Redoute, but the Baron objected.

'Let us have an evening altogether: surely we
have had enough of the Redoute. In my opinion one
of the advantages of the fête is, that there is no New

House to-night. Conversation is a novelty. On a moderate calculation I must have told you to-day at least fifty original anecdotes. I have done my duty. It is the Chevalier's turn now. Come, De Bœffleurs, a choice one!'

'I remember a story Prince Salvinski once told me.'

'No, no, that is too bad; none of that Polish bear's romances; if we have his stories, we may as well have his company.'

'But it is a very curious story,' continued the Chevalier, with a little animation.

'Oh! so is every story, according to the storier.'

'I think, Von Konigstein, you imagine no one can tell a story but yourself,' said De Bœffleurs, actually indignant. Vivian had never heard him speak so much before, and really began to believe that he was not quite an automaton.

'Let us have it!' said St. George.

'It is a story told of a Polish nobleman, a Count somebody: I never can remember their crack-jaw names. Well! the point is this,' said the silent little Chevalier, who, apparently, already repented of the boldness of his offer, and, misdoubting his powers, wished to begin with the end of his tale: 'the point is this, he was playing one day at ecarté with the Governor of Wilna; the stake was trifling, but he had a bet, you see, with the Governor of a thousand roubles; a bet with the Governor's secretary, never mind the amount, say two hundred and fifty, you see; then, he went on the turn-up with the Commandant's wife; and took the pips on the trumps with the Archbishop of Warsaw. To understand the point of the story, you see, you must have a distinct conception how the game stood. You see, St. George, there was the bet with the Governor, one thousand roubles; the Governor's secretary, never mind the amount, say two hundred and fifty; turn-up with the Commandant's lady, and the pips with the Archbishop of Warsaw. Proposed three times, one for the king, the Governor drew ace; the Governor was already three and the ten. When the Governor scored king, the Archbishop gave the odds, drew knave queen one hand. The Count offered to propose fourth time. Governor refused. King to six, ace fell to knave, queen cleared on. Governor lost, besides bets with the whole état-major; the secretary gave his bill; the Commandant's lady pawned her jewels; and the Archbishop was done on the pips!'

'By Jove, what a Salvinski!'

'How many trumps had the Governor?' asked St. George.

'Three,' said the Chevalier.

'Then it is impossible: I do not believe the story; it could not be.'

'I beg your pardon' said the Chevalier; 'you see the Governor had ——'

'By Jove, don't let us have it all over again!' said the Baron. 'Well! if this be your model for an after-dinner anecdote, which ought to be as piquant as an anchovy toast, I will never complain of your silence in future.'

'The story is a true story,' said the Chevalier; 'have you got a pack of cards, Von Konigstein? I will show it you.'

'There is not such a thing in the room,' said the Baron.

'Well, I never heard of a room without a pack of

cards before,' said the Chevalier; 'I will send for one
to my own apartments.'

'Perhaps Ernstorff has got a pack. Here Ernstorff,
have you got a pack of cards ? That's well; bring it
immediately.'

The cards were brought, and the Chevalier began
to fight his battle over again; but could not satisfy
Mr. St. George. 'You see, there was the bet with
the Governor, and the pips, as I said before, with the
Archbishop of Warsaw.'

'My dear De Bœffleurs, let's no more of this. If
you like to have a game of ecarté with St. George,
well and good; but as for quarrelling the whole evenings about some blundering lie of Salvinski's, it really
is too much. You two can play, and I can talk to
Don Vivian, who, by-the-bye, is rather of the rueful
countenance to-night. Why, my dear fellow, I have
not heard your voice this evening: frightened by the
fate of the Archbishop of Warsaw, I suppose ?'

'Ecarté is so devilish dull,' said St. George; 'and
it is such a trouble to deal.'

'I will deal for both, if you like,' said De Bœffleurs; 'I am used to dealing.'

'Oh! no, I won't play ecarté; let us have something in which we can all join.'

'Rouge-et-noir,' suggested the Chevalier, in a careless tone, as if he had no taste for the amusement.

'There is not enough, is there ?' asked St. George.

'Oh! two are enough, you know; one deals, much
more four.'

'Well, I don't care; rouge-et-noir then, let us
have rouge-et-noir. Von Konigstein, what say you
to rouge-et-noir ? De Bœffleurs says we can play it
here very well. Come, Grey.'

'Oh! rouge-et-noir, rouge-et-noir,' said the Baron; 'have not you both had rouge-et-noir enough? Am I not to be allowed one holiday? Well, anything to please you; so rouge-et-noir, if it must be so.'

'If all wish it, I have no objection,' said Vivian.

'Well, then, let us sit down; Ernstorff has, I dare say, another pack of cards, and St. George will be dealer; I know he likes that ceremony.'

'No, no; I appoint the Chevalier.'

'Very well,' said De Bœffleurs, 'the plan will be for two to bank against the table; the table to play on the same colour by joint agreement. You can join me, Von Konigstein, and pay or receive with me, from Mr. St. George and Grey.'

'I will bank with you, if you like Chevalier,' said Vivian.

'Oh! certainly; that is if you like. But perhaps the Baron is more used to banking; you perhaps don't understand it.'

'Perfectly; it appears to me to be very simple.'

'No, don't you bank, Grey,' said St. George. 'I want you to play with me against the Chevalier and the Baron; I like your luck.'

'Luck is very capricious, remember.'

'Oh, no, I like your luck; don't bank.'

'Be it so.'

Playing commenced. An hour elapsed, and the situation of none of the parties was materially different from what it had been when they began the game. Vivian proposed leaving off; but Mr. St. George avowed that he felt very fortunate, and that he had a presentiment that he should win. Another hour elapsed, and he had lost considerably. Eleven o'clock: Vivian's luck had also deserted him. Mr.

St. George was losing desperately. Midnight: Vivian had lost back half his gains on the season. St. George still more desperate, all his coolness had deserted him. He had persisted obstinately against a run on the red; then floundered and got entangled in a seesaw, which alone cost him a thousand.

Ernstorff now brought in refreshments; and for a moment they ceased playing. The Baron opened a bottle of champagne; and St. George and the Chevalier were stretching their legs and composing their minds in very different ways, the first in walking rapidly up and down the room, and the other by lying very quietly at his full length on the sofa; Vivian was employed in building houses with the cards.

'Grey,' said the Chevalier de Bœffleurs, 'I cannot imagine why you do not for a moment try to forget the cards: that is the only way to win. Never sit musing over the table.'

But Grey was not to be persuaded to give up building his pagoda: which, now many stories high, like a more celebrated but scarcely more substantial structure, fell with a crash. Vivian collected the scattered cards into two divisions.

'Now!' said the Baron, seating himself, 'for St. George's revenge.'

The Chevalier and the greatest sufferer took their places.

'Is Ernstorff coming in again, Baron?' asked Vivian.

'No! I think not.'

'Let us be sure; it is disagreeable to be disturbed at this time of night.'

'Lock the door, then,' said St. George.

'A very good plan,' said Vivian; and he locked it accordingly.

'Now, gentlemen,' said Vivian, rising from the table, and putting both packs of cards into his pocket; 'now, gentlemen, I have another game to play.' The Chevalier started on his chair, the Baron turned pale, but both were silent. 'Mr. St. George,' continued Vivian, 'I think that you owe the Chevalier de Bœffleurs about four thousand Napoleons, and to Baron von Konigstein something more than half that sum. I have to inform you that it is unnecessary for you to satisfy the claims of either of these gentlemen, which are founded neither in law nor in honour.'

'Mr. Grey, what am I to understand?' asked the quiet Chevalier de Bœffleurs, with the air of a wolf and the voice of a lion.

'Understand, sir!' answered Vivian, sternly, 'that I am not one who will be bullied by a blackleg.'

'Grey! good God! what do you mean?' asked the Baron.

'That which it is my duty, not my pleasure, to explain, Baron von Konigstein.'

'If you mean to insinuate —' burst forth the Chevalier.

'I mean to insinuate nothing. I leave insinuations and innuendos to *chevaliers d'industrie*. I mean to prove everything.'

Mr. St. George did not speak, but seemed as utterly astounded and overwhelmed as Baron von Konigstein himself, who, with his arms leaning on the table, his hands clasped, and the forefinger of his right hand playing convulsively on his left, was pale as death, and did not even breathe.

'Gentlemen,' said Vivian, 'I shall not detain you long, though I have much to say that is to the purpose. I am perfectly cool, and, believe me, perfectly resolute. Let me recommend to you all the same temperament; it may be better for you. Rest assured, that if you flatter yourselves that I am one to be pigeoned and then bullied, you are mistaken. In one word, I am aware of everything that has been arranged for the reception of Mr. St. George and myself this evening. Your marked cards are in my pocket, and can only be obtained by you with my life. Here are two of us against two; we are equally matched in number, and I, gentlemen, am armed. If I were not, you would not dare to go to extremities. Is it not, then, the wiser course to be temperate, my friends?'

'This is some vile conspiracy of your own, fellow,' said De Bœffleurs: 'marked cards, indeed! a pretty tale, forsooth! The Ministers of a first-rate Power playing with marked cards! The story will gain credit, and on the faith of whom? An adventurer that no one knows, who, having failed this night in his usual tricks, and lost money which he cannot pay, takes advantage of the marked cards, which he has not succeeded in introducing, and pretends, forsooth, that they are those which he has stolen from our table; our own cards being, previously to his accusation, concealed in a secret pocket.'

The impudence of the fellow staggered even Vivian. As for Mr. St. George, he stared like a wild man. Before Vivian could answer him the Baron had broken silence. It was with the greatest effort that he seemed to dig his words out of his breast.

'No, no; this is too much! It is all over! I am lost; but I will not add crime to crime. Your courage and your fortune have saved you, Mr. Grey, and your friend from the designs of villains. And you!

and-twenty hours, has gone for ever. I have no motive, then, to deceive you. You must believe what I speak; even what *I* speak, the most degraded of men. I say again, *never*, never, never, never, never was my honour before sullied, though guilty of a thousand follies. You see before you, gentlemen, the unhappy victim of circumstances; of circumstances which he has in vain struggled to control, to which he has at length fallen a victim. I am not pretending, not for a moment, that my crimes are to be accounted for by an inexorable fate, and not to be expiated by my everlasting misery. No, no! I have been too weak to be virtuous: but I have been tried, tried most bitterly. I am the most unfortunate of men; I was not born to be a villain. Four years have passed since I was banished from my country in which I was honoured, my prospects in life blasted, my peace of mind destroyed; and all because a crime was committed of any participation in which I am as innocent as yourselves. Driven in despair to wander, I tried, in the wild dissipation of Naples, to forget my existence and my misery. I found my fate in the person of this vile Frenchman, who never since has quitted me. Even after two years of madness in that fatal place, my natural disposition rallied; I struggled to save myself; I quitted it. I was already involved to De Bœffleurs; I became still more so, in gaining from him the means of satisfying all claims against me. Alas! I found I had sold myself to a devil, a very devil, with a heart like an adder's. Incapable of a stray generous sensation, he has looked upon mankind during his whole life with the eyes of a bully of a gaming house. I still struggled to free myself from this man; and I indemnified him for his advances by procuring him a place in the mission to which, with the greatest difficulty and perseverance, I had at length obtained my appointment. In public life I yet hoped to forget my private misery. At Frankfort I felt that, though not happy, I might be calm. I determined never again even to run the risk of enduring the slavery of debt. I foreswore, with the most solemn oaths, the gaming table; and had it not been for the perpetual sight of De Bœffleurs, I might, perhaps, have felt at ease; though the remembrance of my blighted prospects, the eternal feeling that I experienced of being born for nobler ends, was quite sufficient perpetually to embitter my existence. The second year of my Frankfort appointment I was tempted to this unhappy place. The unexpected sight of faces which I had known in England, though they called up the most painful associations, strengthened me, nevertheless, in my resolution to be virtuous. My unexpected fortune at the Redoute, the first night, made me forget all my resolves, and has led to all this misery. I make my sad tale brief. I got involved at the New House: De Bœffleurs once more assisted me, though his terms were most severe. Yet, yet again, I was mad enough, vile enough, to risk what I did not possess. I lost to Prince Salvinski and a Russian gentleman a considerable sum on the night before the fête. It is often the custom at the New House, as you know, among men who are acquainted, to pay and receive all losses which are considerable on the next night of meeting. The fête gave me breathing time: it was not necessary to redeem my pledge till the fourth night. I rushed to De Bœffleurs; he refused to assist me, alleging his own losses and his previous advance. What was to be done? No possibility of making any arrangement with Salvinski. Had he won of me as others have done, an arrangement, though painful, would perhaps have been possible; but by a singular fate, whenever I have chanced to be successful, it is of this man that I have won. De Bœffleurs, then, was the only chance. He was inexorable. I prayed to him; I promised him everything; I offered him any terms; in vain! At length, when he had worked me up to the last point of despair, he whispered hope. I listened; let me be quick! why finish? You know I fell!' The Baron again covered his face, and appeared perfectly overwhelmed.

'By God! it is too horrible,' said St. George. 'Grey, let us do something for him.'

'My dear St. George,' said Vivian, 'be calm. You are taken by surprise. I was prepared for all this. Believe me, it is better for you to leave us. I recommend you to retire, and meet me in the morning. Breakfast with me at eight; we can then arrange everything.'

Vivian's conduct had been so decisive, and evidently so well matured, that St. George felt that, in the present case, it was for him only to obey, and he retired with wonder still expressed on his countenance; for he had not yet, in the slightest degree, recovered from the first surprise.

'Baron von Konigstein,' said Vivian to the unhappy man, 'we are alone. Mr. St. George has left the room: you are freed from the painful presence of the cousin of Captain Fane.'

'You know all, then!' exclaimed the Baron quickly, looking up, 'or you have read my secret thoughts. How wonderful! at that very moment I was thinking of my friend. Would I had died with him! You know all, then; and now you must believe me guilty. Yet, at this moment of annihilating sorrow, when I can gain nothing by deceit, I swear — and if I swear falsely, may I fall down a livid corpse at your feet — I swear that I was guiltless of the crime for which I suffered, guiltless as yourself. What may be my fate I know not. Probably a few hours, and all will be over. Yet, before we part, sir, it would be a relief — you would be doing a generous service to a dying man — to bear a message from me to one with whom you are acquainted; to one whom I cannot now name.'

'Lady Madeleine Trevor?'

'Again you have read my thoughts! Lady Madeleine! Is it she who told you of my early history?'

'All that I know is known to many.'

'I must speak! If you have time, if you can listen for half an hour to a miserable being, it would be a consolation to me. I should die with ease if I thought that Lady Madeleine could believe me innocent of that first great offence.'

'Your Excellency may address anything to me, if it be your wish, even at this hour of the night. It may be better; after what has passed, we neither of us can sleep, and this business must be arranged at once.'

'My object is, that Lady Madeleine should receive from me at this moment, at a time when I can have no interest to deceive, an account of the particulars of her cousin's and my friend's death. I sent it written after the horrid event; but she was ill, and Trevor, who was very bitter against me, returned the letters unopened. For four years I have never travelled without these rejected letters; this year I have them not. But you could convey to Lady Madeleine my story as now given to you; to you at this terrible moment.'

'Speak on!'

'I must say one word of my connection with the family to enable you fully to understand the horrid event, of which, if, as I believe, you only know what all know, you can form but a most imperfect conception. When I was Minister at the Court of London I became acquainted, became, indeed, intimate, with Mr. Trevor, then in office, the husband of Lady Madeleine. She was just married. Of myself at that time, I may say that, though depraved, I was not heartless, and that there were moments when I panted to be excellent. Lady Madeleine and myself became friends; she found in me a companion who not only respected her talents and delighted in her conversation, but one who in return was capable of instructing, and was overjoyed to amuse her. I loved her; but when I loved her I ceased to be a libertine. At first I thought that nothing in the world could have tempted me to have allowed her for an instant to imagine that I dared to look upon her in any other light than as a friend; but the negligence, the coldness of Trevor, the overpowering mastery of my own passions, drove me one day past the line, and I wrote that which I dared not utter. It never entered into my mind for an instant to insult such a woman with the commonplace sophistry of a ribald. No! I loved her with all my spirit's strength. I would have sacrificed all my views in life, my ambition, my family, my fortune, my country, to have gained her; and I told her this in terms of respectful adoration. I worshipped the divinity, even while I attempted to profane the altar. When I had sent this letter I was in despair. Conviction of the insanity of my conduct flashed across my mind. I expected never to see her again. There came an answer; I opened it with the greatest agitation; to my surprise, an appointment. Why trouble you with a detail of my feelings, my mad hope, my dark despair! The moment for the interview arrived. I was received neither with affection nor anger. In sorrow she spoke. I listened in despair. I was more madly in love with her than ever. That very love made me give her such evidences of a contrite spirit that I was pardoned. I rose with a resolution to be virtuous, with a determination to be her friend: then I made the fatal promise which you know of, to be doubly the friend of a man whose friend I already was. It was then that I pledged myself to Lady Madeleine to be the guardian spirit of her cousin.' Here the Baron, overpowered by his emotions, leant back in his chair, and ceased to speak. In a few minutes he resumed.

'I did my duty; by all that's sacred, I did my duty! Night and day I was with young Fane. A hundred times he was on the brink of ruin; a hundred times I saved him. One day, one never-to-be-forgotten day, one most dark and damnable day, I called on him, and found him on the point of joining a coterie of desperate character. I remonstrated with him, I entreated, I supplicated him not to go, in vain. At last he agreed to forego his engagement on condition that I dined with him. There were important reasons that day for my not staying with him; yet every consideration vanished when I thought of her for whom I was exerting myself. He was frantic this day; and, imagining that there was no chance of his leaving his home, I did not refuse to drink freely, to drink deeply! My doing so was the only way to keep him at home. As we were passing down Pall Mall we met two foreigners of distinction and a noble of your country; they were men of whom we both knew little. I had myself introduced Fane to the foreigners a few days before, being aware that they were men of high rank. After some conversation they asked us to join them at supper at the house of their English friend. I declined; but nothing could induce Fane to refuse them, and I finally accompanied him. Play was introduced after supper: I made an ineffectual struggle to get Fane home, but I was too full of wine to be energetic. After losing a small sum I got up from the table, and, staggering to a sofa, fell fast asleep. Even as I passed Fane's chair in this condition, my master-thought was evident, and I pulled him by the shoulder: all was useless; I woke to madness!' It was terrible to witness the anguish of Von Konigstein.

'Could you not clear yourself?' asked Vivian, for he felt it necessary to speak.

'Clear myself! Everything told against me. The villains were my friends, not the sufferer's; I was not injured. My dining with him was part of the conspiracy; he was intoxicated previous to his ruin. Conscious of my innocence, quite desperate, but confiding in my character, I accused the guilty trio; they recriminated and answered, and without clearing themselves convinced the public that I was their dissatisfied and disappointed tool. I can speak no more.'

It is awful to witness sudden death; but, oh! how much more awful it is to witness in a moment the. moral fall of a fellow-creature! How tremendous is the quick succession of mastering passions! The firm, the terrifically firm, the madly resolute denial of guilt; that eagerness of protestation which is a sure sign of crime, then the agonising suspense before the threatened proof is produced, the hell of detection, the audible anguish of sorrow, the curses of remorse, the silence of despair! Few of us, unfortunately, have passed through life without having beheld some instance of this instantaneous degradation of human nature. But, oh! how terrible is it when the confessed criminal has been but a moment before our friend! What a contrast to the laugh of joyous companionship is the quivering tear of an agonised frame! how terrible to be prayed to by those whose wishes a moment before we lived only to anticipate!

'Von Konigstein,' said Vivian, after a long silence, 'I feel for you. Had I known this I would have spared both you and myself this night of misery; I would have prevented you from looking back to this day with remorse. You have suffered for that of which you were not guilty; you shall not suffer now for what has passed. Much would I give to see you freed from that wretched knave, whose vile career I was very nearly tempted this evening to have terminated for ever. I shall make the communication you desire, and I will endeavour that it shall be credited; as to the transactions of this evening, the knowledge of them can never transpire to the world. It is the interest of De Bœffleurs to be silent; if he speak no one will credit the tale of such a creature, who, if he speak truth, must proclaim his own infamy. And now for the immediate calls upon your honour; in what sum are you indebted to Prince Salvinski and his friend?'

'Thousands! two, three thousand.'

'I shall then have an opportunity of ridding myself of that the acquisition of which, to me, has been matter of great sorrow. Your honour is saved. I will discharge the claims of Salvinski and his friend.'

'Impossible! I cannot allow —— '

'Stop; in this business I must command. Surely there can be no feelings of delicacy between us two now. If I gave you the treasures of the Indies you would not be under so great an obligation to me as you are already: I say this with pain. I recommend you to leave Ems to-morrow; public business will easily account for your sudden departure. And now, your character is yet safe, you are yet in the prime of life, you have vindicated yourself from that which has preyed upon your mind for years; cease to accuse your fate!' Vivian was about to leave the room when the Baron started from his seat and seized his hand. He would have spoken, but the words died upon his lips, and before he could recover himself Vivian had retired.

CHAPTER XIV.

ESSPER GEORGE TO THE RESCUE.

THE sudden departure of Baron von Konigstein from the Baths excited great surprise and sorrow; all wondered at the cause, and all regretted the effect. The Grand Duke missed his good stories, the rouge-et-noir table his constant presence, and Monsieur le Restaurateur gave up, in consequence, an embryo idea of a fête and fireworks for his own benefit, which agreeable plan he had trusted that, with his Excellency's generous co-operation as patron, he should have had no difficulty in carrying into execution. But no one was more surprised, and more regretted the absence of his Excellency, than his friend Mr. Fitzloom. What could be the reason? Public business, of course; indeed he had learnt as much, confidentially, from Cracowsky. He tried Mr. Grey, but could elicit nothing satisfactory; he pumped Mr. St. George, but produced only the waters of oblivion: Mr. St. George was gifted, when it suited his purpose with a most convenient want of memory. There must be something in the wind, perhaps a war. Was the independence of Greece about to be acknowledged,

or the dependence of Spain about to be terminated?
What first-rate Power had marched a million of sol-
diers into the land of a weak neighbour, on the mere
pretence of exercising the military? What patriots
had had the proud satisfaction of establishing a constitutional government without bloodshed, to be set
aside in the course of the next month in the same
manner? Had a conspiracy for establishing a republic
in Russia been frustrated by the timely information of
the intended first Consuls? Were the Janissaries
learning mathematics, or had Lord Cochrane taken
Constantinople in the James Watt steampacket? One
of these many events must have happened; but
which? At length Fitzloom decided on a general
war. England must interfere either to defeat the ambition of France or to curb the rapacity of Russia, or
to check the arrogance of Austria, or to regenerate
Spain, or to redeem Greece, or to protect Portugal,
or to shield the Brazils, or to uphold the Bible So-
cieties, or to consolidate the Greek Church, or to
monopolise the commerce of Mexico, or to disseminate the principles of free trade, or to keep up her
high character, or to keep up the price of corn. England must interfere. In spite of his conviction, however, Fitzloom did not alter the arrangements of his
tour; he still intended to travel for two years. All he
did was to send immediate orders to his broker in
England to sell two millions of consols. The sale
was of course effected, the example followed, stocks
fell ten per cent., the exchange turned, money became scarce. The public funds of all Europe experienced a great decline, smash went the country banks,
consequent runs on the London, a dozen Baronets
failed in one morning, Portland Place deserted, the

cause of infant Liberty at a terrific discount, the
Greek loan disappeared like a vapour in a storm, all
the new American States refused to pay their divi-
dends, manufactories deserted, the revenue in a decline, the country in despair, Orders in Council,
meetings of Parliament, change of Ministry, and new
loan! Such were the terrific consequences of a diplomatist turning blackleg! The secret history of the
late distress is a lesson to all modern statesmen. Rest
assured that in politics, however tremendous the effects, the causes are often as trifling.

Vivian found his reception by the Trevor party,
the morning after the memorable night, a sufficient
reward for all his anxiety and exertion. St. George, a
generous, open-hearted young man, full of gratitude
to Vivian, and regretting his previous want of cordiality towards him, now delighted in doing full justice
to his coolness, courage, and ability. Lady Madeleine
said a great deal in the most graceful and impressive
manner; but Miss Fane scarcely spoke. Vivian, however, read in her eyes her approbation and her gratitude.

'And now, how came you to discover the whole
plot, Mr. Grey?' asked Lady Madeleine, 'for we have
not yet heard. Was it at the table?'

'They would hardly have had recourse to such
clumsy instruments as would have given us the
chance of detecting the conspiracy by casual observation. No, no; we owe our preservation and our
gratitude to one whom we must hereafter count
among our friends. I was prepared, as I told you,
for everything; and though I had seen similar cards to
those with which they played only a few hours before, it was with difficulty that I satisfied myself at

the table that the cards we lost by were prepared, so wonderful is the contrivance!'

'But who is the unknown friend?' said Miss Fane, with great eagerness.

'I must have the pleasure of keeping you all in suspense,' said Vivian: 'cannot any of you guess?'

'None, none, none!'

'What say you, then, to —— Essper George?'

'Is it possible?'

'It is the fact that he, and he alone, is our pre-server. Soon after my arrival at this place this sin-gular being was seized with the unaccountable fancy of becoming my servant. You all remember his un-expected appearance one day in the saloon. In the evening of the same day, I found him sleeping at the door of my room; and, thinking it high time that he should be taught more discretion, I spoke to him very seriously the next morning respecting his troublesome and eccentric conduct. It was then that I learnt his wish. I objected, of course, to engaging a servant of whose previous character I was ignorant, and of which I could not be informed, and one whose peculiar habits would render both himself and his master notorious. While I declined his services, I also advised him most warmly to give up all idea of deserting his present mode of life, for which I thought him extremely well suited. The consequence of my lecture was, what you all perceived with sur-prise, a great change in Essper's character. He be-came serious, reserved, and retiring, and commenced his career as a respectable character by throwing off his quaint costume. In a short time, by dint of making a few bad bargains, he ingratiated himself with Ernstorff, Von Konigstein's pompous chasseur.

His object in forming this connection was to gain an opportunity of becoming acquainted with the duties of a gentleman's servant, and in this he has succeeded. About a week since, he purchased from Ernstorff a large quantity of cast-off apparel of the Baron's, and other perquisites of a great man's valet; among these were some playing cards which had been borrowed one evening in great haste from the servant of that rascal De Bœffleurs, and never returned. On accidentally examining these cards, Essper detected they were marked. The system on which the marks are formed and understood is so simple and novel, that it was long before I could bring myself to believe that his suspicions were founded even on a probability. At length, however, he convinced me. It is at Vienna, he tells me, that he has met with these cards before. The marks are all on the rim of the cards; and an experienced dealer, that is to say, a blackleg, can with these marks produce any results and combinations which may suit his purpose. Essper tells me that De Bœffleurs is even more skilled in sleight-of-hand than himself. From Ernstorff, Essper learned on the day of the fête that Mr. St. George was to dine with the Chevalier at the Baron's apartments on the morrow, and that there was a chance that I should join them. He suspected that villany was in the wind, and when I retired to my room at a late hour on the night of the fête, I there met him, and it was then that he revealed to me everything which I have told you. Am I not right, then, in calling him our preserver?'

'What can be done for him?' said Lady Madeleine.

'His only wish is already granted; he is my servant. That he will serve me diligently and faithfully I have no doubt. I only wish that he would accept or could appreciate a more worthy reward.'

'Can man be more amply rewarded,' said Miss Fane, 'than by choosing his own remuneration? I think he has shown in his request his accustomed talent. I must go and see him this moment.'

'Say nothing of what has passed; he is prepared for silence from all parties.'

A week, a happy week, passed over, and few minutes of the day found Vivian absent from the side of Violet Fane; and now he thought again of England, of his return to that country under very different circumstances to what he had ever contemplated. Soon, very soon, he trusted to write to his father, to announce to him the revolution in his wishes, the consummation of his hopes. Soon, very soon, he trusted that he should hail his native cliffs, a reclaimed wanderer, with a matured mind and a contented spirit, his sorrows forgotten, his misanthropy laid aside.

CHAPTER XV.

I T WAS about a week after the departure of the Baron that two young Englishmen, who had been college friends of Mr. St. George, arrived at the Baths. These were Mr. Anthony St. Leger and Mr. Adolphus St. John. In the academic shades of Christchurch these three gentlemen had been known as 'All Saints.' Among their youthful companions they bore the more martial style of 'The Three Champions,' St. George, St. John, and St. Anthony.

St. John and St. Anthony had just completed the grand tour, and, after passing the Easter at Rome, had returned through the Tyrol from Italy. Since then they had travelled over most parts of Germany; and now, in the beginning of July, found themselves at the Baths of Ems. Two years' travel had not produced any very beneficial effect on either of these sainted personages. They had gained, by visiting the capitals of all Europe, only a due acquaintance with the follies of each; and the only difference that could be observed in their conduct on their return was, that

their affectation was rather more fantastical, and therefore more amusing.

'Corpo di Bacco, my champion! who ever thought
of meeting thee, thou holy saint! By the eyebrow of
Venus, my spirit rejoiceth!' exclaimed St. Anthony,
whose peculiar affectation was an adoption in English of the Italian oaths.

'This is the sweetest spot, St. Anthony, that we
have found since we left Paradiso; that is, St. George,
in the vulgar, since we quitted Italia. "Italia! O
Italia!" I forget the rest; probably you remember it.
Certainly, a most sweet spot this, quite a Gaspar!'

Art was the peculiar affectation of St. John; he
was, indeed, quite a patron of the Belle Arti, had
scattered his orders through the studios of most of
the celebrated sculptors of Italy, and spoke on all
subjects and all things only with a view to their
capability of forming material for the painter. According to the school of which Mr. St. John was a
disciple, the only use of the human passions is, that
they produce situations for the historical painter; and
nature according to these votaries of τὸ καλὸν, is
only to be valued as affording hints for the more
perfect conceptions of a Claude or a Salvator.

'By the girdle of Venus, a devilish fine woman!'
exclaimed St. Anthony.

'A splendid bit!' ejaculated St. John; 'touched in
with freedom, a grand tournure, great gout in the
swell of the neck. What a study for Retsch!'

'In the name of the Graces, who is it, mio Santo?'

'Ay! name la bellissima Signora.'

'The "fine bit," St. John, is my sister.'

'The devil!'

'Diavolo!'

'Will you introduce us, most holy man?'

This request from both, simultaneously arranging their mustachios.

The two saints were accordingly, in due time, introduced; but finding the attention of Miss Fane always engrossed, and receiving some not very encouraging responses from Lady Madeleine, they voted her ladyship cursedly satirical; and passing a general censure on the annoying coldness of Englishwomen, they were in four-and-twenty hours attached to the suite of the Miss Fitzlooms, to whom they were introduced by St. George as his particular friends, and were received with the most flattering consideration.

'By the aspect of Diana! fine girls,' swore St. Anthony.

'Truly most gorgeous colouring! quite Venetian! Aurelia is a perfect Giorgione!' said St. John.

'Madeleine,' said St. George, one morning, to his sister, 'have you any objection to make up a party with the Fitzlooms to pass a day at Nassau? You know we have often talked of it; and as Violet is so well now, and the weather so delightful, there surely can be no objection. The Fitzlooms are very agreeable people; and though you do not admire the Santi, still, upon my word, when you know them a little more, you will find them very pleasant fellows, and they are extremely good-natured; and just the fellows for such a party. Do not refuse me. I have set my mind upon your joining the party. Pray nod assent; thank you. Now I must go and arrange everything. Let us see: there are seven Fitzlooms; for we cannot count on less than two boys; yourself, Grey, Violet, and myself, four; the Santi; quite enough, a most delightful party. Half a dozen servants and as many donkeys will manage the provisions. Then three light carriages will take us all. "By the wand of Mercury!" as St. Anthony would vow, admirably planned!'

'By the breath of Zephyr! a most lovely day, Miss Fane,' said St. Anthony, on the morning of the intended excursion.

'Quite a Claude!' said St. John.

'Almost as beautiful as an Italian winter day, Mr. St. Leger?' asked Miss Fane.

'Hardly!' said St. Anthony, with a serious air; for he imagined the question to be quite genuine.

The carriages are at the door; into the first ascended Mrs. Fitzloom, two daughters, and the travelling saints. The second bore Lady Madeleine, Mr. Fitzloom, and his two sons; the third division was formed of Mr. St. George and Aurelia Fitzloom, Miss Fane and Vivian.

Away, away, rolled the carriages; the day was beautiful, the sky was without a cloud, and a mild breeze prevented the heat of the sun from being overpowering. All were in high spirits; for St. George had made a capital master of the ceremonies, and had arranged the company in the carriages to their mutual satisfaction. St. Anthony swore, by the soul of Psyche! that Augusta Fitzloom was an angel; and St. John was in equal raptures with Araminta, who had an expression about the eyes which reminded him of Titian's Flora. Mrs. Fitzloom's natural silence did not disturb the uninterrupted jargon of the Santi, whose foppery elicited loud and continued approbation from the fair sisters. The mother sat admiring these sprigs of noble trees. The young Fitzlooms, in crimson cravats, conversed with Lady

Madeleine with a delightful military air; and their
happy parent, as he gazed upon them with satisfied
affection, internally promised them both a commission
in a crack regiment.

The road from Ems to Nassau winds along the
banks of the Lahn, through two leagues of delightful
scenery; at the end of which, springing up from the
peak of a bold and richly-wooded mountain, the lofty
tower of the ancient castle of Nassau meets your
view. Winding walks round the sides of the mountain lead through all the varieties of sylvan scenery,
and command in all points magnificent views of the
surrounding country. These finally bring you to the
old castle, whose spacious chambers, though now
choked up with masses of grey ruin or covered with
underwood, still bear witness to the might of their
former lord! the powerful Baron whose sword gained
for his posterity a throne.

All seemed happy; none happier than Violet Fane.
Never did she look so beautiful as to-day, never was
she so animated, never had she boasted that her pulse
beat more melodious music, or her lively blood danced
a more healthful measure. After examining all the antique chambers of the castle, and discovering, as they
flattered themselves, secret passages, and dark dungeons, and hidden doors, they left this interesting relic
of the middle ages; and soon, by a gradual descent
through delightful shrubberies, they again found themselves at the bottom of the valley. Here they visited
the modern château of Baron von Stein, one of the
most enlightened and able politicians that Germany
has ever produced. As Minister of Prussia, he commenced those reforms which the illustrious Harden-
berg perfected. For upwards of five centuries the

family of Stein have retained their territorial possessions in the valley of the Lahn. Their family castle,
at present a ruin, and formerly a fief of the House of
Nassau, is now only a picturesque object in the pleasure-grounds of the present lord.

The noon had passed some hours before the delighted wanderers complained of fatigue, and by that
time they found themselves in a pleasant green glade
on the skirts of the forest of Nassau. It was nearly
environed by mountains, covered with hanging woods,
which shaded the beautiful valley, and gave it the
appearance of a sylvan amphitheatre. From a rocky
cleft in these green mountains a torrent, dashing down
with impetuous force, and whose fall was almost
concealed by the cloud of spray which it excited,
gave birth to a small and gentle river, whose banks
were fringed with beautiful trees, which prevented the
sun's darts from piercing its coldness, by bowing
their fair heads over its waters. From their extending branches Nature's choristers sent forth many a
lovely lay

Of God's high praise, and of their loves' sweet teen.

Near the banks of this river, the servants, under
the active direction of Essper George, had prepared a
banquet for the party. The cloth had been laid on a
raised work of wood and turf, and rustic seats of the
same material surrounded the picturesque table. It
glowed with materials, and with colours to which
Veronese alone could have done justice: pasties, and
birds, and venison, and groups of fish, gleamy with
prismatic hues, while amid pyramids of fruit rose
goblets of fantastic glass, worthy of the famous wines
they were to receive.

'Well!' said Miss Fane, 'I never will be a member of an adventurous party like the present, of which Albert is not manager.'

'I must not take the whole credit upon myself, Violet; St. John is butler, and St. Leger my vice-chamberlain.'

'Well, I cannot praise Mr. St. John till I have tasted the malvoisie which he has promised; but as for the other part of the entertainment, Mr. St. Leger, I am sure this is a temptation which it 'would be a sin, even in St. Anthony, to withstand.'

'By the body of Bacchus, very good!' swore Mr. St. Leger.

'These mountains,' said Mr. St. John, 'remind me of one of Gaspar's cool valleys. The party, indeed, give it a different character, quite a Watteau!'

'Now, Mrs. Fitzloom,' said St. George, who was in his element, 'let me recommend a little of this pike! Lady Madeleine, I have sent you some lamb. Miss Fitzloom, I hope St. Anthony is taking care of you. Wrightson, plates to Mr. St. Leger. Holy man, and much beloved! send Araminta some chicken. Grey has helped you, Violet? Aurelia, this is for you. William Pitt Fitzloom, I leave you to yourself. George Canning Fitzloom, take care of the ladies near you. Essper George! Where is Essper? St. John, who is your deputy in the wine department? Wrightson! bring those long green bottles out of the river, and put the champagne underneath the willow. Will your Ladyship take some light claret? Mrs. Fitzloom, you must use your tumbler; nothing but tumblers allowed, by Miss Fane's particular request!'

'St. George, thou holy man!' said Miss Fane, 'methinks you are very impertinent. You shall not be my patron saint if you say such words.'

For the next hour there was nothing heard save the calling of servants, the rattling of knives and forks, the drawing of corks, and continued bursts of laughter, which were not occasioned by any brilliant observations, either of the Saints, or any other persons, but merely the result of an exuberance of spirits on the part of every one present.

'Well, Aurelia,' said Lady Madeleine, 'do you prefer our present mode of life to feasting in an old hall, covered with banners and battered shields, and surrounded by mysterious corridors and dark dungeons?' Aurelia was so flattered by the notice of Lady Madeleine, that she made her no answer; probably because she was intent on a plover's egg.

'I think we might all retire to this valley,' said Miss Fane, 'and revive the feudal times with great success. Albert might take us to Nassau Castle, and you, Mr. Fitzloom, might re-fortify the old tower of Stein. With two sons, however, who are about to enter the Guards, I am afraid we must be your vassals. Then what should we do? We could not have wood parties every day; I suppose we should get tired of each other. No! that does seem impossible; do not you all think so?'

Omnes, 'Impossible!'

'We must, however, have some regular pursuit, some cause of constant excitement, some perpetual source of new emotions. New ideas, of course, we must give up; there would be no going to London for the season, for new opinions to astound country cousins on our return. Some pursuit must be in-

vented; we all must have something to do. I have
it! Albert shall be a tyrant.'

'I am very much obliged to you, Violet.'

'Yes! a cruel, unprincipled, vindictive, remorseless
tyrant, with a long black beard, I cannot tell how
long, about twenty thousand times longer than Mr.
St. Leger's mustachios.'

'By the beard of Jove!' swore St. Anthony, as he
almost started from his seat, and arranged with his
thumb and forefinger the delicate Albanian tuft of his
upper lip, 'by the beard of Jove, Miss Fane, I am
obliged to you.'

'Well, then,' continued Violet, 'Albert being a
tyrant, Lady Madeleine must be an unhappy, ill-used,
persecuted woman, living on black bread and green
water, in an unknown dungeon. My part shall be to
discover her imprisonment. Sounds of strange music
attract my attention to a part of the castle which I
have not before frequented. There I shall distinctly
hear a female voice chaunting the "Bridesmaids' Chorus," with Erard's double pedal accompaniment. By
the aid of the confessors of the two families, two
drinking, rattling, impertinent, most corrupt, and most
amusing friars, to wit, our sainted friends ——'

Here both Mr. St. Leger and Mr. St. John bowed
low to Miss Fane.

'A most lively personage is Miss Fane,' whispered
St. Anthony to his neighbour, Miss Fitzloom, 'great
style!'

'Most amusing, delightful girl, great style! rather
a display to-day, I think.'

'Oh, decidedly! and devilish personal, too; some
people wouldn't like it. I have no doubt she will
say something about you next.'

'Oh, I shall be very surprised, indeed, if she does! It may be very well to you, but Miss Fane must be aware——'

Before this pompous sentence could be finished an incident occurred which prevented Miss Fane from proceeding with her allotment of characters, and rendered unnecessary the threatened indignation of Miss Fitzloom.

Miss Fane, as we mentioned, suddenly ceased speaking; the eyes of all were turned in the direction in which she was gazing as if she had seen a ghost.

'What are you looking up at, Violet?' asked St. George.

'Did not you see anything? did not any of you see anything?'

'None, none!'

'Mr. Grey, surely you must have seen it!'

'I saw nothing.'

'It could not be fancy; impossible. I saw it distinctly. I cannot be in a dream. See there! again, on that topmost branch. It moves!'

Some odd shrill sounds, uttered in the voice of a Pulcinello, attracted the notice of them all; and lo! high in the air, behind a lofty chestnut tree, the figure of a Pulcinello did appear, hopping and vaulting in the unsubstantial air. Now it sent forth another shrill, piercing sound, and now, with both its hands, it patted and complacently stroked its ample paunch; dancing all the time with unremitting activity, and wagging its queer head at the astounded guests.

'Who, what can it be?' cried all. The Misses Fitzloom shrieked, and the Santi seemed quite puzzled.

'Who, what can it be?'

Ere time could be given for any one to hazard a conjecture, the figure had advanced from behind the trees, and had spanned in an instant the festal board, with two enormous stilts, on which they now perceived it was mounted. The Misses Fitzloom shrieked again. The figure imitated their cries in his queer voice, and gradually raising one enormous stilt up into the air, stood only on one support, which was planted behind the lovely Araminta.

'O! inimitable Essper George!' exclaimed Violet Fane.

Here Signor Punch commenced a song, which he executed in the tone peculiar to his character, and in a style which drew applauses from all; and then, with a hop, step, and a jump, he was again behind the chestnut tree. In a moment he advanced without his stilts towards the table. Here, on the turf, he again commenced his antics; kicking his nose with his right foot, and his hump with his left one; executing splendid somersets, and cutting every species of caper, and never ceasing for a moment from performing all his movements to the inspiring music of his own melodious voice. At last, jumping up very high in the air, he fell as if all his joints were loosened, and the Misses Fitzloom, imagining that his bones were really broken, shrieked again. But now Essper began the wonderful performance of a dead body possessed by a devil, and in a minute his shattered corpse, apparently without the assistance of any of its members, began to jump and move about the ground with miraculous rapidity. At length it disappeared behind the chestnut tree.

'I really think,' said Mr. St. George, 'it is the most agreeable day I ever passed in all my life.'

'Decidedly!' said St. Anthony. 'St. John, you remember our party to Pæstum with Lady Calabria M'Crater and the Marquis of Agrigentum. It was nothing to this! Nothing! Do you know, I thought that rather dull.'

'Yes, too elaborate; too highly finished; nothing of the pittore improvisatore. A party of this kind should be more sketchy in its style; the outline more free, and less detail.'

'Essper is coming out to-day,' said Vivian to Miss Fane, 'after a long, and, I venture to say, painful forbearance. However, I hope you will excuse him, it seems to amuse us.'

'I think it is delightful. See! here he comes again.'

He now appeared in his original costume; the one in which Vivian first met him at the fair. Bowing, he threw his hand carelessly over his mandolin, and having tried the melody of its strings, sang with great taste, and a sweet voice — sweeter from its contrast with its previous shrill tones — a very pretty romance. All applauded him very warmly, and no one more so than Miss Fane.

'Ah! inimitable Essper George, how can we sufficiently thank you! How well he plays! and his voice is quite beautiful. Oh! could not we dance? would not it be delightful? and he could play on his guitar. Think of the delicious turf!'

Omnes, 'Delightful! delightful!' They rose from the table.

'Violet, my dear,' asked Lady Madeleine, 'what are you going to do?'

'By the toe of Terpsichore!' as Mr. St. Leger would say, 'I am going to dance.'

'But remember to-day you have done so much!

let us be moderate; though you feel so much better, still think what a change to-day has been from your usual habits!'

'But, dearest Lady Madeleine, think of dancing on the turf, and I feel so well!'

'By the Graces! I am for the waltz,' said St. Anthony.

'It has certainly a very free touch to recommend it,' said St. John.

'No, no,' said Violet; 'let us all join in a country dance.' But the Misses Fitzloom preferred a quadrille.

The quadrille was soon formed: Violet made up for not dancing with Vivian at the Grand Duke's. She was most animated, and kept up a successful rivalry with Mr. St. Leger, who evidently prided himself, as Mr. Fitzloom observed, 'on his light fantastic toe.' Now he pirouetted like Paul, and now he attitudinised like Albert; and now Miss Fane eclipsed all his exertions by her inimitable imitations of Ronzi Vestris' rushing and arrowy manner. St. Anthony, in despair, but quite delighted, revealed a secret which had been taught him by a Spanish dancer at Milan; but then Miss Fane vanquished him for ever with the pas de Zephyr of the exquisite Fanny Bias.

The day was fast declining when the carriages arrived; the young people were in no humour to return; and as, when they had once entered the carriage, the day seemed finished for ever, they proposed walking part of the way home. Lady Madeleine made little objection to Violet joining the party, as after the exertion that Miss Fane had been making, a drive in an open carriage might be dangerous; and yet the walk was too long, but all agreed that it would be impossible to shorten it; and, as Violet declared that she was not in the least fatigued, the lesser evil was therefore chosen. The carriages rolled off; at about half way from Ems, the two empty ones were to wait for the walking party. Lady Madeleine smiled with fond affection, as she waved her hand to Violet the moment before she was out of sight.

'And now,' said St. George, 'good people all, instead of returning by the same road, it strikes me, that there must be a way through this little wood; you see there is an excellent path. Before the sun is set we shall have got through it, and it will bring us out, I have no doubt, by the old cottage which you observed, Grey, when we came along. I saw a gate and path there; just where we first got sight of Nassau Castle; there can be no doubt about it. You see it is a regular right-angle, and besides varying the walk, we shall at least gain a quarter of an hour, which, after all, as we have to walk nearly three miles, is an object. It is quite clear, if I have a head for anything, it is for finding my way.'

'I think you have a head for everything,' said Aurelia Fitzloom, in a soft sentimental whisper; 'I am sure we owe all our happiness to-day to you!'

'If I have a head for everything, I have a heart only for one person!'

As every one wished to be convinced, no one offered any argument in opposition to Mr. St. George's view of the case; and some were already in the wood.

'Albert,' said Miss Fane, 'I do not like walking in the wood so late; pray come back.'

'Oh, nonsense, Violet! come. If you do not like to come, you can walk by the road; you will meet us round by the gate, it is only five minutes' walk.'

Ere he had finished speaking, the rest were in the wood, and some had advanced. Vivian strongly recommended Violet not to join them; he was sure that Lady Madeleine would not approve of it; he was sure that it was very dangerous, extremely; and, by-the-bye, while he was talking, which way had they gone? he did not see them. He hallooed; all answered, and a thousand echoes besides. 'We certainly had better go by the road, we shall lose our way if we try to follow them; nothing is so puzzling as walking in woods; we had much better keep to the road.' So by the road they went.

The sun had already sunk behind the mountains, whose undulating forms were thrown into dark shadow against the crimson sky. The thin crescent of the new moon floated over the eastern hills, whose deep woods glowed with the rosy glories of twilight. Over the peak of a purple mountain glittered the solitary star of evening. As the sun dropped, universal silence seemed to pervade the whole face of nature. The voice of the birds was stilled; the breeze, which had refreshed them during the day, died away, as if its office were now completed; and none of the dark sounds and sights of hideous Night yet dared to triumph over the death of Day. Unseen were the circling wings of the fell bat; unheard the screech of the waking owl; silent the drowsy hum of the shade-born beetle! What heart has not acknowledged the influence of this hour, the sweet and soothing hour of twilight! the hour of love, the hour of adoration, the hour of rest! when we think of those we love, only to regret that we have not loved more dearly; when we remember our enemies only to forgive them!

And Vivian and his beautiful companion owned
the magic of this hour, as all must do, by silence.
No word was spoken, yet is silence sometimes a
language. They gazed, and gazed again, and their
full spirits held due communion with the starlit sky,
and the mountains and the woods, and the soft
shadows of the increasing moon. Oh! who can describe what the o'ercharged spirit feels at this sacred
hour, when we almost lose the consciousness of existence, and our souls seem to struggle to pierce futu-
rity! In the forest of the mysterious Odenwald, in
the solitudes of the Bergstrasse, had Vivian at this
hour often found consolation for a bruised spirit,
often in adoring nature had forgotten man. But
now, when he had never felt nature's influence more
powerful; when he had never forgotten man and
man's world more thoroughly; when he was expe-
riencing emotions, which, though undefinable, he felt
to be new; he started when he remembered that all
this was in the presence of a human being! Was it
Hesperus he gazed upon, or something else that
glanced brighter than an Evening star? Even as he
thought that his gaze was fixed on the countenance
of nature, he found that his eyes rested on the face
of nature's loveliest daughter!

'Violet! dearest Violet!'

As in some delicious dream the sleeper is awakened
from his bliss by the sound of his own rapturous
voice, so was Vivian roused by these words from his
reverie, and called back to the world which he had
forgotten. But ere a moment had passed, he was
pouring forth in a rapid voice, and incoherent manner, such words as men speak only once. He spoke
of his early follies, his misfortunes, his misery; of his

AFTER AN ORIGINAL DRAWING BY HERMAN ROUNTREE.

*Alarmed, he raised her off the ground and bore her
to the river-side.*

(See page 55.)

matured views, his settled principles, his plans, his prospects, his hopes, his happiness, his bliss; and when he had ceased, he listened, in his turn, to some small still words, which made him the happiest of human beings. He bent down, he kissed the soft silken cheek which now he could call his own. Her hand was in his; her head sank upon his breast. Suddenly she clung to him with a strong grasp. 'Violet! my own, my dearest; you are overcome. I have been rash, I have been imprudent. Speak, speak, my beloved! say, you are not ill!'

She spoke not, but clung to him with a fearful strength, her head still upon his breast, her full eyes closed. Alarmed, he raised her off the ground, and bore her to the river-side. Water might revive her. But when he tried to lay her a moment on the bank, she clung to him gasping, as a sinking person clings to a stout swimmer. He leant over her; he did not attempt to disengage her arms; and, by degrees, by very slow degrees, her grasp loosened. At last her arms gave way and fell by his side, and her eyes partly opened.

'Thank God! Violet, my own, my beloved, say you are better!'

She answered not, evidently she did not know him, evidently she did not see him. A film was on her sight, and her eye was glassy. He rushed to the water-side, and in a moment he had sprinkled her temples, now covered with a cold dew. Her pulse beat not, her circulation seemed suspended. He rubbed the palms of her hands, he covered her delicate feet with his coat; and then rushing up the bank into the road, he shouted with frantic cries on all sides. No one came, no one was near. Again, with a cry of fearful anguish, he shouted as if an hyæna were feeding on his vitals. No sound; no answer. The nearest cottage was above a mile off. He dared not leave her. Again he rushed down to the water-side. Her eyes were still open, still fixed. Her mouth also was no longer closed. Her hand was stiff, her heart had ceased to beat. He tried with the warmth of his own body to revive her. He shouted, he wept, he prayed. All, all in vain. Again he was in the road, again shouting like an insane being. There was a sound. Hark! It was but the screech of an owl!

Once more at the river-side, once more bending over her with starting eyes, once more the attentive ear listening for the soundless breath. No sound! not even a sigh! Oh! what would he have given for her shriek of anguish! No change had occurred in her position, but the lower part of her face had fallen; and there was a general appearance which struck him with awe. Her body was quite cold, her limbs stiffened. He gazed, and gazed, and gazed. He bent over her with stupor rather than grief stamped on his features. It was very slowly that the dark thought came over his mind, very slowly that the horrible truth seized upon his soul. He gave a loud shriek, and fell on the lifeless body of VIOLET FANE!

BOOK VI.

CHAPTER I.

THE PALACE OF THE WINES.

THE green and bowery summer had passed away. It was midnight when two horsemen pulled up their steeds beneath a wide oak; which, with other lofty trees, skirted the side of a winding road in an extensive forest in the south of Germany.

'By heavens!' said one, who apparently was the master, 'we must even lay our cloaks, I think, under this oak; for the road winds again, and assuredly cannot lead now to our village.'

'A starlit sky in autumn can scarcely be the fittest curtain for one so weak as you, sir; I should recommend travelling on, if we keep on our horses' backs till dawn.'

'But if we are travelling in a directly contrary way to our voiturier, honest as we may suppose him to be, if he find in the morning no paymaster for his job, he may with justice make free with our baggage. And I shall be unusually mistaken if the road we are now pursuing does not lead back to the city.'

(57)

'City, town, or village, you must sleep under no forest tree, sir. Let us ride on. It will be hard if we do not find some huntsman's or ranger's cottage; and for aught we know a neat snug village, or some comfortable old manor-house, which has been in the family for two centuries; and where, with God's blessing, they may chance to have wine as old as the bricks. I know not how you may feel, sir, but a ten hours' ride when I was only prepared for half the time, and that, too, in an autumn night, makes me somewhat desirous of renewing my acquaintance with the kitchen-fire.'

'I could join you in a glass of hock and a slice of venison, I confess, my good fellow; but in a nocturnal ride I am no longer your match. However, if you think it best, we will prick on our steeds for another hour. If it be only for them, I am sure we must soon stop.'

'Ay! do sir; and put your cloak well round you; all is for the best. You are not, I guess, a Sabbath-born child?'

'That am I not, but how would that make our plight worse than it is? Should we be farther off supper?'

'Nearer, perhaps, than you imagine; for we should then have a chance of sharing the spoils of the Spirit Hunter.'

'Ah! Essper, is it so?'

'Truly yes, sir; and were either of us a Sabbath-born child, by holy cross! I would not give much for our chance of a down bed this night.'

Here a great horned owl flew across the road.

'Were I in the north,' said Essper, 'I would sing an Ave Mary against the STUT OZEL.'

'What call you that?' asked Vivian.

''Tis the great bird, sir; the great horned owl, that always flies before the Wild Hunter. And truly, sir, I have passed through many forests in my time, but never yet saw I one where I should sooner expect to hear a midnight bugle. If you will allow me, sir, I will ride by your side. Thank God, at least, it is not the Walpurgis night!'

'I wish to Heaven it were!' said Vivian, 'and that we were on the Brocken. It must be highly amusing!'

'Hush! hush! it is lucky we are not in the Hartz; but we know not where we are, nor who at this moment may be behind us.'

And here Essper began pouring forth a liturgy of his own, half Catholic and half Calvinistic, quite in character with the creed of the country through which they were travelling.

'My horse has stumbled,' continued Essper, 'and yours, sir, is he not shying? There is a confounded cloud over the moon, but I have no sight in the dark if that mass before you be not a devil-stone. The Lord have mercy upon our sinful souls!'

'Peace! Essper,' said Vivian, who was surprised to find him really alarmed; 'I see nothing but a block of granite, no uncommon sight in a German forest.'

'It is a devil-stone, I tell you, sir; there has been some church here, which he has knocked down in the night. Look! is it the moss-people that I see! As sure as I am a hungry sinner, the Wild One is out a-hunting to-night.'

'More luck for us, if we meet him. His dogs, as you say, may gain us a supper. I think our wisest course will be to join the cry.'

'Hush! hush! you would not talk so if you knew what your share of the spoils might be. Ay! if you did, sir, your cheek would be paler, and your very teeth would chatter. I knew one man who was travelling in the forest, just as we are now; it was about this time; and he believed in the Wild Huntsman about as much as you, that is, he liked to talk of the Spirit, merely to have the opportunity of denying that he believed in him; which showed, as I used to say, that his mind was often thinking of it. He was a merry knave, and as firm a hand for a boar-spear as ever I met with, and I have met many. We used to call him, before the accident, Left-handed Hans, but they call him now, sir, the Child-Hunter. Oh! it is a very awful tale, and I would sooner tell it in blazing hall than in free forest. You did not hear any sound to the left, did you?'

'Nothing but the wind, Essper; on with your tale, my man.'

'It is a very awful tale, sir, but I will make short work of it. You see, sir, it was a night just like this; the moon was generally hid, but the stars prevented it from ever being pitch dark. And so, sir, he was travelling alone; he had been up to the castle of the baron, his master; you see, sir, he was head-ranger to his lordship, and he always returned home through the forest. What he was thinking of, I cannot say, but most likely of no good; when all on a sudden he heard the baying of hounds in the distance. Now directly he heard it — I have heard him tell the story a thousand times — directly he heard it, it struck him that it must be the Spirit Huntsman; and though there were many ways to account for the hounds, still he never for a moment doubted

refuse the invitation, and instantly he was galloping
by the side of the Wild Huntsman. Away they flew!
away! away! away! over bog, and over mere; over
ditch, and over hedge; away! away! away! and the
Ranger's horse never failed, but kept by the side of
the Wild Spirit without the least distress; and yet it
is very singular that Hans was about to sell this very
beast only a day before, for a matter of five crowns:
you see, he only kept it just to pick his way at night
from the castle to his own cottage. Well, it is very
odd, but Hans soon lost all fear, for the sport was so
fine and he had such a keen relish for the work,
that, far from being alarmed, he thought himself one
of the luckiest knaves alive. But the oddest thing all
this time was, that Hans never caught sight for one
moment of either buck or boar, although he saw by
the dogs' noses that there was something keen in the
wind, and although he felt that if the hunted beast
were like any that he had himself ever followed before, it must have been run down with such dogs,
quicker than a priest could say a paternoster. At
last, for he had grown quite bold, says Hans to the
Wild Huntsman, "The beasts run quick 'o nights, sir,
I think; it has been a long time, I ween, ere I scampered so far, and saw so little!" Do you know that
the old gentleman was not the least affronted, but
said, in the pleasantest voice imaginable, "A true
huntsman should be patient, Hans; you will see the
game quick enough; look forward, man! what see
you?" And sure enough, your Highness, he did
look forward. It was near the skirts of the forest,
there was a green glade before them, and very few
trees, and therefore he could see far a-head. The
moon was shining very bright, and sure enough,

what did he see? Running as fleet over the turf as a rabbit, was a child. The little figure was quite black in the moonlight, and Hans could not catch its face: in a moment the hell-dogs were on it. Hans quivered like a windy reed, and the Wild One laughed till the very woods echoed. "How like you hunting moss-men?" asked the Spirit. Now when Hans found it was only a moss-man, he took heart again, and said in a shaking voice, that "It is rare good sport in good company;" and then the Spirit jumped off his horse, and said, "Now, Hans, you must watch me well, for I am little used to bag game." He said this with a proudish air, as much as to hint, that had not he expected Hans, he would not have rode out this evening without his groom. So the Wild One jumped on his horse again, and put the bag before him. It was nearly morning when Hans found himself at the door of his own cottage; and, bowing very respectfully to the Spirit Hunter, he thanked him for the sport, and begged his share of the night's spoil. This was all in joke, but Hans had heard that "talk to the devil, and fear the last word;" and so he was determined, now that they were about to part, not to appear to tremble, but to carry it off with a jest. "Truly, Hans," said the Huntsman, "thou art a bold lad, and to encourage thee to speak to wild huntsmen again, I have a mind to give thee for thy pains the whole spoil. Take the bag, knave, a moss-man is good ating; had I time I would give thee a receipt for sauce;" and, so saying, the Spirit rode off, laughing very heartily. Well, sir, Hans was so anxious to examine the contents of the bag, and see what kind of thing a moss-man really was, for he had only caught a glimpse of him in the chase, that instead of going to bed immediately, and saying his prayers, as he should have done, he lighted a lamp and undid the string; and what think you he took out of the bag? As sure as I am a born sinner, his own child!'

''Tis a wonderful tale,' said Vivian; 'and did the unfortunate man tell you this himself?'

'Often and often. I knew Left-handed Hans well. He was ranger, as I said, to a great lord; and was quite a favourite, you see. For some reason or other he got out of favour. Some said that the Baron had found him out a-poaching; and that he used to ride his master's horses a-night. Whether this be true or not, who can say? But, howsoever, Hans went to ruin; and instead of being a flourishing active lad, he was turned out, and went a-begging all through Saxony; and he always told this story as the real history of his misfortunes. Some say he is not as strong in his head as he used to be. However, why should we say it is not a true tale? What is that?' almost shrieked Essper.

Vivian listened, and heard distinctly the distant baying of hounds.

''Tis he!' said Essper; 'now don't speak, sir, don't speak! and if the devil make me join him,— as may be the case, for I am but a cock-brained thing, particularly at midnight,— don't be running after me from any foolish feeling, but take care of yourself, and don't be chattering. To think you should come to this, my precious young master!'

'Cease your blubbering! Do you think that I am to be frightened by the idiot tales of a parcel of old women, and the lies of a gang of detected poachers? Come sir, ride on. We are, most probably, near some huntsman's cottage. That distant baying is the sweetest music I have heard a long while.'

'Don't be rash, sir; don't be rash. If you were to give me fifty crowns now, I could not remember a single line of a single prayer. Ave Maria! it always is so when I most want it. Paternoster! and whenever I have need to remember a song, sure enough I am always thinking of a prayer. "Unser vater, der du bist im himmel, sanctificado se el tu nombra; il tuo regno venga."' Here Essper George was proceeding with a scrap of modern Greek, when the horsemen suddenly came upon one of those broad green vistas which we often see in forests, and which are generally cut, either for the convenience of hunting, or carting wood. It opened on the left side of the road; and at the bottom of it, though apparently at a great distance, a light was visible.

'So much for your Wild Huntsman, friend Essper! I shall be much disappointed if here are not quarters for the night. And see! the moon comes out, a good omen!'

After ten minutes' canter over the noiseless turf, the travellers found themselves before a large and many-windowed mansion. The building formed the farthest side of a quadrangle, which you entered through an ancient and massy gate; on each side of which was a small building, of course the lodges. Essper soon found that the gate was closely fastened; and though he knocked often and loudly, it was with no effect. That the inhabitants of the mansion had not yet retired was certain, for lights were moving in the great house; and one of the lodges was not only very brilliantly illuminated, but full, as Vivian was soon convinced, of clamorous if not jovial guests.

'Now, by the soul of my unknown father!' said the enraged Essper, 'I will make these saucy porters learn their duty. What ho! there; what ho! within! within!' But the only answer he received was the loud reiteration of a rude and roaring chorus, which, as it was now more distinctly and audibly enunciated, evidently for the purpose of enraging the travellers, they detected to be something to the following effect: —

> Then a prayer to St. Peter, a prayer to St. Paul!
> A prayer to St. Jerome, a prayer to them all!
> A prayer to each one of the saintly stock,
> But devotion alone, devotion to Hock!

'A right good burden!' said Essper. The very words had made him recover his temper, and ten thousand times more desirous of gaining admittance. He was off his horse in a moment, and scrambling up the wall with the aid of the iron stanchions, he clambered up to the window. The sudden appearance of his figure startled the inmates of the lodge, and one of them soon staggered to the gate.

'What want you, ye noisy and disturbing varlets? what want you, ye most unhallowed rogues, at such a place, and at such an hour? If you be thieves, look at our bars (here a hiccup). If you be poachers, our master is engaged, and ye may slay all the game in the forest (another hiccup); but if ye be good men and true——'

'We are!' halloed Essper, eagerly.

'You are!' said the porter, in a tone of great surprise; 'then you ought to be ashamed of yourselves for disturbing holy men at their devotions!'

'Is this the way,' said Essper, 'to behave, ye shameless rascals, to a noble and mighty prince, who

happens to have lost his way in your abominable
forest, but who, though he has parted with his suite,
has still in his pocket a purse full of ducats? Would
ye have him robbed by any others but yourselves?
Is this the way you behave to a Prince of the Holy
Roman Empire, a Knight of the Golden Fleece, and a
most particular friend of your own master? Is this
the way to behave to his secretary, who is one of
the merriest fellows living, can sing a jolly song with
any of you, and so bedevil a bottle of Geisenheim
with lemons and brandy that for the soul of ye you
wouldn't know it from the greenest Tokay? Out,
out on ye! you know not what you have lost!'

Ere Essper had finished more than one stout bolt
had been drawn, and the great key had already entered the stouter lock.

'Most honourable sirs!' hiccuped the porter, 'in
our Lady's name enter. I had forgot myself, for in
these autumn nights it is necessary to anticipate the
cold with a glass of cheering liquor; and, God forgive me! if I did not mistake your most mighty
Highnesses for a couple of forest rovers, or small
poachers at least. Thin entertainment here, kind sir
(here the last bolt was withdrawn); a glass of indifferent liquor and a prayer-book. I pass the time
chiefly these cold nights with a few holy-minded
friends at our devotions. You heard us at our prayers,
honourable lords!

> 'A prayer to St. Peter, a prayer to St. Paul!
> A prayer to St. Jerome, a prayer to them all!'

Here the devout porter most reverently crossed himself.

> 'A prayer to each one of the saintly stock,
> But devotion alone, devotion to Hock!'

added Essper George; 'you forget the best part of the burden, my honest friend.'

'Oh!' said the porter with an arch smile, as he opened the lodge door; 'I am glad to find that your honourable Excellencies have a taste for hymns!'

The porter led them into a room, at a round table in which about half-a-dozen individuals were busily engaged in discussing the merits of various agreeable liquors. There was an attempt to get up a show of polite hospitality to Vivian as he entered, but the man who offered him his chair fell to the ground in an unsuccessful struggle to be courteous; and another one, who had filled a large glass for the guest on his entrance, offered him, after a preliminary speech of incoherent compliments, the empty bottle by mistake. The porter and his friends, although they were all drunk, had sense enough to feel that the presence of a Prince of the Holy Roman Empire, a Chevalier of the Golden Fleece, and the particular friend of their master, was not exactly a fit companion for themselves, and was rather a check on the gay freedom of equal companionship; and so, although the exertion was not a little troublesome, the guardian of the gate reeled out of the room to inform his honoured lord of the sudden arrival of a stranger of distinction. Essper George immediately took his place, and ere the master of the lodge had returned the noble secretary had not only given a choice toast, sung a choice song, and been hailed by the grateful plaudits of all present, but had proceeded in his attempt to fulfil the pledge which he had given at the gate to the very letter by calling out lustily for a bottle of Geisenheim, lemons, brandy, and a bowl.

'Fairly and softly, my little son of Bacchus,' said

the porter as he re-entered, 'fairly and softly, and then thou shalt want nothing; but remember I have to perform my duties unto the noble Lord my master, and also to the noble Prince your master. If thou wilt follow me,' continued the porter, reeling as he bowed with the greatest consideration to Vivian; 'if thou wilt follow me, most high and mighty sir, my master will be right glad to have the honour of drinking your health. And as for you, my friends, fairly and softly say I again. We will talk of the Geisenheim anon. Am I to be absent from the first brewing? No, no! fairly and softly; you can drink my health when I am absent in cold liquor, and say those things which you could not well say before my face. But mind, my most righteous and well-beloved, I will have no flattery. Flattery is the destruction of all good fellowship; it is like a qualmish liqueur in the midst of a bottle of wine. Speak your minds, say any little thing that comes first, as thus, "Well, for Hunsdrich, the porter, I must declare that I never heard evil word against him;" or thus, "A very good leg has Hunsdrich the porter, and a tight-made lad altogether; no enemy with the girls, I warrant me;" or thus, "Well, for a good-hearted, good-looking, stout-drinking, virtuous, honourable, handsome, generous, sharp-witted knave, commend me to Hunsdrich the porter;" but not a word more, my friends, not a word more, no flattery. Now, sir, I beg your pardon.'

The porter led the way through a cloistered walk, until they arrived at the door of the great mansion, to which they ascended by a lofty flight of steps; it opened into a large octagonal hall, the sides of which were covered with fowling-pieces, stags' heads, cou-

teaux de chasse, boar-spears, and huge fishing nets.
Passing through this hall, they ascended a noble
staircase, on the first landing-place of which was a
door, which Vivian's conductor opened, and ushering
him into a large and well-lighted chamber, withdrew.
From the centre of this room descended a magnifi-
cently cut chandelier, which threw a graceful light
upon a sumptuous banquet table, at which were
seated eight very singular-looking personages. All of
them wore hunting-dresses of various shades of straw-
coloured cloth, with the exception of one, who sat on
the left hand of the master of the feast, and the
colour of whose costume was a rich crimson purple.
From the top to the bottom of the table extended a
double file of wine-glasses and goblets, of all sizes
and all colours. There you might see brilliant relics
of that ancient ruby-glass the vivid tints of which
seem lost to us for ever. Next to these were
marshalled goblets of Venetian manufacture, of a
cloudy, creamy white; then came the huge hock
glass of some ancient Primate of Mentz, nearly a yard
high, towering above its companions, as the church,
its former master, predominated over the simple lay-
men of the middle ages. Why should we forget a
set of most curious and antique drinking-cups of
painted glass, on whose rare surfaces were emblazoned the Kaiser and ten electors of the old Empire ?

Vivian bowed to the party and stood in silence,
while they stared a scrutinising examination. At
length the master of the feast spoke. He was a very
stout man, with a prodigious paunch, which his
tightened dress set off to great advantage. His face,
and particularly his forehead, was of great breadth.

His eyes were set far apart. His long ears hung
down almost to his shoulders; yet singular as he was,
not only in these, but in many other respects, everything was forgotten when your eyes lighted on his
nose. It was the most prodigious nose that Vivian
ever remembered not only seeing, but hearing or even
reading of. In fact, it was too monstrous for a dream.
This mighty nose seemed to hang almost to its owner's chest.

'Be seated,' said this personage, in no unpleasing
voice, and he pointed to the chair opposite to him.
Vivian took the vacated seat of the Vice-President,
who moved himself to the right. 'Be seated, and
whoever you may be, welcome! If our words be few,
think not that our welcome is scant. We are not
much given to speech, holding it for a principle that
if a man's mouth be open, it should be for the purpose of receiving that which cheers a man's spirit;
not of giving vent to idle words, which, so far as we
have observed, produce no other effect save filling
the world with crude and unprofitable fantasies, and
distracting our attention when we are on the point
of catching those flavours which alone make the
world endurable. Therefore, briefly, but heartily, welcome! Welcome, Sir Stranger, from us, and from all;
and first from us, the Grand Duke of Johannisberger.'
Here his Highness rose, and pulled out a large ruby
tumbler from the file. Each of those present did the
same, without, however, rising, and the late Vice-
President, who sat next to Vivian, invited him to follow their example.

The Grand Duke of Johannisberger brought forward, from beneath the table, an ancient and exquisite
bottle of that choice liquor from which he took his

exhilarating title. The cork was drawn, and the bottle circulated with rapidity; and in three minutes the ruby glasses were filled and emptied, and the Grand Duke's health quaffed by all present.

'Again, Sir Stranger,' continued the Grand Duke, 'briefly, but heartily, welcome! Welcome from us and welcome from all; and first from us, and now from the Archduke of Hockheimer!'

The Archduke of Hockheimer was a thin, sinewy man, with long, carroty hair, eyelashes of the same colour, but of a remarkable length; and mustachios, which, though very thin, were so long that they met under his chin. Vivian could not refrain from noticing the extreme length, whiteness, and apparent sharpness of his teeth. The Archduke did not speak, but, leaning under the table, soon produced a bottle of Hockheimer. He then took from the file one of the Venetian glasses of clouded white. All followed his example; the bottle was sent round, his health was pledged, and the Grand Duke of Johannisberger again spoke:

'Again, Sir Stranger, briefly, but heartily, welcome! Welcome from us and welcome from all; and first from us, and now from the Elector of Steinberg!'

The Elector of Steinberg was a short, but very broad-backed, strong-built man. Though his head was large, his features were small, and appeared smaller from the immense quantity of coarse, shaggy, brown hair which grew over almost every part of his face and fell down upon his shoulders. The Elector was as silent as his predecessor, and quickly produced a bottle of Steinberg. The curious drinking cups of painted glass were immediately withdrawn from the file, the bottle was sent round, the Elector's health was pledged, and the Grand Duke of Johannisberger again spoke:

'Again, Sir Stranger, briefly, but heartily, welcome! Welcome from us and welcome from all; and first from us, and now from the Margrave of Rudesheimer!'

The Margrave of Rudesheimer was a slender man of elegant appearance. As Vivian watched the glance of his speaking eye, and the half-satirical and half-jovial smile which played upon his features, he hardly expected that he would be as silent as his predecessors. But the Margrave spoke no word. He gave a kind of shout of savage exultation as he smacked his lips after dashing off his glass of Rudesheimer; and scarcely noticing the salutations of those who drank his health he threw himself back in his chair, and listened seemingly with a smile of derision, while the Grand Duke of Johannisberger again spoke:

'Again, Sir Stranger, briefly, but heartily, welcome! Welcome from us and welcome from all; and first from us, and now from the Landgrave of Grafenberg!'

The Landgrave of Grafenberg was a rude, awkward-looking person, who, when he rose from his seat, stared like an idiot, and seemed utterly ignorant of what he ought to do. But his quick companion, the Margrave of Rudesheimer, soon thrust a bottle of Grafenberg into the Landgrave's hand, and with some trouble and bustle the Landgrave extracted the cork; and then helping himself sat down, forgetting either to salute, or to return the salutations of those present.

'Again, Sir Stranger, briefly, but heartily, welcome! Welcome from us and welcome from all;

and first from us, and now from the Palsgrave of Geisenheim!'

The Palsgrave of Geisenheim was a dwarf in spectacles. He drew the cork from his bottle like lightning, and mouthed at his companions even while he bowed to them.

'Again, Sir Stranger, briefly, but heartily, welcome! Welcome from us and welcome from all; and first from us, and now from the Count of Markbrunnen!'

The Count of Markbrunnen was a sullen-looking personage, with lips protruding nearly three inches beyond his nose. From each side of his upper jaw projected a large tooth.

'Thanks to Heaven!' said Vivian, as the Grand Duke again spoke; 'thanks to Heaven, here is our last man!'

'Again, Sir Stranger, briefly, but heartily, welcome! Welcome from us and welcome from all; and first from us, and now from the Baron of Asmanshausen!'

The Baron of Asmanshausen sat on the left hand of the Grand Duke of Johannisberger, and was dressed, as we have before said, in an unique costume of crimson purple. The Baron stood, without his boots, about six feet eight. He was a sleek man, with a head not bigger than a child's, and a pair of small, black, beady eyes, of singular brilliancy. The Baron introduced a bottle of the only red wine that the Rhine boasts; but which, for its fragrant and fruity flavour and its brilliant tint, is perhaps not inferior to the sunset glow of Burgundy.

'And now,' continued the Grand Duke, 'having introduced you to all present, sir, we will begin drinking.'

that no treason can exist among those who are not
our sworn subjects? Pity we rather the degeneracy
of this bold-spoken youth, and in the plenitude of our
mercy let us pardon his demand! Know ye, unknown
knight, that you are in the presence of an august society who are here met at one of their accustomed
convocations, whereof the purport is the frequent
quaffing of those most glorious liquors of which the
sacred Rhine is the great father. We profess to find
a perfect commentary on the Pindaric laud of the
strongest element in the circumstance of the banks of
a river being the locality where the juice of the grape
is most delicious, and holding, therefore, that water
is strongest because, in a manner, it giveth birth to
wine, we also hold it as a sacred element, and consequently most religiously refrain from refreshing our
bodies with that sanctified and most undrinkable fluid.
Know ye that we are the children of the Rhine, the
conservators of his flavours, profound in the learning
of his exquisite aroma, and deep students in the
mysteries of his inexplicable näre. Professing not to
be immortal, we find in the exercise of the chase a
noble means to preserve that health which is necessary for the performance of the ceremonies to which
we are pledged. At to-morrow's dawn our bugle
sounds, and thou, stranger, may engage the wild
boar at our side; at to-morrow's noon the castle bell
will toll, and thou, stranger, may eat of the beast
which thou hast conquered; but to feed after midnight, to destroy the power of catching the delicate
flavour, to annihilate the faculty of detecting the undefinable näre, is heresy, most rank and damnable
heresy! Therefore at this hour soundeth no plate or
platter, jingleth no knife or culinary instrument, in

the PALACE OF THE WINES. Yet, in consideration of thy youth, and that on the whole thou hast tasted thy liquor like a proper man, from which we augur the best expectations of the manner in which thou wilt drink it, we feel confident that our brothers of the goblet will permit us to grant thee the substantial solace of a single shoeing horn.'

'Let it be a Dutch herring, then,' said Vivian, 'and as you have souls to be saved grant me one slice of bread.'

'It cannot be,' said the Grand Duke; 'but as we are willing to be indulgent to bold hearts, verily, we will wink at the profanation of a single toast; but you must order an anchovy one, and give secret instructions to the waiting-man to forget the fish. It must be counted as a second shoeing horn, and you will forfeit for the last a bottle of Markbrunnen.'

'And now, illustrious brothers,' continued the Grand Duke, 'let us drink 1726.'

All present gave a single cheer, in which Vivian was obliged to join, and they honoured with a glass of the very year the memory of a celebrated vintage.

'1748!' said the Grand Duke.

Two cheers and the same ceremony.

1766 and 1779 were honoured in the same manner, but when the next toast was drank, Vivian almost observed in the countenances of the Grand Duke and his friends the signs of incipient insanity.

'1783!' hallooed the Grand Duke in a tone of the most triumphant exultation, and his mighty proboscis, as it snuffed the air, almost caused a whirlwind round the room. Hockheimer gave a roar, Steinberg a growl, Rudesheimer a wild laugh, Markbrunnen a loud grunt, Grafenberg a bray, Asmanshausen's long

body moved to and fro with wonderful agitation,
and little Geisenheim's bright eyes glistened through
their glasses as if they were on fire. How ludicrous
is the incipient inebriety of a man who wears spectacles!

Thanks to an excellent constitution, which recent
misery, however, had somewhat shattered, Vivian
bore up against all these attacks; and when they had
got down to 1802, from the excellency of his diges-
tion and the inimitable skill with which he emptied
many of the latter glasses under the table, he was,
perhaps, in better condition than any one in the
room.

And now rose the idiot Grafenberg; Rudesheimer
all the time, with a malicious smile, faintly pulling
him down by the skirt of his coat, as if he were desirous of preventing an exposure which his own advice had brought about. He had been persuading
Grafenberg the whole evening to make a speech.

'My Lord Duke,' brayed the jackass; and then he
stopped dead, and looked round the room with an
unmeaning stare.

'Hear, hear, hear!' was the general cry; but Grafenberg seemed astounded at any one being desirous
of hearing his voice, or for a moment seriously entertaining the idea that he could have anything to
say; and so he stared again, and again, and again,
till at last Rudesheimer, by dint of kicking his shins
under the table, the Margrave the whole time seeming perfectly motionless, at length extracted a sentence from the asinine Landgrave.

'My Lord Duke!' again commenced Grafenberg,
and again he stopped.

'Go on!' shouted all.

great reverence to all present, and a party of devout
Catholics could not have paid greater homage to the
elevated Host than did the various guests to the horn
of the Fairy King. Even the Satanic smile on Rudesheimer's countenance was for a moment subdued,
and all bowed. The Grand Duke then delivered the
mighty cup to his neighbour, the Archduke of Hockheimer, who held it with both hands until his Royal
Highness had emptied into it, with great care, three
bottles of Johannisberger. All rose: the Grand Duke
took the goblet in one hand, and with the other he
dexterously put aside his most inconvenient and enormous nose. Dead silence prevailed, save the roar of
the liquor as it rushed down the Grand Duke's
throat, and resounded through the chamber like the
distant dash of a waterfall. In three minutes the
Chairman had completed his task, the horn had quitted his mouth, his nose had again resumed its usual
situation, and as he handed the cup to the Archduke,
Vivian thought that a material change had taken
place in his countenance since he had quaffed his last
draught. His eyes seemed more apart; his ears
seemed broader and longer; and his nose visibly
lengthened. The Archduke, before he commenced
his draught, ascertained with great scrupulosity that
his predecessor had taken his fair share by draining
the horn as far as the first ring; and then he poured
off with great rapidity his own portion. But though,
in performing the same task, he was quicker than
the master of the party, the draught not only apparently, but audibly, produced upon him a much more
decided effect than it had on the Grand Duke; for
when the second ring was drained the Archduke
gave a loud roar of exultation, and stood up for some

time from his seat, with his hands resting on the
table, over which he leant, as if he were about
to spring upon his opposite neighbour. The cup
was now handed across the table to the Baron of
Asmanshausen. His Lordship performed his task
with ease; but as he withdrew the horn from his
mouth, all present, except Vivian, gave a loud cry of
'Supernaculum!' The Baron smiled with great contempt, as he tossed, with a careless hand, the great
horn upside downwards, and was unable to shed
upon his nail even the one excusable pearl. He
handed the refilled horn to the Elector of Steinberg,
who drank his portion with a growl; but afterwards
seemed so pleased with the facility of his execution
that, instead of delivering it to the next bibber, the
Palsgrave of Markbrunnen, he commenced some
clumsy attempts at a dance of triumph, in which he
certainly would have proceeded, had not the loud
grunts of the surly and thick-lipped Markbrunnen occasioned the interference of the President. Supernaculum now fell to the Margrave of Rudesheimer, who
gave a loud and long-continued laugh as the dwarf
of Geisenheim filled the horn for the third time.

While this ceremony was going on, a thousand
plans had occurred to Vivian for his escape; but all,
on second thoughts, proved impracticable. With
agony he had observed that supernaculum was his
miserable lot. Could he but have foisted it on the
idiot Grafenberg, he might, by his own impudence
and the other's stupidity, have escaped. But he could
not flatter himself that he should be successful in
bringing about this end, for he observed with dismay
that the malicious Rudesheimer had not for a moment ceased watching him with a keen and exulting

glance. Geisenheim performed his task; and ere Vivian could ask for the goblet, Rudesheimer, with a fell laugh, had handed it to Grafenberg. The greedy ass drank his portion with ease, and indeed drank far beyond his limit. The cup was in Vivian's hand, Rudesheimer was roaring supernaculum louder than all; Vivian saw that the covetous Grafenberg had providentially rendered his task comparatively light; but even as it was, he trembled at the idea of drinking at a single draught more than a pint of most vigorous and powerful wine.

'My Lord Duke,' said Vivian, 'you and your companions forget that I am little used to these ceremonies; that I am yet uninitiated in the mysteries of the näre. I have endeavoured to prove myself no chicken-hearted water-drinking craven, and I have more wine within me at this moment than any man yet bore without dinner. I think, therefore, that I have some grounds for requesting indulgence, and I have no doubt that the good sense of yourself and your friends ——'

Ere Vivian could finish, he almost fancied that a well-stocked menagerie had been suddenly emptied in the room. Such roaring, and such growling, and such hissing, could only have been exceeded on some grand feast day in the recesses of a Brazilian forest. Asmanshausen looked as fierce as a boa constrictor before dinner. The proboscis of the Grand Duke heaved to and fro like the trunk of an enraged elephant. Hockheimer glared like a Bengal tiger about to spring upon its prey. Steinberg growled like a Baltic bear. In Markbrunnen Vivian recognised the wild boar he had himself often hunted. Grafenberg brayed like a jackass, and Geisenheim chattered

like an ape. But all was forgotten and unnoticed
when Vivian heard the fell and frantic shouts of the
laughing hyæna, the Margrave of Rudesheimer! Vivian, in despair, dashed the horn of Oberon to his
mouth. One pull, a gasp, another desperate draught;
it was done! and followed by a supernaculum almost
superior to the exulting Asmanshausen's.

A loud shout hailed the exploit, and when the
shout had subsided into silence the voice of the Grand
Duke of Johannisberger was again heard:

'Noble Lords and Princes! I congratulate you on the
acquisition of a congenial co-mate, and the accession
to our society of one who, I now venture to say, will
never disgrace the glorious foundation; but who, on
the contrary, with heaven's blessing and the aid of his
own good palate, will, it is hoped, add to our present knowledge of flavours by the detection of new
ones, and by illustrations drawn from frequent study
and constant observation of the mysterious näre. In
consideration of his long journey and his noble
achievement, I do propose that we drink but very
lightly to-night, and meet by two hours after to-
morrow's dawn, under the moss-man's oak. Nevertheless, before we part, for the refreshment of our
own good bodies, and by way of reward and act of
courtesy unto this noble and accomplished stranger,
let us pledge him in some foreign grape of fame, to
which he may perhaps be more accustomed than unto
the ever-preferable juices of our Father Rhine.' Here
the Grand Duke nodded to little Geisenheim, who in
a moment was at his elbow.

It was in vain that Vivian remonstrated, excused
himself from joining, or assured them that their conduct had already been so peculiarly courteous, that

any further attention was at present unnecessary. A
curiously-cut glass, which on a moderate calculation
Vivian reckoned would hold at least three pints, was
placed before each guest; and a basket, containing
nine bottles of sparkling champagne, première qualité,
was set before his Highness.

'We are no bigots, noble stranger,' said the Grand
Duke, as he took one of the bottles, and scrutinised
the cork with a very keen eye; 'we are no bigots,
and there are moments when we drink champagne,
nor is Burgundy forgotten, nor the soft Bourdeaux,
nor the glowing grape of the sunny Rhône!' His
Highness held the bottle at an oblique angle with the
chandelier. The wire is loosened, whirr! The ex-
ploded cork whizzed through the air, extinguished
one of the burners of the chandelier, and brought the
cut drop which was suspended under it rattling down
among the glasses on the table. The President poured
the foaming fluid into his great goblet, and bowing
to all around, fastened on its contents with as much
eagerness as Arabs hasten to a fountain.

The same operation was performed as regularly
and as skilfully by all except Vivian. Eight burners
were extinguished; eight diamond drops had fallen
clattering on the table; eight human beings had finished a miraculous carouse, by each drinking off a
bottle of sparkling champagne. It was Vivian's turn.
All eyes were fixed on him with the most perfect attention. He was now, indeed, quite desperate; for
had he been able to execute a trick which long practice alone could have enabled any man to perform,
he felt conscious that it was quite out of his power
to taste a single drop of the contents of his bottle.
However, he loosened his wire and held the bottle at

an angle with the chandelier; but the cork flew quite wild, and struck with great force the mighty nose of Johannisberger.

'A forfeit!' cried all.

'Treason, and a forfeit!' cried the Margrave of Rudesheimer.

'A forfeit is sufficient punishment,' said the President; who, however, still felt the smarting effect of the assault on his proboscis. 'You must drink Oberon's horn full of champagne,' he continued.

'Never!' said Vivian. 'Enough of this. I have already conformed in a degree which may injuriously affect my health with your barbarous humours; but there is moderation even in excess. And so, if you please, my Lord, your servant may show me to my apartment, or I shall again mount my horse.'

'You shall not leave this room,' said the President, with great firmness.

'Who shall prevent me?' asked Vivian.

'I will, all will!'

'Now, by heavens! a more insolent and inhospitable old ruffian did I never meet. By the wine you worship, if one of you dare touch me, you shall rue it all your born days; and as for you, sir, if you advance one step towards me, I will take that sausage of a nose of yours and hurl you half round your own castle!'

'Treason!' shouted all, and looked to the chair.

'Treason!' said enraged majesty. The allusion to the nose had done away with all the constitutional doubts which had been sported so moderately at the commencement of the evening.

'Treason!' howled the President: 'instant punishment!'

'What punishment?' asked Asmanshausen.

'Drown him in the new butt of Moselle,' recommended Rudesheimer. The suggestion was immediately adopted. Every one rose: the little Geisenheim
already had hold of Vivian's shoulder; and Grafenberg,
instigated by the cowardly but malicious Rudesheimer,
was about to seize him by the neck. Vivian took the
dwarf and hurled him at the chandelier, in whose
brazen chains the little being got entangled, and there
remained. An unexpected cross-buttocker floored the
incautious and unscientific Grafenberg; and following
up these advantages, Vivian laid open the skull of
his prime enemy, the retreating Margrave of Rudesheimer, with the assistance of the horn of Oberon;
which flew from his hand to the other end of the
room, from the force with which it rebounded from
the cranium of the enemy. All the rest were now on
the advance; but giving a vigorous and unexpected
push to the table, the Johannisberger and Asman-
hausen were thrown over, and the nose of the former
got entangled with the awkward windings of the
Fairy King's horn. Taking advantage of this move,
Vivian rushed to the door. He escaped, but had not
time to secure the lock against the enemy, for the
stout Elector of Steinberg was too quick for him. He
dashed down the stairs with extraordinary agility;
but just as he had gained the large octagonal hall,
the whole of his late boon companions, with the exception of the dwarf of Geisenheim, who was left in
the chandelier, were visible in full chase. Escape was
impossible, and so Vivian, followed by the seven
nobles, headed by the President, described with all
possible rapidity a circle round the hall. He gave
himself up for lost; but, luckily, for him, it never oc-

curred to one of his pursuers to do anything but follow their leader; and as, therefore, they never dodged Vivian, and as, also, he was a much fleeter runner than the fat President, whose pace, of course, regulated the progress of his followers, the party might have gone on at this rate until all of them had dropped from fatigue, had not the occurrence of a ludicrous incident prevented this consummation.

The hall door was suddenly dashed open, and Essper George rushed in, followed in full chase by Hunsdrich and the guests of the lodge, who were the servants of Vivian's pursuers. Essper darted in between Rudesheimer and Markbrunnen, and Hunsdrich and his friends following the same tactics as their lords and masters, without making any attempt to surround and hem in the object of their pursuit, merely followed him in order, describing, but in a contrary direction, a lesser circle within the eternal round of the first party. It was only proper for the servants to give their masters the wall. In spite of their very disagreeable and dangerous situation, it was with difficulty that Vivian refrained from laughter, as he met Essper regularly every half minute at the foot of the great staircase. Suddenly, as Essper passed, he took Vivian by the waist, and with a single jerk placed him on the stairs; and then, with a dexterous dodge, he brought Hunsdrich the porter and the Grand Duke in full contact.

'I have got you at last,' said Hunsdrich, seizing hold of his Grace of Johannisberger by the ears, and mistaking him for Essper.

'I have got you at last,' said his master, grappling, as he supposed, with Vivian. Both struggled: their followers pushed on with impetuous force, the battle was general, the overthrow universal. In a moment all were on the ground; and if any less inebriated or more active individual attempted to rise, Essper immediately brought him down with a boar-spear.

'Give me that large fishing-net,' said Essper to Vivian; 'quick, quick.'

Vivian pulled down a large coarse net, which covered nearly five sides of the room. It was immediately unfolded, and spread over the fallen crew. To fasten it down with half a dozen boar-spears, which they drove into the floor, was the work of a moment. Essper had one pull at the proboscis of the Grand Duke of Johannisberger before he hurried Vivian away; and in ten minutes they were again on their horses' backs and galloping through the starlit wood.

CHAPTER II.

T IS the hour before the labouring bee has left his golden hive; not yet the blooming day buds in the blushing East; not yet has the victorious Lucifer chased from the early sky the fainting splendour of the stars of night. All is silent, save the light breath of morn waking the slumbering leaves. Even now a golden streak breaks over the grey mountains. Hark to shrill chanticleer! As the cock crows the owl ceases. Hark to shrill chanticleer's feathered rival! The mountain lark springs from the sullen earth, and welcomes with his hymn the coming day. The golden streak has expanded into a crimson crescent, and rays of living fire flame over the rose-enamelled East. Man rises sooner than the sun, and already sound the whistle of the ploughman, the song of the mower, and the forge of the smith; and hark to the bugle of the hunter, and the baying of his deep-mouthed hound. The sun is up, the generating sun! and temple, and tower, and tree, the massy wood, and the broad field, and the distant hill, burst into

sudden light; quickly upcurled is the dusky mist from
the shining river; quickly is the cold dew drunk from
the raised heads of the drooping flowers!

A canter by a somewhat clearer light than the one
which had so unfortunately guided himself and his
companion to the Palace of the Wines soon carried
them again to the skirts of the forest, and at this
minute they are emerging on the plain from yonder
dark wood.

'By heavens! Essper, I cannot reach the town
this morning. Was ever anything more unfortunate.
A curse on those drunken fools. What with no rest
and no solid refreshment, and the rivers of hock
that are flowing within me, and the infernal exertion of running round that vile hall, I feel fairly
exhausted, and could at this moment fall from my
saddle. See you no habitation, my good fellow,
where there might be a chance of a breakfast and
a few hours' rest? We are now well out of the
forest. Oh! surely there is smoke from behind those
pines; some good wife, I trust, is by her chimney
corner.'

'If my sense be not destroyed by the fumes of
that mulled Geisenheim, which still haunts me, I
could swear that the smoke is the soul of a burning
weed.'

'A truce to your jokes, good Essper; I really am
very ill. A year ago I could have laughed at our
misfortunes, but now it is very different; and, by
heavens, I must have breakfast! so stir, exert yourself, and, although I die for it, let us canter up to
the smoke.'

'No, dear master, I will ride on before. Do you
follow gently, and if there be a pigeon in the pot in

all Germany, I swear by the patron saint of every
village for fifty miles round, provided they be not
heretics, that you shall taste of its breast-bone this
morning.'

The smoke did issue from a chimney, but the door
of the cottage was shut.

'Hilloa, within!' shouted Essper; 'who shuts the
sun out on a September morning?'

The door was at length slowly opened, and a most
ill-favoured and inhospitable-looking dame demanded,
in a sullen voice, 'What's your will?'

'You pretty creature!' said Essper, who was still
a little tipsy.

The door would have been shut in his face had
not he darted into the house before the woman was
aware.

'Truly, a neat and pleasant dwelling! and you
would have no objection, I guess, to give a handsome young gentleman some little sop of something
just to remind him, you know, that it isn't dinner-
time.'

'We give no sops here: what do you take us for?
and so, my handsome young gentleman, be off, or I
shall call the good man.'

'Why, I am not the handsome young gentleman; that is my master! who, if he were not half-
starved to death, would fall in love with you at first
sight.'

'Your master; is he in the carriage?'

'Carriage! no; on horseback.'

'Travellers?'

'To be sure, dear dame; travellers true.'

'Travellers true, without luggage, and at this time
of morn! Methinks, by your looks, queer fellows,

that you are travellers whom it may be wise for an honest woman not to meet.'

'What! some people have an objection, then, to a forty kreüzer piece on a sunny morning?'

So saying, Essper, in a careless manner, tossed a broad piece in the air, and made it ring on a fellow coin, as he caught it in the palm of his hand when it descended.

'Is that your master?' asked the woman.

'Ay, is it! and the prettiest piece of flesh I have seen this month, except yourself.'

'Well! if the gentleman likes bread he can sit down here,' said the woman, pointing to a bench, and throwing a sour black loaf upon the table.

'Now, sir!' said Essper, wiping the bench with great care, 'lie you here and rest yourself. I have known a marshal sleep upon a harder sofa. Breakfast will be ready immediately.'

'If you cannot eat what you have, you may ride where you can find better cheer.'

'What is bread for a traveller's breakfast? But I daresay my lord will be contented; young men are so easily pleased when there is a pretty girl in the case; you know that, you wench! you do, you little hussy; you are taking advantage of it.'

Something like a smile lit up the face of the sullen woman when she said, 'There may be an egg in the house, but I don't know.'

'But you will soon, you dear creature! What a pretty foot!' bawled Essper after her, as she left the room. 'Now confound this hag; if there be not meat about this house may I keep my mouth shut at our next dinner. What's that in the corner? a boar's tusk! Ay, ay! a huntsman's cottage; and when lived a huntsman on black bread before! Oh! bless your bright eyes for these eggs, and this basin of new milk.'

So saying, Essper took them out of her hand and placed them before Vivian.

'I was saying to myself, my pretty girl, when you were out of the room, "Essper George, good cheer, say thy prayers, and never despair; come what may, you will fall among friends at last, and how do you know that your dream mayn't come true after all? Didn't you dream that you breakfasted in the month of September with a genteel young woman with gold ear-rings? and is not she standing before you now? and did not she do everything in the world to make you comfortable? Did not she give you milk and eggs, and when you complained that you and meat had been but slack friends of late, did not she open her own closet, and give you as fine a piece of hunting beef as was ever set before a Jagd Junker?"'

'I think you will turn me into an innkeeper's wife at last,' said the dame, her stern features relaxing into a smile; and while she spoke she advanced to the great closet, Essper George following her, walking on his toes, lolling out his enormous tongue, and stroking his mock paunch. As she opened it he jumped upon a chair and had examined every shelf in less time than a pistol could flash. 'White bread! fit for a countess; salt! worthy of Poland; boar's head!! no better at Troyes; and hunting beef!!! my dream is true!' and he bore in triumph to Vivian, who was nearly asleep, the ample round of salt and pickled beef well stuffed with all kinds of savoury herbs.

It was nearly an hour before noon ere the travellers had remounted. Their road again entered the
forest which they had been skirting for the last two
days. The huntsmen were abroad; and the fine
weather, his good meal and seasonable rest, and the
inspiriting sounds of the bugle made Vivian feel recovered from his late fatigues.

'That must be a true-hearted huntsman, Essper,
by the sound of his bugle. I never heard one played
with more spirit. Hark! how fine it dies away in
the wood; fainter and fainter, yet how clear! It must
be now half a mile distant.'

'I hear nothing so wonderful,' said Essper, putting
the two middle fingers of his right hand before his
mouth and sounding a note so clear and beautiful, so
exactly imitative of the fall which Vivian had noticed
and admired, that for a moment he imagined that the
huntsman was at his elbow.

'Thou art a cunning knave! do it again.' This
time Essper made the very wood echo. In a few
minutes a horseman galloped up; he was as spruce a
cavalier as ever pricked gay steed on the pliant grass.
He was dressed in a green military uniform, and a
gilt bugle hung by his side; his spear told them that
he was hunting the wild boar. When he saw Vivian
and Essper he suddenly pulled up his horse and
seemed astonished.

'I thought that his Highness had been here,' said
the huntsman.

'No one has passed us, sir,' said Vivian.

'I could have sworn that his bugle sounded from
this very spot,' said the huntsman. 'My ear seldom
deceives me.'

'We heard a bugle to the right, sir,' said Essper.

'Thanks, my friend,' and the huntsman was about to gallop off.

'May I ask the name of his Highness?' said Vivian. 'We are strangers in this country.'

'That may certainly account for your ignorance,' said the huntsman; 'but no one who lives in this land can be unacquainted with his Serene Highness the Prince of Little Lilliput, my illustrious master. I have the honour,' continued the huntsman, 'of being Jagd Junker, or Gentilhomme de la Chasse to his Serene Highness.'

''Tis an office of great dignity,' said Vivian, 'and one that I have no doubt you admirably perform; I will not stop you, sir, to admire your horse.'

The huntsman bowed courteously and galloped off.

'You see, sir,' said Essper George, 'that my bugle has deceived even the Jagd Junker, or Gentilhomme de la Chasse to his Serene Highness the Prince of Little Lilliput himself;' so saying, Essper again sounded his instrument.

'A joke may be carried too far, my good fellow,' said Vivian. 'A true huntsman like myself must not spoil a brother's sport, so silence your bugle.'

Now again galloped up the Jagd Junker, or Gentilhomme de la Chasse to his Serene Highness the Prince of Little Lilliput. He pulled up his horse again apparently as much astounded as ever.

'I thought that his Highness had been here,' said the huntsman.

'No one has passed us,' said Vivian.

'We heard a bugle to the right,' said Essper George.

'I am afraid his Serene Highness must be in distress. The whole suite are off the scent. It must

have been his bugle, for the regulations of this forest
are so strict that no one dare sound a blast but his
Serene Highness.' Away galloped the huntsman.

'Next time I must give you up, Essper,' said Vivian.

'One more blast, good master!' begged Essper, in
a supplicating voice. 'This time to the left; the confusion will be then complete.'

'I command you not,' and so they rode on in silence. But it was one of those days when Essper
could neither be silent nor subdued. Greatly annoyed
at not being permitted to play his bugle, he amused
himself imitating the peculiar sound of every animal
that he met; a young fawn and various birds already
followed him, and even a squirrel had perched on
his horse's neck. And now they came to a small
farmhouse, which was situated in the forest: the yard
here offered great amusement to Essper. He neighed,
and half a dozen horses' heads immediately appeared
over the hedge; another neigh, and they were following him in the road. A dog rushed out to seize the
dangerous stranger and recover his charge, but Essper
gave an amicable bark, and in a second the dog was
jumping by his side and engaged in earnest and
friendly conversation. A loud and continued grunt
soon brought out the pigs, and meeting three or four
cows returning home, a few lowing sounds soon seduced them from keeping their appointment with the
dairymaid. A stupid jackass, who stared with astonishment at the procession, was saluted with a lusty
bray, which immediately induced him to swell the
ranks; and, as Essper passed the poultry-yard, he so
deceitfully informed its inhabitants that they were
about to be fed, that broods of ducks and chickens

were immediately after him. The careful hens were terribly alarmed at the danger which their offspring incurred from the heels and hoofs of the quadrupeds; but while they were in doubt and despair a whole flock of stately geese issued in solemn pomp from another gate of the farmyard, and commenced a cackling conversation with the delighted Essper. So contagious is the force of example, and so great was the confidence which the hens placed in these pompous geese, who were not the first fools whose solemn air has deceived a few old females, that as soon as they perceived them in the train of the horseman they also trotted up to pay their respects at his levée.

But it was not a moment for mirth; for rushing down the road with awful strides appeared two sturdy and enraged husbandmen, one armed with a pike and the other with a pitchfork, and accompanied by a frantic female, who never for a moment ceased hallooing 'Murder, rape, and fire!' everything but 'theft.'

'Now, Essper, here's a pretty scrape!'

'Stop, you rascals!' hallooed Adolph, the herdsman.

'Stop, you gang of thieves!' hallooed Wilhelm, the ploughman.

'Stop, you bloody murderers!' shrieked Phillippa, the indignant mistress of the dairy and the poultryyard.

'Stop, you villains!' hallooed all three. The villains certainly made no attempt to escape, and in half a second the enraged household of the forest farmer would have seized on Essper George; but just at this crisis he uttered loud sounds in the respective lan-

guage of every bird and beast about him, and suddenly they all turned round and counter-marched.
Away rushed the terrified Adolph, the herdsman,
while one of his own cows was on his back. Still
quicker scampered off the scared Wilhelm, the ploughman, while one of his own steeds kicked him in his
rear. Quicker than all these, shouting, screaming,
shrieking, dashed back the unhappy mistress of the
hen-roost, with all her subjects crowding about her;
some on her elbow, some on her head, her lace cap
destroyed, her whole dress disordered. The movements of the crowd were so quick that they were
soon out of sight.

'A trophy!' called out Essper, as he jumped off
his horse and picked up the pike of Adolph, the
herdsman.

'A boar-spear, or I am no huntsman,' said Vivian:
'give it me a moment!' He threw it up into the
air, caught it with ease, poised it with the practised
skill of one well used to handle the weapon, and
with the same delight imprinted on his countenance
as greets the sight of an old friend.

'This forest, Essper, and this spear, make me remember days when I was vain enough to think that
I had been sufficiently visited with sorrow. Ah!
little did I then know of human misery, although I
imagined I had suffered so much!'

As he spoke, the sounds of a man in distress were
heard from the right side of the road.

'Who calls?' cried Essper. A shout was the only
answer. There was no path, but the underwood was
low, and Vivian took his horse, an old forester,
across it with ease. Essper's jibbed; Vivian found
himself in a small green glade of about thirty feet

square. It was thickly surrounded with lofty trees, save at the point where he had entered; and at the farthest corner of it, near some grey rocks, a huntsman was engaged in a desperate contest with a wild boar.

The huntsman was on his right knee, and held his spear with both hands at the furious beast. It was an animal of extraordinary size and power. Its eyes glittered like fire. On the turf to its right a small grey mastiff, of powerful make, lay on its back, bleeding profusely, with its body ripped open. Another dog, a fawn-coloured bitch, had seized on the left ear of the beast; but the under-tusk of the boar, which was nearly a foot long, had penetrated the courageous dog, and the poor creature writhed in agony, even while it attempted to wreak its revenge upon its enemy. The huntsman was nearly exhausted. Had it not been for the courage of the fawn-coloured dog, which, clinging to the boar, prevented it making a full dash at the man, he must have been gored. Vivian was off his horse in a minute, which, frightened at the sight of the wild boar, dashed again over the hedge.

'Keep firm, sir!' said he; 'do not move. I will amuse him behind, and make him turn.'

A graze of Vivian's spear on its back, though it did not materially injure the beast, for there the boar is nearly invulnerable, annoyed it; and dashing off the fawn-coloured dog with great force, it turned on its new assailant. Now there are only two places in which the wild boar can be assailed with any effect; and these are just between the eyes and between the shoulders. Great caution, however, is necessary in aiming these blows, for the boar is very adroit in transfixing the weapon on his snout or his tusks; and if once you miss, particularly if you are not assisted by dogs, which Vivian was not, 'tis all over with you; for the enraged animal rushes in like lightning, and gored you must be.

But Vivian was fresh and cool. The animal suddenly stood still and eyed its new enemy. Vivian was quiet, for he had no objection to give the beast an opportunity of retreating to its den. But retreat was not its object; it suddenly darted at the huntsman, who, however, was not off his guard, though unable, from a slight wound in his knee, to rise. Vivian again annoyed the boar at the rear, and the animal soon returned to him. He made a feint, as if he were about to strike his pike between its eyes. The boar, not feeling a wound which had not been inflicted, and very irritated, rushed at him, and he buried his spear a foot deep between its shoulders. The beast made one fearful struggle, and then fell down quite dead. The fawn-coloured bitch, though terribly wounded, gave a loud bark; and even the other dog, which Vivian thought had been long dead testified its triumphant joy by an almost inarticulate groan. As soon as he was convinced that the boar was really dead, Vivian hastened to the huntsman, and expressed his hope that he was not seriously hurt.

'A trifle, which our surgeon, who is used to these affairs, will quickly cure. Sir! we owe you our life!' said the huntsman, with great dignity, as Vivian assisted him in rising from the ground. He was a tall man, of distinguished appearance; but his dress, which was the usual hunting costume of a German nobleman, did not indicate his quality.

AFTER AN ORIGINAL DRAWING BY HERMAN ROUNTREE.

*The animal suddenly stood still and eyed its new
enemy.*

(See page 100.)

'Sir, we owe you our life!' repeated the stranger; 'five minutes more, and our son must have reigned in Little Lilliput.'

'I have the honour, then, of addressing your Serene Highness. Far from being indebted to me, I feel that I ought to apologise for having so unceremoniously joined your sport.'

'Nonsense, man! We have killed in our time too many of these gentry to be ashamed of owning that, had it not been for you, one of them would at last have revenged the species. But many as are the boars that we have killed or eaten, we never saw a more furious or powerful animal than the present. Why, sir, you must be one of the best hands at the spear in all Christendom!'

'Indifferently good, your Highness: your Highness forgets that the animal was already exhausted by your assault.'

'Why, there is something in that; but it was neatly done, man; it was neatly done. You are fond of the sport, we think?'

'I have had some practice, but illness has so weakened me that I have given up the forest.'

'Pity! and on a second examination we observe that you are no hunter. This coat is not for the free forest; but how came you by the pike?'

'I am travelling to the next post town, to which I have sent on my luggage. I am getting fast to the south; and as for this pike, my servant got it this morning from some peasant in a brawl, and was showing it to me when I heard your Highness call. I really think now that Providence must have sent it. I certainly could not have done you much service with my riding whip. Hilloa! Essper, where are you?'

'Here, noble sir! here, here. Why, what have you got there? The horses have jibbed, and will not stir. I can stay no longer; they may go to the devil!' So saying, Vivian's valet dashed over the underwood, and leaped at the foot of the Prince.

'In God's name, is this thy servant?' asked his Highness.

'In good faith am I,' said Essper; 'his valet, his cook, and his secretary, all in one; and also his Jagd Junker, or Gentilhomme de la Chasse, as a puppy with a bugle horn told me this morning.'

'A merry knave!' said the Prince; 'and talking of a puppy with a bugle horn reminds us how unaccountably we have been deserted to-day by a suite that never yet were wanting. We are indeed astonished. Our bugle, we fear, has turned traitor.' So saying, the Prince executed a blast with great skill, which Vivian immediately recognised as the one which Essper George had imitated.

'And now, my good friend,' said the Prince, 'we cannot hear of your passing through our land without visiting our good castle. We would that we could better testify the obligation that we feel under to you in any other way than by the offer of an hospitality which all gentlemen, by right, can command. But your presence would, indeed, give us sincere pleasure. You must not refuse us. Your looks, as well as your prowess, prove your blood; and we are quite sure no cloth-merchant's order will suffer by your not hurrying to your proposed point of destination. We are not wrong, we think, though your accent is good, in supposing that we are conversing with an English gentleman. But here they come.'

As he spoke, three or four horsemen, at the head of whom was the young huntsman whom the travellers had met in the morning, sprang into the glade.

'Why, Arnelm!' said the Prince, 'when before was the Jagd Junker's ear so bad that he could not discover his master's bugle, even though the wind were against him?'

'In truth, your Highness, we have heard bugles enough this morning. Who is violating the forest laws we know not; but that another bugle is sounding, and played — St. Hubert forgive me for saying so, with as great skill as your Highness'— is certain. Myself, Von Neuwied, and Lintz have been galloping over the whole forest. The rest, I doubt not, will be up directly.' The Jagd Junker blew his own bugle.

In the course of five minutes, about twenty other horsemen, all dressed in the same uniform, had arrived; all complaining of their wild chases after the Prince in every other part of the forest.

'It must be the Wild Huntsman himself!' swore an old hand. This solution of the mystery satisfied all.

'Well, well!' said the Prince; 'whoever it may be, had it not been for the timely presence of this gentleman, you must have changed your green jackets for mourning coats, and our bugle would have sounded no more in the forest of our fathers. Here, Arnelm! cut up the beast, and remember that the left shoulder is the quarter of honour, and belongs to this stranger, not less honoured because unknown.'

All present took off their caps and bowed to Vivian, who took this opportunity of informing the Prince who he was.

'And now,' continued his Highness, 'Mr. Grey will accompany us to our castle; nay, sir, we can take no refusal. We will send on to the town for your luggage. Arnelm, do you look to this! And, honest friend,' said the Prince, turning to Essper George, 'we commend you to the special care of our friend Von Neuwied; and so, gentlemen, with stout hearts and spurs to your steeds, to the castle.'

CHAPTER III.

THE PRINCIPALITY OF LITTLE LILLIPUT.

HE cavalcade proceeded for some time at a brisk but irregular pace, until they arrived at a less wild and wooded part of the forest. The Prince of Little Lilliput reined in his steed as he entered a broad avenue of purple beeches, at the end of which, though at a considerable distance, Vivian perceived the towers and turrets of a Gothic edifice glittering in the sunshine.

'Welcome to Turriparva!' said his Highness.

'I assure your Highness,' said Vivian, 'that I view with no unpleasant feeling the prospect of a reception in any civilised mansion; for to say the truth, for the last eight-and-forty hours Fortune has not favoured me either in my researches after a bed, or that which some think still more important than repose.'

'Is it so?' said the Prince. 'Why, we should have thought by your home-thrust this morning that you were as fresh as the early lark. In good faith, it was a pretty stroke! And whence come you, then, good sir?'

'Know you a most insane and drunken idiot who styles himself the Grand Duke of Johannisberger?'

'No, no!' said the Prince, staring in Vivian's face earnestly, and then laughing. 'And you have actually fallen among that mad crew. A most excellent adventure! Arnelm! why, man, where art thou? Ride up! Behold in the person of this gentleman a new victim to the overwhelming hospitality of our Uncle of the Wines. And did they confer a title on you on the spot? Say, art thou Elector, or Palsgrave, or Baron; or, failing in thy devoirs, as once did our good cousin Arnelm, confess that thou wert ordained with becoming reverence the Archprimate of Puddledrink. Eh! Arnelm, is not that the style thou bearest at the Palace of the Wines?'

'So it would seem, your Highness. I think the title was conferred on me the same night that your Highness mistook the Grand Duke's proboscis for Oberon's horn, and committed treason not yet pardoned.'

'Good! good! thou hast us there. Truly a good memory is often as ready a friend as a sharp wit. Wit is not thy strong point, friend Arnelm; and yet it is strange that in the sharp encounter of ready tongues and idle logomachies thou hast sometimes the advantage. But, nevertheless, rest assured, good cousin Arnelm, that wit is not thy strong point.'

'It is well for me that all are not of the same opinion as your Serene Highness,' said the young Jagd Junker, somewhat nettled; for he prided himself on his repartees.

The prince was much diverted with Vivian's account of his last night's adventure; and our hero learnt from his Highness that his late host was no less a personage than the cousin of the Prince of Little Lilliput, an old German Baron, who passed his time, with some neighbours of congenial temperament, in hunting the wild boar in the morning, and speculating on the flavours of the fine Rhenish wines during the rest of the day. 'He and his companions,' continued the Prince, 'will enable you to form some idea of the German nobility half a century ago. The debauch of last night was the usual carouse which crowned the exploits of each day when we were a boy. The revolution has rendered all these customs obsolete. Would that it had not sent some other things equally out of fashion!'

At this moment the Prince sounded his bugle, and the gates of the castle, which were not more than twenty yards distant, were immediately thrown open. The whole cavalcade set spurs to their steeds, and dashed at full gallop over the hollow-sounding drawbridge into the courtyard of the castle. A crowd of serving-men, in green liveries, instantly appeared, and Arnelm and Von Neuwied, jumping from their saddles, respectively held the stirrup and the bridle of the Prince as he dismounted.

'Where is Master Rodolph?' asked his Highness, with a loud voice.

'So please your Serene Highness, I am here!' answered a very thin treble; and, bustling through the surrounding crowd, came forward the owner of the voice. Master Rodolph was not much above five feet high, but he was nearly as broad as he was long. Though more than middle-aged, an almost infantile smile played upon his broad fair face, to which his small turn-up nose, large green goggle-eyes, and unmeaning mouth gave no expression. His long hair hung over his shoulders, the flaxen locks in some places maturing into grey. In compliance with the taste of his master, this most unsportsman-like-looking steward was clad in a green jerkin, on the right arm of which was embroidered a giant's head, the crest of the Little Lilliputs.

'Truly, Rodolph, we have received some scratch in the chase to-day, and need your assistance. The best of surgeons, we assure you, Mr. Grey, if you require one: and look you that the blue chamber be prepared for this gentleman; and we shall have need of our cabinet this evening. See that all this be done, and inform Prince Maximilian that we would speak with him. And look you, Master Rodolph, there is one in this company — what call you your servant's name, sir? Essper George! 'tis well: look you, Rodolph, see that our friend Essper George be well provided for. We know that we can trust him to your good care. And now gentlemen, at sunset we meet in the Giants' Hall.' So saying, his Highness bowed to the party; and taking Vivian by the arm, and followed by Arnelm and Von Neuwied, he ascended a staircase which opened into the court, and then mounted into a covered gallery which ran round the whole building. The interior wall of the gallery was alternately ornamented with stags' heads or other trophies of the chase, and coats of arms blazoned in stucco. The Prince did the honours of the castle to Vivian with great courtesy. The armoury and the hall, the knights' chamber, and even the donjon-keep, were all examined; and when Vivian had sufficiently admired the antiquity of the structure and the beauty of the situation, the Prince, having proceeded down a long corridor, opened the door into a small cham-

ber, which he introduced to Vivian as his cabinet.
The furniture of this room was rather quaint, and not
unpleasing. The wainscot and ceiling were painted
alike, of a light green colour, and were richly carved
and gilt. The walls were hung with green velvet, of
which material were also the chairs, and a sofa,
which was placed under a large and curiously-cut
looking-glass. The lower panes of the windows of
this room were of stained glass, of vivid tints; but
the upper panes were untinged, in order that the
light should not be disturbed which fell through them
upon two magnificent pictures; one a hunting-piece,
by Schneiders, and the other a portrait of an armed
chieftain on horseback, by Lucas Cranach.

And now the door opened, and Master Rodolph
entered, carrying in his hand a white wand, and bowing very reverently as he ushered in servants bearing
a cold collation. As he entered, it was with difficulty
that he could settle his countenance into the due and
requisite degree of gravity; and so often was the fat
steward on the point of bursting into laughter, as he
arranged the setting out of the refreshments on the
table, that the Prince, with whom he was at the
same time both a favourite and a butt, at last noticed
his unusual and unmanageable risibility.

'Why, Rodolph, what ails thee? Hast thou just
discovered the point of some good saying of yesterday?'

The steward could now contain his laughter no
longer, and he gave vent to his emotion in a most
treble 'He! he! he!'

'Speak, man, in the name of St. Hubert, and on
the word of as stout a huntsman as ever yet crossed
horse. Speak, we say; what ails thee?'

'He! he! he! in truth, a most comical knave! I beg your Serene Highness ten thousand most humble pardons, but, in truth, a more comical knave did I never see. How call you him? Essper George, I think; he! he! he! In truth, your Highness was right when you styled him a merry knave; in truth, a most comical knave; he! he! a very funny knave! He says, your Highness, that I am like a snake in a consumption! he! he! he! In truth, a most comical knave!'

'Well, Rodolph, so long as you do not quarrel with his jokes, they shall pass as true wit. But why comes not our son? Have you bidden the Prince Maximilian to our presence?'

'In truth have I, your Highness; but he was engaged at the moment with Mr. Sievers, and therefore he could not immediately attend my bidding. Nevertheless, he bade me deliver to your Serene Highness his dutiful affection, saying that he would soon have the honour of bending his knee unto your Serene Highness.'

'He never said any such nonsense. At least, if he did, he must be changed since last we hunted.'

'In truth, your Highness, I cannot aver, upon my conscience as a faithful steward, that such were the precise words and exact phraseology of his Highness the Prince Maximilian. But in the time of the good Prince, your father, whose memory be ever blessed, such were the words and style of message which I was schooled and instructed by Mr. von Lexicon, your Serene Highness' most honoured tutor, to bear unto the good Prince your father, whose memory be ever blessed, when I had the great fortune of being your Serene Highness' most particular page, and it

fell to my lot to have the pleasant duty of informing
the good Prince your father, whose memory be ever
blessed——'

'Enough! but Sievers is not Von Lexicon, and
Maximilian, we trust, is——'

'Papa! papa! dearest papa!' shouted a young lad,
as he dashed open the door, and, rushing into the
room, threw his arms round the Prince's neck.

'My darling!' said the father, forgetting at this
moment of genuine feeling the pompous plural in
which he had hitherto spoken of himself. The Prince
fondly kissed his child. The boy was about ten
years of age, exquisitely handsome. Courage, not
audacity, was imprinted on his noble features.

'Papa! may I hunt with you to-morrow?'

'What says Mr. Sievers?'

'Oh! Mr. Sievers says I am excellent; I assure
you, upon my honour, he does. I heard you come
home; but though I was dying to see you, I would
not run out till I had finished my Roman History. I
say, papa! what a grand fellow Brutus was; what a
grand thing it is to be a patriot! I intend to be a
patriot myself, and to kill the Grand Duke of Reisenburg. Who is that?'

'My friend, Max, Mr. Grey. Speak to him.'

'I am happy to see you at Turriparva, sir,' said
the boy, bowing to Vivian with dignity. 'Have you
been hunting with his Highness this morning?'

'I can hardly say I have.'

'Max, I have received a slight wound to-day. Do
not look alarmed; it is slight. I only mention it because, had it not been for this gentleman, it is very
probable you would never have seen your father again.
He has saved my life!'

'Saved your life! saved my papa's life!' said the young Prince, seizing Vivian's hand. 'Oh! sir, what can I do for you? Mr. Sievers!' said the boy, with eagerness, to a gentleman who entered the room; 'Mr. Sievers! here is a young lord who has saved papa's life!'

Mr. Sievers was a tall, thin man, about forty, with a clear sallow complexion, a high forehead, on which a few wrinkles were visible, bright keen eyes, and a quantity of grey curling hair, which was combed back off his forehead, and fell down over, his shoulders. He was introduced to Vivian as the Prince's particular friend; and then he listened, apparently with interest, to his Highness' narrative of the morning's adventure, his danger, and his rescue. Young Maximilian never took his large, dark-blue eyes off his father while he was speaking, and when he had finished the boy rushed to Vivian and threw his arms round his neck. Vivian was delighted with the affection of the child, who whispered to him in a low voice, 'I know what you are!'

'What, my young friend?'

'Ah! I know.'

'But tell me!'

'You thought I should not find out: you are a patriot!'

'I hope I am,' said Vivian; 'but travelling in a foreign country is hardly a proof of it. Perhaps you do not know that I am an Englishman.'

'An Englishman!' said the child, with an air of great disappointment. 'I thought you were a patriot! I am one. Do you know I will tell you a secret. You must promise not to tell, though. Promise, upon your word! Well then,' said the urchin, whispering with **great** energy in Vivian's ear through his hollow fist, 'I hate the Grand Duke of Reisenburg, and I mean to stab him to the heart.' So saying, the little Prince grated his teeth with an expression of bitter detestation.

'What the deuce is the matter with the child?' thought Vivian; but at this moment his conversation with him was interrupted.

'Am I to believe this young gentleman, my dear Sievers,' asked the Prince, 'when he tells me that his conduct has met your approbation?'

'Your son, Prince,' answered Mr. Sievers, 'can only speak truth. His excellence is proved by my praising him to his face.'

The young Maximilian, when Mr. Sievers had ceased speaking, stood blushing, with his eyes fixed on the ground; and the delighted parent, catching his child up in his arms, embraced him with unaffected fondness.

'And now, all this time Master Rodolph is waiting for his patient. By St. Hubert, you can none of you think me very ill! Your pardon, Mr. Grey, for leaving you. My friend Sievers will, I am sure, be delighted to make you feel at ease at Turriparva. Max, come with me!"

Vivian found in Mr. Sievers an interesting companion; nothing of the pedant and much of the philosopher. Their conversation was of course chiefly on topics of local interest, anecdotes of the castle and the country, of Vivian's friends, the drunken Johannisberger and his crew, and such matters; but there was a keenness of satire in some of Mr. Sievers' observations which was highly amusing, and enough passed to make Vivian desire opportunities of conversing with him at greater length, and on subjects of greater interest. They were at present disturbed by Essper George entering the room to inform Vivian that his luggage had arrived from the village, and that the blue chamber was now prepared for his presence.

'We shall meet, I suppose, in the hall, Mr. Sievers?'

'No; I shall not dine there. If you remain at Turriparva, which I trust you will, I shall be happy to see you in my room. If it have no other inducement to gain it the honour of your visit, it has here, at least, the recommendation of singularity; there is, at any rate, no other chamber like it in this good castle.'

The business of the toilet is sooner performed for a hunting party in a German forest than for a state dinner at Château Desir, and Vivian was ready before he was summoned.

'His Serene Highness has commenced his progress towards the hall,' announced Essper George to Vivian in a treble voice, and bowing with ceremony as he offered to lead the way, with a white wand waving in his right hand.

'I shall attend his Highness,' said his master; 'but before I do, if that white wand be not immediately laid aside it will be broken about your back.'

'Broken about my back! what, the wand of office, sir, of your steward! Master Rodolph says that, in truth, a steward is but half himself who hath not his wand: methinks when his rod of office is wanting, his Highness of Lilliput's steward is but unequally divided. In truth, he is stout enough to be Aaron's wand that swallowed up all the rest. But has your nobleness any serious objection to my carrying a wand? It gives such an air!'

The Giants' Hall was a Gothic chamber of imposing appearance; the oaken rafters of the curiously-carved roof rested on the grim heads of gigantic figures of the same material. These statues extended the length of the hall on each side; they were elaborately sculptured and highly polished, and each one held in its outstretched arm a blazing and aromatic torch. Above them, small windows of painted glass admitted a light which was no longer necessary at the banquet to which we are now about to introduce the reader. Over the great entrance doors was a gallery, from which a band of trumpeters, arrayed in ample robes of flowing scarlet, sent forth many a festive and martial strain. More than fifty individuals, all wearing hunting dresses of green cloth on which the giant's head was carefully emblazoned, were already seated in the hall when Vivian entered: he was conducted to the upper part of the chamber, and a seat was allotted him on the left hand of the Prince. His Highness had not arrived, but a chair of state, placed under a crimson canopy, denoted the style of its absent owner and a stool, covered with velvet of the same regal colour, and glistening with gold lace, announced that the presence of Prince Maximilian was expected. While Vivian was musing in astonishment at the evident affectation of royal pomp which pervaded the whole establishment of the Prince of Little Lilliput, the trumpeters in the gallery suddenly commenced a triumphant flourish. All rose as the princely procession entered the hall: first came Master Rodolph twirling his white wand with the practised pride of a drum-major, and looking as pompous as a turkey-cock in a storm; six footmen in splendid liveries, two by two, immediately followed him. A page heralded the Prince Maximilian, and then came the Serene father; the Jagd Junker, and four or five other gentlemen of the court, formed the suite.

His Highness ascended the throne, Prince Maximilian was on his right, and Vivian had the high honour of the left hand; the Jagd Junker seated himself next to our hero. The table was profusely covered, chiefly with the sports of the forest, and the celebrated wild boar was not forgotten. Few minutes had elapsed ere Vivian perceived that his Highness was always served on bended knee; surprised at this custom, which even the mightiest and most despotic monarchs seldom exact, and still more surprised at the contrast which all this state afforded to the natural ease and affable amiability of the Prince, Vivian ventured to ask his neighbour Arnelm whether the banquet of to-day was in celebration of any particular event of general or individual interest.

'By no means,' said the Jagd Junker, 'this is the usual style of the Prince's daily meal, except that to-day there is, perhaps, rather less state and fewer guests than usual, in consequence of many of our fellow-subjects having left us with the purpose of attending a great hunting party, which is now holding in the dominions of his Highness' cousin, the Duke of Micromegas.'

When the more necessary but, as most hold, the less delightful part of banqueting was over, and the numerous serving-men had removed the more numerous dishes of wild boar, red deer, roebuck, and winged game, a stiff Calvinistic-looking personage rose and delivered a long and most grateful grace, to which the sturdy huntsmen listened with a due mixture of piety and impatience. When his starch reverence, who in his black coat looked among the huntsmen very like (as Essper George observed) a black-bird among a set of moulting canaries, had finished, an old man, with long snow-white hair and a beard of the same colour, rose from his seat, and, with a glass in his hand, bowing first to his Highness with great respect and then to his companions with an air of condescension, gave in a stout voice, 'The Prince!' A loud shout was immediately raised, and all quaffed with rapture the health of a ruler whom evidently they adored. Master Rodolph now brought forward an immense silver goblet full of some crafty compound, from its odour doubtless delicious. The Prince held the goblet by its two massive handles, and then said in a loud voice:

'My friends, the giant's head! and he who sneers at its frown may he rue its bristles!'

The toast was welcomed with a cry of triumph. When the noise had subsided the Jagd Junker rose, and prefacing the intended pledge by a few observations as remarkable for the delicacy of their sentiments as the elegance of their expression, he gave, pointing to Vivian, 'The Guest! and may the Prince never want a stout arm at a strong push!' The sentiment was again echoed by the lusty voices of all present, and particularly by his Highness. As Vivian shortly returned thanks and modestly apologised for the German of a foreigner, he could not refrain from remembering the last time when he was placed in the same situation; it was when the treacherous Lord Courtown had drunk success to Mr. Vivian Grey's maiden speech in a bumper of claret at the political orgies of Château Desir.   Could he really be the same individual as the daring youth who then organised the crazy councils of those ambitious, imbecile grey-beards? What was he then? What had happened since? What was he now? He turned from the comparison with feelings of sickening disgust, and it was with difficulty that his countenance could assume the due degree of hilarity which befitted the present occasion.

'Truly Mr. Grey,' said the Prince, 'your German would pass current at Weimar. Arnelm, good cousin Arnelm, we must trouble thy affectionate duty to marshal and regulate the drinking devoirs of our kind subjects to-night; for by the advice of our trusty surgeon, Master Rodolph, of much fame, we shall refrain this night from our accustomed potations, and betake ourselves to the solitude of our cabinet; a solitude in good sooth, unless we can persuade you to accompany us, kind sir,' said the Prince, turning to Mr. Grey. 'Methinks eight-and-forty hours without rest, and a good part spent in the mad walls of our cousin of Johannisberger, are hardly the best preparatives for a drinking bout, unless, after Oberon's horn, ye may fairly be considered to be in practice. Nevertheless, I advise the cabinet and a cup of Rodolph's coffee. What sayest thou?' Vivian acceded to the Prince's proposition with eagerness; and accompanied by Prince Maximilian, and preceded by the little steward, who, surrounded by his serving-men, very much resembled a planet eclipsed by his satellites, they left the hall.

''Tis almost a pity to shut out the moon on such a night,' said the Prince, as he drew a large green velvet curtain from the windows of the cabinet.

"'Tis a magnificent night!' said Vivian; 'how fine the effect of the light is upon the picture of the warrior. The horse seems quite living, and its fierce rider actually frowns upon us.'

'He may well frown,' said the Prince of Little Lilliput, in a voice of deep melancholy; and he hastily redrew the curtain. In a moment he started from the chair on which he had just seated himself, and again admitted the moonlight. 'Am I really afraid of an old picture? No, no; it has not yet come to that.'

This was uttered in a distinct voice, and of course excited the astonishment of Vivian, who, however, had too much discretion to evince his surprise, or to take any measure by which his curiosity might be satisfied.

His companion seemed instantly conscious of the seeming singularity of his expression.

'You are surprised at my words, good sir,' said his Highness, as he paced very rapidly up and down the small chamber; 'you are surprised at my words; but, sir, my ancestor's brow was guarded by a diadem!'

'Which was then well won, Prince, and is now worthily worn.'

'By whom? where? how?' asked the Prince, in a rapid voice. 'Maximilian,' continued his Highness, in a more subdued tone; 'Maximilian, my own love, leave us; go to Mr. Sievers. God bless you, my only boy. Good night!'

'Good night, dearest papa, and down with the Grand Duke of Reisenburg!'

'He echoes the foolish zeal of my fond followers,' said the Prince, as his son left the room. 'The idle parade to which their illegal loyalty still clings; my

own manners, the relics of former days; habits will
not change like stations; all these have deceived you,
sir. You have mistaken me for a monarch; I should
be one. A curse light on me the hour I can mention
it without a burning blush. Oh, shame! shame on
the blood of my father's son! Can my mouth own
that I once was one? Yes, sir! you see before you
the most injured, the least enviable of human beings.
I am a mediatised Prince!'

Vivian had resided too long in Germany to be
ignorant of the meaning of this title, with which,
perhaps, few of our readers may be acquainted. A
mediatised Prince is an unhappy victim of those
Congresses which, among other good and evil, purged
with great effect the ancient German political system.
By the regulations then determined on, that country
was freed at one fell swoop from the vexatious and
harassing dominion of the various petty Princes who
exercised absolute sovereignties over little nations of
fifty thousand souls. These independent sovereigns
became subjects; and either swelled, by their medi-
atisation, the territories of some already powerful po-
tentate, or transmuted into a state of importance
some more fortunate petty ruler than themselves,
whose independence, through the exertions of political intrigue or family influence, had been preserved
inviolate. In most instances, the concurrence of these
little rulers in their worldly degradation was obtained
by a lavish grant of official emoluments or increase of
territorial possessions; and the mediatised Prince, instead of being an impoverished and uninfluential sovereign, became a wealthy and powerful subject. But
so dominant in the heart of man is the love of independent dominion, that even with these temptations

few of the petty princes could have been induced to
have parted with their cherished sceptres, had they
not been conscious that, in case of contumacy, the
resolutions of a Diet would have been enforced by
the armies of an emperor. As it is, few of them
have yet given up the outward and visible signs of
regal sway. The throne is still preserved and the
tiara still revered. They seldom frequent the courts
of their sovereigns, and scarcely condescend to notice
the attentions of their fellow nobility. Most of them
expend their increased revenues in maintaining the
splendour of their little courts at their ancient capitals,
or in swelling the ranks of their retainers at their
solitary forest castles.

The Prince of Little Lilliput was the first mediatised
sovereign that Vivian had ever met. At another time,
and under other circumstances, he might have smiled
at the idle parade and useless pomp which he had
this day witnessed, or moralised on that weakness of
human nature which seemed to consider the inconvenient appendages of a throne as the great end for
which power was to be coveted; but at the present
moment he only saw a kind and, as he believed,
estimable individual disquieted and distressed. It was
painful to witness the agitation of the Prince, and
Vivian felt it necessary to make some observations
which, from his manner, expressed more than they
meant.

'Sir,' said his Highness, 'your sympathy consoles
me. Do not imagine that I can misunderstand it; it
does you honour. You add by this to the many
favours you have already conferred on me by saving
my life and accepting my hospitality. I sincerely hope
that your departure hence will be postponed to the

last possible moment. Your conversation and your company have made me pass a more cheerful day than I am accustomed to. All here love me; but, with the exception of Sievers, I have no companion; and although I esteem his principles and his talents, there is no congeniality in our tastes, or in our tempers. As for the rest, a more devoted band cannot be conceived; but they think only of one thing, the lost dignity of their ruler; and although this concentration of their thoughts on one subject may gratify my pride, it does not elevate my spirits. But this is a subject on which in future we will not converse. One of the curses of my unhappy lot is, that a thousand circumstances daily occur which prevent me forgetting it.'

The Prince rose from the table, and pressing with his right hand on part of the wall, the door of a small closet sprung open; the interior was lined with crimson velvet. He took out of it a cushion of the same regal material, on which reposed, in solitary magnificence, a golden coronet of antique workmanship.

'The crown of my fathers,' said his Highness, as he placed the treasure with great reverence on the table, 'won by fifty battles and lost without a blow! Yet in my youth I was deemed no dastard; and I have shed more blood for my country in one day than he who claims to be my suzerain in the whole of his long career of undeserved prosperity. Ay, this is the curse; the ancestor of my present sovereign was that warrior's serf!' The Prince pointed to the grim chieftain, whose stout helmet Vivian now perceived was encircled by a crown similar to the one which was now lying before him. 'Had I been the subject, had

I been obliged to acknowledge the sway of a Cæsar,
I might have endured it with resignation. Had I
been forced to yield to the legions of an Emperor, a
noble resistance might have consoled me for the
clanking of my chains. But to sink without a struggle,
the victim of political intrigue; to become the bonds-
man of one who was my father's slave; for such was
Reisenburg, even in my own remembrance, our unsuccessful rival; this was too bad. It rankles in my
heart, and unless I can be revenged I shall sink under
it. To have lost my dominions would have been
nothing. But revenge I will have! It is yet in my
power to gain for an enslaved people the liberty
I have myself lost. Yes! the enlightened spirit of the
age shall yet shake the quavering councils of the
Reisenburg cabal. I will, in truth I have already
seconded the just, the unanswerable demands of an
oppressed and insulted people; and, ere six months
are over, I trust to see the convocation of a free and
representative council in the capital of the petty
monarch to whom I have been betrayed. The chief
of Reisenburg has, in his eagerness to gain his grand
ducal crown, somewhat overstepped the mark.

'Besides myself, there are no less than three other
powerful princes whose dominions have been devoted
to the formation of his servile duchy. We are all
animated by the same spirit, all intent upon the same
end. We have all used, and are using, our influence
as powerful nobles to gain for our fellow-subjects
their withheld rights; rights which belong to them as
men, not merely as Germans. Within this week I
have forwarded to the Residence a memorial sub-
scribed by myself, my relatives, the other princes,
and a powerful body of discontented nobles, request-

ing the immediate grant of a constitution similar to those of Wirtemburg and Bavaria. My companions in misfortune are inspirited by my joining them. Had I been wise I should have joined them sooner; but until this moment I have been the dupe of the artful conduct of an unprincipled Minister. My eyes, however, are now open. The Grand Duke and his crafty counsellor, whose name shall not profane my lips, already tremble. Part of the people, emboldened by our representations, have already refused to answer an unconstitutional taxation. I have no doubt that he must yield. Whatever may be the inclination of the Courts of Vienna or St. Petersburg, rest assured that the liberty of Germany will meet with no opponent except political intrigue; and that Metternich is too well acquainted with the spirit which is now only slumbering in the bosom of the German nation to run the slightest risk of exciting it by the presence of foreign legions. No, no! that mode of treatment may do very well for Naples, or Poland, or Spain; but the moment that a Croat or a Cossack shall encamp upon the Rhine or the Elbe, for the purpose of supporting the unadulterated tyranny of their new-fangled Grand Dukes, that moment Germany becomes a great and united nation. The greatest enemy of the prosperity of Germany is the natural disposition of her sons; but that disposition, while it does now, and may for ever, hinder us from being a great people, will at the same time infallibly prevent us from ever becoming a degraded one.'

At this moment, this moment of pleasing anticipation of public virtue and private revenge, Master Rodolph entered, and prevented Vivian from gaining any details of the history of his host. The little round steward informed his master that a horseman had just arrived, bearing for his Highness a despatch of importance, which he insisted upon delivering into the Prince's own hands.

'Whence comes he?' asked his Highness.

'In truth, your Serene Highness, that were hard to say, inasmuch as the messenger refuses to inform us.'

'Admit him.'

A man whose jaded looks proved that he had travelled far that day, was soon ushered into the room, and, bowing to the Prince, delivered to him in silence a letter.

'From whom comes this?' asked the Prince.

'It will itself inform your Highness,' was the only answer.

'My friend, you are a trusty messenger, and have been well trained. Rodolph, look that this gentleman be well lodged and attended.'

'I thank your Highness,' said the messenger, 'but I do not tarry here. I wait no answer, and my only purpose in seeing you was to perform my commission to the letter, by delivering this paper into your own hands.'

'As you please, sir; you must be the best judge of your own time; but we like not strangers to leave our gates while our drawbridge is yet echoing with their entrance steps.'

The Prince and Vivian were again alone. Astonishment and agitation were visible on his Highness's countenance as he threw his eye over the letter. At length he folded it up, put it into his breast-pocket, and tried to resume conversation; but the effort was both evident and unsuccessful. In another moment the letter was again taken out, and again read with not less emotion than accompanied its first perusal.

'I fear I have wearied you, Mr. Grey,' said his Highness; 'it was inconsiderate in me not to remember that you require repose.'

Vivian was not sorry to have an opportunity of retiring, so he quickly took the hint, and wished his Highness agreeable dreams.

mourn over some impressive incident of the night, which is nevertheless forgotten, or to collect some inexplicable plot which has been revealed in sleep, and has fled from the memory as the eyelids have opened. Where is the sweet sleep of the artist? of the lawyer? Where, indeed, of any human being to whom to-morrow brings its necessary duties? Sleep is the enemy of Care, and Care is the constant companion of regular labour, mental or bodily.

But your traveller, your adventurous traveller, careless of the future, reckless of the past, with a mind interested by the world, from the immense and various character which that world presents to him, and not by his own stake in any petty or particular contingency; wearied by delightful fatigue, daily occasioned by varying means and from varying causes; with the consciousness that no prudence can regulate the fortunes of the morrow, and with no curiosity to discover what those fortunes may be, from a conviction that it is utterly impossible to ascertain them; perfectly easy whether he lie in a mountain-hut, or a royal palace; and reckless alike of the terrors and chances of storm and bandits, seeing that he has as fair a chance of meeting both with security and enjoyment; this is the fellow who, throwing himself upon a down couch or his mule's pack-saddle, with equal eagerness and equal *sang froid*, sinks into a repose, in which he is never reminded by the remembrance of an appointment or an engagement for the next day, a duel, a marriage, or a dinner, the three perils of man, that he has the misfortune of being mortal; and wakes not to combat care, but only to feel that he is fresher and more vigorous than he was the night before; and that, come what come may, he is, at any rate, sure this day of seeing different faces, and of improvising his unpremeditated part upon a different scene.

We have now both philosophically accounted and politely apologised for the loud and unfashionable snore which sounded in the blue chamber about five minutes after Vivian Grey had entered that most comfortable apartment. In about twelve hours' time he was scolding Essper George for having presumed to wake him so early, quite unconscious that he had enjoyed anything more than a twenty minutes' doze.

'I should not have come in, sir, only they are all out. They were off by six o'clock this morning, sir; most part at least. The Prince has gone; I do not know whether he went with them, but Master Rodolph has given me——I breakfasted with Master Rodolph. Holy Virgin! what quarters we have got into!'

'To the point; what of the Prince?'

'His Highness has left the castle, and desired Master Rodolph; if your Grace had only seen Master Rodolph tipsy last night; he rolled about like a turbot in a tornado.'

'What of the Prince?'

'The Prince desired this letter to be given to you, sir.'

Vivian read the note, which supposed that, of course, he would not wish to join the chase this morning, and regretted that the writer was obliged to ride out for a few hours to visit a neighbouring nobleman, but requested the pleasure of his guest's company at a private dinner in the cabinet on his return.

After breakfast Vivian called on Mr. Sievers. He found that gentleman busied in his library.

'You never hunt, I suppose, Mr. Sievers?'

'Never. His Highness, I apprehend, is out this morning; the beautiful weather continues; surely we never had such a season. As for myself, I almost have given up my indoor pursuits. The sun is not the light of study. Let us take our caps and have a stroll.'

The gentlemen accordingly left the library, and proceeding through a different gate to that by which Vivian had entered the castle, they came upon a part of the forest in which the timber and brushwood had been in a great measure cleared away; large clumps of trees being left standing on an artificial lawn, and newly-made roads winding about in pleasing irregularity until they were all finally lost in the encircling woods.

'I think you told me,' said Mr. Sievers, 'that you had been long in Germany. What course do you think of taking from here?'

'Straight to Vienna.'

'Ah! a delightful place. If, as I suppose to be the case, you are fond of dissipation and luxury, Vienna is to be preferred to any city with which I am acquainted. And intellectual companions are not wanting there, as some have said. There are one or two houses in which the literary soirées will yield to few in Europe; and I prefer them to most, because there is less pretension and more ease. The Archduke John is a man of considerable talents, and of more considerable acquirements. An excellent geologist! Are you fond of geology?'

'I am not in the least acquainted with the science.'

'Naturally so; at your age, if, in fact, we study at all, we are fond of fancying ourselves moral philosophers, and our study is mankind. Trust me, my dear sir, it is a branch of research soon exhausted; and in a few years you will be very glad, for want of something else to do, to meditate upon stones. See now,' said Mr. Sievers, picking up a stone, 'to what associations does this little piece of quartz give rise! I am already an antediluvian, and instead of a stag bounding by that wood I witness the moving mass of a mammoth. I live in other worlds, which, at the same time, I have the advantage of comparing with the present. Geology is indeed a magnificent study! What excites more the imagination? What exercises more the reason? Can you conceive anything sublimer than the gigantic shadows and the grim wreck of an antediluvian world? Can you devise any plan which will more brace our powers, and develop our mental energies, than the formation of a perfect chain of inductive reasoning to account for these phenomena? What is the boasted communion which the vain poet holds with nature compared with conversation which the geologist perpetually carries on with the elemental world? Gazing on the strata of the earth, he reads the fate of his species. In the undulations of the mountains is revealed to him the history of the past; and in the strength of rivers and the powers of the air he discovers the fortunes of the future. To him, indeed, that future, as well as the past and the present, are alike matter for meditation: for the geologist is the most satisfactory of antiquarians, the most interesting of philosophers, and the most inspired of prophets; demonstrating that which has past by discovery, that which is occurring by obser-

vation, and that which is to come by induction.
When you go to Vienna I will give you a letter to
Frederic Schlegel; we were fellow-students, and are
friends, though for various reasons we do not at
present meet; nevertheless a letter from me will command respect. I will recommend you, however, before you go on to Vienna, to visit Reisenburg.'

'Indeed! from the Prince's account, I should have
thought that there was little to interest me there.'

'His Highness is not an impartial judge. You are
probably acquainted with the disagreeable manner in
which he is connected with that Court. Far from his
opinion being correct, I should say there are few
places in Germany more worthy of a visit than the
little Court near us; and above all things my advice
is that you should not pass it over.'

'I am inclined to follow it. You are right in supposing that I am not ignorant that his Highness has
the misfortune of being a mediatised Prince; but what
is the exact story about him? I have heard some
odd rumours, some——'

'It is a curious story, but I am afraid you will
find it rather long. Nevertheless, if you really visit
Reisenburg, it may be of use to you to know something of the singular characters you will meet there.
In the first place, you say you know that Little Lilliput is a mediatised Prince, and, of course, are precisely aware what that title means. About fifty years
ago, the rival of the illustrious family in whose chief
castle we are both of us now residing was the Margrave of Reisenburg, another petty Prince with territories not so extensive as those of our friend, and
with a population more limited: perhaps fifty thousand souls, half of whom were drunken cousins. The

old Margrave of Reisenburg, who then reigned, was a perfect specimen of the old-fashioned German Prince; he did nothing but hunt and drink and think of the quarterings of his immaculate shield, all duly acquired from some Vandal ancestor as barbarous as himself. His little Margraviate was misgoverned enough for a great empire. Half of his nation, who were his real people, were always starving, and were unable to find crown pieces to maintain the extravagant expenditure of the other moiety, the cousins; who, out of gratitude to their fellow-subjects for their generous support, harassed them with every species of excess. Complaints were of course made to the Margrave, and loud cries for justice resounded at the palace gates. This Prince was an impartial chief magistrate; he prided himself upon his "invariable" principles of justice, and he allowed nothing to influence his decisions. His plan for arranging all differences had the merit of being brief; and if brevity be the soul of wit, it certainly was most unreasonable in his subjects to consider his judgments no joke. He always counted the quarterings in the shields of the respective parties, and decided accordingly. Imagine the speedy redress gained by a muddy-veined peasant against one of the cousins; who, of course, had as many quarterings as the Margrave himself. The defendant was regularly acquitted. At length, a man's house having been burnt down out of mere joke in the night, the owner had the temerity in the morning to accuse one of the privileged, and to produce, at the same time, a shield with exactly one more quartering than the reigning shield itself contained. The Margrave was astounded, the people in raptures, and the cousins in despair. The complainant's shield was examined and counted, and not a flaw discovered. What a dilemma! The chief magistrate consulted with the numerous branches of his family, and the next morning the complainant's head was struck off for high treason, for daring to have one more quartering than his monarch!

'In this way they passed their time about fifty years since in Reisenburg; occasionally, for the sake of variety, declaring war against the inhabitants of Little Lilliput, who, to say the truth, in their habits and pursuits did not materially differ from their neighbours. The Margrave had one son, the present Grand Duke. A due reverence of the great family shield, and a full acquaintance with the invariable principles of justice, were early instilled into him; and the royal stripling made such rapid progress, under the tuition of his amiable parent, that he soon became highly popular with all his relations. At length his popularity became troublesome to his father; and so the old Margrave sent for his son one morning, and informed him that he had dreamed the preceding night that the air of Reisenburg was peculiarly unwholesome for young persons, and therefore he begged him to get out of his dominions as soon as possible. The young Prince had no objection to see something of the world. He flew to a relative whom he had never before visited. This nobleman was one of those individuals who anticipate their age, which, by-the-bye, Mr. Grey, none but noblemen should do; for he who anticipates his century is generally persecuted when living, and is always pilfered when dead. Howbeit, this relation was a philosopher; all about him thought him mad; he, in return, thought all about him fools. He sent the Prince to an University, and gave him for a tutor a young man about ten years older than his pupil. This person's name was Beckendorff. You will hear more of him.

'About three years after the sudden departure of the young Prince, the old Margrave his father and the then reigning Prince of Little Lilliput shot each other through the head in a drunken brawl, after a dinner given in honour of a proclamation of peace between the two countries. The cousins were not much grieved, as they anticipated a fit successor in their former favourite. Splendid preparations were made for the reception of the inheritor of the family shield, and all Reisenburg was poured out to witness the triumphant entrance of their future monarch. At last two horsemen in plain dresses, and on indifferent steeds, rode up to the palace gates, dismounted, and without making any enquiry ordered the attendance of some of the chief nobility in the presence chamber. One of them, a young man, without any preparatory explanation, introduced the Reisenburg chieftains to his companion as his Prince Minister, and commanded them immediately to deliver up their portefeuilles and golden keys to Mr. Beckendorff. The nobles were in dismay, and so astounded that they made no resistance, though the next morning they started in their beds when they remembered that they had delivered their insignia of office to a man without a *von* before his name. They were soon, however, roused from their sorrow and their stupor, by receiving a peremptory order to quit the palace; and as they retired from the walls which they had long considered as their own, they had the mortification of meeting crowds of the common people, their slaves and their victims, hurrying with joyful countenances and triumphant looks to the palace of their Prince, in consequence of an energetic proclamation for the redress of grievances, and an earnest promise to decide cases in future without examining the quarterings of the parties. In a week's time the cousins were all adrift. At length they conspired, but the conspiracy was tardy, they found their former servants armed, and they joined in an unequal struggle; for their opponents were alike animated with hopes of the future and with revenge for the past. The cousins got well beat, and this was not the worst; for Beckendorff took advantage of this unsuccessful treason, which he had himself fomented, and forfeited all their estates; destroying in one hour the system which had palsied, for so many years, the energies of his master's subjects. In time many of the chief nobility were restored to their honours and estates; but the power with which they were again invested was greatly modified, and the privileges of the Commons greatly increased. At this moment the French Revolution broke out. The French crossed the Rhine and carried all before them; and the Prince of Little Lilliput, among other true Germans, made a bold but fruitless resistance. The Margrave of Reisenburg, on the contrary, received the enemy with open arms; he raised a larger body of troops than his due contingent, and exerted himself in every manner to second the views of the Great Nation. In return for his services he was presented with the conquered principality of Little Lilliput and some other adjoining lands; and the Margraviate of Reisenburg, with an increased territory and population, and governed with consummate wisdom, began to be considered the most flourishing of the petty states in the quarter of the empire to which it belonged. On the contrary, our princely and patriotic friend, mortified by the degenerate condition of his country and the prosperity of his rival house, quitted Little Lilliput, and became one of those emigrant princes who abounded during the first years of the Revolution in the northern courts of Europe. Napoleon soon appeared upon the stage; and vanquished Austria, with the French dictating at the gates of her capital, was no longer in a condition to support the dignity of the Empire. The policy of the Margrave of Reisenburg was as little patriotic and quite as consistent as before. Beckendorff became the constant and favoured counsellor of the French Emperor. It was chiefly by his exertions that the celebrated Confederation of the Rhine was carried into effect. The institution of this body excited among many Germans, at the time, loud expressions of indignation; but I believe few impartial and judicious men now look upon that league as any other than one in the formation of which consummate statesmanship was exhibited. In fact, it prevented the subjugation of Germany to France, and by flattering the pride of Napoleon saved the decomposition of our Empire. But how this might be it is not at present necessary for us to enquire. Certain it was, that the pupil of Beckendorff was amply repaid for the advice and exertions of his master and his Minister; and when Napoleon fell the brows of the former Margrave were encircled with a grand ducal crown, and his duchy, while it contained upwards of a million and a half of inhabitants, numbered in its limits some of the most celebrated cities in Germany and many of Germany's most flourishing provinces. But Napoleon fell. The Prince of Little Lilliput and his companions

in patriotism and misfortune returned from their exile
panting with hope and vengeance. A Congress was
held to settle the affairs of agitated Germany. Where
was the Grand Duke of Reisenburg? His hard-
earned crown tottered on his head. Where was his
crafty Minister, the supporter of revolutionary France,
the friend of its Imperial enslaver, the constant enemy
of the House of Austria? At the very Congress
which, according to the expectations of the exiled
Princes, was to restore them to their own dominions,
and to reward their patriotic loyalty with the territories of their revolutionary brethren; yes! at this
very Congress was Beckendorff; not as a suppliant,
not as a victim, but seated at the right hand of Metternich, and watching, with parental affection, the
first interesting and infantile movements of that most
prosperous of political bantlings, the Holy Alliance.
You may well imagine that the Military Grand Duke
had a much better chance in political negotiation
than the emigrant Prince. In addition to this, the
Grand Duke of Reisenburg had married, during the
war, a Princess of a powerful House; and the allied
Sovereigns were eager to gain the future aid and constant co-operation of a mind like Beckendorff's. The
Prince of Little Lilliput, the patriot, was rewarded for
his conduct by being restored to his forfeited possessions; and the next day he became the subject of his
former enemy, the Grand Duke of Reisenburg, the
traitor. What think you of Monsieur Beckendorff?'

'One of the most interesting characters I have
long heard of. But his pupil appears to be a man of
mind.'

'You shall hear. I should, however, first mention
that while Beckendorff has not scrupled to resort to

any measures or adopt any opinions in order to
further the interests of his monarch and his country,
he has in every manner shown that personal aggran-
disement has never been his object. He lives in re-
tirement, scarcely with an attendant, and his moderate
official stipend amply supports his more moderate expenditure. The subjects of the Grand Duke may well
be grateful that they have a Minister without relations
and without favourites. The Grand Duke is, unques-
tionably, a man of talents; but at the same time, perhaps, one of the most weak-minded men that ever
breathed. He was fortunate in meeting with Beckendorff early in life; and as the influence of the Minister
has not for a moment ceased over the mind of the
monarch, to the world the Grand Duke of Reisenburg
has always appeared to be an individual of a strong
mind and consistent conduct. But when you have
lived as much and as intimately in his Court as I
have done, you will find how easily the world may
be deceived. Since the close connection which now
exists between Reisenburg and Austria took place,
Beckendorff has, in a great degree, revived the ancient privileges of blood and birth. A Minister who
has sprung from the people will always conciliate the
aristocracy. Having no family influence of his own,
he endeavours to gain the influence of others; and it
often happens that merit is never less considered than
when merit has made the Minister. A curious instance of this occurs in a neighbouring State. There
the Premier, decidedly a man of great talents, is of
as humble an origin as Beckendorff. With no family
to uphold him, he supports himself by a lavish division of all the places and patronage of the State among
the nobles. If the younger son or brother of a peer

dare to sully his oratorical virginity by a chance observation in the Lower Chamber, the Minister, himself a real orator, immediately rises to congratulate,
in pompous phrase, the House and the country on the
splendid display which has made this night memorable, and on the decided advantages which must ac-
crue both to their own resolutions and the national
interests from the future participation of his noble
friend in their deliberations. All about him are young
nobles, quite unfit for the discharge of their respective duties. His private secretary is unable to coin a
sentence, almost to direct a letter; but he is noble!
The secondary officials cannot be trusted even in the
least critical conjunctures; but they are noble! And
the Prime Minister of a powerful empire is forced to
rise early and be up late; not to meditate on the
present fortunes or future destinies of his country, but
by his personal exertions to compensate for the inefficiency and expiate the blunders of his underlings,
whom his unfortunate want of blood has forced him
to overwhelm with praises which they do not deserve, and duties which they cannot discharge. I do
not wish you to infer that the policy of Beckendorff
has been actuated by the feelings which influence the
Minister whom I have noticed, from whose conduct
in this very respect his own materially differs.

'On the contrary, his connection with Austria is,
in all probability, the primary great cause. However
this may be, certain it is that all offices about the
Court and connected with the army (and I need not
remind you that at a small German Court these situations are often the most important in the State) can
only be filled by the nobility; nor can any person who
has the misfortune of not inheriting the magical mono-

syllable *von* before his name, the shibboleth of nobility and the symbol of territorial pride, violate by their
unhallowed presence the sanctity of Court dinners, or
the as sacred ceremonies of a noble fête. But while
a monopoly of those offices which for their due performance require only a showy exterior or a schooled
address is granted to the nobles, all those State charges
which require the exercise of intellect are now chiefly
filled by the bourgeoisie. At the same time, however, that both our Secretaries of State, many of our
Privy Councillors, war Councillors, forest Councillors,
and finance Councillors, are to be reckoned among
the second class, still not one of these exalted individuals, who from their situations are necessarily in
constant personal communication with the Sovereign,
ever see that Sovereign except in his Cabinet and his
Council-chamber. Beckendorff himself, the Premier,
is the son of a peasant; and of course not noble.
Nobility, which has been proffered him, not only by
his own monarch, but by most of the sovereigns of
Europe, he has invariably refused; and consequently
never appears at Court. The truth is, that, from disposition, he is little inclined to mix with men; and
he has taken advantage of his want of an escutcheon
completely to exempt himself from all those duties of
etiquette which his exalted situation would otherwise
have imposed upon him. None can complain of the
haughtiness of the nobles when, ostensibly, the Minister himself is not exempted from their exclusive regulations. If you go to Reisenburg, you will not
therefore see Beckendorff, who lives, as I have mentioned, in solitude, about thirty miles from the capital;
communicating only with his royal master, the foreign Ministers, and one or two official characters of

his own country. I was myself an inmate of the Court for upwards of two years. During that time I never saw the Minister; and, with the exception of some members of the royal family and the characters I have mentioned, I never knew one person who had even caught a glimpse of the individual who may indeed be said to be regulating their destinies.

'It is at the Court, then,' continued Mr. Sievers, 'when he is no longer under the control of Beckendorff, and in those minor points which are not subjected to the management or influenced by the mind of the Minister, that the true character of the Grand Duke is to be detected. Indeed it may really be said, that the weakness of his mind has been the origin of his fortune. In his early youth his pliant temper adapted itself without a struggle to the barbarous customs and the brutal conduct of his father's Court; that same pliancy of temper prevented him opposing with bigoted obstinacy the exertions of his relation to educate and civilise him; that same pliancy of temper allowed him to become the ready and the enthusiastic disciple of Beckendorff. Had the pupil, when he ascended the throne, left his master behind him, it is very probable that his natural feelings would have led him to oppose the French; and at this moment, instead of being the first of the second-rate powers of Germany, the Grand Duke of Reisenburg might himself have been a mediatised Prince. As it was, the same pliancy of temper which I have noticed enabled him to receive Napoleon, when an Emperor, with outstretched arms; and at this moment does not prevent him from receiving, with equal rapture, the Imperial Archduchess, who will soon be on her road from Vienna to espouse his son; for, to crown his career, Beckendorff has successfully negotiated a marriage between a daughter of the House of Austria and the Crown Prince* of Reisenburg. It is generally believed that the next step of the Diet will be to transmute the father's Grand Ducal coronet into a Regal crown; and perhaps, my good sir, before you reach Vienna, you may have the supreme honour of being presented to his Majesty the King of Reisenburg.'

'But when you talk only of the pupil's pliancy of temper, am I to suppose that in mentioning his talents you were speaking ironically?'

'By no means! The Grand Duke is a scholar; a man of refined taste, a patron of the fine arts, a lover of literature, a promoter of science, and what the world would call a philosopher. His judgment is sound, and generally correct, his powers of discrimination acute, and his knowledge of mankind greater than that of most sovereigns; but with all these advantages he is cursed with such a wavering and indecisive temper, that when, which is usually the case, he has come to a right conclusion, he can never prevail upon himself to carry his theory into practice; and with all his acuteness, his discernment, and his knowledge of the world, his mind is always ready to receive any impression from the person who last addressed him, though he himself be fully aware of the inferiority of his adviser's intellect to his own, or the imperfection of that adviser's knowledge. Never for a moment out of the sight of Beckendorff, the royal pupil has made an admirable political puppet,

* Hereditary Prince is the correct style of the eldest son of a German Grand Duke. I have not used a title which would not be understood by the English reader. Crown Prince is also a German title; but, in strictness, only assumed by the son of a King.

since his talents have always enabled him to understand the part which the Minister had forced him to perform. Thus the world has given the Grand Duke credit, not only for the possession of great talents, but almost for as much firmness of mind and decision of character as his Minister. But since his long-agitated career has become calm and tranquil, and Beckendorff, like a guardian spirit, has ceased to be ever at his elbow, the character of the Grand Duke of Reisenburg begins to be understood. His Court has been, and still is, frequented by all the men of genius in Germany, who are admitted without scruple, even if they be not noble. But the astonishing thing is, that the Grand Duke is always surrounded by every species of political and philosophical quack that you can imagine. Discussions on a free press, on the reformation of the criminal code, on the abolition of commercial duties, and such like interminable topics, are perpetually resounding within the palace of this arbitrary Prince; and the people, fired by the representations of the literary and political journals with which Reisenburg abounds, and whose bold speculations on all subjects elude the vigilance of the censor, by being skilfully amalgamated with a lavish praise of the royal character, are perpetually flattered with the speedy hope of becoming freemen. Suddenly, when all are expecting the grant of a charter or the institution of Chambers, Mr. Beckendorff rides up from his retreat to the Residence, and the next day the whole crowd of philosophers are swept from the royal presence, and the censorship of the press becomes so severe, that for a moment you would fancy that Reisenburg, instead of being, as it boasts itself, the modern Athens, had more right to the title of the modern Bœotia. The people who enjoy an impartial administration of equal laws, who have flourished, and are flourishing, under the wise and moderate rule of their new monarch, have in fact no inclination to exert themselves for the attainment of constitutional liberty in any other way than by their voices. Their barbarous apathy astounds the philosophes; who, in despair, when the people tell them that they are happy and contented, artfully remind them that their happiness depends on the will of a single man; and that, though the present character of the monarch may guarantee present felicity, still they should think of their children, and not less exert themselves for the insurance of the future. These representations, as constantly reiterated as the present system will allow, have at length produced an effect; and political causes of a peculiar nature, combining their influence with these philosophical exertions, have of late frequently frightened the Grand Duke, who, in despair, would perhaps grant a Constitution if Beckendorff would allow him. But the Minister is conscious that the people would not be happier, and do not in fact require one: he looks with a jealous and an evil eye on the charlatanism of all kinds which is now so prevalent at Court: he knows, from the characters of many of these philosophers and patriots, that their private interest is generally the secret spring of their public virtue; that if the Grand Duke, moved by their entreaties or seduced by their flattery, were to yield a little, he would soon be obliged to grant all to their demands and their threats; and finally, Beckendorff has, of late years, so completely interwoven the policy of Reisenburg with that of Austria, that he feels that the rock on which he has determined to found the greatness of his country must be quitted for ever if he yield one jot to the caprice or the weakness of his monarch.'

'But Beckendorff,' said Vivian; 'why can he not crush in the bud the noxious plant which he so much dreads? Why does the press speak in the least to the people? Why is the Grand Duke surrounded by any others except pompous Grand Marshals and empty-headed Lord Chamberlains? I am surprised at this indifference, this want of energy!'

'My dear sir, there are reasons for all things. Rest assured that Beckendorff is not a man to act incautiously or weakly. The Grand Duchess, the mother of the Crown Prince, has been long dead. Beckendorff, who, as a man, has the greatest contempt for women; as a statesman, looks to them as the most precious of political instruments; it was his wish to have married the Grand Duke to the young Princess who is now destined for his son, but for once in his life he failed in influencing his pupil. The truth was, and it is to this cause that we must trace the present disorganised state of the Court, and indeed of the Duchy, that the Grand Duke had secretly married a lady to whom he had long been attached. This lady was a Countess, and his subject; and, as it was impossible by the laws of the kingdom that any one but a member of the reigning family could be allowed to share the throne, his Royal Highness had recourse to a plan which is not uncommon in this country, and espoused the lady with his left hand. The ceremony, which we call here a morganatic marriage, you have, probably, heard of before. The favoured female is, to all intents and purposes, the wife of the monarch, and shares everything except his throne.

She presides at Court, but neither she nor her children assume the style of majesty, although in some instances the latter have been created princes, and acknowledged as heirs apparent when there has been a default in the lineal royal issue. The lady of whom we are speaking, according to the usual custom, has assumed a name derivative from that of her royal husband; and as the Grand Duke's name is Charles, she is styled Madame Carolina.'

'And what kind of lady is Madame Carolina?' asked Vivian.

'Philosophical! piquant! Parisian! a genius, according to her friends; who, as in fact she is a Queen, are of course the whole world. Though a German by family, she is a Frenchwoman by birth. Educated in the spiritual saloons of the French metropolis, she has early imbibed superb ideas of the perfectibility of man, and of the "science" of conversation, on both which subjects you will not be long at Court ere you hear her descant; demonstrating by the brilliancy of her ideas the possibility of the one, and by the fluency of her language her acquaintance with the other. She is much younger than her husband, and, though not exactly a model for Phidias, a fascinating woman. Variety is the talisman by which she commands all hearts and gained her monarch's. She is only consistent in being delightful; but, though changeable, she is not capricious. Each day displays a new accomplishment as regularly as it does a new costume; but as the acquirement seems only valued by its possessor as it may delight others, so the dress seems worn, not so much to gratify her own vanity as to please her friends' tastes. Genius is her idol; and with her

genius is found in everything. She speaks in equal
raptures of an opera dancer and an epic poet. Her
ambition is to converse on all subjects; and by a judicious management of a great mass of miscellaneous
reading, and by indefatigable exertions to render herself mistress of the prominent points of the topics of
the day, she appears to converse on all subjects with
ability. She takes the liveliest interest in the progress of mind, in all quarters of the globe; and im-
agines that she should, at the same time, immortalise
herself and benefit her species, could she only establish
a Quarterly Review in Ashantee and a scientific Ga-
zette at Timbuctoo. Notwithstanding her sudden elevation, no one has ever accused her of arrogance, or
pride, or ostentation. Her liberal principles and her
enlightened views are acknowledged by all. She ad-
vocates equality in her circle of privileged nobles, and
is enthusiastic on the rights of man in a country
where justice is a favour. Her boast is to be surrounded by men of genius, and her delight to corre-
spond with the most celebrated persons of all countries.
She is herself a literary character of no mean celeb-
rity. Few months have elapsed since enraptured
Reisenburg hailed from her glowing pen two neat oc-
tavos, bearing the title of "Memoirs of the Court of
Charlemagne," which give an interesting and accurate
picture of the age, and delight the modern public
with vivid descriptions of the cookery, costume,
and conversation of the eighth century. You smile,
my friend, at Madame Carolina's production. Do
not you agree with me that it requires no mean
talent to convey a picture of the bustle of a levée
during the middle ages? Conceive Sir Oliver looking
in at his club! and fancy the small talk of Roland

during a morning visit! Yet even the fame of this work is to be eclipsed by Madame's forthcoming quarto of "Haroun-al-Raschid and his Times." This, it is whispered, is to be a *chef-d'œuvre*, enriched by a chronological arrangement, by a celebrated oriental scholar, of all the anecdotes in the Arabian Nights relating to the Caliph. It is, of course, the sun of Madame's patronage that has hatched into noxious life the swarm of sciolists who now infest the Court, and who are sapping the husband's political power while they are establishing the wife's literary reputation. So much for Madame Carolina! I need hardly add that during your short stay at Court you will be delighted with her. If ever you know her as well as I do, you will find her vain, superficial, heartless; her sentiment a system, her enthusiasm exaggeration, and her genius merely a clever adoption of the profundity of others.'

'And Beckendorff and the lady are not friendly?' asked Vivian, who was delighted with his communicative companion.

'Beckendorff's is a mind that such a woman cannot comprehend. He treats her with contempt, and, if possible, views her with hatred, for he considers that she has degraded the character of his pupil; while she, on the contrary, wonders by what magic spell he exercises such influence over the conduct of her husband. At first Beckendorff treated her and her circle of illuminati with contemptuous silence; but in politics nothing is contemptible. The Minister, knowing that the people were prosperous and happy, cared little for projected constitutions, and less for metaphysical abstractions; but some circumstances have lately occurred, which, I imagine, have con-

vinced him that for once he has miscalculated. After
the arrangement of the German States, when the
Princes were first mediatised, an attempt was made,
by means of a threatening league, to obtain for these
political victims a very ample share of the power and
patronage of the new State of Reisenburg. This plan
failed from the lukewarmness and indecision of our
good friend of Little Lilliput, who, between ourselves,
was prevented from joining the alliance by the intrigues of Beckendorff. Beckendorff secretly took
measures that the Prince should be promised that, in
case of his keeping backward, he should obtain more
than would fall to his lot by leading the van. The
Prince of Little Lilliput and his peculiar friends accordingly were quiet, and the attempt of the other
chieftains failed. It was then that his Highness found
he had been duped. Beckendorff would not acknowledge the authority, and, of course, did not redeem
the pledge, of his agent. The effect that this affair
produced upon the Prince's mind you can conceive.
Since then he has never frequented Reisenburg, but
constantly resided either at his former capital, now a
provincial town of the Grand Duchy, or at this castle; viewed, you may suppose, with no very cordial
feeling by his companions in misfortune. But the
thirst of revenge will inscribe the bitterest enemies in
the same muster-roll; and the Princes, incited by the
bold carriage of Madame Carolina's philosophical *pro-
tégés*, and induced to believe that Beckendorff's power
is on the wane, have again made overtures to our
friend, without whose powerful assistance they feel
that they have but little chance of success. Observe
how much more men's conduct is influenced by circumstances than principles! When these persons

leagued together before it was with the avowed intention of obtaining a share of the power and patronage of the State: the great body of the people, of course, did not sympathise in that which, after all, to them was a party quarrel, and by the joint exertions of open force and secret intrigue the Court triumphed. But now these same individuals come forward, not as indignant Princes demanding a share of the envied tyranny, but as ardent patriots advocating a people's rights. The public, though I believe that in fact they will make no bodily exertion to acquire a constitutional freedom the absence of which they can only abstractedly feel, have no objection to attain that which they are assured will not injure their situation, provided it be by the risk and exertions of others. So far, therefore, as clamour can support the Princes, they have the people on their side; and as upwards of three hundred thousand of the Grand Ducal subjects are still living on their estates, and still consider themselves as their serfs, they trust that some excesses from this great body may incite the rest of the people to similar outrages. The natural disposition of mankind to imitation, particularly when the act to be imitated is popular, deserves attention. The Court is divided; for the exertions of Madame and the bewitching influence of Fashion have turned the heads even of greybeards: and to give you only one instance, his Excellency the Grand Marshal, *protégé* of the House of Austria, and a favourite of Metternich, the very person to whose interests, and as a reward for whose services, our princely friend was sacrificed by the Minister, has now himself become a pupil in the school of modern philosophy, and drivels out, with equal ignorance and

fervour, enlightened notions on the most obscure subjects. In the midst of all this confusion, the Grand
Duke is timorous, dubious, and uncertain. Beckendorff has a difficult game to play; he may fall at
last. Such, my dear sir, are the tremendous consequences of a weak Prince marrying a blue-stocking!'

'And the Crown Prince, Mr. Sievers, how does
he conduct himself at this interesting moment? or is
his mind so completely engrossed by the anticipation
of his Imperial alliance that he has no thought for
anything but his approaching bride.'

'The Crown Prince, my dear sir, is neither thinking of his bride nor of anything else: he is a hunch-
backed idiot. Of his deformity I have myself been a
witness; and though it is difficult to give an opinion
of the intellect of a being with whom you have
never interchanged a syllable, nevertheless his countenance does not contradict the common creed. I
say the common creed, Mr. Grey, for there are moments when the Crown Prince of Reisenburg is
spoken of by his future subjects in a very different
manner. Whenever any unpopular act is committed,
or any unpopular plan suggested by the Court or
the Grand Duke, then whispers are immediately afloat
that a future Brutus must be looked for in their
Prince; then it is generally understood that his idiocy
is only assumed; and what woman does not detect,
in the glimmerings of his lack-lustre eye, the vivid
sparks of suppressed genius! In a short time the
cloud blows over the Court, dissatisfaction disappears,
and the moment that the monarch is again popular
the unfortunate Crown Prince again becomes the uninfluential object of pity or derision. All immediately forget that his idiocy is only assumed; and

what woman ever ceases from deploring the unhappy lot of the future wife of their impuissant Prince! Such, my dear sir, is the way of mankind! At the first glance it would appear, that in this world monarchs, on the whole, have it pretty well their own way; but reflection will soon enable us not to envy their situations; and speaking as a father, which unfortunately I am not, should I not view with disgust that lot in life which necessarily makes my son my enemy? The Crown Prince of all countries is only a puppet in the hands of the people, to be played against his own father.'

CHAPTER V.

A Delicate Mission.

THE Prince returned home at a late hour, and immediately inquired for Vivian. During dinner, which he hastily despatched, it did not escape our hero's attention that his Highness was unusually silent, and, indeed, agitated.

'When we have finished our meal, my good friend,' at length said the Prince, 'I very much wish to consult with you on a most important business.' Since the explanation of last night, the Prince, in private conversation, had dropped his regal plural.

'I am ready at once,' said Vivian.

'You will think it strange, Mr. Grey, when you become acquainted with the nature of my communication; you will justly consider it most strange, most singular, that I should choose for a confidante and a counsellor in an important business a gentleman with whom I have been acquainted so short a time as yourself. But, sir, I have well weighed, at least I have endeavoured well to weigh, all the circumstances and contingencies which such a confidence would involve; and the result of my reflection is, that

(154)

I will look to you as a friend and adviser, feeling assured that, both from your situation and your disposition, no temptation exists which can induce you to betray or to deceive me.' Though the Prince said this with an appearance of perfect sincerity, he stopped and looked earnestly in his guest's face, as if he would read his secret thoughts, or were desirous of now giving him an opportunity of answering.

'So far as the certainty of your confidence being respected,' answered Vivian, 'I trust your Highness may communicate to me with the most assured spirit. But while my ignorance of men and affairs in this country will ensure you from any treachery on my part, I very much fear that it will also preclude me from affording you any advantageous advice or assistance.'

'On that head,' replied the Prince, 'I am, of course, the best judge. The friend whom I need is a man not ignorant of the world, with a cool head and an impartial mind. Though young, you have said and told me enough to prove that you are not unacquainted with mankind. Of your courage I have already had a convincing proof. In the business in which I require your assistance freedom from national prejudices will materially increase the value of your advice; and, therefore, I am far from being unwilling to consult a person ignorant, according to your own phrase, of men and affairs in this country. Moreover, your education as an Englishman has early led you to exercise your mind on political subjects; and it is in a political business that I require your aid.'

'Am I fated always to be the dry nurse of an embryo faction!' thought Vivian; and he watched earnestly the countenance of the Prince. In a moment he expected to be invited to become a counsellor of the leagued Princes. Either the lamp was burning dim, or the blazing wood fire had suddenly died away, or a mist was over Vivian's eyes; but for a moment he almost imagined that he was sitting opposite his old friend the Marquis of Carabas. The Prince's phrase had given rise to a thousand agonising associations: in an instant Vivian had worked up his mind to a pitch of nervous excitement.

'Political business?' said Vivian, in an agitated voice. 'You could not address a more unfortunate person. I have seen, Prince, too much of politics ever to wish to meddle with them again.'

'You are too quick, my good friend,' continued his Highness. 'I may wish to consult you on political business, and yet have no intention of engaging you in politics, which, indeed, is quite a ridiculous idea. But I see that I was right in supposing that these subjects have engaged your attention.'

'I have seen, in a short time, something of the political world,' answered Vivian, who was almost ashamed of his previous emotion; 'and I thank Heaven daily that I have no chance of again having any connection with it.'

'Well, well! that as it may be. Nevertheless, your experience is only another inducement to me to request your assistance. Do not fear that I wish to embroil you in politics; but I hope you will not refuse, although almost a stranger, to add to the great obligations which I am already under to you, and give me the benefit of your opinion.'

'Your Highness may speak with perfect unreserve, and reckon upon my delivering my genuine sentiments.'

'You have not forgotten, I venture to believe,' said the Prince, 'our short conversation of last night?'

'It was of too interesting a nature easily to escape my memory.'

'Before I can consult you on the subject which at present interests me, it is necessary that I should make you a little acquainted with the present state of public affairs here, and the characters of the principal individuals who control them.'

'So far as an account of the present state of political parties, the history of the Grand Duke's career, and that of his Minister, Mr. Beckendorff, and their reputed characters, will form part of your Highness's narrative, by so much may its length be curtailed and your trouble lessened; for I have at different times picked up, in casual conversation, a great deal of information on these topics. Indeed, you may address me, in this respect, as you would any German gentleman who, not being himself personally interested in public life, is, of course, not acquainted with its most secret details.'

'I did not reckon on this,' said the Prince, in a cheerful voice. 'This is a great advantage, and another reason that I should no longer hesitate to develop to you a certain affair which now occupies my mind. To be short,' continued the Prince, 'it is of the letter which I so mysteriously received last night, and which, as you must have remarked, very much agitated me; it is on this letter that I wish to consult you. Bearing in mind the exact position, the avowed and public position, in which I stand, as connected with the Court, and having a due acquaintance, which you state you have, with the character of Mr. Beckendorff, what think you of this letter?'

So saying, the Prince leant over the table, and handed to Vivian the following epistle:

'TO HIS HIGHNESS THE PRINCE OF LITTLE LILLIPUT.

'I am commanded by his Royal Highness to inform your Highness that his Royal Highness has considered the request which was signed by your Highness and other noblemen, and presented by you to his Royal Highness in a private interview. His Royal Highness commands me to state that that request will receive his most attentive consideration. At the same time, his Royal Highness also commands me to observe that, in bringing about the completion of a result desired by all parties, it is difficult to carry on the necessary communications merely by written documents; and his Royal Highness has therefore commanded me to submit to your Highness the advisability of taking some steps in order to further the possibility of the occurrence of an oral interchange of the sentiments of the respective parties. Being aware, from the position which your Highness has thought proper at present to maintain, and from other causes which are of too delicate a nature to be noticed in any other way except by allusion, that your Highness may feel difficulty in personally communicating with his Royal Highness without consulting the wishes and opinions of the other Princes; a process to which, it must be evident to your Highness, his Royal Highness feels it impossible to submit; and, at the same time, desirous of forwarding the progress of those views which his Royal Highness and your Highness may conjunctively consider calculated to advance the well-being of the State, I have to submit to your

Highness the propriety of considering the propositions contained in the enclosed paper; which, if your Highness keep unconnected with this communication, the purport of this letter will be confined to your Highness.

' " PROPOSITIONS.

' " 1st. That an interview shall take place between your Highness and myself, the object of which shall be the consideration of measures by which, when adopted, the various interests now in agitation shall respectively be regarded.

' " 2nd. That this interview shall be secret; your Highness be incognito."

' If your Highness be disposed to accede to the first proposition, I beg to submit to you that, from the nature of my residence, its situation, and other causes, there will be no fear that any suspicion of the fact of Mr. von Philipson acceding to the two propositions will gain notoriety. This letter will be delivered into your own hands. If Mr. von Philipson determine on acceding to these propositions, he is most probably aware of the general locality in which my residence is situated; and proper measures will be taken that, if Mr. von Philipson honour me with a visit, he shall not be under the necessity of attracting attention by inquiring the way to my house. It is wished that the fact of the second proposition being acceded to should only be known to Mr. von Philipson and myself; but if to be perfectly unattended be considered as an insuperable objection, I consent to his being accompanied by a single friend. I shall be alone.

' BECKENDORFF.'

'Well!' said the Prince, as Vivian finished the letter.

'The best person,' said Vivian, 'to decide upon your Highness consenting to this interview is yourself.'

'That is not the point on which I wish to have the benefit of your opinion; for I have already consented. I rode over this morning to my cousin, the Duke of Micromegas, and despatched from his residence a trusty messenger to Beckendorff. I have agreed to meet him, and to-morrow; but on the express terms that I should not be unattended. Now then,' continued the Prince, with great energy; 'now then, will you be my companion?'

'I!' said Vivian.

'Yes; you, my good friend! you. I should consider myself as safe if I were sleeping in a burning house as I should be were I with Beckendorff alone. Although this is not the first time that we have communicated, I have never yet seen him; and I am fully aware that if the approaching interview were known to my friends, they would consider it high time that my son reigned in my stead. But I am resolved to be firm, to be inflexible. My course is plain. I am not to be again duped by him, which,' continued the Prince, much confused, 'I will not conceal that I have been once.'

'But I!' said Vivian; 'I; what good can I possibly do? It appears to me that if Beckendorff is to be dreaded as you describe, the presence or the attendance of no friend can possibly save you from his crafty plans. But surely, if any one attend you, why not be accompanied by a person whom you have known long, and who knows you well; on whom you can confidently rely, and who may be aware, from a thousand signs and circumstances which will never attract my attention, at what particular and pressing moments you may require prompt and energetic assistance. Such is the companion you want; and surely such an one you may find in Arnelm, Von Neuwied ——'

'Arnelm! Von Neuwied!' said the Prince; 'the best hands at sounding a bugle or spearing a boar in all Reisenburg! Excellent men, forsooth! to guard their master from the diplomatic deceits of the wily Beckendorff! Moreover, were they to have even the slightest suspicion of my intended movement, they would commit rank treason out of pure loyalty, and lock me up in my own cabinet! No, no! they will never do: I want a companion of experience and knowledge of the world, with whom I may converse with some prospect of finding my wavering firmness strengthened, or my misled judgment rightly guided, or my puzzled brain cleared; modes of assistance to which the worthy Jagd Junker is but little accustomed, however quickly he might hasten to my side in a combat or the chase.'

'If these, then, will not do, surely there is one man in this castle who, although he may not be a match for Beckendorff, can be foiled by few others. Mr. Sievers?' said Vivian, with an inquiring eye.

'Sievers!' exclaimed the Prince, with great eagerness; 'the very man! firm, experienced, and sharp-witted; well schooled in political learning, in case I required his assistance in arranging the terms of the intended Charter or the plan of the intended Chambers; for these, of course, are the points on which Beckendorff wishes to consult. But one thing I am determined on: I positively pledge myself to nothing while under Beckendorff's roof. He doubtless antici-

pates, by my visit, to grant the liberties of the people
on his own terms: perhaps Mr. Beckendorff, for once
in his life, may be mistaken. I am not to be deceived twice; and I am determined not to yield the
point of the Treasury being under the control of the
Senate. That is the part of the harness which galls;
and to preserve themselves from this rather inconvenient regulation, without question, my good friend
Beckendorff has hit upon this plan.'

'Then Mr. Sievers will accompany you?' asked
Vivian, calling the Prince's attention to the point of
consultation.

'The very man for it, my dear friend! but although
Beckendorff, most probably respecting my presence,
and taking into consideration the circumstances under
which we meet, would refrain from consigning Sievers to a dungeon; still, although the Minister invites
this interview, and although I have no single inducement to conciliate him, yet it would scarcely be correct, scarcely dignified on my part, to prove, by the
presence of my companion, that I had for a length of
time harboured an individual who, by Beckendorff's
own exertions, was banished from the Grand Duchy.
It would look too much like a bravado.'

'Oh!' said Vivian; 'is it so? And pray of what
was Mr. Sievers guilty?'

'Of high treason against one who was not his
sovereign.'

'How is that?'

'Sievers, who is a man of considerable talents,
was for a long time a professor in one of our great
Universities. The publication of many able works
procured him a reputation which induced Madame
Carolina to use every exertion to gain his attendance

at Court; and a courtier in time the professor became.
At Reisenburg Mr. Sievers was the great authority on
all subjects: philosophical, literary, and political. In
fact, he was the fashion; and, at the head of the
great literary journal which is there published, he
terrified admiring Germany with his profound and
piquant critiques. Unfortunately, like some men as
good, he was unaware that Reisenburg was not an
independent state; and so, on the occasion of Austria attacking Naples, Mr. Sievers took the opportunity
of attacking Austria. His article, eloquent, luminous,
profound, revealed the dark colours of the Austrian
policy, as an artist's lamp brings out the murky tints
of a Spagnoletto. Every one admired Sievers's bitter
sarcasms, enlightened views, and indignant eloquence.
Madame Carolina crowned him with laurel in the
midst of her coterie, and it is said that the Grand
Duke sent him a snuff-box. In a short time the article reached Vienna, and in a still shorter time Mr.
Beckendorff reached the Residence, and insisted on
the author being immediately given up to the Austrian
Government. Madame Carolina was in despair, the
Grand Duke in doubt, and Beckendorff threatened to
resign if the order were not signed. A kind friend,
perhaps his Royal Highness himself, gave Sievers
timely notice, and by rapid flight he reached my castle, and demanded my hospitality. He has lived here
ever since, and has done me a thousand services, not
the least of which is the education which he has
given my son, my glorious Maximilian.'

'And Beckendorff,' asked Vivian; 'has he always
been aware that Sievers was concealed here?'

'That I cannot answer: had he been, it is not im-
probable that he would have winked at it; since it

never has been his policy unnecessarily to annoy a mediatised Prince, or without great occasion to let us feel that our independence is gone—I will not, with such a son as I have, say, for ever.'

'Mr. Sievers of course, then, cannot visit Beckendorff,' said Vivian.

'That is clear,' said the Prince; 'and I therefore trust that now you will no longer refuse my first request.'

It was impossible for Vivian to deny the Prince any longer; and indeed he had no objection (as his Highness could not be better attended) to seize the singular and unexpected opportunity which now offered itself of becoming acquainted with an individual respecting whom his curiosity was much excited. It was a late hour ere the Prince and his friend retired, having arranged everything for the morrow's journey, and conversed on the probable subjects of the approaching interview at great length.

CHAPTER VI.

An Eccentric Prime Minister.

N THE following morning, before sunrise, the Prince's valet roused Vivian from his slumbers. According to the appointment of the preceding evening, Vivian repaired in due time to a certain spot in the park. The Prince reached it at the same moment. A mounted groom, leading two English horses of showy appearance, and each having a travelling case strapped on the back of its saddle, awaited them. His Highness mounted one of the steeds with skilful celerity, although Arnelm and Von Neuwied were not there to do honour to his bridle and his stirrup.

'You must give me an impartial opinion of your courser, my dear friend,' said the Prince to Vivian; 'for if you deem it worthy of being bestridden by you, my son requests that you will do him the honour of accepting it. If so, call it Max; and provided it be as thoroughbred as the donor, you need not change it for Bucephalus.'

'Not unworthy of the son of Ammon!' said Vivian, as he touched the spirited animal with the spur, and proved its fiery action on the springing turf.

A man never feels so proud or so sanguine as when he is bounding on the back of a fine horse. Cares fly with the first curvet, and the very sight of a spur is enough to prevent one committing suicide.

When Vivian and his companion had proceeded about five miles, the Prince pulled up, and giving a sealed letter to the groom, he desired him to leave them. The Prince and Vivian amused themselves by endeavouring to form some conception of the person, manners, and habits of the remarkable man to whom they were on the point of paying so interesting a visit.

'I expect,' said Vivian, 'to be received with folded arms, and a brow lowering with the overwhelming weight of a brain meditating for the control of millions. His letter has prepared us for the mysterious, but not very amusing, style of his conversation. He will be perpetually on his guard not to commit himself; and although public business, and the receipt of papers, by calling him away, will occasionally give us an opportunity of being alone, still I regret that I did not put up in my case some interesting volume, which would have allowed me to feel less tedious those hours during which you will necessarily be employed with him in private consultation.'

After a ride of five hours, the horsemen arrived at a small village.

'Thus far I think I have well piloted you,' said the Prince: 'but I confess my knowledge here ceases; and though I shall disobey the diplomatic instructions of the great man, I must even ask some old woman the way to Mr. Beckendorff's.'

While they were hesitating as to whom they should address, an equestrian, who had already passed

upon a lawn, which formed on the farthest side a terrace, by gradually sloping down to the margin of the river. It was inclosed on the other side, and white pheasants were feeding in its centre. Following the path which skirted the lawn, they arrived at a second gate, which opened into a garden, in which no signs of the taste at present existing in Germany for the English system of picturesque pleasure-grounds were at all visible. The walk was bounded on both sides by tall borders, or rather hedges, of box, cut into the shape of battlements; the sameness of these turrets being occasionally varied by the immovable form of some trusty warder, carved out of yew or laurel. Raised terraces and arched walks, aloes and orange trees mounted on sculptured pedestals, columns of cypress and pyramids of bay, whose dark foliage strikingly contrasted with the marble statues, and the white vases shining in the sun, rose in all directions in methodical confusion. The sound of a fountain was not wanting, and large beds of beautiful flowers abounded. Proceeding through a lofty berçeau, occasional openings in whose curving walks allowed effective glimpses of a bust or a statue, the companions at length came in sight of the house. It was a long, uneven, low building, evidently of ancient architecture. Numerous stacks of tall and fantastically-shaped chimneys rose over three thick and heavy gables, which reached down farther than the middle of the elevation, forming three compartments, one of them including a large and modern bow window, over which clustered in profusion the sweet and glowing blossoms of the clematis and the pomegranate. Indeed, the whole front of the house was so completely covered with a rich scarlet-creeper, that it was diffi-

cult to ascertain of what materials it was built. As
Vivian was admiring a white peacock, which, attracted
by their approach, had taken the opportunity of un-
furling its wheeling train, a man came forward from
the bow window.

In height he was about five feet eight, and of a
spare but well-proportioned figure. He had little
hair, which was powdered, and dressed in a manner
to render more remarkable the elevation of his conical
and polished forehead. His long piercing black eyes
were almost closed, from the fulness of their upper
lids. His cheek was sallow, his nose aquiline, his
mouth compressed. His ears, which were uncovered,
were so small that it would be wrong to pass them
over unnoticed; as, indeed, were his hands and feet,
in form quite feminine. He was dressed in a coat
and waistcoat of black velvet, the latter part of his
costume reaching to his thighs; and in a button-hole
of his coat was a large bunch of tube-rose. The
broad collar of his exquisitely plaited shirt, though
tied round with a wide black ribbon, did not conceal
a neck which agreed well with his beardless chin,
and would not have misbecome a woman. In England we should have called his breeches buckskin.
They were of a pale yellow leather, and suited his
large and spur-armed cavalry boots, which fitted closely
to the legs they covered, reaching over the knees of
the wearer. A ribbon round his neck, tucked into
his waistcoat pocket, was attached to a small French
watch. He swung in his right hand the bow of a
violin; and in the other, the little finger of which was
nearly hid by a large antique ring, he held a white
handkerchief strongly perfumed with violets. Notwithstanding the many feminine characteristics which

I have noticed, either from the expression of the eyes or the formation of the mouth, the countenance of this individual generally conveyed an impression of firmness and energy. This description will not be considered ridiculously minute by those who have never had an opportunity of becoming acquainted with the person of so celebrated a gentleman as Mr. Beckendorff.

He advanced to the Prince with an air which seemed to proclaim that, as his person could not be mistaken, the ceremony of introduction was unnecessary. Bowing in a ceremonious and courtly manner to his Highness, Mr. Beckendorff, in a weak but not unpleasing voice, said that he was 'honoured by the presence of Mr. von Philipson.' The Prince answered his salutation in a manner equally ceremonious and equally courtly; for having no mean opinion of his own diplomatic abilities, his Highness determined that neither by an excess of coldness nor cordiality on his part should the Minister gather the slightest indication of the temper in which he had attended the interview. You see that even the bow of a diplomatist is a serious business!

'Mr. Beckendorff,' said his Highness, 'my letter doubtless informed you that I should avail myself of your permission to be accompanied. Let me have the honour of presenting to you my friend Mr. Grey, an English gentleman.'

As the Prince spoke, Beckendorff stood with his arms crossed behind him, and his chin resting upon his chest, but his eyes at the same time so raised as to look his Highness full in the face. Vivian was so struck by his posture and the expression of his countenance, that he nearly omitted to bow when he was presented. As his name was mentioned, the Minister gave him a sharp, sidelong glance, and moving his head slightly, invited his guests to enter the house. The gentlemen accordingly complied with his request. Passing through the bow window, they found themselves in a well-sized room, the sides of which were covered with shelves filled with richly-bound books. There was nothing in the room which gave the slightest indication that the master of the library was any other than a private gentleman. Not a book, not a chair was out of its place. A purple inkstand of Sèvres, and a highly-tooled morocco portfolio of the same colour, reposed on a marqueterie table, and that was all. No papers, no despatches, no red tape, and no red boxes. Over an ancient chimney, lined with china tiles, on which were represented grotesque figures, cows playing the harp, monkeys acting monarchs, and tall figures all legs, flying with rapidity from pursuers who were all head; over this chimney were suspended some curious pieces of antique armour, among which an Italian dagger, with a chased and jewelled hilt, was the most remarkable and the most precious.

'This,' said Mr. Beckendorff, 'is my library.'

'What a splendid poignard!' said the Prince, who had no taste for books; and he immediately walked up to the chimney-piece. Beckendorff followed him, and taking down the admired weapon from its resting-place, proceeded to lecture on its virtues, its antiquity, and its beauty. Vivian seized this opportunity of taking a rapid glance at the contents of the library. He anticipated interleaved copies of Machiavel, Vattel, and Montesquieu; and the lightest works that he expected to meet with were the lying memoirs of some

intriguing cardinal or the deluding apology of an exiled minister. To his surprise, he found that, without an exception, the collection consisted of poetry
and romance. Somewhat surprised, Vivian looked
with a curious eye on the unlettered backs of a row
of mighty folios on a corner shelf. 'These,' he
thought, 'at least must be royal ordinances, and collected state papers.' The sense of propriety struggled
for a moment with the passion of curiosity; but
nothing is more difficult for the man who loves books
than to refrain from examining a volume which he
fancies may be unknown to him. From the jewelled
dagger Beckendorff had now got to an enamelled
breast-plate. Two to one he should not be observed;
and so, with a desperate pull, Vivian extracted a volume; it was a herbal! He tried another; it was a
collection of dried insects!

'And now,' said Mr. Beckendorff, 'I will show
you my drawing-room.'

He opened a door at the farther end of the library,
and introduced them to a room of a different character. The sun, which was shining brightly, lent additional brilliancy to the rainbow-tinted birds of
paradise, the crimson maccaws, and the green parro-
quets that glistened on the Indian paper, which covered not only the walls, but also the ceiling of the
room. Over the fireplace a black frame, projecting
from the wall, and mournfully contrasting with the
general brilliant appearance of the apartment, inclosed
a picture of a beautiful female; and bending over its
frame, and indeed partly shadowing the countenance,
was the withered branch of a tree. A harpsichord
and several cases of musical instruments were placed
in different parts of the room; and suspended by

broad black ribbons from the wall, on each side of the picture, were a guitar and a tambourine. On a sofa of unusual size lay a Cremona; and as Mr. Beckendorff passed the instrument he threw by its side the bow, which he had hitherto carried in his hand.

'We may as well now take something,' said Mr. Beckendorff, when his guests had sufficiently admired the room; 'my pictures are in my dining-room; let us go there.'

So saying, and armed this time not only with his bow but also with his violin, he retraced his steps through the library, and crossing a small passage which divided the house into two compartments, he opened the door into his dining-room. The moment they entered the room their ears were saluted, and indeed their senses ravished, by what appeared to be a concert of a thousand birds; yet none of the winged choristers were to be seen, and not even a single cage was visible. The room, which was simply furnished, appeared at first rather gloomy; for, though lighted by three windows, the silk blinds were all drawn.

'And now,' said Mr. Beckendorff, raising the first blind, 'you shall see my pictures. At what do you estimate this Breughel?'

The window, which was of stained green glass, gave to the landscape an effect similar to that generally produced by the artist mentioned. The Prince, who was already puzzled by finding one who at the same time was both his host and his enemy so different a character from what he had conceived, and who, being by temper superstitious, considered that this preliminary false opinion of his was rather a bad omen, did not express any great admiration of the gallery of

Mr. Beckendorff; but Vivian, who had no ambitious
hopes or fears to affect his temper, and who was
amused by the character with whom he had become
so unexpectedly acquainted, good-naturedly humoured
the fantasies of the Minister, and said that he preferred his picture to any Breughel he had ever seen.

'I see you have a fine taste,' said Mr. Beckendorff,
with a serious air, but in a courteous tone; 'you
shall see my Claude!'

The rich yellow tint of the second window gave
to the fanciful garden all that was requisite to make
it look Italian.

'Have you ever been in Italy, sir?' asked Beckendorff.

'I have not.'

'You have, Mr. von Philipson?'

'Never south of Germany,' answered the Prince,
who was hungry, and eyed with a rapacious glance
the capital luncheon which he saw prepared for him.

'Well, then, when either of you go, you will, of
course, not miss the Lago Maggiore. Gaze on Isola
Bella at sunset, and you will not view so fair a scene
as this! And now, Mr. von Philipson,' said Beckendorff, 'do me the favour of giving me your opinion of this Honthorst?'

His Highness would rather have given his opinion
of the dish of game which still smoked upon the
table, but which he was mournfully convinced would
not smoke long. 'But,' thought he, 'this is the
last!' and so he admired the effect produced by the
flaming panes, to which Beckendorff swore that no
piece ever painted by Gerard Honthorst, for brilliancy
of colouring and boldness of outline, could be compared. 'Besides,' continued Beckendorff, 'mine are

all animated pictures. See that cypress, waving from the breeze which is now stirring, and look! look at this crimson peacock! look! Mr. von Philipson.'

'I am looking, Mr. von —— I beg pardon, Mr. Beckendorff,' said the Prince, with great dignity, making this slight mistake in the name, either from being unused to converse with such low people as had not the nominal mark of nobility, or to vent his spleen at being so unnecessarily kept from the refreshment which he so much required.

'Mr. von Philipson,' said Beckendorff, suddenly turning round, 'all my fruits and all my vegetables are from my own garden. Let us sit down and help ourselves.'

The only substantial food at table was a great dish of game. The vegetables and the fruits were numerous and superb; and there really appeared to be a fair prospect of the Prince of Little Lilliput making as good a luncheon as if the whole had been conducted under the auspices of Master Rodolph himself, had it not been for the melody of the unseen vocalists, which, probably excited by the sounds of the knives and plates, too evidently increased every moment. But this inconvenience was soon removed by Mr. Beckendorff rising and giving three loud knocks on the door opposite to the one by which they had entered. Immediate silence ensued.

'Clara will change your plate, Mr. von Philipson,' said Beckendorff.

Vivian eagerly looked up, not with the slightest idea that the entrance of Clara would prove that the mysterious picture in the drawing-room was a portrait, but, it must be confessed, with a little curiosity to view the first specimen of the sex who lived under the roof of Mr. Beckendorff. Clara was a hale old woman, with rather an acid expression of countenance, prim in her appearance, and evidently precise in her manners. She placed a bottle and two wineglasses with long thin stems on the table; and having removed the game and changed the plates, she disappeared.

'Pray what wine is this, Mr. Beckendorff?' eagerly asked the Prince.

'I really don't know. I never drink wine.'

'Not know! I never tasted such Tokay in my life!'

'Probably,' said Mr. Beckendorff; 'I think it was a present from the Emperor. I have never tasted it.'

'My dear sir, take a glass!' said the Prince, his naturally jovial temper having made him completely forget whom he was addressing, and the business he had come upon.

'I never drink wine; I am glad you like it; I have no doubt Clara has more.'

'No, no, no! we must be moderate,' said the Prince, who, though a great admirer of a good luncheon, had also a due respect for a good dinner, and consequently had no idea, at this awkward hour in the day, of preventing himself from properly appreciating the future banquet. Moreover, his Highness, taking into consideration the manner in which the game had been dressed, and the marks of refinement and good taste which seemed to pervade every part of the establishment of Mr. Beckendorff, did not imagine that he was much presuming when he conjectured that there was a fair chance of his dinner being something superior.

The sudden arrival and appearance of some new and unexpected guests through the mysterious portal on which Mr. Beckendorff by his three knocks had previously produced such a tranquillising effect, and which he had now himself opened, explained the character of the apartment, which, from its unceasing melody, had so much excited the curiosity of his guests. These new visitors were a crowd of piping bullfinches, Virginia nightingales, trained canaries, Java sparrows, and Indian lorys; which, freed from their cages of golden wire by their fond master, had fled, as was their custom, from his superb aviary to pay their respects and compliments at his daily levée.

'I am glad to see that you like birds, sir,' said Beckendorff to Vivian; for our hero, good-naturedly humouring the tastes of his host, was impartially dividing the luxuries of a peach among a crowd of gaudy and greedy little sparrows. 'You shall see my favourites,' continued Beckendorff; and tapping rather loudly on the table, he held out the forefinger of each hand. Two bullfinches recognised the signal, and immediately hastened to their perch.

'My dear!' trilled out one little songster, and it raised its speaking eyes to its delighted master.

'My love!' warbled the other, marking its affection by looks equally personal.

As these monosyllables were repeated, Beckendorff, with sparkling eyes, triumphantly looked round at Vivian, as if the frequent reiteration were a proof of the sincerity of the affection of these singular friends.

At length, to the Prince's relief, Mr. Beckendorff's feathered friends, having finished their dessert, were sent back to their cages, with a strict injunction not to trouble their master at present with their voices, an injunction which was obeyed to the letter; and when the door was closed few persons could have been persuaded that the next room was an aviary.

'I am proud of my peaches, Mr. von Philipson,' said Beckendorff, recommending the fruit to his guest's attention; then rising from the table, he threw himself on the sofa, and began humming a tune in a low voice. Presently he took up his Cremona, and, using the violin as a guitar, accompanied himself in a beautiful air, but not in a more audible tone. While Mr. Beckendorff was singing he seemed unconscious that any person was in the room; and the Prince, who was not very fond of music, certainly gave him no hint, either by his approbation or his attention, that he was listened to. Vivian, however, like most unhappy men, loved music; and actuated by this feeling, and the interest which he began to take in the character of Mr. Beckendorff, he could not, when that gentleman had finished his air, refrain from very sincerely saying ' encore! '

Beckendorff started and looked round, as if he were for the first moment aware that any being had heard him.

'Encore!' said he, with a kind of sneer; 'who ever could sing or play the same thing twice! Are you fond of music, sir ?'

'Very much so, indeed. I fancied I recognised that air. You are an admirer, I imagine, of Mozart ?'

'I never heard of him; I know nothing of those gentry. But if you really like music, I will play you something worth listening to.'

Mr. Beckendorff began a beautiful air very adagio, gradually increasing the time in a kind of variation, till at last his execution became so rapid that Vivian, surprised at the mere mechanical action, rose from his chair in order better to examine the player's management and motion of his bow. Exquisite as were the tones, enchanting as were the originality of his variations and the perfect harmony of his composition, it was nevertheless extremely difficult to resist smiling at the contortions of his face and figure. Now his body bending to the strain, he was at one moment with his violin raised in the air, and the next instant with the lower nut almost resting upon his foot. At length, by well-proportioned degrees, the air died away into the original soft cadence; and the player, becoming completely entranced in his own performance, finished by sinking back on the sofa, with his bow and violin raised over his head. Vivian would not disturb him by his applause. An instant after, Mr. Beckendorff, throwing down the instrument, rushed through an open window into the garden.

As soon as Beckendorff was out of sight, Vivian looked at the Prince; and his Highness, elevating his eyebrows, screwing up his mouth, and shrugging his shoulders, altogether presented a comical picture of a puzzled man.

'Well, my dear friend,' said he, 'this is rather different from what we expected.'

'Very different; but much more amusing.'

'Humph!' said the Prince, slowly; 'I do not think it exactly requires a ghost to tell us that Mr. Beckendorff is not in the habit of going to court. I do not know how he is accustomed to conduct himself when he is honoured by a visit from the Grand Duke; but I am quite sure that, as regards his treatment of myself, to say the least, the incognito is well observed.'

'Mr. von Philipson,' said the gentleman of whom

were speaking, putting his head in at the win-
, 'you shall see my blue passion-flower. We
take a walk round the garden.'

The Prince gave Vivian a look which seemed to
suppose they must go, and accordingly they stepped
into the garden.

'You do not see my garden in its glory,' said Mr.
Beckendorff, stopping before the bow window of the
library. 'This spot is my strong point; had you been
here earlier in the year, you might have admired with
me my invaluable crescents of tulips; such colours!
such brilliancy! so defined! And last year I had three
king-tulips; their elegantly-formed, creamy cups I have
never seen equalled. And then my double variegated
ranunculuses; my hyacinths of fifty bells, in every tint,
single and double; and my favourite stands of auric-
ulas, so large and powdered that the colour of the
velvet leaves was scarcely discoverable! The blue
passion-flower is, however, now beautiful. You see
that summer-house, sir,' continued he, turning to
Vivian; 'the top is my observatory. You will sleep
in that pavilion to-night, so you had better take notice
how the walk winds.'

The passion-flower was trained against the summer-
house in question.

'There,' said Mr. Beckendorff; and he stood admiring with outstretched arms; 'the latter days of its
beauty, for the autumn frosts will soon stop its
flower. Pray, Mr. von Philipson, are you a botanist?'

'Why,' said the Prince, 'I am a great admirer of
flowers, but I cannot exactly say that——'

'Ah! no botanist. The flower of this beautiful
plant continues only one day, but there is a constant

succession from July to the end of the autumn; and if this fine weather continue —— Pray, sir, how is the wind?'

'I really cannot say,' said the Prince; 'but I think the wind is either ——'

'Do you know, sir?' continued Beckendorff to Vivian.

'I think, sir, that it is ——'

'Westerly. Well! If this weather continue, the succession may still last another month. You will be interested to know, Mr. von Philipson, that the flower comes out at the same joint with the leaf, on a peduncle nearly three inches long; round the centre of it are two radiating crowns; look, look, sir! the inner inclining towards the centre column; now examine this well, and I will be with you in a moment.' So saying, Mr. Beckendorff, running down the walk, jumped over the railing, and in a moment was coursing across the lawn, towards the river, in a chase after a dragon-fly.

Mr. Beckendorff was soon out of sight, and after lingering half-an-hour in the vicinity of the blue passion-flower, the Prince proposed to Vivian that they should quit the spot. 'So far as I can observe,' continued his Highness, 'we might as well quit the house. No wonder that Beckendorff's power is on the wane, for he appears to me to be growing childish. Surely he could not always have been this frivolous creature!'

'I really am so astonished,' said Vivian, 'that it is quite out of my power to assist your Highness in any supposition. But I should recommend you not to be too hasty in your movements. Take care that staying here does not affect the position which you

have taken up, or retard the progress of any measures on which you have determined, and you are
safe. What will it injure you if, with the chance of
achieving the great and patriotic purpose to which
you have devoted your powers and energies, you are
subjected for a few hours to the caprices, or even
rudeness, of any man whatever? If Beckendorff be
the character which the world gives him credit to be,
I do not think he can imagine that you are to be deceived twice; and if he do imagine so, we are convinced that he will be disappointed. If, as you have
supposed, not only his power is on the wane, but his
intellect also, four-and-twenty hours will convince us
of the fact; for in less than that time your Highness
will necessarily have conversation of a more important
nature with him. I recommend, therefore, that we
continue here to-day, although,' added Vivian, smiling, 'I have to sleep in his observatory.'

After walking in the garden about an hour, the
Prince and Vivian again went into the house, imagining that Beckendorff might have returned by another entrance; but he was not there. The Prince
was much annoyed; and Vivian, to amuse himself,
had recourse to the library. After re-examining the
armour, looking at the garden through the painted
windows, conjecturing who might be the original of
the mysterious picture and what could be the meaning of the withered branch, the Prince was fairly
worn out. The precise dinner hour he did not know;
and notwithstanding repeated exertions, he had hitherto been unable to find the blooming Clara. He
could not flatter himself, however, that there were
less than two hours to kill before the great event
took place; and so, heartily wishing himself back

again at Turriparva, he prevailed upon Vivian to
throw aside his book and take another walk.

This time they extended their distance, stretched
out as far as the river, and explored the adjoining
woods; but of Mr. Beckendorff they saw and heard
nothing. At length they again returned: it was getting dusk. They found the bow window of the library closed. They again entered the dining-room,
and, to their surprise, found no preparations for dinner. This time the Prince was more fortunate in his
exertions to procure an interview with Madam Clara,
for that lady almost immediately entered the room.

'Pray, my good madam,' inquired the Prince, 'has
your master returned?'

'Mr. Beckendorff is in the library, sir,' said the
old lady, pompously.

'Indeed! we do not dine in this room, then?'

'Dine, sir!' said the good dame, forgetting her
pomposity in her astonishment.

'Yes, dine,' said the Prince.

'Mr. Beckendorff never takes anything after his
noon meal.'

'Am I to understand, then, that we are to have
no dinner?' asked his Highness, angry and agitated.

'Mr. Beckendorff never takes anything after his
noon meal, sir; but I am sure that if you and your
friend are hungry, sir, I hope there is never a want
in this house.'

'My good lady, I am hungry, very hungry, indeed; and if your master, I mean Mr. von,—that is,
Mr. Beckendorff, has such a bad appetite that he can
satisfy himself with picking, once a day, the breast
of a pheasant,—why, if he expect his friends to be
willing or even able to live on such fare, the least

that I can say is, that he is much mistaken; and so, therefore, my good friend Grey, I think we had better order our horses and be off.'

'No occasion for that, I hope,' said Mrs. Clara, rather alarmed at the Prince's passion; 'no want, I trust, ever here, sir; and I make no doubt you will have dinner as soon as possible; and so, sir, I hope you will not be hasty.'

'Hasty! I have no wish to be hasty; but as for disarranging the whole economy of the house, and getting up an extemporaneous meal for me, I cannot think of it. Mr. Beckendorff may live as he likes, and if I stay here I am contented to live as he does. I do not wish him to change his habits for me, and I shall take care that, after to-day, there will be no necessity for his doing so. However, absolute hunger can make no compliments; and therefore I will thank you, my good madam, to let me and my friend have the remains of that cold game, if they be still in existence, on which we lunched, or, as you term it, took our noon meal, this morning; and which, if it were your own cooking, Mrs. Clara, I assure you, as I observed to my friend at the time, did you infinite credit.'

The Prince, although his gentlemanlike feelings had, in spite of his hunger, dictated a deprecation of Mrs. Clara's making a dinner merely for himself, still thought that a seasonable and deserved compliment to the lady might assist in bringing about a result which, notwithstanding his politeness, he much desired; and that was the production of another specimen of her culinary accomplishments. Having behaved, as he considered, with moderation and dignified civility, he was, it must be confessed, rather astounded when Mrs. Clara, duly acknowledging his compliment by her curtsey, was sorry to inform him that she dared give no refreshment in this house without Mr. Beckendorff's special order.

'Special order! Why! surely your master will not grudge me the cold leg of a pheasant?'

'Mr. Beckendorff is not in the habit of grudging anything,' answered the housekeeper, with offended majesty.

'Then why should he object?' asked the Prince.

'Mr. Beckendorff is the best judge, sir, of the propriety of his own regulations.'

'Well, well!' said Vivian, more interested for his friend than himself, 'there is no difficulty in asking Mr. Beckendorff?'

'None in the least, sir,' answered the housekeeper, 'when he is awake.'

'Awake!' said the Prince, 'why! is he asleep now?'

'Yes, sir, in the library.'

'And how long will he be asleep?' asked the Prince with eagerness.

'It is uncertain; he may be asleep for hours, he may wake in five minutes; all I can do is to watch.'

'But, surely in a case like the present, you can wake your master?'

'I could not wake Mr. Beckendorff, sir, if the house were on fire. No one can enter the room when he is asleep.'

'Then how can you possibly know when he is awake?'

'I shall hear his violin immediately, sir.'

'Well, well! I suppose it must be so. I wish we were in Turriparva; that is all I know. Men of my station have no business to be paying visits to the sons of the Lord knows who! peasants, shopkeepers, and pedagogues!'

As a fire was blazing in the dining-room, which Mrs. Clara informed them Mr. Beckendorff never omitted having every night in the year, the Prince and his friend imagined that they were to remain there, and they consequently did not attempt to disturb the slumbers of their host. Resting his feet on the hobs, his Highness, for the fiftieth time declared that he wished he had never left Turriparva; and just when Vivian was on the point of giving up in despair the hope of consoling him, Mrs. Clara entered and proceeded to lay the cloth.

'Your master is awake, then?' asked the Prince, very quickly.

'Mr. Beckendorff has been long awake, sir! and dinner will be ready immediately.'

His Highness's countenance brightened; and in a short time the supper appearing, the Prince, again fascinated by Mrs. Clara's cookery and Mr. Beckendorff's wine, forgot his chagrin, and regained his temper.

In about a couple of hours Mr. Beckendorff entered.

'I hope that Clara has given you wine you like, Mr. von Philipson?'

'The same bin, I will answer for that.'

Mr. Beckendorff had his violin in his hand, but his dress was much changed. His great boots being pulled off, exhibited the white silk stockings which he invariably wore; and his coat had given place to the easier covering of a brocade dressing-gown. He drew a chair round the fire, between the Prince and

Vivian. It was a late hour, and the room was only lighted by the glimmering coals, for the flames had long died away. Mr. Beckendorff sat for some time without speaking, gazing earnestly on the decaying embers. Indeed, before many minutes had elapsed, complete silence prevailed; for both the endeavours of the Prince and of Vivian to promote conversation had been unsuccessful. At length the master of the house turned round to the Prince, and pointing to a particular mass of coal, said, 'I think, Mr. von Philipson, that is the completest elephant I ever saw. We will ring the bell for some coals, and then have a game of whist.'

The Prince was so surprised by Mr. Beckendorff's remark that he was not sufficiently struck by the strangeness of his proposition, and it was only when he heard Vivian professing his ignorance of the game that it occurred to him that to play at whist was hardly the object for which he had travelled from Turriparva.

'An Englishman not know whist!' said Mr. Beckendorff: 'ridiculous! you do know it. Let us play! Mr. von Philipson, I know, has no objection.'

'But, my good sir,' said the Prince, 'although previous to conversation I may have no objection to join in a little amusement, still it appears to me that it has escaped your memory that whist is a game which requires the co-operation of four persons.'

'Not at all! I take dummy! I am not sure it is not the finest way of playing the game.'

The table was arranged, the lights brought, the cards produced, and the Prince of Little Lilliput, greatly to his surprise, found himself playing whist with Mr. Beckendorff. Nothing could be more dull.

The Minister would neither bet nor stake, and the immense interest which he took in every card that was played ludicrously contrasted with the rather sullen looks of the Prince and the very sleepy ones of Vivian. Whenever Mr. Beckendorff played for dummy he always looked with the most searching eye into the next adversary's face, as if he would read his cards in his features. The first rubber lasted an hour and a half, three long games, which Mr. Beckendorff, to his triumph, hardly won. In the first game of the second rubber Vivian blundered; in the second he revoked; and in the third, having neglected to play, and being loudly called upon, and rated both by his partner and Mr. Beckendorff, he was found to be asleep. Beckendorff threw down his hand with a loud dash, which roused Vivian from his slumber. He apologised for his drowsiness; but said that he was so sleepy that he must retire. The Prince, who longed to be with Beckendorff alone, winked approbation of his intention.

'Well!' said Beckendorff, ' you spoiled the rubber. I shall ring for Clara. Why you all are so fond of going to bed I cannot understand. I have not been to bed these thirty years.'

Vivian made his escape; and Beckendorff, pitying his degeneracy, proposed to the Prince, in a tone which seemed to anticipate that the offer would meet with instantaneous acceptation, double dummy. This, however, was too much.

'No more cards, sir, I thank you,' said the Prince; 'if, however, you have a mind for an hour's conversation, I am quite at your service.'

'I am obliged to you; I never talk. Good night, Mr. von Philipson.'

Mr. Beckendorff left the room. His Highness could contain himself no longer. He rang the bell.

'Pray, Mrs. Clara,' said he, 'where are my horses?'

'Mr. Beckendorff will have no quadrupeds within a mile of the house, except Owlface.'

'How do you mean? Let me see the man-servant.'

'The household consists only of myself, sir.'

'Why! where is my luggage, then?'

'That has been brought up, sir; it is in your room.'

'I tell you I must have my horses.'

'It is quite impossible to-night, sir. I think, sir, you had better retire. Mr. Beckendorff may not be home again these six hours.'

'What! is your master gone out?'

'Yes, sir, he is just gone out to take his ride.'

'Why! where is his horse kept, then?'

'It is Owlface, sir.'

'Owlface, indeed! What! is your master in the habit of riding out at night?'

'Mr. Beckendorff rides out, sir, just when it happens to suit him.'

'It is very odd I cannot ride out when it happens to suit me! However, I will be off to-morrow; and so, if you please, show me my bed-room at once.'

'Your room is the library, sir.'

'The library! Why, there is no bed in the library.'

'We have no beds, sir; but the sofa is made up.'

'No beds! Well! it is only for one night. You are all mad, and I am as mad as you for coming here.'

CHAPTER VII.

An Indignant Prince.

THE morning sun peeping through the window of the little summer-house roused its inmate at an early hour; and finding no signs of Mr. Beckendorff and his guest having yet arisen from their slumbers, Vivian took the opportunity of strolling about the gardens and the grounds. Directing his way along the margin of the river, he soon left the lawn and entered some beautiful meadows, whose dewy verdure glistened in the brightening beams of the early sun. Crossing these, and passing through a gate, he found himself in a rural road, whose lofty hedge-rows, rich with all the varieties of wild fruit and flower, and animated with the cheering presence of the busy birds chirping from every bough and spray, altogether presented a scene which reminded him of the soft beauties of his own country. With some men, to remember is to be sad; and unfortunately for Vivian Grey, there were few objects which with him did not give rise to associations of a painful nature. The strange occurrences of the last few days had recalled, if not revived, the feelings of his boyhood.

His early career flitted across his mind. He would
have stifled the remembrance with a sigh, but man is
the slave of Memory. For a moment he mused over
Power; but then he, shuddering, shrank from the
wearing anxiety, the consuming care, the eternal
vigilance, the constant contrivance, the agonising suspense, the distracting vicissitudes of his past career.
Alas! it is our nature to sicken, from our birth, after
some object of unattainable felicity, to struggle
through the freshest years of our life in an insane
pursuit after some indefinite good, which does not
even exist! But sure and quick is the dark hour
which cools our doting frenzy in the frigid waves of
the ocean of oblivion! We dream of immortality until we die. Ambition! at thy proud and fatal altar we
whisper the secrets of our mighty thoughts, and
breathe the aspirations of our inexpressible desires. A
clouded flame licks up the offering of our ruined
souls, and the sacrifice vanishes in the sable smoke
of Death.

But where are his thoughts wandering? Had he
forgotten that day of darkest despair? There had that
happened to him which had happened to no other
man. He was roused from his reverie by the sound
of a trotting horse. He looked up, but the winding
road prevented him at first from seeing the steed
which evidently was approaching. The sound came
nearer and nearer; and at length, turning a corner,
Mr. Beckendorff came in sight. He was mounted on
a strong-built, rough, and ugly pony, with an obstinate mane, which, defying the exertions of the groom,
fell in equal divisions on both sides of its bottle neck,
and a large white face, which, combined with its
blinking vision, had earned for it the euphonious title

of Owlface. Both master and steed must have travelled hard and far, for both were covered with dust
and mud from top to toe, from mane to hoof. Mr.
Beckendorff seemed surprised at meeting Vivian, and
pulled up his pony as he reached him.

'An early riser, I see, sir.   Where is Mr. von
Philipson?'

'I have not yet seen him, and imagined that both
he and yourself had not yet risen.'

'Hum! how many hours is it to noon?' asked Mr.
Beckendorff, who always spoke astronomically.

'More than four, I imagine.'

'Pray do you prefer the country about here to
Turriparva?'

'Both, I think, are beautiful.'

'You live at Turriparva?' asked Mr. Beckendorff.

'As a guest,' answered Vivian.

'Has it been a fine summer at Turriparva?'

'I believe everywhere.'

'I am afraid Mr. von Philipson finds it rather dull
here?'

'I am not aware of it.'

'He seems a ve–ry ——?' said Beckendorff, looking keenly in his companion's face.   But Vivian did
not supply the desired phrase; and so, the Minister
was forced to finish the sentence himself, 'a very
gentlemanlike sort of man?'   A low bow was the
only response.

'I trust, sir, I may indulge the hope,' continued
Mr. Beckendorff, 'that you will honour me with your
company another day.'

'You are exceedingly obliging!'

'Mr. von Philipson is fond, I think, of a country
life?' said Beckendorff.

'Most men are.'

'I suppose he has no innate objection to live occasionally in a city.'

'Few have.'

'You probably have known him long?'

'Not long enough to wish our acquaintance at an end.'

'Hum!'

They proceeded in silence for some moments, and then Beckendorff again turned round, and this time with a direct question.

'I wonder if Mr. von Philipson can make it convenient to honour me with his company another day. Can you tell me?'

'I think the best person to inform you of that would be his Highness himself,' said Vivian, using his friend's title purposely to show Mr. Beckendorff how ridiculous he considered his present use of the incognito.

'You think so, sir, do you?' answered Beckendorff, sarcastically.

They had now arrived at the gate by which Vivian had reached the road.

'Your course, sir,' said Mr. Beckendorff, 'lies that way. I see, like myself, you are no great talker. We shall meet at breakfast.' So saying, the Minister set spurs to his pony, and was soon out of sight.

When Vivian reached the house, he found the bow window of the library thrown open, and as he approached he saw Mr. Beckendorff enter the room and bow to the Prince. His Highness had passed a good night in spite of not sleeping in a bed, and he was at this moment commencing a delicious breakfast. His ill-humour had consequently vanished. He had made up his mind that Beckendorff was mad; and although he had given up all the secret and flattering hopes which he had dared to entertain when the interview was first arranged, he nevertheless did not regret his visit, which on the whole had been amusing, and had made him acquainted with the person and habits, and, as he believed, the intellectual powers of a man with whom, most probably, he should soon be engaged in open hostility. Vivian took his seat at the breakfast table, and Beckendorff stood conversing with them with his back to the fireplace, and occasionally, during the pauses of conversation, pulling the strings of his violin with his fingers. It did not escape Vivian's observation that the Minister was particularly courteous and even attentive to the Prince; and that he endeavoured by his quick and more communicative answers, and occasionally by a stray observation, to encourage the good humour visible on the cheerful countenance of his guest.

'Have you been long up, Mr. Beckendorff?' asked the Prince; for his host had resumed his dressing-gown and slippers.

'I generally see the sun rise.'

'And yet you retire late! out riding last night, I understand?'

'I never go to bed.'

'Indeed!' said the Prince. 'Well, for my part, without my regular rest I am nothing. Have you breakfasted, Mr. Beckendorff?'

'Clara will bring my breakfast immediately.'

The dame accordingly soon appeared, bearing a tray with a basin of boiling water and one large thick biscuit. This Mr. Beckendorff, having well soaked in the hot fluid, eagerly devoured; and then

taking up his violin, amused himself until his guests
had finished their breakfast.

When Vivian had ended his meal he left the Prince
and Beckendorff alone, determined that his presence
should not be the occasion of the Minister any longer
retarding the commencement of business. The Prince,
who by a private glance had been prepared for his
departure, immediately took the opportunity of asking
Mr. Beckendorff, in a decisive tone, whether he might
flatter himself that he could command his present attention to a subject of importance. Mr. Beckendorff
said that he was always at Mr. von Philipson's service; and drawing a chair opposite him, the Prince
and Mr. Beckendorff now sat on each side of the fireplace.

'Hem!' said the Prince, clearing his throat; and
he looked at Mr. Beckendorff, who sat with his heels
close together, his toes out square, his hands resting
on his knees, which, as well as his elbows, were
turned out, his shoulders bent, his head reclined, and
his eyes glancing.

'Hem!' said the Prince of Little Lilliput. 'In
compliance, Mr. Beckendorff, with your wish, developed in the communication received by me on the
—— inst., I assented in my answer to the arrangement then proposed; the object of which was, to use
your own words, to facilitate the occurrence of an
oral interchange of the sentiments of various parties
interested in certain proceedings, by which interchange it was anticipated that the mutual interests
might be respectively considered and finally arranged.
Prior, Mr. Beckendorff, to either of us going into any
detail upon those points of probable discussion, which
will, in all likelihood, form the fundamental features

of this interview, I wish to recall your attention to the paper which I had the honour of presenting to his Royal Highness, and which is alluded to in your communication of the —— inst. The principal heads of that document I have brought with me, abridged in this paper.'

Here the Prince handed to Mr. Beckendorff a MS. pamphlet, consisting of several sheets closely written. The Minister bowed very graciously as he took it from his Highness's hand, and then, without even looking at it, laid it on the table.

'You, sir, I perceive,' continued the Prince, 'are acquainted with its contents; and it will therefore be unnecessary for me at present to expatiate upon their individual expediency, or to argue for their particular adoption. And, sir, when we observe the progress of the human mind, when we take into consideration the quick march of intellect, and the wide expansion of enlightened views and liberal principles; when we take a bird's-eye view of the history of man from the earliest ages to the present moment, I feel that it would be folly in me to conceive for an instant that the measures developed and recommended in that paper will not finally receive the approbation of his Royal Highness. As to the exact origin of slavery, Mr. Beckendorff, I confess that I am not, at this moment, prepared distinctly to speak. That the Divine Author of our religion was its decided enemy, I am informed, is clear. That the slavery of ancient times was the origin of the feudal service of a more modern period, is a point on which men of learning have not precisely made up their minds. With regard to the exact state of the ancient German people, Tacitus affords us a great deal of most interesting informa-

tion. Whether or not, certain passages which I have
brought with me marked in the Germania are incontestable evidences that our ancestors enjoyed or understood the practice of a wise and well-regulated
representative system, is a point on which I shall be
happy to receive the opinion of so distinguished a
statesman as Mr. Beckendorff. In stepping forward,
as I have felt it my duty to do, as the advocate of
popular rights and national privileges, I am desirous
to prove that I have not become the votary of in-
novation and the professor of revolutionary doctrines.
The passages of the Roman author in question, and
an ancient charter of the Emperor Charlemagne, are,
I consider, decisive and sufficient precedents for the
measures which I have thought proper to sanction by
my approval, and to support by my influence. A
minister, Mr. Beckendorff, must take care that in the
great race of politics the minds of his countrymen do
not leave his own behind them. We must never
forget the powers and capabilities of man. On this
very spot, perhaps, some centuries ago, savages clothed
in skins were committing cannibalism in a forest.
We must not forget, I repeat, that it is the business
of those to whom Providence has allotted the responsible possession of power and influence (that it is their
duty, our duty, Mr. Beckendorff), to become guardians
of our weaker fellow-creatures; that all power is a
trust; that we are accountable for its exercise; that
from the people, and for the people, all springs, and
all must exist; and that, unless we conduct ourselves
with the requisite wisdom, prudence, and propriety,
the whole system of society will be disorganised; and
this country, in particular, will fall a victim to that
system of corruption and misgovernment which has

already occasioned the destruction of the great king-doms mentioned in the Bible, and many other states besides, Greece, Rome, Carthage, &c.'

Thus ended the peroration of an harangue consist-ing of an incoherent arrangement of imperfectly-remembered facts and misunderstood principles; all gleaned by his Highness from the enlightening articles of the Reisenburg journals. Like Brutus, the Prince of Little Lilliput paused for a reply.

'Mr. von Philipson,' said his companion, when his Highness had finished, 'you speak like a man of sense.' Having given this answer, Mr. Beckendorff rose from his seat and walked straight out of the room.

The Prince at first took the answer for a compli-ment; but Mr. Beckendorff not returning, he began to have a faint idea that he was neglected. In this uncertainty he rang the bell for his friend Clara.

'Mrs. Clara! where is your master?'

'Just gone out, sir.'

'How do you mean?'

'He has gone out with his gun, sir.'

'You are quite sure he has gone out?'

'Quite sure, sir. I took him his coat and boots myself.'

'I am to understand, then, that your master has gone out?'

'Yes, sir; Mr. Beckendorff has gone out. He will be home for his noon meal.'

'That is enough! Grey!' called out the indignant Prince, darting into the garden.

'Well, my dear Prince,' said Vivian, 'what can possibly be the matter?'

'The matter! Insanity can be the only excuse; in-sanity can alone account for his preposterous conduct.

We have seen enough of him. The repetition of absurdity is only wearisome. Pray assist me in getting
our horses immediately.'

'Certainly, if you wish it; but remember you
brought me here as your friend and counsellor. As I
have accepted the trust, I cannot help being sensible
of the responsibility. Before, therefore, you finally
resolve upon departure, pray let me be fully acquainted
with the circumstances which have impelled you to
this sudden resolution.'

'Willingly, my good friend, could I only command
my temper; and yet to fall into a passion with a
madman is almost a mark of madness. But his manner and his conduct are so provoking and so puzzling
that I cannot altogether repress my irritability. And
that ridiculous incognito! Why I sometimes begin to
think that I really am Mr. von Philipson! An incognito forsooth! for what? to deceive whom? His
household apparently only consists of two persons,
one of whom has visited me in my own castle; and
the other is a cross old hag, who would not be able
to comprehend my rank if she were aware of it.
But to the point! When you left the room I was determined to be trifled with no longer, and I asked
him, in a firm voice and very marked manner,
whether I might command his immediate attention to
important business. He professed to be at my service. I opened the affair by taking a cursory, yet
definite, review of the principles in which my political conduct had originated, and on which it was
founded. I flattered myself that I had produced an
impression. Sometimes we are in a better cue for
these expositions than at others, and to-day I was
really unusually felicitous. My memory never de-

serted. I was at the same time luminous and profound; and while I was guided by the philosophical
spirit of the present day, I showed, by my various
reading, that I respected the experience of antiquity.
In short, I was satisfied with myself; and with the
exception of one single point about the origin of
slavery, which unfortunately got entangled with the
feudal system, I could not have got on better had
Sievers himself been at my side. Nor did I spare Mr.
Beckendorff; but, on the contrary, I said a few things
which, had he been in his senses, must, I imagine,
have gone home. Do you know I finished by drawing his own character, and showing the inevitable
effects of his ruinous policy: and what do you think
he did ?'

'Left you in a passion ?'

'Not at all. He seemed much struck by what I
had said, and apparently understood it. I have heard
that in some species of insanity the patient is perfectly able to comprehend everything addressed to
him, though at that point his sanity ceases, and he
is unable to answer or to act. This must be Beckendorff's case; for no sooner had I finished than he rose
up immediately, and, saying that I spoke like a man
of sense, abruptly quitted the room. The housekeeper
says he will not be at home again till that infernal
ceremony takes place called the noon meal. Now, do
not you advise me to be off as soon as possible ?'

'It will require some deliberation. Pray did you
not speak to him last night ?'

'Ah! I forgot that I had not been able to speak to
you since then. Well! last night what do you think
he did ? When you were gone, he had the insolence
to congratulate me on the opportunity then afforded

of playing double dummy; and when I declined his proposition, but said that if he wished to have an hour's conversation I was at his service, he coolly told me that he never talked, and bade me good night! Did you ever know such a madman? He never goes to bed. I only had a sofa. How the deuce did you sleep?'

'Well and safely, considering that I was in a summer-house without lock or bolt.'

'Well! I need not ask you now as to your opinion of our immediately getting off. We shall have, however, some trouble about our horses, for he will not allow a quadruped near the house, except some monster of an animal that he rides himself; and, by St. Hubert! I cannot find out where our steeds are. What shall we do?' But Vivian did not answer. 'What are you thinking of?' continued his Highness. 'Why don't you answer?'

'Your Highness must not go,' said Vivian, shaking his head.

'Not go! Why so?'

'Depend upon it you are wrong about Beckendorff. That he is a humourist there is no doubt; but it appears to me to be equally clear that his queer habits and singular mode of life are not of late adoption. What he is now he must have been these ten, perhaps these twenty years, perhaps more; of this there are a thousand proofs about us. As to the overpowering cause which has made him the character he appears at present, it is needless for us to inquire; probably some incident in his private life in all likelihood connected with the mysterious picture. Let us be satisfied with the effect. If the case be as I state it in his private life and habits, Beckendorff must have

been equally incomprehensible and equally singular at
the very time that, in his public capacity, he was
producing such brilliant results as at the present moment. Now then, can we believe him to be insane?
I anticipate your objections. I know you will enlarge
upon the evident absurdity of his inviting his political opponent to his house for a grave consultation on
the most important affairs, and then treating him as
he has done you, when it must be clear to him that
you cannot be again duped, and when he must feel
that, were he to amuse you for as many weeks as he
has days, your plans and your position would not be
injuriously affected. Be it so; probably a humourist
like Beckendorff cannot, even in the most critical
moment, altogether restrain the bent of his capricious
inclinations. However, my dear Prince, I will lay no
stress upon this point. My opinion, indeed my conviction, is that Beckendorff acts from design. I have
considered his conduct well, and I have observed all
that you have seen, and more than you have seen,
and keenly; depend upon it that since you assented
to the interview Beckendorff has been obliged to
shift his intended position for negotiation; some of
the machinery has gone wrong. Fearful, if he had
postponed your visit, you should imagine that he was
only again amusing you, and consequently would
listen to no future overtures, he has allowed you to
attend a conference for which he is not prepared.
That he is making desperate exertions to bring the
business to a point is my firm opinion; and you
would perhaps agree with me were you as convinced
as I am that, since we parted last night, our host
has been to Reisenburg and back again.'

'To Reisenburg and back again!'

'Ay! I rose this morning at an early hour, and imagining that both you and Beckendorff had not yet made your appearance, I escaped from the grounds, intending to explore part of the surrounding country. In my stroll I came to a narrow winding road, which I am convinced lies in the direction towards Reisenburg; there, for some reason or other, I loitered more than an hour, and very probably should have been too late for breakfast had not I been recalled to myself by the approach of a horseman. It was Beckendorff, covered with dust and mud; his horse had been evidently hard ridden. I did not think much of it at the time, because I supposed he might have been out for three or four hours and hard worked, but I nevertheless was struck by his appearance; and when you mentioned that he went out riding at a late hour last night, it immediately occurred to me that had he come home at one or two o'clock it was not very probable that he would have gone out again at four or five. I have no doubt that my conjecture is correct; Beckendorff has been to Reisenburg.'

'You have placed this business in a new and important light,' said the Prince, his expiring hopes reviving; 'what then do you advise me to do?'

'To be quiet. If your own view of the case be right, you can act as well to-morrow or the next day as this moment; on the contrary, if mine be the correct one, a moment may enable Beckendorff himself to bring affairs to a crisis. In either case I should recommend you to be silent, and in no manner to allude any more to the object of your visit. If you speak you only give opportunities to Beckendorff of ascertaining your opinions and your inclinations; and your silence, after such frequent attempts on your side to promote discussion upon business, will soon be discovered by him to be systematic. This will not decrease his opinion of your sagacity and firmness. The first principle of negotiation is to make your adversary respect you.'

After long consultation the Prince determined to follow Vivian's advice; and so firmly did he adhere to his purpose that when he met Mr. Beckendorff at the noon meal, he asked him, with a very unembarrassed voice and manner, 'what sport he had had in the morning.'

The noon meal again consisted of a single dish, as exquisitely dressed, however, as the preceding one. It was a haunch of venison.

'This is my dinner, gentlemen,' said Beckendorff; 'let it be your luncheon. I have ordered your dinner at sunset.'

After having eaten a slice of the haunch, Mr. Beckendorff rose from the table and said, 'We will have our wine in the drawing-room, Mr. von Philipson, and then you will not be disturbed by my birds.'

He left the room.

To the drawing-room, therefore, his two guests soon adjourned; they found him busily employed with his pencil. The Prince thought it must be a chart, or a fortification at least, and was rather surprised when Mr. Beckendorff asked him the magnitude of Mirac in Boötes; and the Prince confessing his utter ignorance of the subject, the Minister threw aside his unfinished planisphere and drew his chair to them at the table. It was with satisfaction that his Highness perceived a bottle of his favourite Tokay; and with no little astonishment he observed that to-day there

were three wine-glasses placed before them. They
were of peculiar beauty, and almost worthy, for their
elegant shapes and great antiquity, of being included
in the collection of the Grand Duke of Johannisberger.

After exhausting their bottle, in which they were
assisted to the extent of one glass by their host, who
drank Mr. von Philipson's health with cordiality, they
assented to Mr. Beckendorff's proposition of visiting
his fruitery.

To the Prince's great relief, dinner-time soon arrived; and having employed a couple of hours on
that meal very satisfactorily, he and Vivian adjourned
to the drawing-room, having previously pledged their
honour to each other that nothing should again induce
them to play dummy whist. Their resolutions and
their promises were needless. Mr. Beckendorff, who
was sitting opposite the fire when they came into
the room, neither by word nor motion acknowledged
that he was aware of their entrance. Vivian found
refuge in a book; and the Prince, after having examined and re-examined the brilliant birds that figured on the drawing-room paper, fell asleep upon the
sofa. Mr. Beckendorff took down the guitar, and
accompanied himself in a low voice for some time;
then he suddenly ceased, and stretching out his legs,
and supporting his thumbs in the armholes of his
waistcoat, he leant back in his chair and remained
motionless, with his eyes fixed upon the picture.
Vivian, in turn, gazed upon this singular being and
the fair pictured form which he seemed to idolise.
Was he, too, unhappy? Had he, too, been bereft in
the hour of his proud and perfect joy? Had he, too,
lost a virgin bride? His agony overcame him, the
book fell from his hand, and he sighed aloud! Mr.

Beckendorff started, and the Prince awoke. Vivian, confounded, and unable to overpower his emotions, uttered some hasty words, explanatory, apologetical, and contradictory, and retired. In his walk to the summer-house a man passed him. In spite of a great cloak, Vivian recognised him as their messenger and guide; and his ample mantle did not conceal his riding boots and the spurs which glistened in the moonlight.

It was an hour past midnight when the door of the summer-house softly opened and Mr. Beckendorff entered. He started when he found Vivian still undressed, and pacing up and down the little chamber. The young man made an effort, when he witnessed an intruder, to compose a countenance whose agitation could not be concealed.

'What, are you up again?' said Mr. Beckendorff. 'Are you ill?'

'Would I were as well in mind as in body! I have not yet been to rest. We cannot command our feelings at all moments, sir; and at this, especially, I felt that I had a right to count upon being alone.'

'I exceedingly regret that I have disturbed you,' said Mr. Beckendorff, in a kind voice, and in a manner which responded to the sympathy of his tone. 'I thought that you had been long asleep. There is a star which I cannot exactly make out. I fancy it must be a comet, and so I ran to the observatory; but let me not disturb you;' and Mr. Beckendorff was retiring.

'You do not disturb me, sir. I cannot sleep: pray ascend.'

'Never mind the star. But if you really have no inclination to sleep, let us sit down and have a little conversation; or perhaps we had better take a stroll. It is a warm night.' As he spoke, Mr. Beckendorff gently put his arm within Vivian's, and led him down the steps.

'Are you an astronomer, sir?' asked Beckendorff.

'I can tell the Great Bear from the Little Dog; but I confess that I look upon the stars rather in a poetical than a scientific spirit.'

'Hum! I confess I do not.'

'There are moments,' continued Vivian, 'when I cannot refrain from believing that these mysterious luminaries have more influence over our fortunes than modern times are disposed to believe. I feel that I am getting less sceptical, perhaps I should say more credulous, every day; but sorrow makes us superstitious.'

'I discard all such fantasies,' said Mr. Beckendorff; 'they only tend to enervate our mental energies and paralyse all human exertion. It is the belief in these, and a thousand other deceits I could mention, which teach man that he is not the master of his own mind, but the ordained victim or the chance sport of circumstances, that makes millions pass through life unimpressive as shadows, and has gained for this existence the stigma of a vanity which it does not deserve.'

'I wish that I could think as you do,' said Vivian; 'but the experience of my life forbids me. Within only these last two years my career has, in so many instances, indicated that I am not the master of my own conduct; that no longer able to resist the conviction which is hourly impressed on me, I recognise in every contingency the preordination of my fate.'

'A delusion of the brain!' said Beckendorff, quickly. 'Fate, Destiny, Chance, particular and special Providence; idle words! Dismiss them all, sir! A man's fate is his own temper; and according to that will be his opinion as to the particular manner in which the course of events is regulated. A consistent man believes in Destiny, a capricious man in Chance.'

'But, sir, what is a man's temper? It may be changed every hour. I started in life with very different feelings from those which I profess at this moment. With great deference to you, I imagine that you mistake the effect for the cause; for surely temper is not the origin, but the result of those circumstances of which we are all the creatures.'

'Sir, I deny it. Man is not the creature of circumstances. Circumstances are the creatures of men. We are free agents, and man is more powerful than matter. I recognise no intervening influence between that of the established course of nature and my own mind. Truth may be distorted, may be stifled, be suppressed. The invention of cunning deceits may, and in most instances does, prevent man from exercising his own powers. They have made him responsible to a realm of shadows, and a suitor in a court of shades. He is ever dreading authority which does not exist, and fearing the occurrence of penalties which there are none to enforce. But the mind that dares to extricate itself from these vulgar prejudices, that proves its loyalty to its Creator by devoting all its adoration to His glory; such a spirit as this becomes a master-mind, and that master-mind will invariably find that circumstances are its slaves.'

'Mr. Beckendorff, yours is a bold philosophy, of which I myself was once a votary. How successful in my service you may judge by finding me a wanderer.'

'Sir! your present age is the age of error: your whole system is founded on a fallacy: you believe that a man's temper can change. I deny it. If you have ever seriously entertained the views which I profess; if, as you lead me to suppose, you have dared to act upon them, and failed; sooner or later, whatever may be your present conviction and your present feelings, you will recur to your original wishes and your original pursuits. With a mind experienced and matured, you may in all probability be successful; and then I suppose, stretching your legs in your easy chair, you will at the same moment be convinced of your own genius, and recognise your own Destiny!'

'With regard to myself, Mr. Beckendorff, I am convinced of the erroneousness of your views. It is my opinion that no one who has dared to think can look upon this world in any other than a mournful spirit. Young as I am, nearly two years have elapsed since, disgusted with the world of politics, I retired to a foreign solitude. At length, with passions subdued, and, as I flatter myself, with a mind matured, convinced of the vanity of all human affairs, I felt emboldened once more partially to mingle with my species. Bitter as my lot had been, I had discovered the origin of my misery in my own unbridled passions; and, tranquil and subdued, I now trusted to pass through life as certain of no fresh sorrows as I was of no fresh joys. And yet, sir, I am at this moment sinking under the infliction of unparalleled misery; misery which I feel I have a right to believe

was undeserved.   But why expatiate to a stranger on
sorrow which must be secret?   I deliver myself up
to my remorseless Fate '

'What is grief?' said Mr. Beckendorff; 'if it be
excited by the fear of some contingency, instead of
grieving, a man should exert his energies and prevent
its occurrence.   If, on the contrary, it be caused by
an event, that which has been occasioned by anything human, by the co-operation of human circumstances, can be, and invariably is, removed by the
same means.   Grief is the agony of an instant; the
indulgence of Grief the blunder of a life.   Mix in
the world, and in a month's time you will speak
to me very differently.   A young man, you meet
with disappointment; in spite of all your exalted notions of your own powers, you immediately sink
under it.   If your belief of your powers were sincere,
you should have proved it by the manner in which
you have struggled against adversity, not merely by
the mode in which you laboured for advancement.
The latter is but a very inferior merit.   If, in fact,
you wish to succeed, success, I repeat, is at your
command.   You talk to me of your experience; and
do you think that my sentiments are the crude opinions of an unpractised man?   Sir! I am not fond of
conversing with any person, and therefore far from
being inclined to maintain an argument in a spirit of
insincerity merely for the sake of a victory of words.
Mark what I say: it is truth.   No Minister ever yet
fell but from his own inefficiency.   If his downfall be
occasioned, as it generally is, by the intrigues of one
of his own creatures, his downfall is merited for having been the dupe of a tool which in all probability
he should never have employed.   If he fall through

the open attacks of his political opponents, his down-fall is equally deserved for having occasioned by his impolicy the formation of a party, for having allowed it to be formed, or for not having crushed it when formed. No conjuncture can possibly occur, however fearful, however tremendous it may appear, from which a man, by his own energy, may not extricate himself, as a mariner by the rattling of his cannon can dissipate the impending water-spout!'

CHAPTER VIII.

T WAS on the third day of the visit to Mr. Beckendorff, just as that gentleman was composing his mind after his noon meal, with his favourite Cremona, and in a moment of rapture raising his instrument high in air, that the door was suddenly dashed open, and Essper George rushed into the room. The intruder, the moment that his eye caught Vivian, flew to his master, and, seizing him by the arm, commenced and continued a loud shout of exultation, accompanying his scream the whole time by a kind of quick dance, which, though not quite as clamorous as the Pyrrhic, nevertheless completely drowned the scientific harmony of Mr. Beckendorff.

So astounded were the three gentlemen by this unexpected entrance, that some moments elapsed ere either of them found words at his command. At length the master of the house spoke.

'Mr. von Philipson, I beg the favour of being informed who this person is?'

The Prince did not answer, but looked at Vivian in great distress; and just as our hero was about to give Mr. Beckendorff the requisite information, Essper George, taking up the parable himself, seized the opportunity of explaining the mystery.

'Who am I? who are you? I am an honest man, and no traitor; and if all were the same, why, then, there would be no rogues in Reisenburg. Who am I? A man. There's an arm! there's a leg! Can you see through a wood by twilight? If so, yours is a better eye than mine. Can you eat an unskinned hare, or dine on the haunch of a bounding stag? If so, your teeth are sharper than mine. Can you hear a robber's footstep when he's kneeling before murder? or can you listen to the snow falling on Midsummer's day? If so, your ears are finer than mine. Can you run with a chamois? can you wrestle with a bear? can you swim with an otter? If so, I'm your match. How many cities have you seen? how many knaves have you gulled? Which is dearest, bread or justice? Why do men pay more for the protection of life than life itself? Is cheatery a staple at Constantinople, as it is at Vienna? and what's the difference between a Baltic merchant and a Greek pirate? Tell me all this, and I will tell you who went in mourning in the moon at the death of the last comet. Who am I, indeed!'

The embarrassment of the Prince and Vivian while Essper George addressed to Mr. Beckendorff these choice queries was indescribable. Once Vivian tried to check him, but in vain. He did not repeat his attempt, for he was sufficiently employed in restraining his own agitation and keeping his own countenance; for in spite of the mortification and anger that Essper's appearance had excited in him, still an unfortunate but innate taste for the ludicrous did not allow him

to be perfectly insensible to the humour of the scene.
Mr. Beckendorff listened quietly till Essper had finished; then he rose.

'Mr. von Philipson,' said he, 'as a personal favour
to yourself, and to my own great inconvenience, I
consented that in this interview you should be attended by a friend. I did not reckon upon your servant, and it is impossible that I can tolerate his presence
for a moment. You know how I live, and that my
sole attendant is a female. I allow no male servants
within this house. Even when his Royal Highness
honours me with his presence he is unattended. I
desire that I am immediately released from the presence
of this buffoon.'

So saying, Mr. Beckendorff left the room.

'Who are you?' said Essper following him, with
his back bent, his head on his chest, and his eyes
glancing. The imitation was perfect.

'Essper,' said Vivian, 'your conduct is inexcus-
able, the mischief that you have done irreparable, and
your punishment shall be severe.'

'Severe! Why, what day did my master sell his
gratitude for a silver groschen! Is this the return for
finding you out, and saving you from a thousand
times more desperate gang than that Baron at Ems!
Severe indeed will be your lot when you are in a
dungeon in Reisenburg Castle, with black bread for
roast venison and sour water for Rhenish!'

'Why, what are you talking about?'

'Talking about! About treason, and arch traitors,
and an old scoundrel who lives in a lone lane, and
dares not look you straight in the face. Why, his
very blink is enough to hang him without trial!'

'Essper, cease immediately this rhodomontade,

and then in distinct terms inform his Highness and myself of the causes of this unparalleled intrusion.'

The impressiveness of Vivian's manner produced a proper effect; and except that he spoke somewhat affectedly slow and ridiculously precise, Essper George delivered himself with great clearness.

'You see, sir, you never let me know that you were going to leave, and so when I found that you did not come back, I made bold to speak to Mr. Arnelm when he came home from hunting; but I could not get enough breath out of him to stop a ladybird on a rose-leaf. I did not much like it, your honour, for I was among strangers, and so were you, you know. Well, then, I went to Master Rodolph: he was very kind to me, and seeing me in low spirits, and thinking me, I suppose, in love, or in debt, or that I had done some piece of mischief, or had something or other preying on my mind, he comes to me, and says, "Essper," said he; you remember Master Rodolph's voice, sir?'

'To the point. Never let me hear Master Rodolph's name again.'

'Yes, sir! Well, well! he said to me, "Come and dine with me in my room;" says I, "I will." A good offer should never be refused, unless we have a better one at the same time. Whereupon, after dinner, Master Rodolph said to me, "We will have a bottle of Burgundy for a treat." You see, sir, we were rather sick of the Rhenish. Well, sir, we were free with the wine; and Master Rodolph, who is never easy except when he knows everything, must be trying, you see, to get out of me what it was that made me so down in the mouth. I, seeing this, thought I would put off the secret to another bottle;

which being produced, I did not conceal from him any longer what was making me so low. "Rodolph," said I, "I do not like my young master going out in this odd way: he is of a temper to get into scrapes, and I should like very much to know what he and the Prince (saving your Highness's presence) are after. They have been shut up in that cabinet these two nights, and though I walked by the door pretty often, devil a bit of a word ever came through the key-hole; and so you see, Rodolph," said I, "it requires a bottle or two of Burgundy to keep my spirits up." Well, your Highness, strange to say, no sooner had I spoken than Master Rodolph put his head across the little table; we dined at the little table on the right hand of the room as you enter——'

'Go on.'

'I am going on. Well! he put his head across the little table, and said to me in a low whisper, cocking his odd-looking eye at the same time, "I tell you what, Essper, you are a deuced sharp fellow!" and so, giving a shake of his head and another wink of his eye, he was quiet. I smelt a rat, but I did not begin to pump directly; but after the third bottle, "Rodolph," said I, "with regard to your last observation (for we had not spoken lately, Burgundy being too fat a wine for talking), we are both of us sharp fellows. I dare say, now, you and I are thinking of the same thing." "No doubt of it," said Rodolph. And so, sir, he agreed to tell me what he was thinking of, on condition that I should be equally frank afterwards. Well, then, he told me that there were sad goings on at Turriparva.'

'The deuce!' said the Prince.

'Let him tell his story,' said Vivian.

'Sad goings on at Turriparva! He wished that his Highness would hunt more and attend less to politics; and then he told me, quite confidentially, that his Highness the Prince, and Heaven knows how many other Princes besides, had leagued together, and were going to dethrone the Grand Duke, and that his master was to be made King, and he, Master Rodolph, Prime Minister. Hearing all this, and duly allowing for a tale over a bottle, I made no doubt, as I find to be the case, that you, good master, were about to be led into some mischief; and as I know that conspiracies are always unsuccessful, I have done my best to save my master; and I beseech you, upon my knees, to get out of the scrape as soon as you possibly can.' Here Essper George threw himself at Vivian's feet, and entreated him to quit the house immediately.

'Was ever anything so absurd and so mischievous!' ejaculated the Prince; and then he conversed with Vivian for some time in a whisper. 'Essper,' at length Vivian said, 'you have committed one of the most perfect and most injurious blunders that you could possibly perpetrate. The mischief which may result from your imprudent conduct is incalculable. How long is it since you have thought proper to regulate your conduct on the absurd falsehoods of a drunken steward? His Highness and myself wish to consult in private; but on no account leave the house. Now mind me; if you leave this house without my permission, you forfeit the little chance which remains of being retained in my service.'

'Where am I to go, sir?'

'Stay in the passage.'

'Suppose (here he imitated Beckendorff) comes to me.'

'Then open the door and come into this room.'

'Well,' said the Prince, when the door was at length shut, 'one thing is quite clear. He does not know who Beckendorff is.'

'So far satisfactory; but I feel the force of your Highness's observations. It is a most puzzling case. To send him back to Turriparva would be madness: the whole affair would be immediately revealed over another bottle of Burgundy with Master Rodolph; in fact, your Highness's visit would be a secret to no one in the country, your host would be soon discovered, and the evil consequences are incalculable. I know no one to send him to at Reisenburg; and if I did, it appears to me that the same objections equally apply to his proceeding to that city as to his returning to Turriparva. What is to be done? Surely some demon must have inspired him. We cannot now request Beckendorff to allow him to stay here; and if we did, I am convinced, from his tone and manner, that nothing could induce him to comply with our wish. The only course to be pursued is certainly an annoying one; but, so far as I can judge, it is the only mode by which very serious mischief can be prevented. Let me proceed forthwith to Reisenburg with Essper. Placed immediately under my eye, and solemnly adjured by me to silence, I think I can answer, particularly when I give him a gentle hint of the station of Beckendorff, for his preserving the confidence with which it will now be our policy partially to entrust him. It is, to say the least, awkward and distressing to leave you alone; but what is to be done? It does not appear that I can now be of any material service to you. I have assisted you as much as, and more than, we could reasonably have supposed it would have been in my power to have done, by throwing some light upon the character and situation of Beckendorff. With the clue to his conduct which my chance meeting with him yesterday morning has afforded us, the only point for your Highness to determine is as to the length of time you will resolve to wait for his communication. As to your final agreement together, with your Highness's settled views and decided purpose, all the difficulty of negotiation will be on his side. Whatever, my dear Prince,' continued Vivian, with a significant voice and marked emphasis, 'whatever, my dear Prince, may be your secret wishes, be assured that to attain them in your present negotiation you have only to be firm. Let nothing divert you from your purpose, and the termination of this interview must be gratifying to you.'

The Prince of Little Lilliput was very disinclined to part with his shrewd counsellor, who had already done him considerable service, and he strongly opposed Vivian's proposition. His opposition, however, like that of most other persons, was unaccompanied by any suggestion of his own. And as both agreed that something must be done, it of course ended in the Prince being of opinion that Vivian's advice must be followed. The Prince was really much affected by this sudden and unexpected parting with one for whom, though he had known him so short a time, he began to entertain a sincere regard. 'I owe you my life,' said the Prince, 'and perhaps more than my life; and here we are about suddenly to part, never to meet again. I wish I could get you to make Turriparva your home. You should have your own suite of rooms, your own horses, your own servants, and never feel for an instant that you were not master of all around you. In truth,' continued the Prince, with great earnestness, 'I wish, my dear friend, you would really think seriously of this. You know you could visit Vienna, and even Italy, and yet return to me. Max would be delighted to see you: he loves you already; and Sievers and his library would be at your command. Agree to my proposition, dear friend.'

'I cannot express to your Highness how sensible I am of your kindness. Your friendship I sincerely value and shall never forget; but I am too unhappy and unlucky a being to burden any one with my constant presence. Adieu! or will you go with me to Beckendorff ?'

'Oh, go with you by all means! But,' said the Prince, taking a ruby ring of great antiquity off his finger, 'I should feel happy if you would wear this for my sake.'

The Prince was so much affected at the thoughts of parting with Vivian that he could scarcely speak. Vivian accepted the ring with a cordiality which the kind-hearted donor deserved; and yet our hero unfortunately had had rather too much experience of the world not to be aware that, most probably, in less than another week, his affectionate friend would not be able to recall his name under an hour's recollection. Such are friends! The moment that we are not, at their side we are neglected, and the moment that, we die we are forgotten!

They found Mr. Beckendorff in his library. In apprising Mr. Beckendorff of his intention of immediately quitting his roof, Vivian did not omit to state the causes of his sudden departure. These not only accounted for the abruptness of his movement, but also gave Beckendorff an opportunity of preventing its necessity, by allowing Essper to remain. But the opportunity was not seized by Mr. Beckendorff. The truth was, that gentleman had a particular wish to see Vivian out of his house. In allowing the Prince of Little Lilliput to be attended during the interview by a friend, Beckendorff had prepared himself for the reception of some brawny Jagd Junker, or some thick-headed chamberlain, who he reckoned would act rather as an incumbrance than an aid to his opponent. It was with great mortification, therefore, that he found him accompanied by a shrewd, experienced, wary, and educated Englishman. A man like Beckendorff soon discovered that Vivian Grey's was no common mind. His conversation with him of the last night had given him some notion of his powers, and the moment that Beckendorff saw Essper George enter the house he determined that he should be the cause of Vivian leaving it. There was also another and weighty reason for Mr. Beckendorff desiring that the Prince of Little Lilliput should at this moment be left to himself.

'Mr. Grey will ride on to Reisenburg immediately,' said the Prince, 'and, my dear friend, you may depend upon having your luggage by the day after to-morrow. I shall be at Turriparva early to-morrow, and it will be my first care.'

This was said in a loud voice, and both gentlemen watched Mr. Beckendorff's countenance as the information was given; but no emotion was visible.

'Well, sir, good morning to you,' said Mr. Beckendorff; 'I am sorry you are going. Had I known it sooner I would have given you a letter. Mr. von Philipson,' said Beckendorff, 'do me the favour of looking over that paper.' So saying, Mr. Beckendorff put some official report into the Prince's hand; and while his Highness's attention was attracted by this sudden request, Mr. Beckendorff laid his finger on Vivian's arm, and said in a lower tone, 'I shall take care that you find a powerful friend at Reisenburg!'

BOOK VII.

CHAPTER I.

A S VIVIAN left the room Mr. Beckendorff was seized with an unusual desire to converse with the Prince of Little Lilliput, and his Highness was consequently debarred the consolation of walking with his friend as far as the horses. At the little gate Vivian and Essper encountered the only male attendant who was allowed to approach the house of Mr. Beckendorff. As Vivian quietly walked his horse up the rough turf road, he could not refrain from recurring to his conversation of the previous night; and when he called to mind the adventures of the last six days, he had new cause to wonder at, and perhaps to lament over, his singular fate. In that short time he had saved the life of a powerful Prince, and being immediately signalled out, without any exertion on his part, as the object of that Prince's friendship, the moment he arrives at his castle, by a wonderful contingency, he becomes the depositary of state secrets, and assists in a consultation of importance with one of the most powerful Ministers in Europe. And now the object of so much friendship, confidence, and honour, he is suddenly on the road to the capital of the State of which his late host is the Prime Minister and his friend the chief subject, without even the convenience of a common letter of introduction; and with little prospect of viewing, with even the usual advantages of a common traveller, one of the most interesting of European Courts.

When he had proceeded about half-way up the turf lane he found a private road to his right, which, with that spirit of adventure for which Englishmen are celebrated, he immediately resolved must not only lead to Reisenburg, but also carry him to that city much sooner than the regular high road. He had not advanced far up this road before he came to the gate at which he had parted with Beckendorff on the morning that gentleman had roused him so unexpectedly from his reverie in a green lane. He was surprised to find a horseman dismounting at the gate. Struck by this singular circumstance, the appearance of the stranger was not unnoticed. He was a tall and well proportioned man, and as the traveller passed he stared Vivian so fully in the face that our hero did not fail to remark his handsome countenance, the expression of which, however, was rather vacant and unpleasing. He was dressed in a riding-coat exactly similar to the one always worn by Beckendorff's messenger, and had Vivian not seen him so distinctly he would have mistaken him for that person. The stranger was rather indifferently mounted, and carried his cloak and a small portmanteau at the back of his saddle.

'I suppose it is the butler,' said Essper George, who now spoke for the first time since his dismissal from the room. Vivian did not answer him; not because he entertained any angry feeling on account of his exceedingly unpleasant visit. By no means: it was impossible for a man like Vivian Grey to cherish an irritated feeling for a second. But he did not exchange a syllable with Essper George, merely because he was not in the humour to speak. He could not refrain from musing on the singular events of the last few days; and, above all, the character of Beckendorff particularly engrossed his meditation. Their conversation of the preceding night excited in his mind new feelings of wonder, and revived emotions which he thought were dead or everlastingly dormant. Apparently, the philosophy on which Beckendorff had regulated his career, and by which he had arrived at his pitch of greatness, was exactly the same with which he himself, Vivian Grey, had started in life; which he had found so fatal in its consequences; which he believed to be so vain in its principles. How was this? What radical error had he committed? It required little consideration. Thirty, and more than thirty, years had passed over the head of Beckendorff ere the world felt his power, or indeed was conscious of his existence. A deep student, not only of man in detail, but of man in groups; not only of individuals, but of nations; Beckendorff had hived up his ample knowledge of all subjects which could interest his fellow-creatures, and when that opportunity which in this world occurs to all men occurred to Beckendorff he was prepared. With acquirements equal to his genius, Beckendorff depended only upon himself, and succeeded. Vivian Grey, with a mind inferior to no man's, dashed on the stage, in years a boy, though in feelings a man. Brilliant as might have been his genius, his acquirements necessarily were insufficient. He could not depend only upon himself; a consequent necessity arose to have recourse to the assistance of others; to inspire them with feelings which they could not share; and humour and manage the petty weaknesses which he himself could not experience. His colleagues were, at the same time, to work for the gratification of their own private interests, the most palpable of all abstract things; and to carry into execution a great purpose, which their feeble minds, interested only by the first point, cared not to comprehend. The unnatural combination failed, and its originator fell. To believe that he could recur again to the hopes, the feelings, the pursuits of his boyhood, he felt to be the vainest of delusions. It was the expectation of a man like Beckendorff, whose career, though difficult, though hazardous, had been uniformly successful; of a man who mistook cares for grief, and anxiety for sorrow.

The travellers entered the city at sunset. Proceeding through an ancient and unseemly town, full of long, narrow, and ill-paved streets, and black unevenly built houses, they ascended the hill, on the top of which was situated the new and Residence town of Reisenburg. The proud palace, the white squares, the architectural streets, the new churches, the elegant opera house, the splendid hotels, and the gay public gardens, full of busts, vases, and statues, and surrounded by an iron railing cast out of the cannon taken from both sides during the war by the Reisenburg troops, and now formed into pikes and fasces, glittering with gilded heads: all these, shining in the setting sun, produced an effect which, at any time and in any place, would have been beautiful and striking; but on the present occasion were still more so, from the remarkable contrast they afforded to the ancient, gloomy, and filthy town through which Vivian had just passed, and where, from the lowness of its situation, the sun had already set. There was as much difference between the old and new town of Reisenburg as between the old barbarous Margrave and the new and noble Grand Duke.

On the second day after his arrival at Reisenburg, Vivian received the following letter from the Prince of Little Lilliput. His luggage did not accompany the epistle.

'MY DEAR FRIEND,

'By the time you have received this I shall have returned to Turriparva. My visit to a certain gentleman was prolonged for one day. I never can convey to you by words the sense I entertain of the value of your friendship and of your services; I trust that time will afford me opportunities of testifying it by my actions. I return home by the same road by which we came; you remember how excellent the road was, as indeed are all the roads in Reisenburg; that must be confessed by all. I fear that the most partial admirers of the old régime cannot say as much for the convenience of travelling in the time of our fathers. Good roads are most excellent things, and one of the first marks of civilisation and prosperity. The Emperor Napoleon, who, it must be confessed, had, after all, no common mind, was celebrated for his roads. You have doubtless admired the Route Napoleon on the Rhine, and if you travel into Italy I am informed

that you will be equally, and even more, struck by
the passage over the Simplon and the other Italian
roads. Reisenburg has certainly kept pace with the
spirit of the time; nobody can deny that; and I confess to you that the more I consider the subject it
appears to me that the happiness, prosperity, and
content of a state are the best evidences of the wisdom and beneficent rule of a government. Many
things are very excellent in theory, which are quite
the reverse in practice, and even ludicrous. And
while we should do our most to promote the cause
and uphold the interests of rational liberty, still, at
the same time, we should ever be on our guard
against the crude ideas and revolutionary systems of
those who are quite inexperienced in that sort of
particular knowledge which is necessary for all statesmen. Nothing is so easy as to make things look
fine on paper; we should never forget that: there is
a great difference between high-sounding generalities
and laborious details. Is it reasonable to expect that
men who have passed their lives dreaming in col-
leges and old musty studies should be at all calculated to take the head of affairs, or know what
measures those at the head of affairs ought to adopt?
I think not. A certain personage, who by-the-bye is
one of the most clear-headed and most perfect men
of business that I ever had the pleasure of being acquainted with; a real practical man, in short; he tells
me that Professor Skyrocket, whom you will most
likely see at Reisenburg, wrote an article in the Military Quarterly Review, which is published there, on
the probable expenses of a war between Austria and
Prussia, and forgot the commissariat altogether. Did
you ever know anything so ridiculous? What busi-

ness have such fellows to meddle with affairs of
state? They should certainly be put down: that, I
think, none can deny. A liberal spirit in government
is certainly a most excellent thing; but we must always remember that liberty may degenerate into
licentiousness. Liberty is certainly an excellent thing,
that all admit; but, as a certain person very well
observed, so is physic, and yet it is not to be given
at all times, but only when the frame is in a state to
require it. People may be as unprepared for a wise
and discreet use of liberty, as a vulgar person may
be for the management of a great estate unexpectedly
inherited: there is a great deal in this, and, in my
opinion, there are cases in which to force liberty
down a people's throat is presenting them, not with
a blessing, but a curse. I shall send your luggage
on immediately; it is very probable that I may be in
town at the end of the week, for a short time. I
wish much to see and to consult you, and therefore
hope that you will not leave Reisenburg before you see

'Your faithful and obliged friend,

'LITTLE LILLIPUT.'

Two days after the receipt of this letter Essper
George ran into the room with a much less solemn
physiognomy than he had thought proper to assume
since his master's arrival at Reisenburg.

'Lord, sir! whom do you think I have just met?'

'Whom?' asked Vivian with eagerness, for, as is
always the case when such questions are asked us,
he was thinking of every person in the world except
the right one. 'It might be ——'

'To think that I should see him!' continued Essper.

'It is a man, then,' thought Vivian; 'who is it at
once, Essper?'

'I thought you would not guess, sir! It will quite
cure you to hear it; Master Rodolph!'

'Master Rodolph!'

'Ay! and there's great news in the wind.'

'Which of course you have confidentially extracted
from him. Pray let us have it.'

'The Prince of Little Lilliput is coming to Reisenburg,' said Essper.

'Well! I had some idea of that before,' said Vivian.

'Oh! then, you know it all, sir, I suppose,' said
Essper, with a look of great disappointment.

'I know nothing more than I have mentioned,'
said his master.

'What! do you not know, sir, that the Prince has
come over; that he is going to live at Court; and be,
Heaven knows what! That he is to carry a staff
every day before the Grand Duke at dinner; does not
my master know that?'

'I know nothing of all this; and so tell me in
plain German what the case is.'

'Well, then,' continued Essper, 'I suppose you do
not know that his Highness the Prince is to be his
Excellency the Grand Marshal, that unfortunate but
principal officer of state having received his dismissal
yesterday. They are coming up immediately. Not a
moment is to be lost, which seems to me very odd.
Master Rodolph is arranging everything; and he has
this morning purchased from his master's predecessor
his palace, furniture, wines, and pictures; in short,
his whole establishment: the late Grand Marshal consoling himself for his loss of office, and revenging

himself on his successor, by selling him his property at a hundred per cent. profit. However, Master Rodolph seems quite contented with his bargain; and your luggage is come, sir. His Highness, the Prince, will be in town at the end of the week; and all the men are to be put in new livery. Mr. Arnelm is to be his Highness's chamberlain, and Von Neuwied master of the horse. So you see, sir, you were right; and that old puss-in-boots was no traitor, after all. Upon my soul, I did not much believe you, sir, until I heard all this good news.'

CHAPTER II.

BOUT a week after his arrival at Reisenburg, as Vivian was at breakfast, the door opened, and Mr. Sievers entered.

'I did not think that our next meeting would be in this city,' said Mr. Sievers, smiling.

'His Highness, of course, informed me of your arrival,' said Vivian, as he greeted him cordially.

'You, I understand, are the diplomatist whom I am to thank for finding myself again at Reisenburg. Let me, at the same time, express my gratitude for your kind offices to me, and congratulate you on the brilliancy of your talents for negotiation. Little did I think when I was giving you, the other day, an account of Mr. Beckendorff, that the information would have been of such service to you.'

'I am afraid you have nothing to thank me for; though, certainly, had the office of arranging the terms between the parties devolved on me, my first thoughts would have been for a gentleman for whom I have so much regard and respect as Mr. Sievers.'

'Sir! I feel honoured: you already speak like a finished courtier. Pray, what is to be your office?'

'I fear Mr. Beckendorff will not resign in my favour; and my ambition is so exalted that I cannot condescend to take anything under the Premiership.'

'You are not to be tempted by a Grand Marshalship!' said Mr. Sievers. 'You hardly expected, when you were at Turriparva, to witness such a rapid termination of the patriotism of our good friend. I think you said you have seen him since your arrival: the interview must have been piquant!'

'Not at all. I immediately congratulated him on the judicious arrangements which had been concluded; and, to relieve his awkwardness, took some credit to myself for having partially assisted in bringing about the result. The subject was not again mentioned, and I dare say never will be.'

'It is a curious business,' said Sievers. 'The Prince is a man who, rather than have given me up to the Grand Duke; me, with whom he was not connected, and who, of my own accord, sought his hospitality; sooner, I repeat, than have delivered me up, he would have had his castle razed to the ground and fifty swords through his heart; and yet, without the slightest compunction, has this same man deserted, with the greatest coolness, the party of which, ten days ago, he was the zealous leader. How can you account for this, except it be, as I have long suspected, that in politics there positively is no feeling of honour? Every one is conscious that not only himself, but his colleagues and his rivals, are working for their own private purpose; and that however a party may apparently be assisting in bringing about a result of common benefit, that nevertheless, and in fact, each is conscious that he is the tool of another. With such an understanding, treason is an unexpected affair; and the only point to consider is, who shall be so unfortunate as to be the deserted, instead of the deserter. It is only fair to his Highness to state that Beckendorff gave him incontestable evidence that he had had a private interview with every one of the mediatised Princes. They were the dupes of the wily Minister. In these negotiations he became acquainted with their plans and characters, and could estimate the probability of their success. The golden bribe, which was in turn dandled before the eyes of all, had been always reserved for the most powerful, our friend. His secession and the consequent desertion of his relatives destroy the party for ever; while, at the same time, that party have not even the consolation of a good conscience to uphold them in their adversity; but feel that in case of their clamour, or of any attempt to stir up the people by their hollow patriotism, it is in the power of the Minister to expose and crush them for ever.

'All this,' said Vivian, 'makes me the more rejoice that our friend has got out of their clutches; he will make an excellent Grand Marshal; and you must not forget, my dear sir, that he did not forget you. To tell you the truth, although I did not flatter myself that I should benefit during my stay at Reisenburg by his influence, I am not the least surprised at the termination of our visit to Mr. Beckendorff. I have seen too many of these affairs not to have been quite aware, the whole time, that it would require very little trouble, and very few sacrifices on the part of Mr. Beckendorff, to quash the whole cabal. By-the-bye, our visit to him was highly amusing; he is a singular man.'

'He has had, nevertheless,' said Sievers, 'a difficult part to play. Had it not been for you, the Prince would have perhaps imagined that he was only trifling with him again, and terminated the interview abruptly and in disgust. Having brought the Grand Duke to terms, and having arranged the interview, Beckendorff of course imagined that all was finished. The very day that you arrived at his house he had received despatches from his Royal Highness, recalling his promise, and revoking Beckendorff's authority to use his unlimited discretion in this business. The difficulty then was to avoid discussion with the Prince, with whom he was not prepared to negotiate; and, at the same time, without letting his Highness out of his sight, to induce the Grand Duke to resume his old view of the case. The first night that you were there Beckendorff rode up to Reisenburg, saw the Grand Duke, was refused, through the intrigues of Madame Carolina, the requested authority, and resigned his power. When he was a mile on his return, he was summoned back to the palace; and his Royal Highness asked, as a favour from his tutor, four-and-twenty hours' consideration. This Beckendorff granted, on the condition that, in case the Grand Duke assented to the terms proposed, his Royal Highness should himself be the bearer of the proposition; and that there should be no more written promises to recall, and no more written authorities to revoke. The terms were hard, but Beckendorff was inflexible. On the second night of your visit a messenger arrived with a despatch, advising Beckendorff of the intended arrival of his Royal Highness on the next morning. The ludicrous intrusion of your amusing servant prevented you from being present at the great interview,

in which I understand Beckendorff for the moment
laid aside all his caprices. Our friend acted with
great firmness and energy. He would not be satisfied
even with the personal pledge and written promise of
the Grand Duke, but demanded that he should receive
the seals of office within a week; so that, had the
Court not been sincere, his situation with his former
party would not have been injured. It is astonishing
how very acute even a dull man is when his own interests are at stake! Had his Highness been the agent
of another person, he would probably have committed
many blunders, have made disadvantageous terms, or
perhaps have been thoroughly duped. Self-interest is
the finest eye-water.'

'And what says Madame Carolina to all this?'

'Oh! according to custom, she has changed already, and thinks the whole business admirably arranged. His Highness is her grand favourite, and my
little pupil Max her pet. I think, however, on the
whole, the boy is fondest of the Grand Duke, whom,
if you remember, he was always informing you in
confidence that he intended to assassinate. And as
for your obedient servant,' said Sievers bowing, 'here
am I once more the Aristarchus of her coterie. Her
friends, by-the-bye, view the accession of the Prince
with no pleased eyes; and, anticipating that his junc-
ture with the Minister is only a prelude to their final
dispersion, they are compensating for the approaching
termination of their career by unusual violence and
fresh fervour, stinging like mosquitoes before a storm,
conscious of their impending destruction from the
clearance of the atmosphere. As for myself, I have
nothing more to do with them. Liberty and philosophy are fine words; but until I find men are pre-

AFTER AN ORIGINAL DRAWING BY HERMAN ROUNTREE.

The gentlemen accordingly left the hotel, and proceeding down the street of the New Town, they came into a large square.

(See page 237.)

pared to cultivate them both in a wiser spirit I shall remain quiet. I have no idea of being banished and imprisoned because a parcel of knaves are making a vile use of the truths which I disseminate. In my opinion, philosophers have said enough; now let men act. But all this time I have forgotten to ask you how you like Reisenburg.'

'I can hardly say; with the exception of yesterday, when I rode Max round the ramparts, I have not been once out of the hotel. But to-day I feel so well that, if you are disposed for a lounge, I should like it above all things.'

'I am quite at your service; but I must not forget that I am the bearer of a missive to you from his Excellency the Grand Marshal. You are invited to join the court dinner to-day, and be presented——'

'Really, my dear sir, an invalid——'

'Well! if you do not like it, you must make your excuses to him; but it really is the pleasantest way of commencing your acquaintance at Court, and only allowed to distingués; among which, as you are the friend of the new Grand Marshal, you are of course considered. No one is petted so much as a political apostate, except, perhaps, a religious one; so at present we are all in high feather. You had better dine at the palace to-day. Everything quite easy; and, by an agreeable relaxation of state, neither swords, bags, nor trains are necessary. Have you seen the palace? I suppose not. We will look at it, and then call on the Prince.'

The gentlemen accordingly left the hotel; and proceeding down the principal street of the New Town, they came into a large square, or Place d'Armes. A couple of regiments of infantry were exercising in it.

'A specimen of our standing army,' said Sievers.
'In the war time, this little State brought thirty
thousand highly-disciplined and well-appointed troops
into the field. This efficient contingent was, at the
same time, the origin of our national prosperity and
our national debt. For we have a national debt, sir!
I assure you we are proud of it, and consider it the
most decided sign of being a great people. Our
force in times of peace is, of course, much reduced.
We have, however, still eight thousand men, who
are perfectly unnecessary. The most curious thing is,
that, to keep up the patronage of the Court and
please the nobility, though we have cut down our
army two-thirds, we have never reduced the number
of our generals; and so, at this moment, among our
eight thousand men, we count about forty general
officers, being one to every two hundred privates.
We have, however, which perhaps you would not
suspect, one military genius among our multitude of
heroes. The Count von Sohnspeer is worthy of being one of Napoleon's marshals. Who he is no one
exactly knows; some say an illegitimate son of Beckendorff. Certain it is that he owes his nobility to
his sword; and as certain is it that he is to be
counted among the very few who share the Minister's
confidence. Von Sohnspeer has certainly performed
a thousand brilliant exploits; yet, in my opinion, the
not least splendid day of his life was that of the battle of Leipsic. He was on the side of the French,
and fought against the Allies with desperate fury.
When he saw that all was over, and the Allies triumphant, calling out "Germany for ever!" he dashed
against his former friends, and captured from the flying Gauls a hundred pieces of cannon. He hastened

to the tent of the Emperors with his blood-red sword in his hand, and at the same time congratulated them on the triumph of their cause, and presented them with his hard-earned trophies. The manœuvre was perfectly successful; and the troops of Reisenburg, complimented as true Germans, were pitied for their former unhappy fate in being forced to fight against their fatherland, and were immediately enrolled in the allied army; as such, they received a due share of all the plunder. He is a grand genius, young Master von Sohnspeer?'

'Decidedly! Worthy of being a companion of the fighting bastards of the middle ages. This is a fine square.'

'Very grand indeed! Precedents for some of the architectural combinations could hardly be found at Athens or Rome; nevertheless the general effect is magnificent. Do you admire this plan of making every elevation of an order consonant with the purpose of the building? See, for instance, on the opposite side of the square is the palace. The Corinthian order, which is evident in all its details, suits well the character of the structure. It accords with royal pomp and elegance, with fêtes and banquets, and interior magnificence. On the other hand, what a happy contrast is afforded to this gorgeous structure by the severe simplicity of this Tuscan Palace of Justice. The School of Arts, in the farthest corner of the square, is properly entered through an Ionic portico. Let us go into the palace. Here not only does our monarch reside, but (an arrangement which I much admire) here are deposited, in a gallery worthy of the treasures it contains, our superb collection of pictures. They are the private property of his Royal Highness;

but, as is usually the case under despotic Princes, the people, equally his property, are flattered by the collection being styled the "Public Gallery." '

The hour of the court dinner at Reisenburg was two o'clock, about which time, in England, a man first remembers the fatal necessity of shaving; though, by-the-bye, this allusion is not a very happy one, for in this country shaving is a ceremony at present somewhat obsolete. At two o'clock, however, our hero, accompanying the Grand Marshal and Mr. Sievers, reached the palace. In the saloon were assembled various guests, chiefly attached to the Court. Immediately after the arrival of our party, the Grand Duke and Madame Carolina, followed by their chamberlains and ladies-in-waiting, entered. The little Prince Maximilian strutted in between his Royal Highness and his fair consort, having hold of a hand of each. The urchin was much changed in appearance since Vivian first saw him; he was dressed in the complete uniform of a captain of the Royal Guards, having been presented with a commission on the day of his arrival at Court. A brilliant star glittered on his scarlet coat, and paled the splendour of his golden epaulettes. The duties, however, of the princely captain were at present confined to the pleasing exertion of carrying the bon-bon box of Madame Carolina, the contents of which were chiefly reserved for his own gratification. In the Grand Duke Vivian was not surprised to recognise the horseman whom he had met in the private road on the morning of his departure from Mr. Beckendorff's; his conversation with Sievers had prepared him for this. Madame Carolina was in appearance Parisian of the highest order: that is to say, an exquisite figure and an indescribable tournure,

an invisible foot, a countenance full of *esprit* and intelligence, without a single regular feature, and large
and very bright black eyes. Madame's hair was of
the same colour, and arranged in the most effective
manner. Her cashmere would have graced the Feast
of Roses, and so engrossed your attention that it was
long before you observed the rest of her costume, in
which, however, traces of a creative genius were immediately visible; in short, Madame Carolina was not
fashionable, but fashion herself. In a subsequent
chapter, at a ball which we have in preparation, we
will make up for this brief notice of her costume by
publishing her court dress. For the sake of our fair
readers, however, we will not pass over the ornament
in her hair. The comb which supported her elaborate curls was invisible, except at each end, whence
it threw out a large Psyche's wing of golden web,
the eyes of which were formed of rubies encircled
with turquoises.

The royal party made a progress round the circle. Madame Carolina first presented her delicate and
faintly-rouged cheek to the hump-backed Crown
Prince, who scarcely raised his eyes from the ground
as he performed the accustomed courtesy. One or
two royal relatives, who were on a visit at the
palace, were honoured by the same compliment.
The Grand Duke bowed graciously and gracefully to
every individual; and his lady accompanied the bow
by a speech, which was at the same time personal
and piquant. The first great duty of a monarch is to
know how to bow skilfully! nothing is more difficult,
and nothing more important. A royal bow may often
quell a rebellion, and sometimes crush a conspiracy.
It should at the same time be both general and indi-

vidual; equally addressed to the company assembled, and to every single person in the assembly. Our own sovereign bows to perfection. His bow is eloquent, and will always render an oration on his part unnecessary; which is a great point, for harangues are not regal. Nothing is more undignified than to make a speech. It is from the first an acknowledgment that you are under the necessity of explaining, or conciliating, or convincing, or confuting; in short, that you are not omnipotent, but opposed.

The bow of the Grand Duke of Reisenburg was a first-rate bow, and always produced a great sensation with the people, particularly if it were followed up by a proclamation for a public fête or fireworks; then his Royal Highness's popularity was at its height. But Madame Carolina, after having by a few magic sentences persuaded the whole room that she took a peculiar interest in the happiness of every individual present, has reached Vivian, who stood next to his friend the Grand Marshal. He was presented by that great officer, and received most graciously. For a moment the room thought that his Royal Highness was about to speak; but he only smiled. Madame Carolina, however, said a great deal; and stood not less than sixty seconds complimenting the English nation, and particularly the specimen of that celebrated people who now had the honour of being presented to her. No one spoke more in a given time than Madame Carolina; and as, while the eloquent words fell from her deep red lips, her bright eyes were invariably fixed on those of the person she addressed, what she did say, as invariably, was very effective. Vivian had only time to give a nod of recognition to his friend Max, for the company, arm-in-arm, now

formed into a procession to the dining saloon.
Vivian was parted from the Grand Marshal, who, as
the highest officer of state present, followed immediately after the Grand Duke. Our hero's companion
was Mr. Sievers. Although it was not a state dinner, the party, from being swelled by the suites of
the royal visitors, was numerous; and as the Court
occupied the centre of the table, Vivian was too distant to listen to the conversation of Madame, who,
however, he well perceived, from the animation of
her countenance, was delighted and delighting. The
Grand Duke spoke little, but listened, like a lover of
three days, to the accents of his accomplished consort.
The arrangement of a German dinner promotes conversation. The numerous dishes are at once placed
upon the table; and when the curious eye has well
examined their contents, the whole dinner, untouched,
disappears. Although this circumstance is rather
alarming to a novice, his terror soon gives place to
self-congratulation when he finds the banquet re-
appear, each dish completely carved and cut up.

'Not being Sunday,' said Mr. Sievers, 'there is no
opera to-night. We are to meet again, I believe, at
the palace in a few hours, at Madame Carolina's
soirée. In the meantime, you had better accompany
his Excellency to the public gardens; that is the fashionable drive. I shall go home and smoke a pipe.'

The circle of the public gardens of Reisenburg exhibited exactly, although upon a smaller scale, the
same fashions and the same frivolities, the same characters and the same affectations, as the Hyde Park of
London, or the Champs Elysées of Paris, the Prater
of Vienna, the Corso of Rome or Milan, or the Cas-
cine of Florence. There was the female leader of *ton*,

hated by her own sex and adored by the other, and
ruling both; ruling both by the same principle of action, and by the influence of the same quality which
creates the arbitress of fashion in all countries, by
courage to break through the conventional customs of
an artificial class, and by talents to ridicule all those
who dare follow her innovating example; attracting
universal notice by her own singularity, and at the
same time conciliating the support of those from
whom she dares to differ, by employing her influence
in preventing others from violating their laws. The
arbitress of fashion is one who is allowed to be
singular, in order that she may suppress singularity;
she is exempted from all laws; but, by receiving the
dictatorship, she ensures the despotism. Then there
was that mysterious being whose influence is perhaps
even more surprising than the dominion of the female
despot of manners, for she wields a power which can
be analysed and comprehended; I mean the male
authority in coats, cravats, and chargers; who, without fortune and without rank, and sometimes merely
through the bold obtrusion of a fantastic taste, becomes the glass of fashion in which even royal dukes
and the most aristocratic nobles hasten to adjust
themselves, and the mould by which the ingenious
youth of a whole nation is enthusiastically formed.
There is a Brummel in every country.

Vivian, who, after a round or two with the Grand
Marshal, had mounted Max, was presented by the
young Count von Bernstorff, the son of the Grand
Chamberlain, to whose care he had been specially
commended by the Prince, to the lovely Countess von
S——. The examination of this high authority was
rigid and her report satisfactory. When Vivian quitted

the side of her britzska half a dozen dandies immediately rode up to learn the result, and, on being informed, they simultaneously cantered up to young
Von Bernstorff, and requested to have the honour of
being introduced to his highly interesting friend. All
these exquisites wore white hats lined with crimson,
in consequence of the head of the all-influential Emilius von Aslingen having, on the preceding day, been
kept sacred from the profaning air by that most
tasteful covering. The young lords were loud in
their commendations of this latest evidence of Von
Aslingen's happy genius, and rallied with unmerciful
spirit the unfortunate Von Bernstorff for not having
yet mounted the all-perfect chapeau. Like all Von
Aslingen's introductions, it was as remarkable for
good taste as for striking singularity; they had no
doubt it would have a great run, exactly the style of
thing for a hot autumn, and it suited so admirably
with the claret-coloured riding coat which Madame
considered Von Aslingen's *chef-d'œuvre.* Inimitable
Von Aslingen! As they were in these raptures, to
Vivian's delight and to their dismay, the object
of their admiration appeared. Our hero was, of
course, anxious to see so interesting a character; but
he could scarcely believe that he, in fact, beheld the
ingenious introducer of white and crimson hats, and
the still happier inventor of those *chef-d'œuvres,*
claret-coloured riding coats, when his attention was
directed to a horseman who wore a peculiarly high
heavy black hat and a frogged and furred frock, but-
toned up, although it was a most sultry day, to his
very nose. How singular is the slavery of fashion!
Notwithstanding their mortification, the unexpected
costume of Von Aslingen appeared only to increase

the young lords' admiration of his character and accomplishments; and instead of feeling that he was an
insolent pretender, whose fame originated in his in-
sulting their tastes, and existed only by their suffer-
ance, all cantered away with the determination of
wearing on the next day, even if it were to cost
them each a calenture, furs enough to keep a man
warm during a winter party at St. Petersburg, not
that winter parties ever take place there; on the contrary, before the winter sets in, the Court moves on
to Moscow, which, from its situation and its climate,
will always, in fact, continue the real capital of Russia.

The royal carriage, drawn by six horses and backed
by three men servants, who would not have disgraced the fairy equipage of Cinderella, has now left
the gardens.

CHAPTER III.

MADAME CAROLINA held her soirée
in her own private apartments, the
Grand Duke himself appearing in
the capacity of a visitor. The company was numerous and brilliant.
His Royal Highness, surrounded by
a select circle, dignified one corner of the saloon;
Madame Carolina at the other end of the room,
in the midst of poets, philosophers, and politicians,
in turn decided upon the most interesting and important topics of poetry, philosophy, and politics.
Boston, and Zwicken, and whist interested some, and
puzzles and other ingenious games others. A few
were above conversing, or gambling, or guessing;
superior intelligences, who would neither be interested
nor amused, among these Emilius von Aslingen was
most prominent. He leant against a door in full uniform, with his vacant eyes fixed on no object. The
others were only awkward copies of an easy original;
and among these, stiff or stretching, lounging on a
chaise-lounge, or posted against the wall, Vivian's
quick eye recognized more than one of the unhappy
votaries of white hats lined with crimson.

When Vivian made his bow to the Grand Duke he was surprised by his Royal Highness coming forward a few steps from the surrounding circle and extending to him his hand. His Royal Highness continued conversing with him for upwards of a quarter of an hour; expressed the great pleasure he felt at seeing at his Court a gentleman of whose abilities he had the highest opinion; and, after a variety of agreeable compliments (compliments are doubly agreeable from crowned heads), the Grand Duke retired to a game of Boston with his royal visitors. Vivian's reception made a sensation through the room. Various rumours were immediately afloat.

'Who can he be?'

'Don't you know? Oh! most curious story. Killed a boar as big as a bonasus, which was ravaging half Reisenburg, and saved the lives of his Excellency the Grand Marshal and his whole suite.'

'What is that about the Grand Marshal and a boar as big as a bonasus? Quite wrong; natural son of Beckendorff; know it for a fact. Don't you see he is being introduced to Von Sohnspeer! brothers, you know, managed the whole business about the leagued Princes; not a son of Beckendorff, only a particular friend; the son of the late General ——, I forget his name exactly. Killed at Leipsic, you know; that famous general; what was his name? that very famous general; don't you remember? Never mind; well! he is his son; father particular friend of Beckendorff; college friend, brought up the orphan; very handsome of him! They say he does handsome things sometimes.'

'Ah! well, I've heard so too; and so this young man is to be the new under-secretary! very much approved by the Countess von S——.'

'No, it can't be! your story is quite wrong. He
is an Englishman.'

'An Englishman! no!'

'Yes he is. I had it from Madame; high rank
incog.; going to Vienna; secret mission.'

'Something to do with Greece, of course; independence recognised?'

'Oh! certainly; pay a tribute to the Porte, and
governed by a hospodar. Admirable arrangement!
have to support their own government and a foreign
one besides!'

It was with pleasure that Vivian at length observed Mr. Sievers enter the room, and extricating
himself from the enlightened and enthusiastic crowd
who were disserting around the tribunal of Madame,
he hastened to his amusing friend.

'Ah! my dear sir, how glad I am to see you! I
have, since we met last, been introduced to your
fashionable ruler, and some of her most fashionable
slaves. I have been honoured by a long conversation
with his Royal Highness, and have listened to some
of the most eloquent of the Carolina coterie. What
a Babel! there all are, at the same time, talkers and
listeners. To what a pitch of perfection may the
"science" of conversation be carried! My mind teems
with original ideas, to which I can annex no definite
meaning. What a variety of contradictory theories,
which are all apparently sound! I begin to suspect
that there is a great difference between reasoning and
reason!'

'Your suspicion is well founded, my dear sir,' said
Mr. Sievers; 'and I know no circumstance which
would sooner prove it than listening for a few minutes to this little man in a snuff-coloured coat near

me. But I will save you from so terrible a demonstration. He has been endeavouring to catch my eye these last ten minutes, and I have as studiously avoided seeing him. Let us move.'

'Willingly; who may this fear-inspiring monster be?'

'A philosopher,' said Mr. Sievers, 'as most of us call ourselves here; that is to say, his profession is to observe the course of Nature; and if by chance he can discover any slight deviation of the good dame from the path which our ignorance has marked out as her only track, he claps his hands, cries εὕρηκα! and is dubbed "illustrious" on the spot. Such is the world's reward for a great discovery, which generally, in a twelvemonth's time, is found out to be a blunder of the philosopher, and not an eccentricity of Nature. I am not underrating those great men who, by deep study, or rather by some mysterious inspiration, have produced combinations and effected results which have materially assisted the progress of civilisation and the security of our happiness. No, no! to them be due adoration. Would that the reverence of posterity could be some consolation to these great spirits for neglect and persecution when they lived! I have invariably observed of great natural philosophers, that if they lived in former ages they were persecuted as magicians, and in periods which profess to be more enlightened they have always been ridiculed as quacks. The succeeding century the real quack arises. He adopts and developes the suppressed, and despised, and forgotten discovery of his unfortunate predecessor! and Fame trumpets this resurrection-man of science with as loud a blast of rapture as if, instead of being merely the accidental animator of the corpse, he were the cunning artist himself who had devised and executed the miraculous machinery which the other had only wound up.'

'But in this country,' said Vivian, 'surely you have no reason to complain of the want of moral philosophers, or of the respect paid to them. The country of Kant —— of ——'

'Yes, yes! we have plenty of metaphysicians, if you mean them. Watch that lively-looking gentleman, who is stuffing *kalte schale* so voraciously in the corner. The leader of the Idealists, a pupil of the celebrated Fichte! To gain an idea of his character, know that he out-Herods his master; and Fichte is to Kant what Kant is to the unenlightened vulgar. You can now form a slight conception of the spiritual nature of our friend who is stuffing *kalte schale*. The first principle of his school is to reject all expressions which incline in the slightest degree to substantiality. Existence, is in his opinion, a word too absolute. Being, principle, essence, are terms scarcely sufficiently ethereal even to indicate the subtile shadowings of his opinions. Some say that he dreads the contact of all real things, and that he makes it the study of his life to avoid them. Matter is his great enemy. When you converse with him you lose all consciousness of this world. My dear sir,' continued Mr. Sievers, 'observe how exquisitely Nature revenges herself upon these capricious and fantastic children. Believe me, Nature is the most brilliant of wits; and that no repartees that were ever inspired by hate, or wine, or beauty, ever equalled the calm effects of her indomitable power upon those who are rejecting her authority. You understand me? Methinks that the best answer to the idealism of M. Fichte is to see his pupil devouring *kalte schale!*'

'And this is really one of your great lights?'

'Verily! His works are the most famous and the most unreadable in all Germany. Surely you have heard of his "Treatise on Man?" A treatise on a subject in which every one is interested, written in a style which no one can understand.'

'You think, then,' said Vivian, 'that posterity may rank the German metaphysicians with the later Platonists?'

'I hardly know; they are a body of men not less acute, but I doubt whether they will be as celebrated. In this age of print, notoriety is more attainable than in the age of manuscript; but lasting fame certainly is not. That tall thin man in black that just bowed to me is the editor of one of our great Reisenburg reviews. The journal he edits is one of the most successful periodical publications ever set afloat. Among its contributors may assuredly be classed many men of eminent talents; yet to their abilities the surprising success and influence of this work is scarcely to be ascribed. It is the result rather of the consistent spirit which has always inspired its masterly critiques. One principle has ever regulated its management; it is a simple rule, but an effective one: every author is reviewed by his personal enemy. You may imagine the point of the critique; but you would hardly credit, if I were to inform you, the circulation of the review. You will tell me that you are not surprised, and talk of the natural appetite of our species for malice and slander. Be not too quick. The rival of this review, both in influence and in sale, is conducted on as simple a principle, but not

a similar one. In this journal every author is reviewed by his personal friend; of course, perfect
panegyric. Each number is flattering as a lover's
tale; every article an *éloge*. What say you to this?
These are the influential literary and political journals
of Reisenburg. There was yet another; it was edited
by an eloquent scholar; all its contributors were, at
the same time, brilliant and profound. It numbered
among its writers some of the most celebrated names
in Germany; its critiques and articles were as impartial as they were able, as sincere as they were sound;
it never paid the expense of the first number. As
philanthropists and admirers of our species, my dear
sir, these are gratifying results; they satisfactorily
demonstrate that mankind have no innate desire for
scandal, calumny, and backbiting; it only proves that
they have an innate desire to be gulled and deceived.'

'And who is that?' said Vivian.

'That is Von Chronicle, our great historical novelist. When I first came to Reisenburg, now eight
years ago, the popular writer of fiction was a man,
the most probable of whose numerous romances was
one in which the hero sold his shadow to a demon
over the dice-box; then married an unknown woman
in a churchyard; afterwards wedded a river nymph;
and, having committed bigamy, finally stabbed himself, to enable his first wife to marry his own father.
He and his works are quite obsolete; and the star of
his genius, with those of many others, has paled before the superior brilliancy of that literary comet, Mr.
von Chronicle. According to Von Chronicle, we
have all, for a long time, been under a mistake. We
have ever considered that the first point to be studied
in novel writing is character: miserable error! It is

costume. Variety of incident, novelty, and nice discrimination of character; interest of story, and all those points which we have hitherto looked upon as necessary qualities of a fine novel, vanish before the superior attractions of variety of dresses, exquisite descriptions of the cloak of a signor, or the trunk-hose of a serving man.

'Amuse yourself while you are at Reisenburg by turning over some volumes which every one is reading; Von Chronicle's last great historical novel. The subject is a magnificent one, Rienzi; yet it is strange that the hero only appears in the first and the last scenes. You look astonished. Ah! I see you are not a great historical novelist. You forget the effect which is produced by the contrast of the costume of Master Nicholas, the notary in the quarter of the Jews, and that of Rienzi, the tribune, in his robe of purple, at his coronation in the Capitol. Conceive the effect, the contrast. With that coronation Von Chronicle's novel terminates; for, as he well observes, after that, what is there in the career of Rienzi which would afford matter for the novelist? Nothing! All that afterwards occurs is a mere contest of passions and a development of character; but where is a procession, a triumph, or a marriage?

'One of Von Chronicle's great characters in this novel is a Cardinal. It was only last night that I was fortunate enough to have the beauties of the work pointed out to me by the author himself. He entreated, and gained my permission to read to me what he himself considered "the great scene." I settled myself in my chair, took out my handkerchief, and prepared my mind for the worst. While I was anticipating the terrors of a heroine he introduced me to his Cardinal. Thirty pages were devoted to the description of the prelate's costume. Although clothed in purple, still, by a skilful adjustment of the drapery, Von Chronicle managed to bring in six other petticoats. I thought this beginning would never finish, but to my surprise, when he had got to the seventh petticoat, he shut his book, and leaning over the table, asked me what I thought of his "great scene." "My friend," said I, "you are not only the greatest historical novelist that ever lived, but that ever will live."'

'I shall certainly get Rienzi,' said Vivian; 'it seems to me to be an original work.'

'Von Chronicle tells me that he looks upon it as his masterpiece, and that it may be considered as the highest point of perfection to which his system of novel-writing can be carried. Not a single name is given in the work, down even to the rabble, for which he has not contemporary authority; but what he is particularly proud of are his oaths. Nothing, he tells me, has cost him more trouble than the management of the swearing; and the Romans you know, are a most profane nation. The great difficulty to be avoided was using the ejaculations of two different ages. The "'sblood" of the sixteenth century must not be confounded with the "zounds" of the seventeenth. Enough of Von Chronicle! The most amusing thing,' continued Mr. Sievers, 'is to contrast this mode of writing works of fiction with the prevalent and fashionable method of writing works of history. Contrast the "Rienzi" of Von Chronicle with the "Haroun-al-Raschid" of Madame Carolina. Here we write novels like history, and history like novels: all our facts are fancy, and all our imagination reality.' So saying, Mr. Sievers rose, and, wishing Vivian good night, quitted the room. He was one of those prudent geniuses who always leave off with a point.

Mr. Sievers had not left Vivian more than a minute when the little Prince Maximilian came up and bowed to him in a condescending manner. Our hero, who had not yet had an opportunity of speaking with him, thanked him cordially for his handsome present, and asked him how he liked the Court.

'Oh, delightful! I pass all my time with the Grand Duke and Madame:' and here the young apostate settled his military stock and arranged the girdle of his sword. 'Madame Carolina,' continued he, 'has commanded me to inform you that she desires the pleasure of your attendance.'

The summons was immediately obeyed, and Vivian had the honour of a long conversation with the interesting consort of the Grand Duke. He was, for a considerable time, complimented by her enthusiastic panegyric of England, her original ideas of the character and genius of Lord Byron, her veneration for Sir Humphry Davy, and her admiration of Sir Walter Scott. Not remiss was Vivian in paying, in his happiest manner, due compliments to the fair and royal authoress of the Court of Charlemagne. While she spoke his native tongue, he admired her accurate English; and while she professed to have derived her imperfect knowledge of his perfect language from a study of its best authors, she avowed her belief of the impossibility of ever speaking it correctly without the assistance of a native. Conversation became more interesting.

When Vivian left the palace he was not unmindful of an engagement to return there the next day, to give a first lesson in English pronunciation to Madame Carolina.

CHAPTER IV.

A ROYAL BLUE-STOCKING.

VIVIAN duly kept his appointment with Madame Carolina. The chamberlain ushered him into a library, where Madame Carolina was seated at a large table covered with books and manuscripts. Her costume and her countenance were equally engaging. Fascination was alike in her smile, and her sash, her bow, and her buckle. What a delightful pupil to perfect in English pronunciation! Madame pointed, with a pride pleasing to Vivian's feelings as an Englishman, to her shelves, graced with the most eminent of English writers. Madame Carolina was not like one of those admirers of English literature whom you often meet on the Continent: people who think that Beattie's "Minstrel" is our most modern and fashionable poem; that the "Night Thoughts" is the masterpiece of our literature; and that Richardson is our only novelist. Oh, no! Madame Carolina would not have disgraced May Fair. She knew Childe Harold by rote, and had even peeped into Don Juan. Her admiration of the Edinburgh and Quarterly Reviews was great and similar. To a Continental liberal, indeed, even the Toryism of the Quarterly is philosophy; and not an Under-Secretary ever yet massacred a radical innovator without giving loose to some sentiments and sentences which are considered rank treason in the meridian of Vienna.

After some conversation, in which Madame evinced eagerness to gain details about the persons and manners of our most eminent literary characters, she naturally began to speak of the literary productions of other countries; and in short, ere an hour was passed, Vivian Grey, instead of giving a lesson in English pronunciation to the consort of the Grand Duke of Reisenburg, found himself listening, in an easy chair, and with folded arms, to a long treatise by that lady ''de l'Esprit de Conversation.'' It was a most brilliant dissertation. Her kindness in reading it to him was most particular; nevertheless, for unexpected blessings we are not always sufficiently grateful.

Another hour was consumed by the treatise. How she refined! what unexpected distinctions! what exquisite discrimination of national character! what skilful eulogium of her own! Nothing could be more splendid than her elaborate character of a repartee; it would have sufficed for an epic poem. At length Madame Carolina ceased ''de l'Esprit de Conversation,'' and Vivian was successful in concealing his weariness and in testifying his admiration. 'The evil is over,' thought he; 'I may as well gain credit for my good taste.' The lesson in English pronunciation, however, was not yet terminated. Madame was charmed with our hero's uncommon discrimination and extraordinary talents. He was the most skilful and the most agreeable critic with whom she had ever been acquainted. How invaluable must the opinion of such a person be to her on her great work! No one had yet seen a line of it; but there are moments when we are irresistibly impelled to seek a confidante; that confidante was before her. The morocco case was unlocked, and the manuscript of Haroun-al-Raschid revealed to the enraptured eye of Vivian Grey.

'I flatter myself,' said Madame Carolina, 'that this work will create a great sensation; not only in Germany. It abounds, I think, with interesting story, engaging incidents, and animated and effective descriptions. I have not, of course, been able to obtain any new matter respecting his Sublimity the Caliph. Between ourselves, I do not think this very important. So far as I have observed, we have matter enough in this world on every possible subject already. It is manner in which the literature of all nations is deficient. It appears to me that the great point for persons of genius now to direct their attention to is the expansion of matter. This I conceive to be the great secret; and this must be effected by the art of picturesque writing. For instance, my dear Mr. Grey, I will open the Arabian Nights' Entertainments, merely for an exemplification, at the one hundred and eighty-fifth night; good! Let us attend to the following passage: —

'"In the reign of the Caliph Haroun-al-Raschid, there was at Bagdad a druggist, called Alboussan Ebn Thaher, a very rich, handsome man. He had more wit and politeness than people of his profession ordinarily have. His integrity, sincerity, and jovial humour made him beloved and sought after by all sorts of people. The Caliph, who knew his merit, had entire confidence in him. He had so great an esteem for him that he entrusted him with the care to provide his favourite ladies with all the things they stood in need of. He chose for them their clothes, furniture, and jewels, with admirable taste. His good qualities and the favour of the Caliph made the sons of Emirs and other officers of the first rank be always about him. His house was the rendezvous of all the nobility of the Court."

'What capabilities lurk in this dry passage!' exclaimed Madame Carolina; 'I touch it with my pen, and transform it into a chapter. It shall be one of those that I will read to you. The description of Alboussan alone demands ten pages. There is no doubt that his countenance was oriental. The tale says that he was handsome: I paint him with his eastern eye, his thin arched brow, his fragrant beard, his graceful mustachio. The tale says he was rich: I have authorities for the costume of men of his dignity in contemporary writers. In my history he appears in an upper garment of green velvet, and loose trousers of pink satin; a jewelled dagger lies in his golden girdle; his slippers are of the richest embroidery; and he never omits the bath of roses daily. On this system — which in my opinion elicits truth, for by it you are enabled to form a conception of the manners of the age — on this system I proceed throughout the paragraph. Conceive my account of his house being the "rendezvous of all the nobility of the Court." What a brilliant scene! what variety of dress and character! what splendour! what luxury! what magnificence! Imagine the detail of the banquet; which, by-the-bye, gives me an opportunity of inserting, after the manner of your own Gibbon, "a dissertation on sherbet." What think you of the art of picturesque writing?'

'Admirable!' said Vivian; 'Von Chronicle him-self——'

'How can you mention the name of that odious man?' almost shrieked Madame Carolina, forgetting the dignity of her semi-regal character in the jealous feelings of the author. 'How can you mention him? A scribbler without a spark, not only of genius, but even of common invention. A miserable fellow, who seems to do nothing but clothe and amplify, in his own fantastic style, the details of a parcel of old chronicles!'

Madame's indignation reminded Vivian of a true but rather vulgar proverb of his own country; and he extricated himself from his very awkward situation with a dexterity worthy of his former years.

'Von Chronicle himself,' said Vivian; 'Von Chronicle himself, as I was going to observe, will be the most mortified of all on the appearance of your work. He cannot be so blinded by self-conceit as to fail to observe that your history is a thousand times more interesting than his fiction. Ah! Madame, if you can thus spread enchantment over the hitherto weary page of history, what must be your work of imagination!'

CHAPTER V.

VIVIAN MEETS A FAIR UNKNOWN.

IVIAN met Emilius von Aslingen in his ride through the gardens. As that distinguished personage at present patronised the English nation, and astounded the Reisenburg natives by driving an English mail, riding English horses, and ruling English grooms, he deigned to be exceedingly courteous to our hero, whom he had publicly declared at the soirée of the preceding night to be 'very good style.' Such a character from such a man raised Vivian even more in the estimation of the Reisenburg world than his flattering reception by the Grand Duke and his cordial greeting by Madame Carolina.

'Shall you be at the Grand Marshal's to-night?' asked Vivian.

'Ah! that is the new man, the man who was mediatised, is not it?'

'The Prince of Little Lilliput.'

'Yes!' drawled out Mr. von Aslingen. 'I shall go if I have courage enough; but they say his servants wear skins, and he has got a tail.'

The ball-room was splendidly illuminated. The whole of the Royal Family was present, and did honour to their new officer of state; his Royal Highness all smiles, and his consort all diamonds. Stars and uniforms, ribbons and orders, abounded. The diplomatic body wore the dresses of their respective Courts. Emilius von Aslingen, having given out in the morning that he should appear as a captain in the Royal Guards, the young lords and fops of fashion were consequently ultra military. They were not a little annoyed when, late in the evening, their model lounged in, wearing the rich scarlet uniform of a Knight of Malta, of which newly-revived order Von Aslingen, who had served half a campaign against the Turks, was a member.

The Royal Family had arrived only a few minutes: dancing had not yet commenced. Vivian was at the top of the room, honoured by the notice of Madame Carolina, who complained of his yesterday's absence from the palace. Suddenly the universal hum and buzz which are always sounding in a crowded room were stilled; and all present, arrested in their conversation and pursuits, stood with their heads turned towards the great door. Thither also Vivian looked, and, wonderstruck, beheld — Mr. Beckendorff. His singular appearance, for, with the exception of his cavalry boots, he presented the same figure as when he first came forward to receive the Prince of Little Lilliput and Vivian on the lawn, immediately attracted universal attention; but in this crowded room there were a few who, either from actual experience or accurate information, were not ignorant that this personage was the Prime Minister. The report spread like wildfire. Even the etiquette of a German ball-room, honoured as it was by the presence of the Court, was no restraint to the curiosity and wonder of all present. Yes! even Emilius von Aslingen raised his glass to his eye. But great as was Vivian's astonishment, it was not only occasioned by this unexpected appearance of his former host. Mr. Beckendorff was not alone: a woman was leaning on his left arm. A quick glance in a moment convinced Vivian that she was not the original of the mysterious picture. The companion of Beckendorff was very young. Her full voluptuous growth gave you, for a moment, the impression that she was somewhat low in stature; but it was only for a moment, for the lady was by no means short. Her beauty it is impossible to describe. It was of a kind that baffles all phrases, nor have I a single simile at command to make it more clear or more confused. Her luxurious form, her blonde complexion, her silken hair, would have all become the languishing sultana; but then her eyes, they banished all idea of the seraglio, and were the most decidedly European, though the most brilliant, that ever glanced; eagles might have proved their young at them. To a countenance which otherwise would have been calm, and perhaps pensive, they gave an expression of extreme vivacity and unusual animation, and perhaps of restlessness and arrogance; it might have been courage. The lady was dressed in the costume of a Chanoinesse of a *Couvent des dames nobles;* an institution to which Protestant and Catholic ladies are alike admitted. The orange-coloured cordon of her canonry was slung gracefully over her plain black silk dress, and a diamond cross hung below her waist.

Mr. Beckendorff and his fair companion were instantly welcomed by the Grand Marshal; and Arnelm and half-a-dozen chamberlains, all in new uniforms, and extremely agitated, did their utmost, by their exertions in clearing the way, to prevent the Prime Minister of Reisenburg from paying his respects to his Sovereign. At length, however, Mr. Beckendorff reached the top of the room, and presented the young lady to his Royal Highness, and also to Madame Carolina. Vivian had retired on their approach, and now found himself among a set of young officers, idolators of Von Aslingen, and of white hats lined with crimson. 'Who can she be?' was the universal question. Though all by the query acknowledged their ignorance, yet it is singular that, at the same time, every one was prepared with a response to it. Such are the sources of accurate information!

'And that is Beckendorff, is it?' exclaimed the young Count of Eberstein; 'and his daughter, of course! Well; there is nothing like being a plebeian and a Prime Minister! I suppose Beckendorff will bring an anonymous friend to Court next.'

'She cannot be his daughter,' said Bernstorff. 'To be a Chanoinesse of that order, remember, she must be noble.'

'Then she must be his niece,' answered the young Count of Eberstein. 'I think I do remember some confused story about a sister of Beckendorff who ran away with some Wirtemberg Baron. What was that story, Gernsbach?'

'No, it was not his sister,' said the Baron of Gernsbach; 'it was his aunt, I think.'

'Beckendorff's aunt; what an idea! As if he ever had an aunt! Men of his calibre make themselves

out of mud. They have no relations. Well, never
mind; there was some story, I am sure, about some
woman or other. Depend upon it that this girl is the
child of that woman, whether she be aunt, niece, or
daughter. I shall go and tell every one that I know
the whole business; this girl is the daughter of some
woman or other.' So saying, away walked the young
Count of Eberstein, to disseminate in all directions
the important conclusion at which his logical head
had allowed him to arrive.

'Von Weinbren,' said the Baron of Gernsbach,
'how can you account for this mysterious appearance
of the Premier?'

'Oh! when men are on the decline they do desperate things. I suppose it is to please the rene-
gado.'

'Hush! there's the Englishman behind you.'

'*On dit*, another child of Beckendorff.'

'Oh no! secret mission.'

'Ah! indeed.'

'Here comes Von Aslingen! Well, great Emilius!
how solve you this mystery?'

'What mystery? Is there one?'

'I allude to this wonderful appearance of Beckendorff.'

'Beckendorff! what a name! Who is he?'

'Nonsense! the Premier.'

'Well!'

'You have seen him, of course; he is here. Have
you just come in?'

'Beckendorff here!' said Von Aslingen, in a tone
of affected horror; 'I did not know that the fellow
was to be visited. It is all over with Reisenburg. I
shall go to Vienna to-morrow.'

But hark! the sprightly music calls to the dance; and first the stately Polonaise, an easy gradation between walking and dancing. To the surprise of the whole room and the indignation of many of the high nobles, the Crown Prince of Reisenburg led off the Polonaise with the unknown fair one. Such an attention to Beckendorff was a distressing proof of present power and favour. The Polonaise is a dignified promenade, with which German balls invariably commence. The cavaliers, with an air of studied grace, offer their right hands to their fair partners; and the whole party, in a long file, accurately follow the leading couple through all their scientific evolutions, as they wind through every part of the room. Waltzes in sets speedily followed the Polonaise; and the unknown, who was now an object of universal attention, danced with Count von Sohnspeer, another of Beckendorff's numerous progeny, if the reader remember. How scurvily are poor single gentlemen who live alone treated by the candid tongues of their fellow-creatures! The commander-in-chief of the Reisenburg troops was certainly a partner of a different complexion from the young lady's previous one. The Crown Prince had undertaken his duty with reluctance, and had performed it without grace; not a single word had he exchanged with his partner during the promenade, and his genuine listlessness was even more offensive than affected apathy. Von Sohnspeer, on the contrary, danced in the true Vienna style, and whirled like a dervish. All our good English prejudices against the soft, the swimming, the sentimental, melting, undulating, dangerous waltz would quickly disappear, if we only executed the dreaded manœuvres in the true Austrian style. One

might as soon expect our daughters to get sentimental in a swing.

Vivian did not choose to presume upon his late
acquaintance with Mr. Beckendorff, as it had not
been sought by that gentleman, and he consequently
did not pay his respects to the Minister.   Mr. Beckendorff continued at the top of the room, standing
between the state chairs of his Royal Highness and
Madame Carolina, and occasionally addressing an observation to his Sovereign and answering one of the
lady's.   Had Mr. Beckendorff been in the habit of attending balls nightly he could not have exhibited
more perfect nonchalance.   There he stood, with his
arms crossed behind him, his chin resting on his
breast, and his raised eyes glancing!

'My dear Prince,' said Vivian to the Grand Marshal, 'you are just the person I want to speak to.
How came you to invite Beckendorff, and how came
he to accept the invitation?'

'My dear friend,' said his Highness, shrugging his
shoulders, 'wonders will never cease.   I never invited
him; I should just as soon have thought of inviting
old Johannisberger.'

'Were not you aware, then, of his intention?'

'Not in the least! you should rather say attention;
for, I assure you, I consider it a most particular one.
It is quite astonishing, my dear friend, how I mistook that man's character.   He really is one of the
most gentlemanlike, polite, and excellent persons I
know; no more mad than you are!   And as for his
power being on the decline, we know the nonsense
of that!'

'Better than most persons, I suspect.   Sievers, of
course is not here?'

'No! you have heard about him, I suppose?'

'Heard! heard what?'

'Not heard! well, he told me yesterday, and said he was going to call upon you directly to let you know.'

'Know what?'

'He is a very sensible man, Sievers; and I am very glad at last that he is likely to succeed in the world. All men have their little imprudences, and he was a little too hot once. What of that? He has come to his senses, so have I; and I hope you will never lose yours!'

'But pray, my dear Prince, tell me what has happened to Sievers.'

'He is going to Vienna immediately, and will be very useful there, I have no doubt. He has got a good place, and I am sure he will do his duty. They cannot have an abler man.'

'Vienna! that is the last city in the world in which I should expect to find Mr. Sievers. What place can he have? and what services can he perform there?'

'Many! he is to be editor of the Austrian Observer, and censor of the Austrian Press. I thought he would do well at last. All men have their imprudent day. I had. I cannot stop now. I must go and speak to the Countess von S——.'

As Vivian was doubting whether he should most grieve or laugh at this singular termination of Mr. Sievers' career, his arm was suddenly touched, and on turning round he found it was by Mr. Beckendorff.

'There is another strong argument, sir,' said the Minister, without any of the usual phrases of recognition; 'there is another strong argument against your doctrine of Destiny.' And then Mr. Becken-dorff, taking Vivian by the arm, began walking up and down part of the saloon with him; and in a few minutes, quite forgetting the scene of the discussion, he was involved in metaphysics. This incident cre-ated another great sensation, and whispers of 'secret mission, Secretary of State, decidedly a son,' &c. &c. &c. were in an instant afloat in all parts of the room.

The approach of his Royal Highness extricated Vivian from an argument which was as profound as it was interminable; and as Mr. Beckendorff retired with the Grand Duke into a recess in the ball-room, Vivian was requested by Von Neuwied to attend his Excellency the Grand Marshal.

'My dear friend,' said the Prince, 'I saw you talk-ing with a certain person. I did not say anything to you when I passed you before; but, to tell you the truth now, I was a little annoyed that he had not spoken to you. I knew you were as proud as Lucifer, and would not salute him yourself; and between our-selves I had no great wish you should, for, not to conceal it, he did not even mention your name. But the reason of this is now quite evident, and you must confess he is remarkably courteous. You know, if you remember, we thought that incognito was a little affected; rather annoying, if you recollect. I remem-ber in the green lane you gave him a gentle cut about it. It was spirited, and I dare say did good. Well! what I was going to say about that is this; I dare say now, after all,' continued his Excellency, with a knowing look, 'a certain person had very good rea-sons for that; not that he ever told them to me, nor that I have the slightest idea of them; but when a person is really so exceedingly polite and attentive, I

always think he would never do anything disagreeable without a cause; and it was exceedingly disagreeable, if you remember, my dear friend. I never
knew to whom he was speaking. Von Philipson indeed! Well! we did not think, the day we were
floundering down that turf road, that it would end in
this. Rather a more brilliant scene than the Giants'
Hall at Turriparva, I think, eh? But all men have
their imprudent days; the best way is to forget them.
There was poor Sievers; who ever did more imprudent things than he? and now it is likely he will do
very well in the world, eh? What I want of you
my dear friend, is this. There is that girl who came
with Beckendorff; who the deuce she is, I don't
know: let us hope the best! We must pay her every
attention. I dare say she is his daughter. You have
not forgotten the portrait. Well! we all were gay
once. All men have their imprudent day; why should
not Beckendorff? Speaks rather in his favour, I think.
Well, this girl; his Royal Highness very kindly made
the Crown Prince walk the Polonaise with her; very
kind of him, and very proper. What attention can
be too great for the daughter or friend of such a
man! a man who, in two words, may be said to have
made Reisenburg. For what was Reisenburg before
Beckendorff? Ah! what? Perhaps we were happier
then, after all; and then there was no Royal Highness
to bow to; no person to be condescending, except
ourselves. But never mind! we will forget. After
all, this life has its charms. What a brilliant scene!
But this girl, every attention should be paid her.
The Crown Prince was so kind as to walk the Polonaise with her. And Von Sohnspeer; he is a brute,
to be sure; but then he is a Field Marshal. Now, I

think, considering what has taken place between Beckendorff and yourself, and the very distinguished manner in which he recognised you; I think, that after all this, and considering everything, the etiquette is for you, particularly as you are a foreigner, and my personal friend — indeed, my most particular friend, for in fact, I owe everything to you, my life, and more than my life — I think, I repeat, considering all this, that the least you can do is to ask her to dance with you; and I, as the host, will introduce you. I am sorry, my dear friend,' continued his Excellency, with a look of great regret, 'to introduce you to——; but we will not speak about it. We have no right to complain of Mr. Beckendorff. No person could possibly behave to us in a manner more gentlemanlike.'

After an introductory speech in his Excellency's happiest manner, and in which an eulogium of Vivian and a compliment to the fair unknown got almost as completely entangled as the origin of slavery and the history of the feudal system in his more celebrated harangue, Vivian found himself waltzing with the anonymous beauty. The Grand Marshal, during the process of introduction, had given the young lady every opportunity of declaring her name; but every opportunity was thrown away. 'She must be incog.,' whispered his Excellency. 'Miss von Philipson, I suppose?'

Vivian was not a little desirous of discovering the nature of the relationship or connection between Beckendorff and his partner. The rapid waltz allowed no pause for conversation; but after the dance Vivian seated himself at her side, with the determination of not quickly deserting it. The lady did not even allow him the satisfaction of commencing the conversation; for no sooner was she seated than she begged to know who the person was with whom she had previously waltzed. The history of Count von Sohnspeer amused her; and no sooner had Vivian finished his anecdote than the lady said, 'Ah! I see you are an amusing person. Now tell me the history of everybody in the room.'

'Really,' said Vivian, 'I fear I shall forfeit my reputation of being amusing very speedily, for I am almost as great a stranger at this Court as you appear to be yourself. Count von Sohnspeer is too celebrated a personage at Reisenburg to have allowed even me to be long ignorant of his history; and as for the rest, so far as I can judge, they are most of them as obscure as myself, and not nearly as interesting as you are!'

'Are you an Englishman?' asked the lady.

'I am.'

'I supposed so, both from your travelling and your appearance: I think the English countenance very peculiar.'

'Indeed! we do not flatter ourselves so at home.'

'Yes! it is peculiar,' said the lady, in a tone which seemed to imply that contradiction was unusual; 'and I think that you are all handsome! I admire the English, which in this part of the world is singular; the South, you know, is generally *francisé*.'

'I am aware of that,' said Vivian. 'There, for instance, pointing to a pompous-looking personage who at that moment strutted by; 'there, for instance, is the most *francisé* person in all Reisenburg! that is our Grand Chamberlain. He considers himself a felicitous copy of Louis the Fourteenth! He allows nothing in his opinions and phrases but what is orthodox. As it generally happens in such cases, his orthodoxy is rather obsolete.'

'Who is that Knight of Malta?' asked the lady.

'The most powerful individual in the room,' answered Vivian.

'Who can he be?' asked the lady, with eagerness.

'Behold him and tremble!' rejoined Vivian: 'for with him it rests to decide whether you are civilised or a savage; whether you are to be abhorred or admired; idolised or despised. Nay, do not be alarmed! there are a few heretics, even in Reisenburg, who, like myself, value from conviction, and not from fashion, and who will be ever ready, in spite of a Von Aslingen anathema, to evince our admiration where it is due.'

The lady pleaded fatigue as an excuse for not again dancing; and Vivian did not quit her side. Her lively remarks, piquant observations, and singular questions highly amused him: and he was flattered by the evident gratification which his conversation afforded her. It was chiefly of the principal members of the Court that she spoke: she was delighted with Vivian's glowing character of Madame Carolina, whom she said she had this evening seen for the first time. Who this unknown could be was a question which often occurred to him; and the singularity of a man like Beckendorff suddenly breaking through his habits and outraging the whole system of his existence, to please a daughter, or niece, or female cousin, did not fail to strike him.

'I have the honour of being acquainted with Mr. Beckendorff,' said Vivian. This was the first time that the Minister's name had been mentioned.

'I perceived you talking with him,' was the answer.

'You are staying, I suppose, at Mr. Beckendorff's?'

'Not at present.'

'You have, of course, been at his retreat; delightful place!'

'Yes!'

'Are you an ornithologist?' asked Vivian, smiling.

'Not at all scientific; but I, of course, can now tell a lory from a Java sparrow, and a bullfinch from a canary. The first day I was there, I never shall forget the surprise I experienced, when, after the noon meal being finished, the aviary door was opened. After that I always let the creatures out myself; and one day I opened all the cages at once. If you could but have witnessed the scene! I am sure you would have been quite delighted with it. As for poor Mr. Beckendorff, I thought even he would have gone out of his mind; and when I brought in the white peacock he actually left the room in despair. Pray how do you like Madame Clara and Owlface too? Which do you think the most beautiful? I am no great favourite with the old lady. Indeed, it was very kind of Mr. Beckendorff to bear with everything as he did: I am sure he is not much used to lady visitors.'

'I trust that your visit to him will not be very short?'

'My stay at Reisenburg will not be very long,' said the young lady, with rather a grave countenance. 'Have you been here any time?'

'About a fortnight; it was a mere chance my coming at all. I was going on straight to Vienna.'

'To Vienna, indeed! Well, I am glad you did not miss Reisenburg; you must not quit it now. You know that this is not the Vienna season?'

'I am aware of it; but I am such a restless person that I never regulate my movements by those of other people.'

'But surely you find Reisenburg agreeable?'

'Very much so; but I am a confirmed wanderer.'

'Why are you?' asked the lady, with great naïveté.

Vivian looked grave; and the lady, as if she were sensible of having unintentionally occasioned him a painful recollection, again expressed her wish that he should not immediately quit the Court, and trusted that circumstances would not prevent him from acceding to her desire.

'It does not even depend upon circumstances,' said Vivian; 'the whim of the moment is my only principle of action, and therefore I may be off to-night, or be here a month hence.'

'Oh! pray stay then,' said his companion eagerly; 'I expect you to stay now. If you could only have an idea what a relief conversing with you is, after having been dragged by the Crown Prince and whirled by that Von Sohnspeer! Heigho! I could almost sigh at the very remembrance of that doleful Polonaise.'

The lady ended with a faint laugh a sentence which apparently had been commenced in no light vein. She did not cease speaking, but continued to request Vivian to remain at Reisenburg at least as long as herself. Her frequent requests were perfectly unnecessary, for the promise had been pledged at the first hint of her wish; but this was not the only time during the evening that Vivian had remarked that his interesting companion occasionally talked without apparently being sensible that she was conversing.

The young Count of Eberstein, who, to use his own phrase, was 'sadly involved,' and consequently desirous of being appointed a forest Councillor, thought that he should secure his appointment by condescending to notice the person whom he delicately styled 'the Minister's female relative.' To his great mortification and surprise, the honour was declined; and 'the female relative,' being unwilling to dance again, but perhaps feeling it necessary to break off her conversation with her late partner, it having already lasted an unusual time, highly gratified his Excellency the Grand Marshal by declaring that she would dance with Prince Maximilian. 'This, to say the least, was very attentive of Miss von Philipson.'

Little Max, who had just tact enough to discover that to be the partner of the fair incognita was the place of honour of the evening, now considered himself by much the most important personage in the room. In fact, he was only second to Emilius von Aslingen. The evident contest which was ever taking place between his natural feelings as a boy and his acquired habits as a courtier made him an amusing companion. He talked of the Gardens and the opera in a style not unworthy of the young Count of Eberstein. He thought that Madame Carolina was as charming as usual to-night; but, on the contrary, that the Countess von S—— was looking rather ill, and this put him in mind of her ladyship's new equipage; and then, apropos to equipages, what did his companion think of the new fashion of the Hungarian harness ? His lively and kind companion encouraged the boy's tattle; and, emboldened by her good nature, he soon forgot his artificial speeches, and was quickly rattling on about Turriparva, and his horses, and his dogs, and his park, and his guns, and his grooms. Soon after the waltz, the lady, taking the arm of the young Prince, walked up to Mr. Beckendorff. He received her with great attention, and led her to Madame Carolina, who rose, seated Mr. Beckendorff's 'female relative' by her side, and evidently said something extremely agreeable.

CHAPTER VI.

<small>INTERESTING STUDIES.</small>

VIVIAN had promised Madame Carolina a second English lesson on the day after the Grand Marshal's fête. The progress which the lady had made, and the talent which the gentleman had evinced during the first, had rendered Madame the most enthusiastic of pupils, and Vivian, in her estimation, the ablest of instructors. Madame Carolina's passion was patronage: to discover concealed merit, to encourage neglected genius, to reveal the mysteries of the world to a novice in mankind, or, in short, to make herself very agreeable to any one whom she fancied to be very interesting, was the great business and the great delight of her existence. No sooner had her eyes lighted on Vivian Grey than she determined to patronise. His country, his appearance, the romantic manner in which he had become connected with the Court, all pleased her lively imagination. She was intuitively acquainted with his whole history, and in an instant he was the hero of a romance, of which the presence of the principal character compensated, we may suppose, for the somewhat indefinite details.

<small>(279)</small>

His taste and literary acquirements completed the spell by which Madame Carolina was willingly enchanted. A low Dutch professor, whose luminous genius rendered unnecessary the ceremony of shaving; and a dumb dwarf, in whose interesting appearance was forgotten its perfect idiocy; a prosy improvisatore, and a South American savage, were all superseded by the appearance of Vivian Grey.

As Madame Carolina was, in fact, a charming woman, our hero had no objection to humour her harmless foibles; and not contented with making notes in an interleaved copy of her Charlemagne, he even promised to read Haroun-al-Raschid in manuscript. The consequence of his courtesy and the reward of his taste was unbounded favour. Apartments in the palace were offered him, and declined; and when Madame Carolina had become acquainted with sufficient of his real history to know that, on his part, neither wish nor necessity existed to return immediately to his own country, she tempted him to remain at Reisenburg by an offer of a place at Court; and doubtless, had he been willing, Vivian might in time have become a Lord Chamberlain, or perhaps even a Field Marshal.

On entering the room the morning in question he found Madame Carolina writing. At the end of the apartment a lady ceased, on his appearance, humming an air to which she was dancing, and at the same time imitating castanets. Madame received Vivian with expressions of delight, saying also, in a peculiar and confidential manner, that she was just sealing up a packet for him, the preface of Haroun; and then she presented him to 'the Baroness!' The lady who was lately dancing came forward. It was his unknown partner of the preceding night. 'The Baroness' extended her hand to Vivian, and unaffectedly expressed her great pleasure at seeing him again. Vivian trusted that she was not fatigued by the fête, and asked after Mr. Beckendorff. Madame Carolina was busily engaged at the moment in duly securing the precious preface. The Baroness said that Mr. Beckendorff had returned home, but that Madame Carolina had kindly insisted upon her staying at the palace. She was not the least wearied. Last night had been one of the most agreeable she had ever spent; at least she supposed she ought to say so: for if she had experienced a tedious or mournful feeling for a moment, it was hardly for what was then passing so much as for——'

'Pray, Mr. Grey,' said Madame Carolina, interrupting them, 'have you heard about our new ballet?'

'No.'

'I do not think you have ever been to our opera. To-morrow is opera night, and you must not be again away. We pride ourselves here very much upon our opera.'

'We estimate it even in England,' said Vivian, 'as possessing perhaps the most perfect orchestra now organised.'

'The orchestra is perfect. His Royal Highness is such an excellent musician, and he has spared no trouble or expense in forming it: he has always superintended it himself. But I confess I admire our ballet department still more. I expect you to be delighted with it. You will perhaps be gratified to know that the subject of our new splendid ballet, which is to be produced to-morrow, is from a great work of your illustrious poet, my Lord Byron.'

'From which?'

'The Corsair. Ah! what a sublime work! what passion! what energy! what knowledge of feminine feeling! what contrast of character! what sentiments! what situations! I wish this were opera night; Gulnare! my favourite character; beautiful! How do you think they will dress her?'

'Are you an admirer of our Byron?' asked Vivian of the Baroness.

'I think he is a very handsome man. I once saw him at the carnival at Venice.'

'But his works; his grand works! *ma chère petite*,' said Madame Carolina, in her sweetest tone; 'you have read his works?'

'Not a line,' answered the Baroness, with great naïveté; 'I never saw them.'

'*Pauvre enfant!*' said Madame Carolina; 'I will employ you, then, while you are here.'

'I never read,' said the Baroness; 'I cannot bear it. I like poetry and romances, but I like somebody to read to me.'

'Very just,' said Madame Carolina; 'we can judge with greater accuracy of the merit of a composition when it reaches our mind merely through the medium of the human voice. The soul is an essence, invisible and indivisible. In this respect the voice of man resembles the principle of his existence; since few will deny, though there are some materialists who will deny everything, that the human voice is both impalpable and audible only in one place at the same time. Hence, I ask, is it illogical to infer its indivisibility? The soul and the voice, then, are similar in two great attributes; there is a secret harmony in their spiritual construction. In the early ages of mankind a beautiful tradition was afloat that the soul and the voice were one and the same. We may perhaps recognise in this fanciful belief the effect of the fascinating and imaginative philosophy of the East; that mysterious portion of the globe,' continued Madame Carolina, 'from which we should frankly confess that we derive everything: for the South is but the pupil of the East, through the mediation of Egypt. Of this opinion,' said Madame with fervour, 'I have no doubt: of this opinion,' continued the lady with enthusiasm, 'I have boldly avowed myself a votary in a dissertation appended to the second volume of Haroun: for this opinion I would die at the stake! Oh, lovely East! why was I not oriental! Land where the voice of the nightingale is never mute! Land of the cedar and the citron, the turtle and the myrtle, of ever-blooming flowers and ever-shining skies! Illustrious East! Cradle of Philosophy! My dearest Baroness, why do not you feel as I do? From the East we obtain everything!'

'Indeed!' said the Baroness, with simplicity; 'I thought we only got shawls.'

This puzzling answer was only noticed by Vivian; for the truth is, Madame Carolina was one of those individuals who never attend to any person's answers. Always thinking of herself, she only asked questions that she herself might supply the responses. And now having made, as she flattered herself, a splendid display to her favourite critic, she began to consider what had given rise to her oration. Lord Byron and the ballet again occurred to her; and as the Baroness, at least, was not unwilling to listen, and as she herself had no manuscript of her own which she particularly wished to be perused, she proposed that Vivian should read to them part of The

Corsair, and in the original tongue. Madame Carolina opened the volume at the first prison scene between Gulnare and Conrad. It was her favourite.
Vivian read with care and feeling. Madame was in
raptures, and the Baroness, although she did not
understand a single syllable, seemed almost equally
delighted. At length Vivian came to this passage:

> My love stern Seyd's! Oh, no, no, not my love!
> Yet much this heart, that strives no more, once strove
> To meet his passion; but it would not be.
> I felt, I feel, love dwells with, with the free.
> I am a slave, a favour'd slave at best,
> To share his splendour, and seem very blest!
> Oft must my soul the question undergo,
> Of, 'Dost thou love? and burn to answer, 'No!'
> Oh! hard it is that fondness to sustain,
> And struggle not to feel averse in vain;
> But harder still the heart's recoil to bear,
> And hide from one, perhaps another there;
> He takes the hand I give not nor withhold,
> Its pulse nor checked nor quickened, calmly cold:
> And when resign'd, it drops a lifeless weight
> From one I never loved enough to hate.
> No warmth these lips return by his imprest,
> And chill'd remembrance shudders o'er the rest.
> Yes, had I ever prov'd that passion's zeal,
> The change to hatred were at least to feel:
> But still, he goes unmourn'd, returns unsought,
> And oft when present, absent from my thought.
> Or when reflection comes, and come it must,
> I fear that henceforth 'twill but bring disgust:
> I am his slave; but, in despite of pride,
> 'Twere worse than bondage to become his bride.

'Superb!' said Madame, in a voice of enthusiasm;
'how true! what passion! what energy! what sentiments! what knowledge of feminine feeling! Read it
again, I pray: it is my favourite passage.'

'What is this passage about?' asked the Baroness, with some anxiety; 'tell me.'

'I have a French translation, *ma mignonne*,' said Madame; 'you shall have it afterwards.'

'No! I detest reading,' said the young lady, with an imperious air; 'translate it to me at once.'

'You are rather a self-willed beauty!' thought Vivian; 'but your eyes are so brilliant that nothing must be refused you!' and so he translated it.

On its conclusion Madame was again in raptures. The Baroness was not less affected, but she said nothing. She appeared agitated; she changed colour, raised her beautiful eyes with an expression of sorrow, looked at Vivian earnestly, and then walked to the other end of the room. In a few moments she returned to her seat.

'I wish you would tell me the story,' she said, with earnestness.

'I have a French translation, *ma belle!*' said Madame Carolina; 'at present I wish to trouble Mr. Grey with a few questions.' Madame Carolina led Vivian into a recess.

'I am sorry we are troubled with this sweet little savage; but I think she has talent, though evidently quite uneducated. We must do what we can for her. Her ignorance of all breeding is amusing, but then I think she has a natural elegance. We shall soon polish her. His Royal Highness is so anxious that every attention should be paid to her. Beckendorff, you know, is a man of the greatest genius.' (Madame Carolina had lowered her tone about the Minister since the Prince of Little Lilliput's apostasy.) 'The country is greatly indebted to him. This, between ourselves, is his daughter. At least I have no doubt of it. Beckendorff was once married, to a lady of great rank, died early, beautiful woman, very interesting! His Royal Highness had a great regard for her. The Premier, in his bereavement, turned humourist, and has brought up this lovely girl in the oddest possible manner; nobody knows where. Now that he finds it necessary to bring her forward, he, of course, is quite at a loss. His Royal Highness has applied to me. There was a little coldness before between the Minister and myself. It is now quite removed. I must do what I can for her. I think she must marry Von Sohnspeer, who is no more Beckendorff's son than you are: or young Eberstein, or young Bernstorff, or young Gernsbach. We must do something for her. I offered her last night to Emilius von Aslingen; but he said that, unfortunately, he was just importing a savage or two of his own from the Brazils, and consequently was not in want of her.'

A chamberlain now entered, to announce the speedy arrival of his Royal Highness. The Baroness, without ceremony, expressed her great regret that he was coming, as now she should not hear the wished-for story. Madame Carolina reproved her, and the reproof was endured rather than submitted to.

His Royal Highness entered, and was accompanied by the Crown Prince. He greeted the young lady with great kindness; and even the Crown Prince, inspired by his father's unusual warmth, made a shuffling kind of bow and a stuttering kind of speech. Vivian was about to retire on the entrance of the Grand Duke, but Madame Carolina prevented him from going, and his Royal Highness, turning round, very graciously seconded her desire, and added that

Mr. Grey was the very gentleman with whom he was desirous of meeting.

'I am anxious,' said he to Vivian, in rather a low tone, 'to make Reisenburg agreeable to Mr. Beckendorff's fair friend. As you are one of the few who are honoured by his intimacy, and are familiar with some of our state secrets,' added the Grand Duke with a smile, 'I am sure it will give you pleasure to assist me in the execution of my wishes.'

His Royal Highness proposed that the ladies should ride; and he himself, with the Crown Prince and Mr. Grey, would attend them. Madame Carolina expressed her willingness; but the Baroness, like all forward girls unused to the world, suddenly grew at the same time both timid and disobliging. She looked sullen and discontented, and coolly said that she did not feel in the humour to ride for at least these two hours. To Vivian's surprise, even the Grand Duke humoured her fancy, and declared that he should then be happy to attend them after the Court dinner. Until that time Vivian was amused by Madame, and the Grand Duke exclusively devoted himself to the Baroness. His Royal Highness was in his happiest mood, and his winning manners and elegant conversation soon chased away the cloud which, for a moment, had settled on the young lady's fair brow.

CHAPTER VII.

THE ROYAL OPERA.

HE Grand Duke of Reisenburg was an enthusiastic lover of music, and his people were consequently music mad. The whole city were fiddling day and night, or blowing trumpets, oboes, and bassoons. Sunday, however, was the most harmonious day in the week. The opera amused the Court and the wealthiest citizens, and few private houses could not boast their family concert or small party of performers. In the tea-gardens, of which there were many in the suburbs of the city, bearing the euphonious, romantic, and fashionable titles of Tivoli, Arcadia, and Vauxhall, a strong and amateur orchestra was never wanting. Strolling through the city on a Sunday afternoon, many a pleasing picture of innocent domestic enjoyment might be observed. In the arbour of a garden a very stout man, with a fair, broad, good-natured, solid German face, may be seen perspiring under the scientific exertion of the French horn; himself wisely disembarrassed of the needless incumbrance of his pea-green coat and showy waistcoat, which lay neatly folded by his side; while his

(288)

large and sleepy blue eyes actually gleam with enthusiasm. His daughter, a soft and delicate girl, touches the light guitar; catching the notes of the music from the opened opera, which is placed before the father on a massy music-stand. Her voice joins in melody with her mother, who, like all German mothers, seems only her daughter's self, subdued by an additional twenty years. The bow of one violin is handled with the air of a master by an elder brother; while a younger one, an university student, grows sentimental over the flute. The same instrument is also played by a tall and tender-looking young man in black, who stands behind the parents, next to the daughter, and occasionally looks off his music-book to gaze on his young mistress's eyes. He is a clerk in a public office; and on next Michaelmas day, if he succeed, as he hopes, in gaining a small addition to his salary, he will be still more entitled to join in the Sunday family concert. Such is one of the numerous groups, the sight of which must, assuredly, give pleasure to every man who delights in seeing his fellow-creatures refreshed after their weekly labours by such calm and rational enjoyment. We would gladly linger among such scenes; and, moreover, the humours of a *guinguette* are not unworthy of our attention; but we must introduce the reader to a more important party.

The Court chapel and the Court dinner are over. We are in the opera-house of Reisenburg; and, of course, rise as the royal party enters. The house, which is of moderate size, was fitted up with splendour; we hardly know whether we should say with great taste; for, although not merely the scenery, but indeed every part of the house, was painted by

eminent artists, the style of the ornaments was rather
patriotic than tasteful. The house had been built immediately after the war, at a period when Reisenburg,
flushed with the success of its thirty thousand men,
imagined itself to be a great military nation. Trophies, standards, cannon, eagles, consequently appeared
in every corner of the opera-house; and quite superseded lyres, and timbrels, and tragic daggers, and
comic masks. The royal box was constructed in the
form of a tent, and held nearly fifty persons. It was
exactly in the centre of the house, its floor over the
back of the pit, and its roof reaching to the top of
the second circle; its crimson hangings were re-
strained by ropes of gold, and the whole was sur-
mounted by a large and radiant crown. The house
was merely lighted by a chandelier from the centre.

The opera for the evening was Rossini's Otello.
As soon as the Grand Duke entered the overture
commenced, his Royal Highness coming forward to
the front of the box and himself directing the musi-
cians, keeping time earnestly with his right hand, in
which was a long black opera-glass. This he occasionally used, but merely to look at the orchestra, not,
assuredly, to detect a negligent or inefficient per-
former; for in the schooled orchestra of Reisenburg it
would have been impossible even for the eagle eye
of his Royal Highness, assisted as it was by his long
black opera-glass, or for his fine ear, matured as it
was by the most complete study, to discover there
either inattention or feebleness. The house was perfectly silent; for when the monarch directs the orchestra the world goes to the opera to listen. Perfect
silence at Reisenburg, then, was etiquette and the
fashion. Between the acts of the opera, however,

the ballet was performed; and then everybody might talk, and laugh, and remark as much as they chose.

The Grand Duke prided himself as much upon the accuracy of his scenery and dresses and decorations as upon the exquisite skill of his performers. In truth, an opera at Reisenburg was a spectacle which could not fail to be interesting to a man of taste. When the curtain drew up the first scene presented a view of old Brabantio's house. It was accurately copied from one of the sumptuous structures of Scamozzi, or Sansovino, or Palladio, which adorn the Grand Canal of Venice. In the distance rose the domes of St. Mark and the lofty Campanile. Vivian could not fail to be delighted with this beautiful work of art, for such indeed it should be styled. He was more surprised, however, but not less pleased, on the entrance of Othello himself. In England we are accustomed to deck this adventurous Moor in the costume of his native country; but is this correct? The Grand Duke of Reisenburg thought not. Othello was an adventurer; at an early age he entered, as many foreigners did, into the service of Venice. In that service he rose to the highest dignities, became General of her armies and of her fleets, and finally the Viceroy of her favourite kingdom. Is it natural to suppose that such a man should have retained, during his successful career, the manners and dress of his original country? Ought we not rather to admit that, had he done so, his career would, in fact, not have been successful? In all probability, he imitated to affectation the manners of the country which he had adopted. It is not probable that in such or in any age the turbaned Moor would have been treated with great deference by the common Christian soldier of

Venice; or, indeed, that the scandal of a heathen leading the armies of one of the most powerful of European States would have been tolerated for an instant by indignant Christendom. If Shylock even, the Jew merchant, confined to his quarter, and herding with his own sect, were bearded on the Rialto, in what spirit would the Venetians have witnessed their doge and nobles, whom they ranked above kings, holding equal converse, and loading with the most splendid honours of the Republic a follower of Mahound? Such were the sentiments of the Grand Duke of Reisenburg on this subject, a subject interesting to Englishmen; and I confess I think that they are worthy of attention. In accordance with his opinions, the actor who performed Othello appeared in the full dress of a Venetian magnifico of the middle ages; a fit companion for Cornaro, or Grimani, or Barberigo, or Foscari.

The first act of the opera was finished. The Baroness expressed to Vivian her great delight at its being over, as she was extremely desirous of learning the story of the ballet, which she had not yet been able to acquire. His translation of yesterday had greatly interested her. Vivian shortly gave her the outline of the story of Conrad. She listened with much attention, but made no remark.

The ballet at Reisenburg was not merely a vehicle for the display of dancing. It professed by gesture and action, aided by music, to influence the minds of the spectators not less than the regular drama. Of this exhibition dancing was a casual ornament, as it is of life. It took place therefore only on fitting occasions, and grew out, in a natural manner, from some event in the history represented. For instance,

suppose the story of Othello the subject of the ballet.
The dancing, in all probability, would be introduced
at a grand entertainment given in celebration of the
Moor's arrival at Cyprus. All this would be in character. Our feelings would not be outraged by a husband chassezing forward to murder his wife, or by
seeing the pillow pressed over the innocent Desde-
mona by the impulse of a pirouette. In most cases,
therefore, the chief performers in this species of spectacle are not even dancers. This, however, may not
always be the case. If Diana be the heroine, poetical probability will not be offended by the goddess
joining in the chaste dance with her huntress nymphs;
and were the Baiadere of Goethe made the subject of
a ballet, the Indian dancing girl would naturally be
the heroine both of the drama and the poem. There
are few performances more affecting than the serious
pantomime of a master. In some of the most interesting situations it is in fact even more natural than
the oral drama, logically it is more perfect; for the
soliloquy is actually thought before us, and the magic
of the representation not destroyed by the sound of
the human voice at a moment when we all know
man never speaks.

The curtain again rises. Sounds of revelry and
triumph are heard from the Pirate Isle. They cele-
brate recent success. Various groups, accurately attired in the costume of the Greek islands, are seated
on the rocky foreground. On the left rises Medora's
tower, on a craggy steep; and on the right gleams
the blue Ægean. A procession of women enters. It
heralds the presence of Conrad and Medora; they
honour the festivity of their rude subjects. The pirates and the women join in the national dance; and

afterwards eight warriors, completely armed, move in
a warlike measure, keeping time to the music with
their bucklers and clattering sabres. Suddenly the
dance ceases; a sail is in sight. The nearest pirates
rush to the strand, and assist the disembarkation of
their welcome comrades. The commander of the
vessel comes forward with an agitated step and
gloomy countenance. He kneels to Conrad and de-
livers him a scroll, which the chieftain reads with
suppressed agitation. In a moment the faithful Juan
is at his side, the contents of the scroll revealed, the
dance broken up, and preparations made to sail in an
hour's time to the city of the Pacha. The stage is
cleared, and Conrad and Medora are alone. The
mysterious leader is wrapt in the deepest abstraction.
He stands with folded arms, and eyes fixed on the
yellow sand. A gentle pressure on his arm calls him
back to recollection; he starts, and turns to the intruder with a gloomy brow. He sees Medora, and
his frown sinks into a sad smile. 'And must we
part again! this hour, this very hour; it cannot be!'
She clings to him with agony, and kneels to him
with adoration. No hope! no hope! a quick return
promised with an air of foreboding fate. His stern
arm encircles her waist. He chases the heavy tear
from her fair cheek, and while he bids her be glad
in his absence with her handmaids peals the sad
thunder of the signal gun. She throws herself upon
him. The frantic quickness of her motion strikingly
contrasts with the former stupor of her appearance.
She will not part. Her face is buried in his breast;
her long fair hair floats over his shoulders. He is almost unnerved; but at this moment the ship sails on;
the crew and their afflicted wives enter; the page

brings to Lord Conrad his cloak, his carbine, and his bugle. He tears himself from her embrace, and without daring to look behind him bounds over the rocks, and is in the ship. The vessel moves, the wives of the pirates continue on the beach, waving their scarfs to their desolate husbands. In the foreground Medora, motionless, stands rooted to the strand, and might have inspired Phidias with a personification of Despair.

In a hall of unparalleled splendour stern Seyd reclines on innumerable pillows, placed on a carpet of golden cloth. His bearded chiefs are ranged around. The chambers are brilliantly illuminated, and an opening at the farther end of the apartments exhibits a portion of the shining city and the glittering galleys. Gulnare, covered with a silver veil, which reaches even to her feet, is ushered into the presence of the Pacha. Even the haughty Seyd rises to honour his beautiful favourite. He draws the precious veil from her blushing features and places her on his right hand. The dancing girls now appear, and then are introduced the principal artists. Now takes place the scientific part of the ballet; and here might Bias, or Noblet, or Ronzi Vestris, or her graceful husband, or the classical Albert, or the bounding Paul, vault without stint, and attitudinise without restraint, and not in the least impair the effect of the tragic tale. The Dervise, of course, appears; the galleys, of course, are fired; and Seyd, of course, retreats. A change in the scenery gives us the blazing Harem, the rescue of its inmates, the deliverance of Gulnare, the capture of Conrad.

It is the prison scene. On a mat, covered with irons, lies the forlorn Conrad. The flitting flame of a solitary lamp hardly reveals the heavy bars of the huge grate that forms the entrance to its cell. For some minutes nothing stirs. The mind of the spectator is allowed to become fully aware of the hopeless misery of the hero. His career is ended, secure is his dungeon, trusty his guards, overpowering his chains. To-morrow he wakes to be impaled. A gentle noise, so gentle that the spectator almost deems it unintentional, is now heard. A white figure appears behind the dusky gate; is it a guard or a torturer? The gate softly opens, and a female comes forward. Gulnare was represented by a girl with the body of a Peri and the soul of a poetess. The Harem Queen advances with an agitated step; she holds in her left hand a lamp, and in the girdle of her light dress is a dagger. She reaches with a soundless step the captive. He is asleep. Ay! he sleeps, while thousands are weeping over his ravage or his ruin; and she, in restlessness, is wandering here! A thousand thoughts are seen coursing over her flushed brow; she looks to the audience, and her dark eye asks why this Corsair is so dear to her. She turns again, and raises the lamp with her long white arm, that the light may fall on the captive's countenance. She gazes, without moving, on the sleeper, touches the dagger with a slow and tremulous hand, and starts from the contact with terror. She again touches it; it is drawn from her vest; it falls to the ground. He wakes; he stares with wonder; he sees a female not less fair than Medora. Confused, she tells him her station; she tells him that her pity is as certain as his doom. He avows his readiness to die; he appears undaunted, he thinks of Medora, he buries his face in his hands. She grows pale as he avows he loves —— another. She cannot

conceal her own passion. He, wondering, confesses
that he supposed her love was his enemy's, was Seyd's.
Gulnare shudders at the name; she draws herself up
to her full stature, she smiles in bitterness:

My love stern Seyd's! Oh, no, no, not my love!

The acting was perfect. The house burst into unusual shouts of admiration. Madame Carolina applauded with her little finger on her fan. The Grand
Duke himself gave the signal for applause. Vivian
never felt before that words were useless. His hand
was suddenly pressed. He turned round; it was the
Baroness. She was leaning back in her chair; and
though she did her utmost to conceal her agitated
countenance, a tear coursed down her cheek big as
the miserable Medora's!

CHAPTER VIII.

REVIEW OF THE TROOPS.

N THE evening of the opera arrived at Court part of the suite of the young Archduchess, the betrothed of the Crown Prince of Reisenburg. These consisted of an old grey-headed General, who had taught her Imperial Highness the manual exercise; and her tutor and confessor, an ancient and toothless Bishop. Their youthful mistress was to follow them in a few days; and this arrival of such a distinguished portion of her suite was the signal for the commencement of a long series of sumptuous festivities. After interchanging a number of compliments and a few snuff-boxes, the new guests were invited by his Royal Highness to attend a review, which was to take place the next morning, of five thousand troops and fifty Generals.

The Reisenburg army was the best appointed in Europe. Never were men seen with breasts more plumply padded, mustachios better trained, or such spotless gaiters. The Grand Duke himself was a military genius, and had invented a new cut for the collars of the Cavalry. His Royal Highness was par-

ticularly desirous of astonishing the old grey-headed
governor of his future daughter by the skilful evolutions and imposing appearance of his legions. The
affair was to be of the most refined nature, and the
whole was to be concluded by a mock battle, in
which the spectators were to be treated by a display
of the most exquisite evolutions and complicated
movements which human beings ever yet invented to
destroy others or to escape destruction. Field Marshal
Count von Sohnspeer, the Commander-in-Chief of all
the forces of his Royal Highness the Grand Duke of
Reisenburg, condescended, at the particular request of
his Sovereign, to conduct the whole affair himself.

At first it was rather difficult to distinguish between the army and the staff; for Darius, in the
Straits of Issus, was not more sumptuously and
numerously attended than Count von Sohnspeer.
Wherever he moved he was followed by a train of
waving plumes and radiant epaulettes, and foaming
chargers and shining steel. In fact, he looked like a
large military comet. Had the fate of Reisenburg depended on the result of the day, the Field Marshal,
and his Generals, and aides-de-camp, and orderlies,
could not have looked more agitated and more in
earnest. Von Sohnspeer had not less than four horses
in the field, on every one of which he seemed to appear in the space of five minutes. Now he was
dashing along the line of the Lancers on a black
charger, and now round the column of the Cuirassiers on a white one. He exhorted the *tirailleurs* on
a chestnut, and added fresh courage to the ardour of
the artillery on a bay.

It was a splendid day. The bands of the respective regiments played triumphant tunes as each

marched on the field. The gradual arrival of the troops was picturesque. Distant music was heard, and a corps of Infantry soon made its appearance. A light bugle sounded, and a body of *tirailleurs* issued from the shade of a neighbouring wood. The kettle-drums and clarions heralded the presence of a troop of cavalry; and an advanced guard of light horse told that the artillery were about to follow. The arms and standards of the troops shone in the sun; military music sounded in all parts of the field; un-ceasing was the bellow of the martial drum and the blast of the blood-stirring trumpet. Clouds of dust ever and anon excited in the distance denoted the arrival of a regiment of cavalry. Even now one ap-proaches; it is the Red Lancers. How gracefully their Colonel, the young Count óf Eberstein, bounds on his barb! Has Theseus turned Centaur? His spur and bridle seem rather the emblems of sovereignty than the instruments of government: he neither chas-tises nor directs. The rider moves without motion, and the horse judges without guidance. It would seem that the man had borrowed the beast's body, and the beast the man's mind. His regiment has formed upon the field, their stout lances erected like a young and leafless grove; but although now in line, it is with difficulty that they can subject the spirit of their warlike steeds. The trumpet has caught the ear of the horses; they stand with open nostrils, al-ready breathing war ere they can see an enemy; and now dashing up one leg, and now the other, they seem to complain of Nature that she has made them of anything earthly.

The troops have all arrived; there is an unusual bustle in the field. Von Sohnspeer is again changing

his horse, giving directions while he is mounting
to at least a dozen aides-de-camp. Orderlies are
scampering over every part of the field. Another
flag, quite new, and of large size, is unfurled by the
Field Marshal's pavilion. A signal gun! the music
in the whole field is hushed: a short silence of agitating suspense, another gun, and another! All the
bands of all the regiments burst forth at the same
moment into the national air: the Court dash into
the field!

Madame Carolina, the Baroness, the Countess von
S——, and some other ladies, wore habits of the
uniform of the Royal Guards. Both Madame and the
Baroness were perfect horsewomen; and the excited
spirits of Mr. Beckendorff's female relative, both during her ride and her dashing run over the field, amidst
the firing of cannon and the crash of drums and
trumpets, strikingly contrasted with her agitation and
depression of the preceding night.

'Your Excellency loves the tented field, I think!'
said Vivian, who was at her side.

'I love war! it is a diversion for kings!' was the
answer. 'How fine the breast-plates and helmets of
those cuirassiers glisten in the sun!' continued the
lady. 'Do you see Von Sohnspeer? I wonder if the
Crown Prince be with him!'

'I think he is.'

'Indeed! Ah! can he interest himself in anything? He seemed apathy itself at the opera last
night. I never saw him smile, or move, and have
scarcely heard his voice! but if he love war, if he be
a soldier, if he be thinking of other things than a
pantomime and a ball, 'tis well! very well for his
country! Perhaps he is a hero?'

At this moment the Crown Prince, who was of Von Sohnspeer's staff, slowly rode up to the royal party.

'Rudolph!' said the Grand Duke, 'do you head your regiment to-day?'

'No,' was the muttered answer.

The Grand Duke moved his horse to his son, and spoke to him in a low tone, evidently with earnestness. Apparently he was expostulating with him; but the effect of the royal exhortation was only to render the Prince's brow more gloomy, and the expression of his withered features more sullen and more sad. The Baroness watched the father and son as they were conversing with keen attention. When the Crown Prince, in violation of his father's wishes, fell into the party, and allowed his regiment to be headed by the Lieutenant-colonel, the young lady raised her lustrous eyes to heaven with that same expression of sorrow or resignation which had so much interested Vivian on the morning that he had translated to her the moving passage in the Corsair.

But the field is nearly cleared, and the mimic war has commenced. On the right appears a large body of cavalry, consisting of cuirassiers and dragoons. A vanguard of light cavalry and lancers, under the command of the Count of Eberstein, is ordered out, from this body, to harass the enemy, a strong body of infantry supposed to be advancing. Several squadrons of light horse immediately spring forward; they form themselves into line, they wheel into column, and endeavour, by well-directed manœuvres, to outflank the strong wing of the advancing enemy. After succeeding in executing all that was committed to them, and after having skirmished in the van of their own army, so as to give time for all necessary dispositions of the line of battle, the vanguard suddenly retreats between the brigades of the cavalry of the line; the prepared battery of cannon is unmasked; and a tremendous concentric fire opened on the line of the advancing foe. Taking advantage of the confusion created by this unexpected salute of his artillery, Von Sohnspeer, who commands the cavalry, gives the word to 'Charge!'

The whole body of cavalry immediately charge in masses; the extended line of the enemy is as immediately broken. But the infantry, who are commanded by one of the royal relatives and visitors, the Prince of Pike and Powdren, dexterously form into squares and commence a masterly retreat in square battalions. At length they take up a more favourable position than the former one. They are again galled by the artillery, who have proportionately advanced, and again charged by the cavalry in their huge masses. And now the squares of infantry partially give way. They admit the cavalry, but the exulting horse find, to their dismay, that the enemy are not routed, but that there are yet inner squares formed at salient angles. The cavalry for a moment retire, but it is only to give opportunity to their artillery to rake the obstinate foes. The execution of the battery is fearful. Headed by their commander, the whole body of cuirassiers and dragoons again charge with renewed energy and concentrated force. The infantry are thrown into the greatest confusion, and commence a rout, increased and rendered irremediable by the lancers and hussars, the former vanguard, who now, seizing on the favourable moment, again rush forward, increasing the effect of the charge of the whole army, overtaking the fugitives with their lances, and securing the prisoners.

The victorious Von Sohnspeer, followed by his staff, now galloped up to receive the congratulations of his Sovereign.

'Where are your prisoners, Field Marshal?' asked his Royal Highness, with a flattering smile.

'What is the ransom of our unfortunate guest?' asked Madame Carolina.

'I hope we shall have another affair,' said the Baroness, with a flushed face and glowing eyes.

But the Commander-in-Chief must not tarry to bandy compliments. He is again wanted in the field. The whole troops have formed in line. Some most scientific evolutions are now executed. With them we will not weary the reader, nor dilate on the comparative advantages of forming *en cremaillière* and *en echiquier;* nor upon the duties of *tirailleurs*, nor upon concentric fires and eccentric movements, nor upon deploying, nor upon enfilading, nor upon oblique fronts, nor upon *échelons*. The day finished by the whole of the troops again forming in line and passing in order before the Commander-in-Chief, to give him an opportunity of observing their discipline and inspecting their equipments.

The review being finished, Count von Sohnspeer and his staff joined the royal party; and after walking their horses round the field, they proceeded to his pavilion, where refreshments were prepared for them. The Field Marshal, flattered by the interest which the young Baroness had taken in the business of the day, and the acquaintance which she evidently possessed of the more obvious details of military tactics, was inclined to be particularly courteous to her;

but the object of his admiration did not encourage attentions by which half the ladies of the Court would have thought themselves as highly honoured as by those of the Grand Duke himself; so powerful a person was the Field Marshal, and so little inclined by temper to cultivate the graces of the fair sex.

'In the tent keep by my side,' said the Baroness to Vivian. 'Although I am fond of heroes, Von Sohnspeer is not to my taste. I know not why I flatter you so by my notice, for I suppose, like all Englishmen, you are not a soldier? I thought so. Never mind! you ride well enough for a field marshal. I really think I could give you a commission without much stickling of my conscience. No, no! I should like you nearer me. I have a good mind to make you my master of the horse; that is to say, when I am entitled to have one.'

As Vivian acknowledged the young Baroness's compliment by becoming emotion, and vowed that an office near her person would be the consummation of all his wishes, his eye caught the lady's: she blushed deeply, looked down upon her horse's neck, and then turned away her head.

Von Sohnspeer's pavilion excellently became the successful leader of the army of Reisenburg. Trophies taken from all sides decked its interior. The black eagle of Austria formed part of its roof, and the brazen eagle of Gaul supported part of the side. The grey-headed General looked rather grim when he saw a flag belonging to a troop which perhaps he had himself once commanded. He vented his indignation to the toothless Bishop, who crossed his breast with his fingers, covered with diamonds, and preached temperance and moderation in inarticulate sounds.

During the collation the conversation was principally military. Madame Carolina, who was entirely ignorant of the subject of discourse, enchanted all the officers present by appearing to be the most interested person in the tent. Nothing could exceed the elegance of her eulogium of *petit guerre.* The old grey General talked much about the 'good old times,' by which he meant the thirty years of plunder, bloodshed, and destruction, which were occasioned by the French Revolution. He gloated on the recollections of horror, which he feared would never occur again. The Archduke Charles and Prince Schwartzenburg were the gods of his idolatry, and Nadasti's hussars and Wurmser's dragoons the inferior divinities of his bloody heaven. One evolution of the morning, a discovery made by Von Sohnspeer himself, in the deploying of cavalry, created a great sensation; and it was settled that it would have been of great use to Desaix and Clairfait in the Netherlands affair of some eight-and-twenty years ago, and was not equalled even by Seidlitz' cavalry in the affair with the Russians at Zorndorff. In short, every 'affair' of any character during the late war was fought over again in the tent of Field Marshal von Sohnspeer. At length from the Archduke Charles and Prince Schwartzenburg, the old grey-headed General got to Polybius and Monsieur Folard; and the Grand Duke now thinking that the 'affair' was taking too serious a turn, broke up the party. Madame Carolina and most of the ladies used their carriages on their return. They were nearly fifteen miles from the city; but the Baroness, in spite of the most earnest solicitations, would remount her charger.

They cantered home, the Baroness in unusual spir-

its, Vivian thinking very much of his fair companion. Her character puzzled him. That she was not
the lovely simpleton that Madame Carolina believed
her to be, he had little doubt. Some people have
great knowledge of society and little of mankind.
Madame Carolina was one of these. She viewed her
species through only one medium. That the Baroness was a woman of acute feeling, Vivian could not
doubt. Her conduct at the opera, which had escaped every one's attention, made this evident. That
she had seen more of the world than her previous
conversation had given him to believe, was equally
clear by her conduct and conversation this morning.
He determined to become more acquainted with her
character. Her evident partiality to his company
would not render the execution of his purpose very
difficult. At any rate, if he discovered nothing, it
was something to do: it would at least amuse him.

In the evening he joined a large party at the palace. He looked immediately for the Baroness. She
was surrounded by the dandies. Their attentions she
treated with contempt, and ridiculed their compliments without mercy. Without obtruding himself on
her notice, Vivian joined her circle, and witnessed
her demolition of the young Count of Eberstein with
great amusement. Emilius von Aslingen was not
there; for having made the interesting savage the
fashion, she was no longer worthy of his attention,
and consequently deserted. The young lady soon observed Vivian; and saying, without the least embarrassment that she was delighted to see him, she
begged him to share her *chaise-longue*. Her envious
levée witnessed the preference with dismay; and as
the object of their attention did not now notice their

remarks, even by her expressed contempt, one by one fell away. Vivian and the Baroness were left alone, and conversed much together. The lady displayed, on every subject, engaging ignorance, and requested information on obvious topics with artless naïveté. Vivian was convinced that her ignorance was not affected, and equally sure that it could not arise from imbecility of intellect; for while she surprised him by her crude questions, and her want of acquaintance with all those topics which generally form the staple of conversation, she equally amused him with her poignant wit, and the imperious and energetic manner in which she instantly expected satisfactory information on every possible subject.

CHAPTER IX.

A Brilliant Bal Masqué.

N THE day after the review a fancy-dress ball was to be given at Court. It was to be an entertainment of a peculiar nature. The lively genius of Madame Carolina, wearied of the commonplace effect generally produced by this species of amusement, in which usually a stray Turk and a wandering Pole looked sedate and singular among crowds of Spanish girls, Swiss peasants, and gentlemen in uniforms, had invented something novel. Her idea was ingenious. To use her own sublime phrase, she determined that the party should represent 'an age!' Great difficulty was experienced in fixing upon the century which was to be honoured. At first a poetical idea was started of having something primeval, perhaps antediluvian; but Noah, or even Father Abraham, were thought characters hardly sufficiently romantic for a fancy-dress ball, and consequently the earliest postdiluvian ages were soon under consideration. Nimrod, or Sardanapalus, were distinguished personages, and might be well represented by the Master of the Staghounds, or the Master of the Revels; but then the want of an interesting lady character was a great objection.

Semiramis, though not without style in her own way, was not sufficiently Parisian for Madame Carolina. New ages were proposed and new objections started; and so the 'Committee of Selection,' which consisted of Madame herself, the Countess von S——, and a few other dames of fashion, gradually slided through the four great empires. Athens was not aristocratic enough, and then the women were nothing. In spite of her admiration of the character of Aspasia, Madame Carolina somewhat doubted the possibility of persuading the ladies of the Court of Reisenburg to appear in the characters of history. Rome presented great capabilities, and greater difficulties. Finding themselves, after many days' sitting and study, still very far from coming to a decision, Madame called in the aid of the Grand Duke, who proposed 'something national.' The proposition was plausible; but, according to Madame Carolina, Germany, until her own time, had been only a land of barbarism and barbarians; and therefore in such a country, in a national point of view, what could there be interesting? The middle ages, as they are usually styled, in spite of the Emperor Charlemagne, 'that oasis in the desert of barbarism,' to use her own eloquent and original image, were her particular aversion. 'The age of chivalry is past!' was as constant an exclamation of Madame Carolina as it was of Mr. Burke. 'The age of chivalry is past; and very fortunate that it is. What resources could they have had in the age of chivalry? an age without either moral or experimental philosophy; an age in which they were equally ignorant of the doctrine of association of ideas, and of the doctrine of electricity; and when they were as devoid of a knowledge of the incalculable powers of the human mind as of the incalculable powers of steam!' Had Madame Carolina been the consort of an Italian grand duke, selection would not be difficult; and, to inquire no farther, the court of the Medici alone would afford them everything they wanted. But Germany never had any character, and never produced nor had been the resort of illustrious men and interesting persons. What was to be done? The age of Frederick the Great was the only thing; and then that was so recent, and would offend the Austrians: it could not be thought of.

At last, when the 'Committee of Selection' was almost in despair, some one proposed a period which not only would be German, not only would compliment the House of Austria, but, what was of still greater importance, would allow of every contemporary character of interest of every nation, the age of Charles the Fifth! The suggestion was received with enthusiasm, and adopted on the spot. 'The Committee of Selection' was immediately dissolved, and its members as immediately formed themselves into a 'Committee of Arrangement.' Lists of all the persons of any fame, distinction, or notoriety, who had lived either in the empire of Germany, the kingdoms of Spain, Portugal, France, or England, the Italian States, the Netherlands, the Americas, and, in short, in every country in the known world, were immediately formed. Von Chronicle, rewarded for his last historical novel by a ribbon and the title of Baron, was appointed secretary to the 'Committee of Costume.' All guests who received a card of invitation were desired, on or before a certain day, to send in the title of their adopted character and a sketch of their intended dress, that their plans might receive the sanction of the ladies of the 'Committee of Arrangement,' and their dresses the approbation of the secretary of costume. By this method the chance and inconvenience of two persons selecting and appearing in the same character were destroyed and prevented. After exciting the usual jealousies, intrigues, dissatisfaction, and ill-blood, by the influence and imperturbable temper of Madame Carolina, everything was arranged; Emilius von Aslingen being the only person who set both the Committees of Arrangement and Costume at defiance, and treated the repeated applications of their respected secretary with contemptuous silence. The indignant Baron von Chronicle entreated the strong interference of the 'Committee of Arrangement,' but Emilius von Aslingen was too powerful an individual to be treated by others as he treated them. Had the fancy-dress ball of the Sovereign been attended by all his subjects, with the exception of this Captain in his Guards, the whole affair might have been a failure; would have been dark in spite of the glare of ten thousand lamps and the glories of all the jewels of his state; would have been dull, although each guest were wittier than Pasquin himself; and very vulgar, although attended by lords of as many quarterings as the ancient shield of his own antediluvian house! All, therefore, that the ladies of the 'Committee of Arrangement' could do, was to enclose to the rebellious Von Aslingen a list of the expected characters, and a resolution passed in consequence of his contumacy, that no person or persons was, or were, to appear as either or any of these characters, unless he, or they, could produce a ticket, or tickets, granted by a member of the 'Committee of Arrangement,' and countersigned by the secretary of the 'Committee of Costume.' At the same time that these vigorous measures were resolved on, no persons spoke of Emilius von Aslingen's rebellious conduct in terms of greater admiration than the ladies of the Committee themselves. If possible, he in consequence became even a more influential and popular personage than before, and his conduct procured him almost the adoration of persons who, had they dared to imitate him, would have been instantly crushed, and would have been banished society principally by the exertions of the very individual whom they had the presumption to mimic.

In the gardens of the palace was a spacious amphitheatre, cut out in green seats, for the spectators of the plays which, during the summer months, were sometimes performed there by the Court. There was a stage in the same taste, with rows of trees for side-scenes, and a great number of arbours and summer-rooms, surrounded by lofty hedges of laurel, for the actors to retire and dress in. Connected with this 'rural theatre,' for such was its title, were many labyrinths, and groves, and arched walks, in the same style. More than twelve large fountains were in the immediate vicinity of this theatre. At the end of one walk a sea-horse spouted its element through its nostrils; and in another, Neptune turned an ocean out of a vase. Seated on a rock, Arcadia's half-goat god, the deity of silly sheep and silly poets, sent forth trickling streams through his rustic pipes; and in the centre of a green grove, an enamoured Salmacis, bathing in a pellucid basin, seemed watching for her Hermaphrodite.

It was in this rural theatre and its fanciful confines that Madame Carolina and her councillors resolved

that their magic should, for a night, not only stop
the course of time, but recall past centuries. It was
certainly rather late ₁in the year for choosing such a
spot for the scene of their enchantment; but the season, as we have often had occasion to remark in the
course of these volumes, was singularly fine; and indeed at this moment the nights were as warm, and
as clear from mist and dew, as they are during an
Italian midsummer.

But it is eight o'clock; we are already rather late.
Is that a figure by Holbein, just started out of the
canvas, that I am about to meet? Stand aside! It is
a page of the Emperor Charles the Fifth! The Court
is on its way to the theatre. The theatre and the
gardens are brilliantly illuminated. The effect of the
thousands of coloured lamps, in all parts of the foliage,
is very beautiful. The moon is up, and a million
stars! If it be not quite as light as day, it is just
light enough for pleasure. You could not perhaps
endorse a bill of exchange, or engross a parchment,
by this light; but then it is just the light to read a
love-letter by, and do a thousand other things besides.

All hail to the Emperor! we would give his costume were it not rather too much in the style of the
Von Chronicles. Reader! you have seen a portrait of
Charles by Holbein: very well; what need is there of
a description? No lack was there in this gay scene
of massy chains and curious collars, nor of cloth of
gold, nor of cloth of silver! No lack was there of
trembling plumes and costly hose! No lack was there
of crimson velvet, and russet velvet, and tawny
velvet, and purple velvet, and plunket velvet, and of
scarlet cloth, and green taffeta, and cloth of silk em-

broidered! No lack was there of garments of estate, and of quaint chemews, nor of short crimson cloaks, covered with pearls and precious stones! No lack was there of party-coloured splendour, of purple velvet embroidered with white, and white satin dresses embroidered with black! No lack was there of splendid koyfes of damask, or kerchiefs of fine Cyprus; nor of points of Venice silver of ducat fineness, nor of garlands of friars' knots, nor of coloured satins, nor of bleeding hearts embroidered on the bravery of dolorous lovers, nor of quaint sentences of wailing gallantry! But for the details, are they not to be found in those much-neglected and much-plundered persons, the old chroniclers? and will they not sufficiently appear in the most inventive portion of the next great historical novel?

The Grand Duke looked the Emperor. Our friend the Grand Marshal was Francis the First; and Arnelm and Von Neuwied figured as the Marshal of Montmorency and the Marshal Lautrec. The old toothless Bishop did justice to Clement the Seventh; and his companion, the ancient General, looked grim as Pompeo Colonna. A prince of the House of Nassau, one of the royal visitors, represented his adventurous ancestor the Prince of Orange. Von Sohnspeer was that haughty and accomplished rebel, the Constable of Bourbon. The young Baron Gernsbach was worthy of the seraglio, as he stalked along as Solyman the Magnificent, with all the family jewels belonging to his dowager mother shining in his superb turban. Our friend the Count of Eberstein personified chivalry, in the person of Bayard. The younger Bernstorff, the intimate friend of Gernsbach, attended his sumptuous sovereign as that Turkish Paul Jones, Barbarossa. An

Italian Prince was Andrew Doria. The Grand Chamberlain, our *francisé* acquaintance, and who affected a love of literature, was the Protestant Elector of Saxony. His train consisted of the principal litterateurs of Reisenburg. The Editor of the 'Attack-all Review,' who originally had been a Catholic, but who had been skilfully converted some years ago, when he thought Catholicism was on the decline, was Martin Luther, an individual whom, both in his apostasy and fierceness, he much and only resembled: on the contrary, the editor of the 'Praise-all Review' appeared as the mild and meek Melanchthon. Mr. Sievers, not yet at Vienna, was Erasmus. Ariosto, Guicciardini, Ronsard, Rabelais, Machiavel, Pietro Aretino, Garcilasso de la Vega, Sannazaro, and Paracelsus, afforded names to many nameless critics. Two Generals, brothers, appeared as Cortes and Pizarro. The noble Director of the Gallery was Albert Dürer, and his deputy Hans Holbein. The Court painter, a wretched mimic of the modern French school, did justice to the character of Correggio; and an indifferent sculptor looked sublime as Michael Angelo.

Von Chronicle had persuaded the Prince of Pike and Powdren, one of his warmest admirers, to appear as Henry the Eighth of England. His Highness was one of those true North German patriots who think their own country a very garden of Eden, and verily believe that original sin is to be finally put an end to in a large sandy plain between Berlin and Hanover. The Prince of Pike and Powdren passed his whole life in patriotically sighing for the concentration of all Germany into one great nation, and in secretly trusting that, if ever the consummation took place, the North would be rewarded for their condescending union by a monopoly of all the privileges of the Empire. Such a character was of course extremely desirous of figuring to-night in a style peculiarly national. The persuasions of Von Chronicle, however, prevailed, and induced his Highness of Pike and Powdren to dismiss his idea of appearing as the ancient Arminius, although it was with great regret that the Prince gave up his plan of personating his favourite hero, with hair down to his middle and skins up to his chin. Nothing would content Von Chronicle but that his kind patron should represent a crowned head: anything else was beneath him. The patriotism of the Prince disappeared before the flattery of the novelist, like the bloom of a plum before the breath of a boy, when he polishes the powdered fruit ere he devours it. No sooner had his Highness agreed to be changed into bluff Harry than the secret purpose of his adviser was immediately detected. No Court confessor, seduced by the vision of a red hat, ever betrayed the secrets of his sovereign with greater fervour than did Von Chronicle labour for the Cardinal's costume, which was the consequence of the Prince of Pike and Powdren undertaking the English monarch. To-night, proud as was the part of the Prince as regal Harry, his strut was a shamble compared with the imperious stalk of Von Chronicle as the arrogant and ambitious Wolsey. The Cardinal in Rienzi was nothing to him; for to-night Wolsey had as many pages as the other had petticoats!

But, most ungallant of scribblers! *Place aux dames!* Surely Madame Carolina, as the beautiful and accomplished Margaret of Navarre, might well command, even without a mandate, your homage and your admiration! The lovely Queen seemed the very goddess of smiles and repartee; young Max, as her page, carried at her side a painted volume of her own poetry. The arm of the favourite sister of Francis, who it will be remembered once fascinated even the Emperor, was linked in that of Cæsar's natural daughter, her beautiful namesake, the bright-eyed Margaret of Austria. Conversing with these royal dames, and indeed apparently in attendance upon them, was a young gallant of courtly bearing, and attired in a fantastic dress. It is Clement Marot, 'the Poet of Princes and the Prince of Poets,' as he was styled by his own admiring age; he offers to the critical inspection of the nimble-witted Navarre a few lines in celebration of her beauty and the night's festivity; one of those short Marotique poems once so celebrated; perhaps a page culled from those gay and airy psalms which, with characteristic gallantry, he dedicated 'to the Dames of France!' Observe well the fashionable bard! Marot was a true poet, and in his day not merely read by queens and honoured by courtiers: observe him well; for the character is supported by our Vivian Grey. It was with great difficulty that Madame Carolina had found a character for her favourite, for the lists were all filled before his arrival at Reisenburg. She at first wished him to appear as some celebrated Englishman of the time, but no character of sufficient importance could be discovered. All our countrymen in contact or connection with the Emperor Charles were churchmen and civilians; and Sir Nicholas Carew and the other fops of the reign of Henry the Eighth, who, after the visit to Paris, were even more ridiculously *francisé* than the Grand Chamberlain of Reisenburg himself, were not, after mature deliberation, considered entitled to the honour of being ranked in Madame Carolina's age of Charles the Fifth.

But who is this, surrounded by her ladies and her chamberlains and her secretaries? Four pages in dresses of cloth of gold, and each the son of a prince of the French blood, support her train; a crown encircles locks grey as much from thought as from time, but which require no show of loyalty to prove that they belong to a mother of princes; that ample forehead, aquiline nose, and the keen glance of her piercing eye denote the Queen as much as the regality of her gait and her numerous and splendid train. The young Queen of Navarre hastens to proffer her duty to the mother of Francis, the celebrated Louise of Savoy; and exquisitely did the young and lovely Countess of S—— personate the most celebrated of female diplomatists.

We have forgotten one character; the repeated commands of his father and the constant entreaties of Madame Carolina had at length prevailed upon the Crown Prince to shuffle himself into a fancy dress. No sooner had he gratified them by his hard-wrung consent than Baron von Chronicle called upon him with drawings of the costume of the Prince of Asturias, afterwards Philip the Second of Spain. If we for a moment forgot so important a personage as the future Grand Duke, it must have been because he supported his character so ably that no one for an instant believed that it was an assumed one; standing near the side scenes of the amphitheatre, with his gloomy brow, sad eye, protruding under-lip, and arms hanging straight by his sides, he looked a bigot without hope, and a tyrant without purpose.

The first hour is over, and the guests are all assembled. As yet they content themselves with promenading round the amphitheatre; for before they can think of dance or stroll, each of them must be duly acquainted with the other's dress. It was a most splendid scene. The Queen of Navarre has now been presented to the Emperor, and, leaning on his arm, they head the promenade. The Emperor had given the hand of Margaret of Austria to his legitimate son; but the Crown Prince, though he continued in silence by the side of the young Baroness, soon resigned a hand which did not struggle to retain his. Clement Marot was about to fall back into a less conspicuous part of the procession; but the Grand Duke, witnessing the regret of his loved consort, condescendingly said, 'We cannot afford to lose our poet;' and so Vivian found himself walking behind Madame Carolina, and on the left side of the young Baroness. Louise of Savoy followed with her son, the King of France; most of the ladies of the Court, and a crowd of officers, among them Montmorency and De Lautrec, after their Majesties. The King of England moves by; his state unnoticed in the superior magnificence of Wolsey. Pompeo Colonna apologises to Pope Clement for having besieged His Holiness in the Castle of St. Angelo. The Elector of Saxony and the Prince of Orange follow. Solyman the Magnificent is attended by his Admiral; and Bayard's pure spirit almost quivers at the whispered treason of the Constable of Bourbon. Luther and Melanchthon, Erasmus and Rabelais, Cortez and Pizarro, Correggio and Michael Angelo, and a long train of dames and dons of all nations, succeed; so long that the amphitheatre cannot hold them, and the procession, that all may walk over the stage, makes a short progress through an adjoining summer-room.

Just as the Emperor and the fair Queen are in the middle of the stage, a wounded warrior with a face pale as an eclipsed moon, a helmet on which is painted the sign of his sacred order, a black mantle thrown over his left shoulder, but not concealing his armour, a sword in his right hand and an outstretched crucifix in his left, rushes on the scene. The procession suddenly halts; all recognise Emilius von Aslingen! and Madame Carolina blushes through her rouge when she perceives that so celebrated, 'so interesting a character' as Ignatius Loyola, the Founder of the Jesuits, has not been included in the all-comprehensive lists of her committee.

2 B. D.—21

CHAPTER X.

ENRY of England led the Polonaise with Louise of Savoy; Margaret of Austria would not join in it: waltzing quickly followed. The Emperor seldom left the side of the Queen of Navarre, and often conversed with her Majesty's poet. The Prince of Asturias hovered for a moment round his father's daughter, as if he were summoning resolution to ask her to waltz. Once, indeed, he opened his mouth; could it have been to speak? But the young Margaret gave no encouragement to this unusual exertion; and Philip of Asturias, looking, if possible, more sad and sombre than before, skulked away. The Crown Prince left the gardens, and now a smile lit up every face, except that of the young Baroness. The gracious Grand Duke, unwilling to see a gloomy countenance anywhere to-night, turned to Vivian, who was speaking to Madame Carolina, and said, 'Gentle poet, would that thou hadst some *chanson* or courtly compliment to chase the cloud which hovers on the brow of our much-loved daughter of Austria! Your popularity, sir,' continued the Grand Duke, dropping his mock heroic vein and speaking in a much lower tone, 'your popularity, sir, among the ladies of the Court, cannot be increased by any panegyric of mine; nor am I insensible, believe me, to the assiduity and skill with which you have complied with my wishes in making our Court agreeable to the relative of a man to whom we owe so much as Mr. Beckendorff. I am informed, Mr. Grey,' continued his Royal Highness, 'that you have no intention of very speedily returning to your country; I wish that I could count you among my peculiar attendants. If you have an objection to live in the palace without performing your quota of duty to the State, we shall have no difficulty in finding you an office, and clothing you in our official costume. Think of this!' So saying, with a gracious smile, his Royal Highness, leading Madame Carolina, commenced a walk round the gardens.

The young Baroness did not follow them. Solyman the Magnificent, and Bayard the irreproachable, and Barbarossa the pirate, and Bourbon the rebel, immediately surrounded her. Few persons were higher *ton* than the Turkish Emperor and his Admiral; few persons talked more agreeable nonsense than the Knight *sans peur et sans reproche;* no person was more important than the warlike Constable; but their attention, their amusement, and their homage were to-night thrown away on the object of their observance. The Baroness listened to them without interest, and answered them with brevity. She did not even condescend, as she had done before, to enter into a war of words, to mortify their vanity or exercise their wit. She treated them neither with contempt nor courtesy. If no smile welcomed their remarks, at least her silence was not scornful, and the most shallow-headed prater that fluttered around her felt that he was received with dignity and not with disdain. Awed by her conduct, not one of them dared to be flippant, and every one of them soon became dull. The ornaments of the Court of Reisenburg, the arbiters of *ton* and the lords of taste, stared with astonishment at each other when they found, to their mutual surprise, that at one moment, in such a select party, universal silence pervaded. In this state of affairs, every one felt that his dignity required his speedy disappearance from the lady's presence. The Orientals, taking advantage of Bourbon's returning once more to the charge with an often unanswered remark, coolly walked away: the Chevalier made an adroit and honourable retreat by joining a passing party; and the Constable was the only one who, being left in solitude and silence, was finally obliged to make a formal bow and retire discomfited from the side of the only woman with whom he had ever condescended to fall in love. Leaning against the trunk of a tree at some little distance, Vivian Grey watched the formation and dissolution of the young Baroness's levée with lively interest. His eyes met the lady's as she raised them from the ground on Von Sohnspeer quitting her. She immediately beckoned to Vivian, but without her usual smile. He was directly at her side, but she did not speak. At last he said, 'This is a most brilliant scene!'

'You think so, do you?' answered the lady, in a tone and manner which almost made Vivian believe, for a moment, that his friend Mr. Beckendorff was at his side.

'Decidedly his daughter!' thought he.

'You are not gay to-night?' said Vivian.

'Why should I be?' said the lady, in a manner which would have made Vivian imagine that his presence was as disagreeable to her as that of Count von Sohnspeer, had not the lady herself invited his company.

'I suppose the scene is very brilliant,' continued the Baroness, after a few moments' silence. 'At least all here seem to think so, except two persons.'

'And who are they?' asked Vivian.

'Myself and —— the Crown Prince. I am almost sorry that I did not dance with him. There seems a wonderful similarity in our dispositions.'

'You are pleased to be severe to-night.'

'And who shall complain when the first person that I satirize is myself?'

'It is most considerate in you,' said Vivian, 'to undertake such an office; for it is one which you yourself are alone capable of fulfilling. The only person that can ever satirize your Excellency is yourself; and I think even then that, in spite of your candour, your self-examination must please us with a self-panegyric.'

'Nay, a truce to compliments: at least let me hear better things from you. I cannot any longer endure the glare of these lamps and dresses! your arm! Let us walk for a few minutes in the more retired and cooler parts of the gardens.'

The Baroness and Vivian left the amphitheatre by a different path to that by which the Grand Duke and Madame Carolina had quitted it. They found the walks quite solitary; for the royal party, which was small, contained the only persons who had yet left the stage.

Vivian and his companion strolled about for some time, conversing on subjects of casual interest. The Baroness, though no longer absent, either in her manner or her conversation, seemed depressed; and Vivian, while he flattered himself that he was more entertaining than usual, felt, to his mortification, that the lady was not entertained.

'I am afraid you find it dull here,' said he; 'shall we return?'

'Oh, no; do not let us return! We have so short a time to be together that we must not allow even one hour to be dull.'

As Vivian was about to reply,' he heard the joyous voice of young Maximilian; it sounded very near. The royal party was approaching. The Baroness expressed her earnest desire to avoid it; and as to advance or to retreat, in these labyrinthine walks, was almost equally hazardous, they retired into one of those green recesses which we have before mentioned; indeed it was the very evergreen grove in the centre of which the nymph of the fountain watched for her loved Carian youth. A shower of moonlight fell on the marble statue, and showed the nymph in an attitude of consummate skill: her modesty struggling with her desire, and herself crouching in her hitherto pure waters, while her anxious ear listens for the bounding step of the regardless huntsman.

'The air is cooler here,' said the Baroness, 'or the sound of the falling water is peculiarly refreshing to my senses. They have passed. I rejoice that we did not return; I do not think that I could have remained among those lamps another moment. How singular actually to view with aversion a scene which appears to enchant all!'

'A scene which I should have thought would have been particularly charming to you,' said Vivian; 'you are dispirited to-night!'

'Am I?' said the Baroness. 'I ought not to be; not to be more dispirited than I ever am. To-night I expected pleasure; nothing has happened which I did not expect, and everything which I did. And yet I am sad! Do you think that happiness can ever be sad? I think it must be so. But whether I am sorrowful or happy I can hardly tell; for it is only within these few days that I have known either grief or joy.'

'It must be counted an eventful period in your existence which reckons in its brief hours a first acquaintance with such passions!' said Vivian, with a searching eye and inquiring voice.

'Yes; an eventful period, certainly an eventful period,' answered the Baroness, with a thoughtful air and in measured words.

'I cannot bear to see a cloud upon that brow!' said Vivian. 'Have you forgotten how much was to be done to-night? How eagerly you looked forward to its arrival? How bitterly we were to regret the termination of the mimic empire?'

'I have forgotten nothing; would that I had! I will not look grave. I will be gay; and yet, when I remember how soon other mockery besides this splendid pageant must be terminated, why should I look gay? Why may I not weep?'

'Nay, if we are to moralise on worldly felicity, I fear that instead of inspiriting you, which is my wish, I shall prove but a too congenial companion. But such a theme is not for you.'

'And why should it be for one who, though he lecture me with such gravity and gracefulness, can scarcely be entitled to play the part of mentor by the weight of years?' said the Baroness with a smile; 'for one who, I trust, who I should think, as little deserved, and was as little inured to, sorrow as myself!'

'To find that you have cause to grieve,' said Vivian, 'and to learn from you, at the same time, your opinion of my own lot, prove what I have too often had the sad opportunity of observing, that the face of man is scarcely more genuine and less deceitful than these masquerade dresses which we now wear.'

'But you are not unhappy?' asked the Baroness with a quick voice.

'Not now,' said Vivian.

His companion seated herself on the marble balustrade which surrounded the fountain: she did not immediately speak again, and Vivian was silent, for he was watching her motionless countenance as her large brilliant eyes gazed with earnestness on the falling water sparkling in the moonlight. Surely it was not the mysterious portrait at Beckendorff's that he beheld!

She turned. She exclaimed in an agitated voice, 'O friend! too lately found, why have we met to part?'

'To part, dearest!' said he, in a low and rapid voice, and he gently took her hand; 'to part! and why should we part? why ——'

'Ask not; your question is agony!' She tried to withdraw her hand, he pressed it with renewed energy, it remained in his, she turned away her head, and both were silent.

'O! lady,' said Vivian, as he knelt at her side, 'why are we not happy?'

His arm is round her waist, gently he bends his head, their speaking eyes meet, and their trembling lips cling into a kiss!

A seal of love and purity and faith! and the chaste moon need not have blushed as she lit up the countenances of the lovers.

'O! lady, why are we not happy?'

'We are, we are: is not this happiness, is not this joy, is not this bliss? Bliss,' she continued, in a low broken voice, 'to which I have no right, no title. Oh! quit, quit my hand! Happiness is not for me!' She extricated herself from his arm, and sprang upon her feet. Alarm, rather than affection, was visible on her agitated features. It seemed to cost her a great effort to collect her scattered senses; the effort was made with pain, but with success.

'Forgive me,' she said, in a hurried and indistinct tone; 'forgive me! I would speak, but cannot, not now at least; we have been long away, too long; our absence will be remarked to-night; to-night we must give up to the gratification of others, but I will speak. For yours, for my own sake, let us — let us go. You know that we are to be very gay to-night, and gay we will be. Who shall prevent us? At least the present hour is our own; and when the future ones must be so sad, why — why trifle with this?'

CHAPTER XI.

More Mystery.

HE reader is not to suppose that Vivian Grey thought of the young Baroness merely in the rapid scenes which we have sketched. There were few moments in the day in which her image did not occupy his thoughts, and which, indeed, he did not spend in her presence. From the first her character had interested him. His accidental but extraordinary acquaintance with Beckendorff made him view any individual connected with that singular man with a far more curious feeling than could influence the young nobles of the Court, who were ignorant of the Minister's personal character. There was an evident mystery about the character and situation of the Baroness, which well accorded with the eccentric and romantic career of the Prime Minister of Reisenburg. Of the precise nature of her connection with Beckendorff Vivian was wholly ignorant. The world spoke of her as his daughter, and the affirmation of Madame Carolina confirmed the world's report. Her name was still unknown to him; and although during the few moments that they had enjoyed an opportunity of conversing together alone, Vivian had made every exertion of which good breeding, impelled by curiosity, is capable, and had devised many little artifices with which a schooled address is well acquainted to obtain it, his exertions had hitherto been unsuccessful. If there was a mystery, the young lady was competent to preserve it; and with all her naïveté, her interesting ignorance of the world, and her evidently uncontrollable spirit, no hasty word ever fell from her cautious lips which threw any light on the objects of his enquiry. Though impetuous, she was never indiscreet, and often displayed a caution which was little in accordance with her youth and temper. The last night had witnessed the only moment in which her passions seemed for a time to have struggled with, and to have overcome, her judgment; but it was only for a moment. That display of overpowering feeling had cost Vivian a sleepless night; and he is at this instant pacing up and down the chamber of his hotel, thinking of that which he had imagined could exercise his thoughts no more.

She was beautiful; she loved him; she was unhappy! To be loved by any woman is flattering to the feelings of every man, no matter how deeply he may have quaffed the bitter goblet of worldly knowledge. The praise of a fool is incense to the wisest of us; and though we believe ourselves brokenhearted, it still delights us to find that we are loved. The memory of Violet Fane was still as fresh, as sweet, to the mind of Vivian Grey as when he pressed her blushing cheek for the first and only time. To love again, really to love as he had done, he once thought was impossible; he thought so still. The character of the Baroness had interested him

from the first. Her ignorance of mankind, and her
perfect acquaintance with the polished forms of society; her extreme beauty, her mysterious rank, her
proud spirit and impetuous feelings; her occasional
pensiveness, her extreme waywardness, had astonished, perplexed, and enchanted him. But he had
never felt in love. It never for a moment had entered into his mind that his lonely bosom could again
be a fit resting-place for one so lovely and so young.
Scared at the misery which had always followed in
his track, he would have shuddered ere he again
asked a human being to share his sad and blighted
fortunes. The partiality of the Baroness for his society, without flattering his vanity, or giving rise to
thoughts more serious than how he could most completely enchant for her the passing hour, had certainly made the time passed in her presence the least
gloomy which he had lately experienced. At the
same moment that he left the saloon of the palace he
had supposed that his image quitted her remembrance; and if she had again welcomed him with
cheerfulness and cordiality, he had felt that his reception was owing to not being, perhaps, quite as
frivolous as the Count of Eberstein, and rather more
amusing than the Baron of Gernsbach.

It was therefore with the greatest astonishment
that, last night, he had found that he was loved,
loved, too, by this beautiful and haughty girl, who
had treated the advances of the most distinguished
nobles with ill-concealed scorn, and who had so presumed upon her dubious relationship to the bour-
geois Minister that nothing but her own surpassing
loveliness and her parent's all-engrossing influence
could have excused or authorised her conduct.

Vivian had yielded to the magic of the moment, and had returned the feelings apparently no sooner expressed than withdrawn. Had he left the gardens of the palace the Baroness's plighted lover he might perhaps have deplored his rash engagement, and the sacred image of his first and hallowed love might have risen up in judgment against his violated affection; but how had he and the interesting stranger parted? He was rejected, even while his affection was returned; and while her flattering voice told him that he alone could make her happy, she had mournfully declared that happiness could not be hers. How was this? Could she be another's? Her agitation at the opera, often the object of his thought, quickly occurred to him! It must be so. Ah! another's! and who this rival? this proud possessor of a heart which could not beat for him? Madame Carolina's declaration that the Baroness must be married off was at this moment remembered: her marked observation, that Von Sohnspeer was no son of Beckendorff's, not forgotten. The Field Marshal, too, was the valued friend of the Minister; and it did not fail to occur to Vivian that it was not Von Sohnspeer's fault that his attendance on the Baroness was not as constant as his own. Indeed, the unusual gallantry of the Commander-in-Chief had been the subject of many a joke among the young lords of the Court, and the reception of his addresses by their unmerciful object not unobserved or unspared. But as for poor Von Sohnspeer, what could be expected, as Emilius von Aslingen observed, 'from a man whose softest compliment was as long, loud, and obscure as a birthday salute!'

No sooner was the affair clear to Vivian, no sooner was he convinced that a powerful obstacle existed to the love or union of himself and the Baroness, than he began to ask what right the interests of third persons had to interfere between the mutual affection of any individuals. He thought of her in the moonlight garden, struggling with her pure and natural passion. He thought of her exceeding beauty, her exceeding love. He beheld this rare and lovely creature in the embrace of Von Sohnspeer. He turned from the picture in disgust and indignation. She was his. Nature had decreed it. She should be the bride of no other man. Sooner than yield her up he would beard Beckendorff himself in his own retreat, and run every hazard and meet every danger which the ardent imagination of a lover could conceive. Was he madly to reject the happiness which Providence, or destiny, or chance had at length offered him? If the romance of boyhood could never be realised, at least with this engaging being for his companion, he might pass through his remaining years in calmness and in peace. His trials were perhaps over. Alas! this is the last delusion of unhappy men!

Vivian called at the Palace, but the fatigues of the preceding night prevented either of the ladies from being visible. In the evening he joined a small and select circle. The party, indeed, only consisted of the Grand Duke, Madame, their visitors, and the usual attendants, himself and Von Sohnspeer. The quiet of the little circle did not more strikingly contrast with the noise, and glare, and splendour of the last night than did Vivian's subdued reception by the Baroness with her agitated demeanour in the garden. She was cordial, but calm. He found it quite impossible to gain even one moment's private conversation with her. Madame Carolina monopo-

lised his attention, as much to favour the views of
the Field Marshal as to discuss the comparative
merits of Pope as a moralist and a poet; and Vivian
had the mortification of observing his odious rival,
whom he now thoroughly detested, discharge without ceasing his royal salutes in the impatient ear of
Beckendorff's lovely daughter.

Towards the conclusion of the evening a chamberlain entered the room and whispered his mission
to the Baroness. She immediately arose and quitted
the apartment. As the party was breaking up she
again entered. Her countenance was agitated, Madame Carolina was in the act of being overwhelmed
with the compliments of the Grand Marshal, and
Vivian seized the opportunity of reaching the Baroness. After a few hurried sentences she dropped her
glove. Vivian gave it her. So many persons were
round them that it was impossible to converse except on the most common topics. The glove was
again dropped.

'I see,' said the Baroness, with a meaning look,
'that you are but a recreant knight, or else you
would not part with a lady's glove so easily.'

Vivian gave a rapid glance round the room. No
one was observing him, and the glove was immediately concealed. He hurried home, rushed up the
staircase of the hotel, ordered lights, locked the door,
and with a sensation of indescribable anxiety, tore
the precious glove from his bosom, seized, opened,
and read the enclosed and following note. It was
written in pencil, in a hurried hand, and some of the
words were repeated:—

'I leave the Court to-night. He is here himself.
No art can postpone my departure. Much, much, I

wish to see you; to say, to say, to you. He is to
have an interview with the Grand Duke to-morrow
morning. Dare you come to his place in his absence? You know the private road. He goes by
the high road, and calls in his way on a Forest
Councillor: it is the white house by the barrier; you
know it! Watch him to-morrow morning; about
nine or ten I should think: here, here; and then for
heaven's sake let me see you. Dare everything! Fail
not! Mind, by the private road: beware the other!
You know the ground. God bless you!

'SYBILLA.'

CHAPTER XII.

Mr. Beckendorff Interferes.

IVIAN read the note over a thousand times. He could not retire to rest. He called Essper George, and gave him all necessary directions for the morning. About three o'clock Vivian lay down on a sofa, and slept for a few hours. He started often in his short and feverish slumber. His dreams were unceasing and inexplicable. At first Von Sohnspeer was their natural hero; but soon the scene shifted. Vivian was at Ems, walking under the well-remembered lime-trees, and with the Baroness. Suddenly, although it was mid-day, the sun became large, blood-red, and fell out of the heavens; his companion screamed, a man rushed forward with a drawn sword. It was the idiot Crown Prince of Reisenburg. Vivian tried to oppose him, but without success. The infuriated ruffian sheathed his weapon in the heart of the Baroness. Vivian shrieked, and fell upon her body, and, to his horror, found himself embracing the cold corpse of Violet Fane!

Vivian and Essper mounted their horses about seven o'clock. At eight they had reached a small inn

near the Forest Councillor's house, where Vivian was
to remain until Essper had watched the entrance of
the Minister. It was a few minutes past nine when
Essper returned with the joyful intelligence that Owlface and his master had been seen to enter the Courtyard. Vivian immediately mounted Max, and telling
Essper to keep a sharp watch, he set spurs to his
horse.

'Now, Max, my good steed, each minute is
golden; serve thy master well!' He patted the horse's
neck, the animal's erected ears proved how well it
understood its master's wishes; and taking advantage
of the loose bridle, which was confidently allowed it,
the horse sprang rather than galloped to the Minister's residence. Nearly an hour, however, was lost in
gaining the private road, for Vivian, after the caution
in the Baroness's letter, did not dare the high road.

He is galloping up the winding rural lane, where
he met Beckendorff on the second morning of his
visit. He has reached the little gate, and following
the example of the Grand Duke, ties Max at the entrance. He dashes over the meadows; not following
the path, but crossing straight through the long and
dewy grass, he leaps over the light iron railing; he
is rushing up the walk; he takes a rapid glance in
passing, at the little summer-house; the blue passion-
flower is still blooming, the house is in sight; a white
handkerchief is waving from the drawing-room window! He sees it; fresh wings are added to its course;
he dashes through a bed of flowers, frightens the
white peacock, darts through the library window, is
in the drawing-room.

The Baroness was there: pale and agitated she
stood beneath the mysterious picture, with one arm

leaning on the old carved mantelpiece. Overcome by her emotions, she did not move forward to meet him as he entered; but Vivian observed neither her constraint nor her agitation.

'Sybilla! dearest Sybilla! say you are mine!'

He seized her hand. She struggled not to disengage herself; her head sank upon her arm, which rested upon his shoulder. Overpowered, she sobbed convulsively. He endeavoured to calm her, but her agitation increased; and minutes elapsed ere she seemed to be even sensible of his presence. At length she became more calm, and apparently making a struggle to compose herself, she raised her head and said, 'This is very weak: let us walk for a moment about the room!'

At this moment Vivian was seized by the throat with a strong grasp. He turned round; it was Mr. Beckendorff, with a face deadly white, his full eyes darting from their sockets like a hungry snake's, and the famous Italian dagger in his right hand.

'Villain!' said he, in the low voice of fatal passion; 'Villain, is this your destiny?'

Vivian's first thoughts were for the Baroness; and turning his head from Beckendorff, he looked with the eye of anxious love to his companion. But, instead of fainting, instead of being overwhelmed by this terrible interruption, she seemed, on the contrary, to have suddenly regained her natural spirit and self-possession. The blood had returned to her hitherto pale cheek, and the fire to an eye before dull with weeping. She extricated herself immediately from Vivian's encircling arm, and by so doing enabled him to have struggled, had it been necessary, more equally with the powerful grasp of his assailant.

'Stand off, sir!' said the Baroness, with an air of inexpressible dignity, and a voice which even at this crisis seemed to anticipate that it would be obeyed. 'Stand off, sir! stand off, I command you!'

Beckendorff for one moment was motionless: he then gave her a look of piercing earnestness, threw Vivian, rather than released him from his hold, and flung the dagger with a bitter smile, into the corner of the room. 'Well, madam!' said he, in a choking voice, 'you are obeyed!'

'Mr. Grey,' continued the Baroness, 'I regret that this outrage should have been experienced by you because you have dared to serve me. My presence should have preserved you from this contumely; but what are we to expect from those who pride themselves upon being the sons of slaves! You shall hear further from me.' So saying, the lady, bowing to Vivian, and sweeping by the Minister with a glance of indescribable disdain, quitted the apartment. As she was on the point of leaving the room, Vivian was standing against the wall, with a pale face and folded arms, Beckendorff, with his back to the window, his eyes fixed on the ground; and Vivian, to his astonishment, perceived, what escaped the Minister's notice, that while the lady bade him adieu with one hand she made rapid signs with the other to some unknown person in the garden.

Mr. Beckendorff and Vivian were left alone, and the latter was the first to break silence.

'Mr. Beckendorff,' said he, in a calm voice, 'considering the circumstances under which you have found me in your house this morning, I should have known how to excuse and to forget any irritable expressions which a moment of ungovernable passion might have inspired. I should have passed them over unnoticed. But your unjustifiable behaviour has exceeded that line of demarcation which sympathy with human feelings allows even men of honour to recognise. You have disgraced both me and yourself by giving me a blow. It is, as that lady well styled it, an outrage; an outrage which the blood of any other man but yourself could only obliterate from my memory; but while I am inclined to be indulgent to your exalted station and your peculiar character, I at the same time expect, and now wait for, an apology.'

'An apology!' said Beckendorff, now beginning to stamp up and down the room; 'an apology! Shall it be made to you, sir, or the Archduchess?'

'The Archduchess!' said Vivian. 'Good God! what can you mean! Did I hear you right?'

'I said the Archduchess,' answered Beckendorff, with firmness; 'a Princess of the House of Austria, and the pledged wife of his Royal Highness the Crown Prince of Reisenburg. Perhaps you may now think that other persons have to apologise?'

'Mr. Beckendorff,' said Vivian, 'I am overwhelmed; I declare, upon my honour——'

'Stop, sir! you have said too much already——'

'But, Mr. Beckendorff, surely you will allow me to explain——'

'Sir! there is no need of explanation. I know everything; more than you do yourself. You can have nothing to explain to me! and I presume you are now fully aware of the impossibility of again speaking to her. It is at present within an hour of noon. Before sunset you must be twenty miles from the Court; so far you will be attended. Do not answer me; you know my power. A remonstrance only, and I write to Vienna: your progress shall be stopped throughout the South of Europe. For her sake this business will be hushed up. An important and secret mission will be the accredited reason of your leaving Reisenburg. This will be confirmed by your official attendant, who will be an envoy's courier. Farewell!'

As Mr. Beckendorff quitted the room, his confidential servant, the messenger of Turriparva, entered, and with the most respectful bow informed Vivian that the horses were ready. In about three hours' time Vivian Grey, followed by the Government messenger, stopped at his hotel. The landlord and waiters bowed with increased obsequiousness on seeing him so attended, and in a few minutes Reisenburg was ringing with the news that his appointment to the Under-Secretaryship of State was now 'a settled thing.'

BOOK VIII.

CHAPTER I.

THE CAPRICE OF A PRINCESS.

THE landlord of the Grand Hotel of the Four Nations at Reisenburg was somewhat consoled for the sudden departure of his distinguished guest by selling the plenipotentiary a travelling carriage lately taken for a doubtful bill from a gambling Russian General at a large profit. In this convenient vehicle, in the course of a couple of hours after his arrival in the city, was Mr. Vivian Grey borne through the gate of the Allies. Essper George, who had reached the hotel about half an hour after his master, followed behind the carriage on his hack, leading Max. The courier cleared the road before, and expedited the arrival of the special envoy of the Grand Duke of Reisenburg at the point of his destination by ordering the horses, clearing the barriers, and paying the postilions in advance. Vivian had never travelled before with such style and speed.

Our hero covered himself up with his cloak and drew his travelling cap over his eyes, though it was one of the hottest days of this singularly hot autumn. Entranced in a reverie, the only figure that occurred to his mind was the young Archduchess, and the only sounds that dwelt on his ear were the words of Beckendorff; but neither to the person of the first nor to the voice of the second did he annex any definite idea.

After some hours' travelling, which to Vivian seemed both an age and a minute, he was roused from his stupor by the door of his calèche being opened. He shook himself as a man does who has wakened from a benumbing and heavy sleep, although his eyes were the whole time wide open. The disturbing intruder was his courier, who, bowing, with his hat in hand, informed his Excellency that he was now on the frontier of Reisenburg; regretting that he was under the necessity of quitting his Excellency, he begged to present him with his passport. 'It is made out for Vienna,' continued the messenger. 'A private pass, sir, of the Prime Minister, and will entitle you to the greatest consideration.'

The carriage was soon again advancing rapidly to the next post-house, when, after they had proceeded about a half a mile, Essper George calling loudly from behind, the drivers suddenly stopped. Just as Vivian, to whose tortured mind the rapid movement of the carriage was some relief, for it produced an excitement which prevented thought, was about to enquire the cause of this stoppage, Essper George rode up to the calèche.

'Kind sir!' said he, with a peculiar look, 'I have a packet for you.'

'A packet! from whom? speak! give it me!'

'Hush! softly, good master. Here am I about to

commit rank treason for your sake, and a hasty word is the only reward of my rashness.'

'Nay, nay,good Essper, try me not now!'

'I will not, kind sir! but the truth is, I could not give you the packet while that double-faced knave was with us, or even while he was in sight. "In good truth," as Master Rodolph was wont to say——!'

'But of this packet?'

'"Fairly and softly," good sir! as Hunsdrich the porter said when I would have drunk the mulled wine, while he was on the cold staircase——'

'Essper! do you mean to enrage me?'

'"By St. Hubert!" as that worthy gentleman the Grand Marshal was in the habit of swearing, I——'

'This is too much; what are the idle sayings of these people to me?'

'Nay, nay, kind sir! they do but show that each of us has his own way of telling a story, and that he who would hear a tale must let the teller's breath come out of his own nostrils.'

'Well, Essper, speak on! Stranger things have happened to me than to be reproved by my own servant.'

'Nay, kind master! say not a bitter word to me because you have slipped out of a scrape with your head on your shoulders. The packet is from Mr. Beckendorff's daughter.'

'Ah! why did you not give it me before?'

'Why do I give it you now? Because I am a fool; that is why. What! you wanted it when that double-faced scoundrel was watching every eyelash of yours as it moved from the breath of a fly? a fel-

low who can see as well at the back of his head as
from his face. I should like to poke out his front
eyes, to put him on an equality with the rest of
mankind. He it was who let the old gentleman
know of your visit this morning, and I suspect that
he has been nearer your limbs of late than you have
imagined. Every dog has his day, and the oldest
pig must look for the knife! The Devil was once
cheated on Sunday, and I have been too sharp for
Puss in boots and his mouse-trap! Prowling about
the Forest Councillor's house, I saw your new servant, sir, gallop in, and his old master soon gallop
out. I was off as quick as they, but was obliged to
leave my horse within two miles of the house, and
then trust to my legs. I crept through the shrubs
like a land tortoise; but, of course, too late to warn
you. However, I was in for the death, and making
signs to the young lady, who directly saw that I was
a friend; bless her! she is as quick as a partridge; I
left you to settle it with papa, and, after all, did that
which I suppose you intended, sir, to do yourself;
made my way into the young lady's bedchamber.'

'Hold your tongue, sir! and give me the packet.'

'There it is, and now we will go on; but we
must stay an hour at the next post, if your honour
pleases not to sleep there; for both Max and my
own hack have had a sharp day's work.'

Vivian tore open the packet. It contained a long
letter, written on the night of her return to Beckendorff's; she had stayed up the whole night writing.
It was to have been forwarded to Vivian, in case of
their not being able to meet. In the enclosure were
a few hurried lines, written since the catastrophe.
They were these: 'May this safely reach you! Can

you ever forgive me? The enclosed, you will see, was intended for you, in case of our not meeting. It anticipated sorrow; yet what were its anticipations to our reality!'

The Archduchess's letter was evidently written under the influence of agitated feelings. We omit it; because, as the mystery of her character is now explained, a great portion of her communication would be irrelevant to our tale. She spoke of her exalted station as a woman, that station which so many women envy, in a spirit of agonising bitterness. A royal princess is only the most flattered of state victims. She is a political sacrifice, by which enraged governments are appeased, wavering allies conciliated and ancient amities confirmed. Debarred by her rank and her education from looking forward to that exchange of equal affection which is the great end and charm of female existence, no individual finds more fatally and feels more keenly that pomp is not felicity, and splendour not content.

Deprived of all those sources of happiness which seem inherent in woman, the wife of the Sovereign sometimes seeks in politics and in pleasure a means of excitement which may purchase oblivion. But the political queen is a rare character; she must possess an intellect of unusual power, and her lot must be considered as an exception in the fortunes of female royalty. Even the political queen generally closes an agitated career with a broken heart. And for the unhappy votary of pleasure, who owns her cold duty to a royal husband, we must not forget that even in the most dissipated courts the conduct of the queen is expected to be decorous, and that the instances are not rare where the wife of the monarch has died on the scaffold, or in a dungeon, or in exile, because she dared to be indiscreet where all were debauched. But for the great majority of royal wives, they exist without a passion; they have nothing to hope, nothing to fear, nothing to envy, nothing to want, nothing to confide, nothing to hate, and nothing to love. Even their duties, though multitudinous, are mechanical, and, while they require much attention, occasion no anxiety. Amusement is their moment of greatest emotion, and for them amusement is rare; for amusement is the result of equal companionship. Thus situated, they are doomed to become frivolous in their pursuits and formal in their manners, and the Court chaplain or the Court confessor is the only person who can prove they have a soul, by convincing them that it will be saved.

The young Archduchess had assented to the proposition of marriage with the Crown Prince of Reisenburg without opposition, as she was convinced that requesting her assent was only a courteous form of requiring her compliance. There was nothing outrageous to her feelings in marrying a man whom she had never seen, because her education, from her tenderest years, had daily prepared her for such an event. Moreover, she was aware that, if she succeeded in escaping from the offers of the Crown Prince of Reisenburg, she would soon be under the necessity of assenting to those of some other suitor; and if proximity to her own country, accordance with its sentiments and manners, and previous connection with her own house, were taken into consideration, an union with the family of Reisenburg was even desirable. It was to be preferred, at least, to one which brought with it a foreign husband and a for-

eign clime, a strange language and strange customs.
The Archduchess, a girl of ardent feelings and lively
mind, had not, however, agreed to become that all-
commanding slave, a Queen, without a stipulation.
She required that she might be allowed, previous to
her marriage, to visit her future Court incognita.
This singular and unparalleled proposition was not
easily acceded to: but the opposition with which
it was received only tended to make the young
Princess more determined to be gratified in her caprice. Her Imperial Highness did not pretend that
any end was to be obtained by this unusual proce-
dure, and indeed she had no definite purpose in requesting it to be permitted. It was originally the
mere whim of the moment, and had it not been
strongly opposed it would not have been strenuously
insisted upon. As it was, the young Archduchess
persisted, threatened, and grew obstinate; and the
grey-headed negotiators of the marriage, desirous of
its speedy completion, and not having a more tract-
able tool ready to supply her place, at length yielded
to her bold importunity. Great difficulty, however,
was experienced in carrying her wishes into execution. By what means and in what character she was
to appear at Court, so as not to excite suspicion or
occasion discovery, were often discussed, without being resolved upon. At length it became necessary to
consult Mr. Beckendorff. The upper lip of the Prime
Minister of Reisenburg curled as the Imperial Minister
detailed the caprice and contumacy of the Princess,
and treating with the greatest contempt this girlish
whim, Mr. Beckendorff ridiculed those by whom it
had been humoured with no suppressed derision.
The consequence of his conduct was an interview

with the future Grand Duchess, and the consequence of his interview an unexpected undertaking on his part to arrange the visit according to her Highness's desires.

The Archduchess had not yet seen the Crown Prince; but six miniatures and a whole-length portrait had prepared her for not meeting an Adonis or a Baron Trenck, and that was all; for never had the Correggio of the age of Charles the Fifth better substantiated his claims to the office of Court painter than by these accurate semblances of his Royal Highness, in which his hump was subdued into a Grecian bend, and his lack-lustre eyes seemed beaming with tenderness and admiration. His betrothed bride stipulated with Mr. Beckendorff that the fact of her visit should be known only to himself and the Grand Duke; and before she appeared at Court she had received the personal pledge both of himself and his Royal Highness that the affair should be kept a complete secret from the Crown Prince.

Most probably, on her first introduction to her future husband, all the romantic plans of the young Archduchess to excite an involuntary interest in his heart vanished; but how this may be, it is needless for us to enquire, for that same night introduced another character into her romance for whom she was perfectly unprepared, and whose appearance totally disorganised its plot.

Her inconsiderate, her unjustifiable conduct, in tampering with that individual's happiness and affection, was what the young and haughty Archduchess deplored in the most energetic, the most feeling, and the most humble spirit; and anticipating that after this painful disclosure they would never meet again, she declared that for his sake alone she regretted what had passed, and praying that he might be happier than herself, she supplicated to be forgiven and forgotten.

Vivian read the Archduchess's letter over and over again, and then put it in his breast. At first he thought that he had lived to shed another tear; but he was mistaken. In a few minutes he found himself quite roused from his late overwhelming stupor. Remorse or regret for the past, care or caution for the future, seemed at the same moment to have fled from his mind. He looked up to Heaven with a wild smile, half of despair and half of defiance. It seemed to imply that Fate had now done her worst, and that he had at last the satisfaction of knowing himself to be the most unfortunate and unhappy being that ever existed. When a man at the same time believes in and sneers at his destiny we may be sure that he considers his condition past redemption.

CHAPTER II.

STRANGE BEDFELLOWS.

THEY stopped for an hour at the next post, according to Essper's suggestion. Indeed, he proposed resting there for the night, for both men and beasts much required repose; but Vivian panted to reach Vienna, to which city two days' travelling would now carry him. His passions were so roused, and his powers of reflection so annihilated, that while he had determined to act desperately, he was unable to resolve upon anything desperate. Whether, on his arrival at the Austrian capital, he should plunge into dissipation or into the Danube was equally uncertain. He had some thought of joining the Greeks or Turks, no matter which, probably the latter, or perhaps of serving in the Americas. The idea of returning to England never once entered his mind: he expected to find letters from his father at Vienna, and he almost regretted it; for, in his excessive misery, it was painful to be conscious that a being still breathed who was his friend.

It was a fine moonlight night, but the road was mountainous; and in spite of all the encouragement of Vivian, and all the consequent exertions of the postilion, they were upwards of two hours and a half going these eight miles. To get on any farther to-night was quite impossible. Essper's horse was fairly knocked up, and even Max visibly distressed. The post-house was fortunately an inn. It was not at a village, and, as far as the travellers could learn, not near one, and its appearance did not promise very pleasing accommodation. Essper, who had scarcely tasted food for nearly eighteen hours, was not highly delighted with the prospect before them. His anxiety, however, was not merely selfish: he was as desirous that his young master should be refreshed by a good night's rest as himself, and anticipating that he should have to exercise his skill in making a couch for Vivian in the carriage, he proceeded to cross-examine the postmaster on the possibility of his accommodating them. The host was a pious-looking personage, in a black velvet cap, with a singularly meek and charitable expression of countenance. His long black hair was exquisitely braided, and he wore round his neck a collar of pewter medals, all which had been recently sprinkled with holy water and blessed under the petticoat of the saintly Virgin; for the postmaster had only just returned from a pilgrimage to the celebrated shrine of the Black Lady of Altoting.

'Good friend!' said Essper, looking him cunningly in the face, 'I fear that we must order horses on: you can hardly accommodate two?'

'Good friend!' answered the innkeeper and he crossed himself very reverently at the same time, 'it is not for man to fear, but to hope.'

'If your beds were as good as your adages,' said Essper George, laughing, 'in good truth, as a friend of mine would say, I would sleep here to-night.'

'Prithee, friend,' continued the innkeeper, kissing a medal of his collar very devoutly, 'what accommodation dost thou lack?'

'Why,' said Essper, 'in the way of accommodation, little, for two excellent beds will content us; but in the way of refreshment, by St. Hubert! as another friend of mine would swear, he would be a bold man who would engage to be as hungry before his dinner as I shall be after my supper.'

'Friend!' said the innkeeper, 'Our Lady forbid that thou shouldst leave our walls to-night: for the accommodation, we have more than sufficient; and as for the refreshment, by Holy Mass! we had a priest tarry here last night, and he left his rosary behind. I will comfort my soul, by telling my beads over the kitchen-fire, and for every Paternoster my wife shall give thee a rasher of kid, and for every Ave a tumbler of Augsburg, which Our Lady forget me, if I did not myself purchase but yesterday se'nnight from the pious fathers of the Convent of St. Florian!'

'I take thee at thy word, honest sir,' said Essper. 'By the Creed! I liked thy appearance from the first; nor wilt thou find me unwilling, when my voice has taken its supper, to join thee in some pious hymn or holy canticle. And now for the beds!'

'There is the green room, the best bedroom in my house,' said the innkeeper. 'Holy Mary forget me if in that same bed have not stretched their legs more valourous generals, more holy prelates, and more distinguished councillors of our Lord the Emperor, than in any bed in all Austria.'

'That, then, for my master, and for myself——'

'H-u-m!' said the host, looking very earnestly in Essper's face; 'I should have thought that thou wert

one more anxious after dish and flagon than curtain
and eider-down!'

'By my Mother! I love good cheer,' said Essper
earnestly, 'and want it more at this moment than
any knave that ever yet starved: but if thou hast not
a bed to let me stretch my legs on after four-and-
twenty hours' hard riding, by holy Virgin! I will
have horses on to Vienna.'

'Our Black Lady forbid!' said the innkeeper, with
a quick voice, and with rather a dismayed look;
'said I that thou shouldst not have a bed? St. Florian
desert me if I and my wife would not sooner sleep
in the chimney-corner than thou shouldst miss one
wink of thy slumbers!'

'In one word, have you a bed?'

'Have I a bed? Where slept, I should like to
know, the Vice-Principal of the Convent of Molk on
the day before the last holy Ascension? The waters
were out in the morning; and when will my wife
forget what his reverence was pleased to say when he
took his leave: "Good woman!" said he, "my duty
calls me; but the weather is cold; and between ourselves, I am used to great feasts, and I should have
no objection, if I were privileged, to stay and to eat
again of thy red cabbage and cream!" What say you
to that? Do you think we have got beds now?
You shall sleep to-night, sir, like an Aulic Councillor!'

This adroit introduction of the red cabbage and
cream settled every thing; when men are wearied
and famished they have no inclination to be incredu-
lous, and in a few moments Vivian was informed by
his servant that the promised accommodation was satisfactory; and having locked up the carriage, and

wheeled it into a small outhouse, he and Essper were
ushered by their host into a room which, as is usual
in small German inns in the South, served at the
same time both for kitchen and saloon. The fire was
lit in a platform of brick, raised in the centre of the
floor: the sky was visible through the chimney,
which, although of a great breadth below, gradually
narrowed to the top. A family of wandering Bohemians, consisting of the father and mother and three
children, were seated on the platform when Vivian
entered; the man was playing on a coarse wooden
harp, without which the Bohemians seldom travel.
The music ceased as the new guests came into the
room, and the Bohemian courteously offered his place
at the fire to our hero, who, however, declined disturbing the family group. A small table and a couple
of chairs were placed in a corner of the room by the
innkeeper's wife, a bustling active dame, who apparently found no difficulty in laying the cloth, dust-
ing the furniture, and cooking the supper at the same
time. At this table Vivian and his servant seated
themselves; nor, indeed, did the cookery discredit the
panegyric of the Reverend Vice-Principal of the Convent of Molk.

Alike wearied in mind and body, Vivian soon
asked for his bed, which, though not exactly fitted
for an Aulic Councillor, as the good host perpetually
avowed it to be, nevertheless afforded decent accommodation.

The Bohemian family retired to the hayloft, and
Essper George would have followed his master's example, had not the kind mistress of the house
tempted him to stay behind by the production of a
new platter of rashers: indeed, he never remembered

meeting with such hospitable people as the postmaster and his wife. They had evidently taken a fancy to him, and, though extremely wearied, the lively little Essper endeavoured, between his quick mouthfuls and long draughts, to reward and encourage their kindness by many a good story and sharp joke. With all these both mine host and his wife were exceedingly amused, seldom containing their laughter, and frequently protesting, by the sanctity of various saints, that this was the pleasantest night and Essper the pleasantest fellow that they had ever met with.

'Eat, eat, my friend!' said his host! 'by the Mass! thou hast travelled far; and fill thy glass, and pledge with me Our Black Lady of Altoting. By Holy Cross! I have hung up this week in her chapel a garland of silk roses, and have ordered to be burnt before her shrine three pounds of perfumed wax tapers! Fill again, fill again! and thou too, good mistress; a hard day's work hast thou had, a glass of wine will do thee no harm! join me with our new friend! Pledge we together the Holy Fathers of St. Florian, my worldly patrons and my spiritual pastors: let us pray that his reverence the Sub-Prior may not have his Christmas attack of gout in the stomach, and a better health to poor Father Felix! Fill again, fill again! this Augsburg is somewhat acid; we will have a bottle of Hungary. Mistress, fetch us the bell-glasses, and here to the Reverend Vice-Principal of Molk! our good friend: when will my wife forget what he said to her on the morning of last holy Ascension! Fill again, fill again!'

Inspired by the convivial spirit of the pious and jolly postmaster, Essper George soon forgot his threatened visit to his bedroom, and ate and drank, laughed and joked, as if he were again with his friend, Master Rodolph: but wearied Nature at length avenged herself for this unnatural exertion, and leaning back in his chair, he was, in the course of an hour, overcome by one of those dead and heavy slumbers the effect of the united influence of fatigue and intemperance; in short, it was like the midnight sleep of a fox-hunter.

No sooner had our pious votary of the Black Lady of Altoting observed the effect of his Hungary wine than, making a well-understood sign to his wife, he took up the chair of Essper in his brawny arms, and, preceded by Mrs. Postmistress with a lantern, he left the room with his guest. Essper's hostess led and lighted the way to an outhouse, which occasionally served as a coach-house, a stable, and a lumber-room. It had no window, and the lantern afforded the only light which exhibited its present contents. In one corner was a donkey tied up, belonging to the Bohemian. Under a hayrack was a large child's cradle: it was of a remarkable size, having been made for twins. Near it was a low wooden sheep-tank, half filled with water, and which had been placed there for the refreshment of the dog and his feathered friends, who were roosting in the rack.

The pious innkeeper very gently lowered to the ground the chair on which Essper was soundly sleeping; and then, having crossed himself, he took up our friend with great tenderness and solicitude, and dexterously fitted him in the huge cradle.

About an hour past midnight Essper George awoke. He was lying on his back, and very unwell; and on trying to move, found that he was rocking. His late adventure was obliterated from his memory; and the strange movement, united with his peculiar indisposition, left him no doubt that he was on board ship! As is often the case when we are tipsy or nervous, Essper had been woke by the fright of falling from some immense height; and finding that his legs had no sensation, for they were quite benumbed, he concluded that he had fallen down the hatchway, that his legs were broken, and himself jammed in between some logs of wood in the hold, and so he began to cry lustily to those above to come down to his rescue.

'O, Essper George!' thought he, 'how came you to set foot on salt timber again! Had not you had enough of it in the Mediterranean and the Turkish seas, that you must be getting aboard this lubberly Dutch galliot! for I am sure she's Dutch by being so low in the water. Well, they may talk of a sea-life, but for my part, I never saw the use of the sea. Many a sad heart it has caused, and many a sick stomach has it occasioned! The boldest sailor climbs on board with a heavy soul, and leaps on land with a light spirit. O! thou indifferent ape of Earth! thy houses are of wood and thy horses of canvas; thy roads have no landmarks and thy highways no inns; thy hills are green without grass and wet without showers! and as for food, what art thou, O, bully Ocean! but the stable of horse-fishes, the stall of cow-fishes, the sty of hog-fishes, and the kennel of dog-fishes! Commend me to a fresh-water dish for meagre days! Sea-weeds stewed with chalk may be savoury stuff for a merman; but, for my part, give me red cabbage and cream: and as for drink, a man may live in the midst of thee his whole life and die for thirst at the end of it! Besides, thou blasphemous salt lake, where is thy religion? Where are thy churches, thou heretic?' So saying Essper made a desperate effort to crawl up the hold. His exertion set the cradle rocking with renewed violence; and at last dashing against the sheep-tank, that pastoral piece of furniture was overset, and part of its contents poured upon the inmate of the cradle.

'Sprung a leak in the hold, by St. Nicholas!' bawled out Essper George. 'Caulkers ahoy!'

At this moment three or four fowls, roused by the fall of the tank and the consequent shouts of Essper, began fluttering about the rack, and at last perched upon the cradle. 'The live stock got loose!' shouted Essper, 'and the breeze getting stiffer every instant! Where is the captain? I will see him. I am not one of the crew: I belong to the Court! I must have cracked my skull when I fell like a lubber down that confounded hatchway! Egad! I feel as if I had been asleep, and been dreaming I was at Court.'

The sound of heavy footsteps was now over his head. These noises were at once an additional proof that he was in the hold, and an additional stimulus to his calls to those on deck. In fact, these sounds were occasioned by the Bohemians, who always rose before break of day; and consequently, in a few minutes, the door of the stable opened and the Bohemian, with a lantern in his hand, entered.

'What do you want?' cried Essper.

'I want my donkey.'

'You do?' said Essper. 'You're the Purser, I suppose, detected keeping a jackass among the poultry! eating all the food of our live stock, and we having kid every day. Though both my legs are off, I'll have a fling at you!' and so saying, Essper, aided by the light of the lantern, scrambled out of the cradle, and taking up the sheep-tank, sent it straight at the astonished Bohemian's head. The aim was good, and the man fell; more, however, from fright than injury. Seizing his lantern, which had fallen out of his hand, Essper escaped through the stable door and rushed into the house. He found himself in the kitchen. The noise of his entrance roused the landlord and his wife, who had been sleeping by the fire; since, not having a single bed besides their own, they had given that up to Vivian. The countenance of the innkeeper effectually dispelled the clouds which had been fast clearing off from Essper's intellect. Giving one wide stare, and then rubbing his eyes, the truth lighted upon him, and so he sent the Bohemian's lantern at his landlord's head. The postmaster seized the poker and the postmistress a faggot, and as the Bohemian, who had now recovered himself, had entered in the rear, Essper George stood a fair chance of receiving a thorough drubbing, had not his master, roused by the suspicious noises and angry sounds which had reached his room, entered the kitchen with his pistols.

CHAPTER III.

VIVIAN ASSISTS AT A WEDDING.

S IT was now morning, Vivian did not again retire to rest, but took advantage of the disturbance in the inn to continue his route at an earlier hour than he had previously intended.

Essper, when he found himself safely mounted, lagged behind a few minutes to vent his spleen against the innkeeper's wife.

'May St. Florian confound me, madam!' said Essper, addressing himself to the lady in the window 'if ever I beheld so ugly a witch as yourself! Pious friend! thy chaplet of roses was ill bestowed, and thou needest not have travelled so far to light thy wax tapers at the shrine of the Black Lady at Altoting; for, by the beauty of holiness! an image of ebony is mother-of-pearl to that soot-face whom thou callest thy wife. Fare thee well! thou couple of saintly sinners! and may the next traveller who tarries in the den of thieves qualify thee for canonisation by thy wife's admiring pastor, the cabbage-eating Vice-Principal of Molk.'

Before the end of an hour they had to ford a rivulet running between two high banks. The scenery just here was particularly lovely, and Vivian's attention was so engrossed by it that he did not observe the danger which he was about to incur.

On the left of the road a high range of rocky mountains abruptly descended into an open but broken country, and the other side of the road was occasionally bounded by low undulating hills, partially covered with dwarf woods, not high enough to obstruct the view of the distant horizon. Rocky knolls jutted out near the base of the mountains; and on the top of one of them, overlooked by a gigantic grey peak, stood an ancient and still inhabited feudal castle. Round the base of this insulated rock a rustic village peeped above the encircling nut-woods, its rising smoke softening the hard features of the naked crag. On the side of the village nearest to Vivian a bold sheet of water discharged itself in three separate falls between the ravine of a wooded mountain, and flowing round the village as a fine broad river, expanded before it reached the foundation of the castled rock into a long and deep lake, which was also fed by numerous streams, the gulleys only of which were now visible down the steep sides of the mountains, their springs having been long dried up.

Vivian's view was interrupted by his sudden descent into the bed of the rivulet, one of the numerous branches of the mountain torrent, and by a crash which as immediately ensued. The spring of his carriage was broken. The carriage fell over, but Vivian sustained no injury; and while Essper George rode forward to the village for assistance, his master helped the postilion to extricate the horses and secure them on the opposite bank. They had done all that was in their power some time before Essper returned; and

Vivian, who had seated himself on some tangled beech-roots, was prevented growing impatient by contemplating the enchanting scenery. The postilion, on the contrary, who had travelled this road every day of his life, and who found no gratification in gazing upon rocks, woods, and waterfalls, lit his pipe, and occasionally talked to his horses. So essential an attribute of the beautiful is novelty! Essper at length made his appearance, attended by five or six peasants, dressed in holiday costume, with some fanciful decorations; their broad hats wreathed with wild flowers, their short brown jackets covered with buttons and fringe, and various coloured ribbons streaming from their knees.

'Well, sir! the grandson is born the day the grandfather dies! a cloudy morning has often a bright sunset! and though we are now sticking, in a ditch, by the aid of St. Florian we may be soon feasting in a castle! Come, my merry men, I did not bring you here to show your ribbons; the sooner you help us out of this scrape the sooner you will be again dancing with the pretty maidens on the green! Lend a hand!'

The calèche appeared to be so much shattered that they only ventured to put in one horse; and Vivian, leaving his carriage in charge of Essper and the postilion, mounted Max, and rode to the village, attended by the peasants. He learnt from them on the way that they were celebrating the marriage of the daughter of their lord, who, having been informed of the accident, had commanded them to go immediately to the gentleman's assistance, and then conduct him to the castle.

They crossed the river over a light stone bridge

of three arches, the key-stone of the centre one being decorated with a splendidly sculptured shield.

'This bridge appears to be very recently built,'
said Vivian to one of his conductors.

'It was opened, sir, for the first time yesterday,
to admit the bridegroom of my young lady, and the
foundation stone was laid on the day she was born.'

'I see that your good lord was determined that
it should be a solid structure.'

'Why, sir, it was necessary that the foundation
should be strong, because three succeeding winters it
was washed away by the rush of that mountain torrent. Turn this way, if you please, sir, through the
village.'

Vivian was much struck by the appearance of the
little settlement as he rode through it. It did not
consist of more than fifty houses, but they were all
detached, and each beautifully embowered in trees.
The end of the village came upon a large rising
green, leading up to the only accessible side of the
castle. It presented a most animated scene, being
covered with various groups, all intent upon different
rustic amusements. An immense pole, the stem of a
gigantic fir-tree, was fixed nearly in the centre of the
green, and crowned with a chaplet, the reward of
the most active young man of the village, whose
agility might enable him to display his gallantry by
presenting it to his mistress, she being allowed to
wear it during the remainder of the sports. The
middle-aged men were proving their strength by raising weights; while the elders of the village joined in
the calmer and more scientific diversion of skittles,
which in Austria are played with bowls and pins of
very great size. Others were dancing; others sitting

under tents, chattering or taking refreshments. Some
were walking in pairs, anticipating speedy celebration of a wedding day happier to them, if less gay
to others. Even the tenderest infants on this festive
day seemed conscious of some unusual cause of excitement, and many an urchin, throwing himself forward in a vain attempt to catch an elder brother or
a laughing sister, tried the strength of his leading-
strings, and rolled over, crowing in the soft grass.

At the end of the green a splendid tent was
erected, with a large white bridal flag waving from
its top, embroidered in gold, with a true lover's
knot. From this pavilion came forth, to welcome the
strangers, the lord of the village. He was a tall but
thin bending figure, with a florid benevolent countenance, and a quantity of long white hair. This ven-
erable person cordially offered his hand to Vivian,
regretted his accident, but expressed much pleasure
that he had come to partake of their happiness.
'Yesterday,' continued he, 'was my daughter's wedding day, and both myself and our humble friends
are endeavouring to forget, in this festive scene, our
approaching loss and separation. If you had come
yesterday you would have assisted at the opening of
my new bridge. Pray what do you think of it?
But I will show it to you myself, which I assure
you will give me great pleasure; at present let me introduce you to my family, who will be quite happy
to see you. It is a pity that you have missed the
Regatta; my daughter is just going to reward the
successful candidate. You see the boats upon
the lake; the one with the white and purple streamer
was the conqueror. You will have the pleasure, too,
of seeing my son-in-law; I am sure you will like

him; he quite enjoys our sports. We shall have a
fête champêtre to-morrow, and a dance on the green
to-night.'

The old gentleman paused for want of breath, and
having stood a moment to recover himself, he introduced his new guests to the inmates of the tent:
first, his maiden sister, a softened fac-simile of himself; behind her stood his beautiful and blushing
daughter, the youthful bride, wearing on her head a
coronal of white roses, and supported by three bridesmaids, the only relief to whose snowy dresses were
large bouquets on their left side. The bridegroom
was at first shaded by the curtain; but as he came
forward Vivian started when he recognised his Hei-
delberg friend, Eugene von Konigstein!

Their mutual delight and astonishment were so
great that for an instant neither of them could speak;
but when the old man learnt from his son-in-law
that the stranger was his most valued and intimate
friend, and one to whom he was under great personal obligations, he absolutely declared that he
would have the wedding, to witness which appeared
to him the height of human felicity, solemnised over
again. The bride blushed, the bridesmaids tittered,
the joy was universal.

Vivian enquired after the Baron. He learnt from
Eugene that he had quitted Europe about a month,
having sailed as Minister to one of the New American States. 'My uncle,' continued the young man,
'was neither well nor in spirits before his departure. I cannot understand why he plagues himself
so about politics; however, I trust he will like his
new appointment. You found him, I am sure, a delightful companion.'

'Come! you two young gentlemen,' said the father-in-law, 'put off your chat till the evening. The business of the day stops, for I see the procession coming forward to receive the Regatta prize. Now, my dear! where is the scarf? You know what to say? Remember, I particularly wish to do honour to the victor! The sight of all these happy faces makes me feel quite young again. I declare I think I shall live a hundred years!'

The procession advanced. First came a band of young children strewing flowers, then followed four stout boys carrying a large purple and white banner. The victor, proudly preceding the other candidates, strutted forward, with his hat on one side, a light scull decorated with purple and white ribbons in his right hand, and his left arm round his wife's waist. The wife, a beautiful young woman, to whom were clinging two fat flaxen-headed children, was the most interesting figure in the procession. Her tight dark bodice set off her round full figure, and her short red petticoat displayed her springy foot and ancle. Her neatly braided and plaited hair was partly concealed by a silk cap, covered with gold-spangled gauze, flattened rather at the top, and finished at the back of the head with a large bow. This costly head-gear, the highest fashion of her class, was presented to the wearer by the bride, and was destined to be kept for festivals. After the victor and his wife came six girls and six boys, at the side of whom walked a very bustling personage in black, who seemed extremely interested about the decorum of the procession. A long train of villagers succeeded.

'Well!' said the old lord to Vivian, 'this must be a very gratifying sight to you! How fortunate that your carriage broke down just at my castle! I think my dear girl is acquitting herself admirably. Ah! Eugene is a happy fellow, and I have no doubt that she will be happy too. The young sailor receives his honors very properly: they are as nice a family as I know. Observe, they are moving off now to make way for the pretty girls and boys. That person in black is our Abbé, as benevolent, worthy a creature as ever lived! and very clever too: you will see in a minute. Now they are going to give us a little bridal chorus, after the old fashion, and it is all the Abbé's doing. I understand that there is an elegant allusion to my new bridge in it, which I think will please you. Who ever thought that bridge would be opened for my girl's wedding? Well! I am glad that it was not finished before. But we must be silent! You will notice that part about the bridge; it is the fifth verse, I am told, beginning with something about Hymen, and ending with something about roses.'

By this time the procession had formed a semi-circle before the tent, the Abbé standing in the middle, with a paper in his hand, and dividing the two bands of choristers. He gave a signal with his cane, and the girls commenced: —

Chorus of Maidens.

Hours fly! it is Morn; he has left the bed of love! She follows him with a strained eye when his figure is no longer seen; she leans her head upon her arm. She is faithful to him as the lake to the mountain!

Chorus of Youths.

Hours fly! it is Noon; fierce is the restless sun! While he labours he thinks of her! while he controls others he will obey her! A strong man subdued by love is like a vineyard silvered by the moon!

Chorus of Youths and Maidens.

Hours fly! it is Eve; the soft star lights him to his home; she meets him as his shadow falls on the threshold! she smiles, and their child, stretching forth its tender hands from its mother's bosom, struggles to lisp 'Father!'

Chorus of Maidens.

Years glide! it is Youth; they sit within a secret bower. Purity is in her raptured eyes, Faith in his warm embrace. He must fly! He kisses his farewell: the fresh tears are on her cheek! He has gathered a lily with the dew upon its leaves!

Chorus of Youths.

Years glide! it is Manhood. He is in the fierce Camp: he is in the deceitful Court. He must mingle sometimes with others, that he may be always with her! In the false world, she is to him like a green olive among rocks!

Chorus of Youths and Maidens.

Years glide! it is Old Age. They sit beneath a branching elm. As the moon rises on the sunset green, their children dance before them! Her hand is in his; they look upon their children, and then upon each other!

'The fellow has some fancy,' said the old lord, 'but given, I think, to conceits. I did not exactly catch the passage about the bridge, but I have no doubt it was all right.'

Vivian was now invited to the pavilion, where refreshments were prepared. Here our hero was introduced to many other guests, relations of the family, who were on a visit at the castle, and who had been on the lake at the moment of his arrival.

'This gentleman,' said the old lord, pointing to Vivian, 'is my son's friend, and I am quite sure that you are all delighted to see him. He arrived here accidentally, his carriage having fortunately broken down in passing one of the streams. All those rivulets should have bridges built over them! I could look at my new bridge for ever. I often ask myself, "Now, how can such a piece of masonry ever be destroyed?" It seems quite impossible, does not it? We all know that everything has an end; and yet, whenever I look at that bridge, I often think that it can only end when all things end.'

In the evening they all waltzed upon the green. The large yellow moon had risen, and a more agreeable sight than to witness two or three hundred persons so gaily occupied, and in such a scene, is not easy to imagine. How beautiful was the stern old castle, softened by the moonlight, the illumined lake, the richly-silvered foliage of the woods, and the white brilliant cataract!

As the castle was quite full of visitors, its hospitable master had lodged Vivian for the night at the cottage of one of his favourite tenants. Nothing would give greater pleasure to Vivian than this circumstance, nor more annoyance to the worthy old gentleman.

The cottage belonged to the victor in the Regatta, who himself conducted the visitor to his dwelling. Vivian did not press Essper's leaving the revellers, so great an acquisition did he seem to their sports! teaching them a thousand new games, and playing all manner of antics; but perhaps none of his powers surprised them more than the extraordinary facility and freedom with which he had acquired and used all their names. The cottager's pretty wife had gone home an hour before her husband, to put her two fair-haired children to bed and prepare her guest's accommodation for the night. Nothing could be more romantic and lovely than the situation of the cottage. It stood just on the gentle slope of the mountain's base, not a hundred yards from the lower waterfall. It was in the middle of a patch of highly-cultivated ground, which bore creditable evidence to the industry of its proprietor. Fruit trees, Turkey corn, vines, and flax flourished in luxuriance. The dwelling itself was covered with myrtle and arbutus, and the tall lemon-plant perfumed the window of the sitting-room. The casement of Vivian's chamber opened full on the foaming cataract. The distant murmur of the mighty waterfall, the gentle sighing of the trees, the soothing influence of the moonlight, and the faint sounds occasionally caught of dying revelry, the joyous exclamation of some successful candidate in the day's games, the song of some returning lover, the plash of an oar in the lake: all combined to produce that pensive mood in which we find ourselves involuntarily reviewing the history of our life.

As Vivian was musing over the last harassing months of his burthensome existence he could not help feeling that there was only one person in the world on whom his memory could dwell with solace and satisfaction, and this person was Lady Madeleine Trevor!

It was true that with her he had passed some agonising hours; but he could not forget the angelic resignation with which her own affliction had been borne, and the soothing converse by which his had been alleviated. This train of thought was pursued till his aching mind sunk into indefiniteness. He sat for some little time almost unconscious of existence, till the crying of a child, waked by its father's return, brought him back to the present scene. His thoughts naturally ran to his friend Eugene. Surely this youthful bridegroom might reckon upon happiness! Again Lady Madeleine recurred to him. Suddenly he observed a wonderful appearance in the sky. The moon was paled in the high heavens, and surrounded by luminous rings, almost as vividly tinted as the rainbow, spreading and growing fainter, till they covered nearly half the firmament. It was a glorious and almost unprecedented halo!

CHAPTER IV.

A FRIGHTFUL CATASTROPHE.

HE sun rose red, the air was thick and hot. Anticipating that the day would be very oppressive, Vivian and Essper were on their horses' backs at an early hour. Already, however, many of the rustic revellers were about, and preparations were commencing for the fête champêtre, which this day was to close the wedding festivities. Many and sad were the looks which Essper George cast behind him at the old castle on the lake. 'No good luck can come of it!' said he to his horse; for Vivian did not encourage conversation. 'O! master of mine, when wilt thou know the meaning of good quarters! To leave such a place, and at such a time! Why, Turriparva was nothing to it! The day before marriage and the hour before death is when a man thinks least of his purse and most of his neighbour. O! man, man, what art thou, that the eye of a girl can make thee so pass all discretion that thou wilt sacrifice for the whim of a moment good cheer enough to make thee last an age!'

Vivian had intended to stop and breakfast after riding about ten miles; but he had not proceeded half

that way when, from the extreme sultriness of the
morning, he found it impossible to advance without
refreshment. Max, also, to his rider's surprise, was
much distressed; and, on turning round to his servant, Vivian found Essper's hack panting and puffing,
and breaking out, as if, instead of commencing their
day's work, they were near reaching their point of
destination.

'Why, how now, Essper? One would think that
we had been riding all night. What ails the beast?'

'In truth, sir, that which ails its rider; the poor
dumb brute has more sense than some who have the
gift of speech. Who ever heard of a horse leaving
good quarters without much regretting the indiscre-
tion?'

'The closeness of the air is so oppressive that I
do not wonder at even Max being distressed. Perhaps when the sun is higher, and has cleared away
the vapours, it may be more endurable: as it is, I
think we had better stop at once and breakfast here.
This wood is as inviting as, I trust, are the contents
of your basket!'

'St. Florian devour them!' said Essper, in a very
pious voice, 'if I agree not with you, sir; and as for
the basket, although we have left the land of milk
and honey, by the blessing of our Black Lady! I
have that within it which would put courage in the
heart of a caught mouse. Although we may not
breakfast on bridecake and beccaficos, yet is a neat's
tongue better than a fox's tail; and I have ever held
a bottle of Rhenish to be superior to rain-water, even
though the element be filtered through a gutter. Nor,
by All Saints! have I forgotten a bottle of Kerchen
Wasser from the Black Forest, nor a keg of Dantzic

brandy, a glass of which, when travelling at night, I am ever accustomed to take after my prayers; for I have always observed that, though devotion doth sufficiently warm up the soul, the body all the time is rather the colder for stopping under a tree to tell its beads.'

The travellers accordingly led their horses a few yards into the wood, and soon met, as they had expected, with a small green glade. It was surrounded, except at the slight opening by which they had entered it, with fine Spanish chestnut trees, which now, loaded with their large brown fruit, rich and ripe, clustered in the starry foliage, afforded a retreat as beautiful to the eye as its shade was grateful to their senses. Vivian dismounted, and, stretching out his legs, leant back against the trunk of a tree; and Essper, having fastened Max and his own horse to some branches, proceeded to display his stores. Vivian was silent, thoughtful, and scarcely tasted anything: Essper George, on the contrary, was in unusual and even troublesome spirits, and had not his appetite necessarily produced a few pauses in his almost perpetual rattle, the patience of his master would have been fairly worn out. At length Essper had devoured the whole supply; and as Vivian not only did not encourage his remarks, but even in a peremptory manner had desired his silence, he was fain to amuse himself by trying to catch in his mouth a large brilliant fly which every instant was dancing before him. Two individuals more singularly contrasting in their appearance than the master and the servant could scarcely be conceived; and Vivian, lying with his back against a tree, with his legs stretched out, his arms folded, and his eyes fixed on the ground; and

AFTER AN ORIGINAL DRAWING BY HERMAN ROUNTREE.

*Two individuals more singularly contrasting in
their appearance than the master and the
servant could scarcely be conceived.*

(See page 376.)

Essper, though seated, in perpetual motion, and shifting his posture with feverish restlessness, now looking over his shoulder for the fly, then making an unsuccessful bite at it, and then, wearied with his frequent failures, amusing himself with acting Punch with his thumbs; altogether presented two figures, which might have been considered as not inapt personifications of the rival systems of Ideality and Materialism.

At length Essper became silent for the sake of variety, and imagining, from his master's example, that there must be some sweets in meditation hitherto undiscovered by him, he imitated Vivian's posture! So perverse is human nature, that the moment Vivian was aware that Essper was perfectly silent, he began to feel an inclination to converse with him.

'Why, Essper!' said he, looking up and smiling, 'this is the first time during our acquaintance that I have ever seen thought upon your brow. What can now be puzzling your wild brain?'

'I was thinking, sir,' said Essper, with a very solemn look, 'that if there were a deceased field-mouse here I would moralise on death.'

'What! turned philosopher!'

'Ay! sir, it appears to me,' said he, taking up a husk which lay on the turf, 'that there is not a nut-shell in Christendom which may not become matter for very grave meditation!'

'Can you expound that?'

'Verily, sir, the whole philosophy of life seems to me to consist in discovering the kernel. When you see a courtier out of favour or a merchant out of credit, when you see a soldier without pillage, a sailor without prize money, and a lawyer without papers, a bachelor with nephews, and an old maid with nieces, be assured the nut is not worth the cracking, and send it to the winds, as I do this husk at present.'

'Why, Essper!' said Vivian, laughing, 'considering that you have taken your degree so lately, you wear the Doctor's cap with authority! Instead of being in your noviciate, one would think that you had been a philosopher long enough to have outlived your system.'

'Bless you, sir, for philosophy, I sucked it in with my mother's milk. Nature then gave me the hint, which I have ever since acted on, and I hold that the sum of all learning consists in milking another man's cow. So much for the recent acquisition of my philosophy! I gained it, you see, sir, with the first wink of my eye; and though I lost a great portion of it by sea-sickness, in the Mediterranean, nevertheless, since I served your Lordship, I have resumed my old habits, and do opine that this vain globe is but a large foot-ball, to be kicked and cuffed about by moody philosophers!'

'You must have seen a great deal in your life, Essper,' said Vivian.

'Like all great travellers,' said Essper, 'I have seen more than I remember, and remember more than I have seen.'

'Have you any objection to go to the East again?' asked Vivian. 'It would require but little persuasion to lead me there.'

'I would rather go to a place where the religion is easier; I wish, sir, you would take me to England!'

'Nay, not there with me, if with others.'

'With you, or with none.'

'I cannot conceive, Essper, what can induce you to tie up your fortunes with those of such a sad-looking personage as myself.'

'In truth, sir, there is no accounting for tastes. My grandmother loved a brindled cat!'

'Your grandmother, Essper! Nothing would amuse me more than to be introduced to your family.'

'My family, sir, are nothing more nor less than what all of us must be counted, worms of five feet long, mortal angels, the world's epitome, heaps of atoms which Nature has kneaded with blood into solid flesh, little worlds of living clay, sparks of heaven, inches of earth, Nature's quintessence, moving dust, the little all, smooth-faced cherubim, in whose souls the King of stars has drawn the image of Himself!'

'And how many years has breathed the worm of five feet long that I am now speaking to?'

'Good my lord, I was no head at calculating from a boy; but I do remember that I am two days older than one of the planets.'

'How is that?'

'There was one born in the sky, sir, the day I was christened with a Turkish crescent.'

'Come, Essper,' said Vivian, who was rather interested by the conversation; Essper, having, until this morning, skilfully avoided any discourse upon the subject of his birth or family, adroitly turning the conversation whenever it chanced to approach these subjects, and silencing enquiries, if commenced, by some ludicrous and evidently fictitious answer. 'Come, Essper,' said Vivian, 'I feel by no means in the humour to quit this shady retreat. You and I have now known each other long, and gone through much together. It is but fair that I should become better acquainted with one who, to me, is not only a faithful servant, but what is more valuable, a faithful friend, I might now almost add, my only one. What say you to whiling away a passing hour by giving me some sketch of your curious and adventurous life? If there be anything that you wish to conceal, pass it over; but no invention, nothing but the truth, if you please; the whole truth, if you like.'

'Why, sweet sir, as for this odd knot of soul and body, which none but the hand of Heaven could have twined, it was first seen, I believe, near the very spot where we are now sitting; for my mother, when I saw her first and last, lived in Bohemia. She was an Egyptian, and came herself from the Levant. I lived a week, sir, in the seraglio, when I was at Constantinople, and I saw there the brightest women of all countries, Georgians, and Circassians, and Poles; in truth, sir, nature's masterpieces. And yet, by the Gods of all nations! there was not one of them half so lovely as the lady who gave me this tongue!' Here Essper exhibited at full length the enormous feature which had so much enraged the one-eyed sergeant at Frankfort.

'When I first remember myself,' he continued, 'I was playing with some other gipsy-boys in the midst of a forest. Here was our settlement! It was large and powerful. My mother, probably from her beauty, possessed great influence, particularly among the men; and yet I found not among them all a father. On the contrary, every one of my companions had a man whom he reverenced as his parent, and who taught him to steal; but I was called

by the whole tribe the mother-son, and was honest
from my first year out of mere wilfulness; at least, if
I stole anything, it was always from our own people. Many were the quarrels I occasioned, since,
presuming on my mother's love and power, I never
called mischief a scrape; but acting just as my fancy
took me, I left those who suffered by my conduct to
apologise for my ill-behaviour. Being thus an idle,
unprofitable, impudent and injurious member of
this pure community, they determined one day to
cast me out from their bosom; and in spite of my
mother's exertions and entreaties, the ungrateful vi-
pers succeeded in their purpose. As a compliment
to my parent, they allowed me to tender my resignation, instead of receiving my expulsion. My dear
mother gave me a donkey, a wallet, and a ducat, a
great deal of advice about my future conduct, and,
what was more interesting to me, much information
about my birth.

'"Sweet child of my womb!" said my mother,
pressing me to her bosom; "be proud of thy white
hands and straight nose! Thou gottest them not
from me, and thou shalt take them from whence
they came. Thy father is a Hungarian Prince; and
though I would not have parted with thee, had I
thought that thou wouldst ever have prospered in
our life, even if he had made thee his child of the
law and lord of his castle, still, as thou canst not
tarry with us, haste thou to him! Give him this
ring and this lock of hair; tell him none have seen
them but the father, the mother, and the child! He
will look on them, and remember the days that are
passed; and thou shalt be unto him as a hope for his
lusty years and a prop for his old age."

'My mother gave me all necessary directions, which I well remember, and much more advice, which I directly forgot.

'Although tempted, now that I was a free man, to follow my own fancy, I still was too curious to see what kind of a person was my unknown father to deviate either from my route or my maternal instructions, and in a fortnight's time I had reached my future principality.

'The sun sank behind the proud castle of my princely father as, trotting slowly along upon my humble beast, with my wallet slung at my side, I approached it through his park. A guard, consisting of twenty or thirty men in magnificent uniforms, was lounging at the portal. I —— but, sir, sir, what is the meaning of this darkness? I always made a vow to myself that I never would tell my history. Ah! what ails me?'

A large eagle fell dead at their feet.

'Protect me, master!' screamed Essper, seizing Vivian by the shoulder; 'what is coming? I cannot stand; the earth seems to tremble! Is it the wind that roars and rages? or is it ten thousand cannon blowing this globe to atoms?'

'It is — it must be the wind!' said Vivian, agitated. 'We are not safe under these trees: look to the horses!'

'I will,' said Essper, 'if I can stand. Out of the forest! Ah, look at Max!'

Vivian turned, and beheld his spirited horse raised on his hind legs, and dashing his fore feet against the trunk of a tree to which they had tied him. The terrified and furious creature was struggling to disengage himself, and would probably have sustained or inflicted some terrible injury, had not the wind suddenly hushed. Covered with foam, he stood panting while Vivian patted and encouraged him. Essper's less spirited beast had, from the first, crouched upon the earth, covered with sweat, his limbs quivering and his tongue hanging out.

'Master!' said Essper, 'what shall we do? Is there any chance of getting back to the castle? I am sure our very lives are in danger. See that tremendous cloud! It looks like eternal night! Whither shall we go; what shall we do?'

'Make for the castle!' said Vivian, mounting.

They had just got into the road when another terrific gust of wind nearly took them off their horses, and blinded them with the clouds of sand which it drove out of the crevices of the mountains.

They looked round on every side; and hope gave way before the scene of desolation. Immense branches were shivered from the largest trees; small ones were entirely stripped of their leaves; the long grass was bowed to the earth; the waters were whirled in eddies out of the little rivulets; birds deserting their nests to seek shelter in the crevices of the rocks, unable to stem the driving air, flapped their wings and fell upon the earth: the frightened animals in the plain, almost suffocated by the impetuosity of the wind, sought safety, and found destruction: some of the largest trees were torn up by the roots; the sluices of the mountains were filled, and innumerable torrents rushed down the before empty gulleys. The heavens now open, and lightning and thunder contend with the horrors of the wind!

In a moment all was again hushed. Dead silence succeeded the bellow of the thunder, the roar of the wind, the rush of the waters, the moaning of the beasts, the screaming of the birds! Nothing was heard save the splash of the agitated lake as it beat up against the black rocks which girt it in.

'Master!' again said Essper, 'is this the day of doom?'

'Keep by my side, Essper; keep close, make the best of this pause: let us but reach the village!'

Scarcely had Vivian spoken when greater darkness enveloped the trembling earth. Again the heavens were rent with lightning, which nothing could have quenched but the descending deluge. Cataracts poured down from the lowering firmament. In an instant the horses dashed round; beast and rider, blinded and stifled by the gushing rain, and gasping for breath. Shelter was nowhere. The quivering beasts reared, and snorted, and sank upon their knees. The horsemen were dismounted. Vivian succeeded in hood-winking Max, who was still furious: the other horse appeared nearly exhausted. Essper, beside himself with terror, could only hang over his neck.

Another awful calm.

'Courage, Essper!' said Vivian. 'We are still safe: look up, man! the storm cannot last long thus; and see! I am sure the clouds are breaking.'

The heavy mass of vapour which had seemed to threaten the earth with instant destruction suddenly parted. The red and lurid sun was visible, but his light and heat were quenched in the still impending waters.

'Mount, Essper!' said Vivian, 'this is our only chance: five minutes' good speed will take us to the village.'

Encouraged by his master's example, Essper once more got upon his horse, and the panting animals, relieved by the cessation of the hurricane, carried them at a fair pace towards the village, considering that their road was now impeded by the overflowing of the lake.

'Master!' said Essper, 'cannot we get out of these waters?'

He had scarcely spoken before a terrific burst, a noise, they knew not what, a rush they could not understand, a vibration which shook them on their horses, made them start back and again dismount. Every terror sank before the appalling roar of the cataract. It seemed that the mighty mountain, unable to support its weight of waters, shook to the foundation. A lake had burst on its summit, and the cataract became a falling ocean. The source of the great deep appeared to be discharging itself over the range of mountains; the great grey peak tottered on its foundations! It shook! it fell! and buried in its ruins the castle, the village, and the bridge!

Vivian with starting eyes beheld the whole washed away; instinct gave him energy to throw himself on the back of his horse: a breath, and he had leaped up the nearest hill! Essper George, in a state of distraction, was madly laughing as he climbed to the top of a high tree: his horse was carried off in the drowning waters, which had now reached the road.

'The desolation is complete!' thought Vivian. At this moment the wind again rose, the rain again descended, the heavens again opened, the lightning again flashed! An amethystine flame hung upon rocks and waters, and through the raging elements a yellow fork darted its fatal point at Essper's resting-place. The tree fell! Vivian's horse, with a maddened snort, dashed down the hill; his master, senseless, clung to his neck; the frantic animal was past all government; he stood upright in the air, flung his rider, and fell dead!

Here leave we Vivian. It was my wish to have detailed, in the present portion of this work, the singular adventures which befell him in one of the most delightful of modern cities, light-hearted Vienna! But his history has expanded under my pen, and I fear that I have, even now, too much presumed upon an attention which I am not entitled to command. I am, as yet, but standing without the gate of the garden of romance. True it is, that as I gaze through the ivory bars of its golden portal, I would fain believe that, following my roving fancy, I might arrive at some green retreats hitherto unexplored, and loiter among some leafy bowers where none have lingered before me. But these expectations may be as vain as those dreams of youth over which all have mourned. The disappointment of manhood succeeds to the delusion of youth: let us hope that the heritage of old age is not despair.